Praise for
Simon the Fiddler

"The reader is treated to a kind of alchemy on the page when character, setting and song converge at all the right notes, generating an authentic humanity that is worth remembering and celebrating."
—*New York Times*

"Jiles's sparse but lyrical writing is a joy to read. . . . A beautifully written book and a worthy follow-up to *News of the World*."
—Associated Press

"Imbued with the dust, grit, and grime of Galveston at the close of the Civil War, *Simon the Fiddler* immerses readers in the challenges of Reconstruction. Jiles brings her singular voice to the young couple's travails, her written word as lyrical and musical as Simon's bow raking over his strings. Loyal Jiles readers and fans of Anthony Doerr's *All the Light We Cannot See* and Elizabeth Strout's *Olive Kitteridge* will adore the author's latest masterpiece."
—*Booklist* (starred review)

"Luminescent prose. . . . Jiles's timeworn territory provides a cozy escape."
—*Los Angeles Times*

"Endearing. . . . And when the final battle royal arrives in San Antonio, it's just the rousing ballad we want to hear."
—*Washington Post*

"Jiles's limber tale satisfies with welcome splashes of comedy and romance."
—*Publishers Weekly*

"Vividly evocative and steeped in American folkways: more great work from a master storyteller." —*Kirkus Reviews* (starred review)

"In *Simon the Fiddler* we once again accompany a cast of intriguing characters on a suspenseful Texas-based quest just after the Civil War. . . . A crackling-good adventure tale."

—*Star Tribune* (Minneapolis)

"[Jiles's] description of Simon and Doris traveling on separate journeys across the Texas landscape is superb, causing us to feel the elation and sense of possibility that rises in the hearts of man, woman and beast in setting out on the road."

—*Wall Street Journal*

"Beautifully told with lyrical descriptions, the novel illuminates the everyday struggles of the era." —*Christian Science Monitor*

"Jiles makes Texas in the 1800s hot and palpable for her readers, edgy and lawless, but the story also sings with melody."

—BookTrib

SIMON

THE

FIDDLER

ALSO BY PAULETTE JILES

News of the World

Lighthouse Island

The Color of Lightning

Stormy Weather

Enemy Women

Sitting in the Club Car Drinking Rum and Karma-Kola

SIMON THE FIDDLER

A Novel

PAULETTE JILES

WILLIAM MORROW
An Imprint of HarperCollins*Publishers*

This is a work of fiction. Names, characters, places, and incidents are products of the author's imagination or are used fictitiously and are not to be construed as real. Any resemblance to actual events, locales, organizations, or persons, living or dead, is entirely coincidental.

HarperCollins books may be purchased for educational, business, or sales promotional use. For information, please email the Special Markets Department at SPsales@harpercollins.com.

A hardcover edition of this book was published in 2020 by William Morrow, an imprint of HarperCollins Publishers.

FIRST WILLIAM MORROW PAPERBACK EDITION PUBLISHED 2021.

Library of Congress Cataloging-in-Publication Data has been applied for.

ISBN 978-0-06-296675-9

21 22 23 24 25 LSC 10 9 8 7 6 5 4 3 2

SIMON

THE

FIDDLER

CHAPTER ONE

SIMON THE FIDDLER HAD managed to evade the Confederate conscription men because he looked much younger than he was and he did everything he could to further that impression. His hair was reddish brown and curly; he was short and spare. He always shaved close so that he had no beard shadow. He could pass for fifteen years of age if not in direct sunlight. And often people protected him because they liked his music and did not care to see him dragged off for a soldier.

In an unseasonably hot October he had been engaged to play at a barbecue near Marshall in East Texas, in plantation country. Horses were tied at random in the shade of the tall loblolly pines, among the fires and the drifting layers of smoke. Black servants moved with pitchers of iced drinks and men and women sat with plates in their hands to listen to Simon play "Jock of Hazeldean"; light and poignant strains so different from the war news, the tattered letters arriving from the ruins of Atlanta with accounts of its burning and its dead.

Simon stood on a flatbed wagon and poured the notes out into the overheated air, unmoving, straight-backed, his hat cocked forward over his face. He had a high-boned face, bright hair, and light eyes and his music was enchanting.

A banjo player sat at the edge of the wagon. He was an old man who tipped his head carefully as if there were water in it and it might spill over. He was trying to hear where it was that Simon was going with the melody and to follow if he could. Simon drew out the last note with a strong vibrato and bowed to the applause, and when he raised his head he searched out the edges of the crowd like a hunted man.

After a moment he laid his bow tip on the old man's shoulder to get his attention and smiled. "How are you doing?" he said in a loud voice. "Could be you want a cold drink. They have ice, I saw it in a pitcher."

"All right." The old man nodded. "Yessir, doing fine, but I think they done come." The old man kept on nodding. He was cotton-headed and partially blind.

"Who done come?"

"The conscription people."

Simon was still and silent for a heartbeat, two heartbeats. Then he said, "Well Goddamn them."

He said this in a low voice because there were ladies present. He would have liked to fall backward into a water tank and sink, clothes and all, but it looked like he was going to be on the run again, abandoning this well-paid job and the lovely girl wearing a blue bonnet sitting in the front row with a rapt, appreciative face. He shoved his fiddle into the case, quickly snapped the bow into its groove, and slammed the case shut. He laid his hand on the old banjo player's shoulder.

"I'm gone," he said. "Take the money."

"No, sir, that ain't fair." The old man's banjo was crudely made and had no resonator, but he had done his best with it. He turned his head in Simon's general direction. "That ain't fair to you."

"Yes, it is." Simon grabbed his fiddle case by the handle and jumped off the flatbed. "I'm about done with those people. If I had a weapon I'd be loading it."

"Son, listen, you don't want to do that."

Now the plantation owner came hurrying through the crowd, past elderly men, past women sitting carefully with their hoop skirts arranged over armless chairs. He took Simon by the arm.

"Come now," he said. "Come with me right now."

Several of the ladies half-stood. They wanted to know what was the matter. These laments so rudely interrupted and the child had not even eaten yet. Simon pressed through the crowd saying excuse me, excuse me and took off at a running walk behind the man.

"Conscription men. I didn't invite them." The man was dressed as the planters always dressed at these barbecues, in a cutaway and trousers with foot straps and a beaver hat big as a church bell. "They were not given an invitation. They are ruffians, these people." Simon marched at his heels in a jerky, furious pace.

"Yes, but I'm not of age for a soldier," Simon said.

It was a bald-faced lie. They were going at long strides away from the plantation grounds and toward a sawmill operation back in the pines. Past stumps, past Virginia creeper blazing green in the sun.

"The hell you are not," the man said. He strode on down a red-dirt path and far above rain crows bent down to watch all they did and then spoke to one another with noises like clocks. "You're lying like a dog trottin'." And then, "I can tell by the backs of yo hains."

Simon stormed along behind the planter, vines slapping at his face. "You know what, I'm about done running. Next they're going to take that old man with the banjo. Jesus!"

"Hush," the planter said. "We are losing this war hand over fist. It's about done. Just keep your britches on."

Simon didn't hear him, partly because he was behind and partly because he was tangled in his own outrage. "If you had a weapon, I would borrow it from you."

"Here we are."

It was an icehouse, dug into the red East Texas dirt and roofed by a plank shed. Down in the pit were blocks of ice under deep layers of sawdust. "Find yoseff a spot down in there and cover up with that sawdust." He held out an invitational hand.

Simon's face had taken on a flat, smooth expression, his mouth in a stubborn straight line. "Wait. I'd just as soon get into a fight with them as run." He looked back down the path among the pines with a determined glare. "If you have a pistol then give me the loan of it."

"I will not." The man picked up a bucket. He spoke like people spoke in Savannah or Mobile, coastal Southerners, dropping *r*'s like loose buttons. "We've got many a soldier but we are short on fiddlers. I don't want shooting at random here at my wife's musical event. Can you shoot anyhow?"

"No," Simon admitted. "Not very well."

"There you go. They'd take you one way or the other. They'd put you in the front rank and you'd take a ball in the head first off. Get down there. Your time is running short, here."

Simon held on to the door frame, leaned his trim and limber body over the pit and looked down into the dark gaps between ice blocks. "Wait, wait, God, there's a *corpse* down in there!"

"I heard you had a quick temper but you just hold on to it for now." The planter stepped forward into the gloom of the low-ceilinged shack to see into the pit. "Pugnacious, hotheaded, and what? That wad of clothes? That's Miss Lucy's, she's freezing out the lice."

"There's *hair*!"

"She's freezing the lice out of her wig too. She was out administering to the poor. Now cover up. I'm going to get the hatchet and take some ice back for an excuse to come here."

Simon stared at the wadded clothes half-buried in sawdust. It seemed rather intimate to get down among a woman's unmentionables and her skirt and her wig. He said, "Ah, I don't believe I am acquainted with Miss Lucy."

"No normal man would *want* to be acquainted with Miss Lucy. Now get your behind down there."

It was a drop of five feet or so. Simon jammed his hat down tight, held the fiddle case under one arm, and jumped. He landed in an explosion of sawdust, got to his feet, and kicked himself a hole in it. He spent a good hour in a gap between the ice blocks, covered over with sawdust and frozen lingerie. He listened intently to the noises from outside: mockingbirds, a mule clearing its long nose in a hoarse snort, a rattling noise in the brush. He held the fiddle case to his chest. That was in October of 1864 and the atmosphere outside was so hot it seemed the air was afire.

In his patched homespun checkered shirt Simon was perishing with cold when they finally came to tell him it was safe to come out. Several young women stood in the doorway and called to him, offered their hands to help him up. They fluttered around him, laughing, dusting off the sawdust with their handkerchiefs. Simon smiled and stood with his arms held straight out to the side, redheaded and engaging and at liberty for the time being. His tension and indignation were all knocked away by the girls and their flying handkerchiefs. The one with the very jaunty blue bonnet took it off and used it to beat the sawdust from his back and he almost said, *Sweetheart, you have permission to beat me half to death with that bonnet,* but he did not and only turned and took their hands one after another to say goodbye. They said it would be a tale to tell your grandchildren, near freezing to death on a hot day in October, in the middle of the war.

He played throughout Central and East Texas in saloons and pleasure palaces, for weddings and funerals. Simon had a hair-trigger temper and he knew it, and all his life it had been impressed upon him to contain himself because he could end up in jail with his fiddle confiscated or stolen. The last thing he ought to do was get into a brawl with the conscription men. So he lived in the bright strains of mountain music and the reflective, running pools of the Irish light airs that brought peace to his mind and to his audiences; peace soon forgotten, always returned to.

He played for a wedding of twins at a church near Long Point and a funeral in Nacogdoches, he played "Song of the Spirits" in a very low dive in Saint Augustine, where the piercing wind of a Southern winter storm tore through a broken pane and furloughed men who carried grave, ineradicable wounds listened with still faces. This was all in the East Texas country, near the Louisiana border, where people still had money; money from cotton smuggled through the coastal blockades. Wherever he lifted his fiddle to his shoulder he commanded a good price and he saved every coin carefully, because when the war was over, he was going to buy a piece of land, live on it with a beautiful and accomplished wife, and play increasingly complex pieces of music. Hard cash and children would, somehow, come of their own accord.

It was not so much that he was a good player, because most of the people who crowded the saloons and dance halls couldn't tell a good fiddle player from Adam's off ox, but because his repertoire seemed to be without end. He had a bottomless supply of waltzes, jigs, reels, hornpipes, and slow airs. Some of the slow airs could bring men and women to a standstill, their eyes brimming with tears for a remembered love or a certain long-lost valley at twilight or another country without war, taken by emotions of loss and exile for which they had no words. He stood straight and still as he had been taught by the fiddlers on the Ohio. Writhing and bending when playing fiddle was distracting, it was undignified. With his hat low over his eyes and his bow flashing in lantern light he brought up melodies clean and clear from some inexhaustible source. He tried to stay out of fights, smiled and accepted compliments, collected his pay in silver pesos, and slipped through the hands of the conscription men with music trailing behind him, harmless and elven and utterly unmilitary.

But they finally got him in March of 1865 in the town of Victoria at J. A. Fenning's Public House on Brazos Street. Victoria was near the Gulf of Mexico, a body of water that Simon had always longed to see; the horizonless ocean itself. A drunk in a pair of striped pants kept insisting he be allowed to play Simon's fiddle. He was drunk enough to come up on the stage crying out that he could play as well as anybody and Simon held both bow and fiddle behind himself and said, *Back off, back off, listen to me, back off,* and his eyes were intent on the man, in the darkness beneath his hat brim. But the drunk would not back off even with the customers shouting at him.

At last Simon laid his bow and fiddle on top of the piano, turned back to the man, and shoved him, hard. "I told you twice, Goddammit, *no*." By this time several of the drunk's friends were grappling with him to get him off the tiny stage and then they began to argue among themselves as to the best method of removing him. The arguing men then started fighting with one another. The bar owner pulled out a shotgun and laid it on the bar. More shouting. The drunk, with reaching clawlike hands, surged with slow menace toward the fiddle.

Simon elbowed a man out of his way, snatched up a spindly chair that was meant for the pianist, who had not showed up, and, his patience gone, braced his feet wide and smashed it down on the man's head with all his strength.

The noise and the shouting caused two conscription men to

come running in off the street to see what was up. Simon had a look of sheer wrath on his face and a broken piece of the chair in his hand. Many of the men in the saloon were of conscription age and they cleared out of the bar from every exit, but Simon was delayed by shutting his fiddle up in the case and they got him. So that was the end of his freedom for the next while.

The two conscription men lifted him right off the stage. He was wise enough not to fight with them. Wisdom comes to us at odd times and this was one of them. They let him collect his money, his coat, his fiddle case with the rosin and tuning fork and the paper package of extra strings, and his clothes in his carpetbag with razor, soap, his other pair of socks. He grabbed his hat, which was a good fur-felt hat with a three-inch brim that had lasted him since he left Paducah, Kentucky. They said they wanted him for a regimental band, they didn't care how old he was. He could have been a titty-sucking baby in his mother's arms but if he could play music then they had just the right place for him.

At the encampment outside of town on the Guadalupe River he gave a false name, Simon Walters. This was so that he would be at the end of any list or muster roll and would therefore have time to think of what to do if some group he was in was called up for some task, such as fighting or kitchen duty. He gave his place of birth as Paducah, Kentucky, lied about his age, had no pass to present, and then put on the worn, patched, second-hand Confederate uniform they handed to him. The coat was a homespun butternut shell jacket with lighter patches where some insignia had been cut off and the buttons were from a Union uniform. They were brass and had the Federal eagle and the shield on them. The sort of thing that gives one pause. He wore his checkered shirt under the jacket and vest as standards had fallen amazingly here at the end of the war. He managed to trade his carpetbag for a rucksack.

They gave him a blanket. He found a pair of suspenders to keep the pants up. The pants sagged around his legs like stiff woolen pipe, but the pockets were enormous and he could carry all sorts of stuff in them.

He ended up with Giddings's regiment under Captain Robinson down on the Rio Grande. They were bivouacked inland, so Simon still had yet to see the Gulf of Mexico. They were given very little to eat. He marched into camp along with fifteen other conscripts and a wagon of supplies, their mules so thin that the caracara eagles had followed them all the way down.

The Yankees held the port at the mouth of the Rio Grande. Where the great river flowed into the Gulf of Mexico a sandy island had formed called Brazos de Santiago, and the Yankees languished there on that island among the docks and warehouses, along with two actual houses occupied by officers and their wives. All buildings leaned downwind in the blown sand, the unending roar of the surf. The Confederates under Giddings were encamped five miles west, up the river, Simon among them. Nobody was moving. Nobody wanted to fight. The war was ending. There was no reason to get killed.

He was assigned to a shelter made of canvas and carrizo cane along with others in the regimental band: the bugler and the drummer and a man of about forty or so who played the Irish tin whistle. He had a dark beard and hair like coal, a top hat tipped over his nose. Something had happened to his right hand. He gave Simon a nod and went back to rolling a cigarette in a piece of the Galveston newspaper.

"Well," said Simon. He pulled off his rucksack and stood unsmiling, holding the straps.

"Well, here's another one," said the bugler.

The drummer said, "Is that a fiddle case?"

"No," said Simon. "It's a dead baby." His gaze swept over them with a cool look from his light eyes, the way he would assess an audience for its volatility, its mood, its ability to pay.

The bugler shoved a wooden box aside, pushed a heap of blankets into a corner, and held out an invitational hand. "Here you go. You're wondering when we're going to eat." He glanced at Simon's lean body under the shell jacket and his thin face.

"More like what." Simon commandeered the box by putting his rucksack on it and sat down on the dirt floor. He was weak with hunger and the heat and was determined not to show it. He cocked up his knees and laid his hands in his lap.

"Beans and cornbread. Sometimes hominy."

"It's food." Simon watched as the bugler went back to sewing a patch on a trouser knee. He turned up the canteen they had issued him and drank the last few drops. Then in a cautious tone, like a man telling of a dream he had once had, he said, "They told me the Gulf of Mexico isn't too far from here." He wiped his mouth on his cuff. "I'd very much like to see it."

"The sergeants," said the dark man, "are not yet allowing the men to go on sightseeing tours." He lit up. "After the surrender you could take a stroll down there and indulge yourself in sportive play upon the gleaming sands."

"You reckon?"

"At this point anything is possible." The dark man lay back in his shirtsleeves and grimy suspenders while smoke drifted from his mouth.

That evening after the beans and cornbread Simon laid out his possessions carefully, each one in exactly the same place whether he was sleeping in the storage room of J. A. Fenning's Public House in Victoria or a crowded army tent on the Rio Grande. He placed his good Kentucky hat on top of his rucksack, laid out his razor and comb on the box and covered them with a handkerchief, and stored his tuning fork, rosin, and extra strings in the case along with his expensive and precious Markneukirche fiddle.

"And so my name is *Damon,*" the dark man said. "Like a demon." His skin was bluish pale, colorless. He was tall and narrow in the shoulders, his long feet stuck out into their tent space in two different shoes. "Damon Lessing."

Simon shifted on his hardtack box, cocked his head. He regarded Damon with a drawn, spare face, no expression.

"Simon Walters. And leave my rucksack where it is."

"Well now, I thought I'd lay out a hand of cards on it."

"I said leave it alone."

Damon glanced at him and parted a deck of cards into two halves. "You have a dangerous look on your face, fiddler. The sergeants make sharpshooters out of men like you. 'Ghastly grim and ancient Raven wandering from the Nightly shore . . .' Very well. I am reduced to the Missouri Shuffle." Damon made the cards snap together, rolled another cigarette, and handed it to Simon. "Calm down, son." Simon thanked him and smoked it, and so they were nominally friends, or at least not ready to shoot each other.

Simon wore the regulation forage cap pulled down over his forehead and left his good hat in the tent. He formed up for drill with the others on the flat sandy stretches while enormous towering clouds built up over the Gulf and sailed inland carrying, it seemed to him, secret messages about blue storms and pirates and tales of giant unknown fish.

Every evening through the months of April and May the wind came up out of the Gulf at nine o'clock like a transparent armada set loose on the world of deep south Texas. Simon could hear the Rio Grande River just beside camp where the Mexican women came to wash their white laundry in the brown water. He could hear the bells of churches on the other side. The wind bowed the thick stands of carrizo cane and the horses ate slowly. Egrets rose up with long leisurely strokes of their wings.

They were all badly armed; they were assigned old Springfield smoothbores of Mexican War issue and the dark man with the pennywhistle had only a percussion revolver made by Dance and Brothers that he kept in his rucksack. Simon loaded, knelt, and fired with the others and his cap flew off with the recoil. They drilled there in the bright, cauterized desert, learned the manual of arms, to the rear march, and dress right dress. Simon had trouble with the last and behind him from the ranks came yells of "Other arm! Other arm!" The sergeant tried to get Simon to play his fiddle for marches. At morning drill the sergeant shouted his name.

"Walters! Front and center!"

Simon was staring out over the river cane, watching the plumed heads bend to the western wind.

"Walters!"

Damon jabbed him in the kidneys with a knuckle. "Simon. That's you. Apparently."

"By God it is me. Yes, sir?" He stepped out to front and center.

The sergeant asked him to get his fiddle for the drill.

"No, sir, I will not."

The sergeant looked him up and down with a raking glance. A short redheaded fiddler with square shoulders and a trim waist, pale skin burnt a dusty brown, a mutinous expression on his face. The sergeant considered. Discipline was slipping; desertion throughout the entire Confederate Army was growing by the day, so the sergeant did not have him stripped to the waist and tied to a buckboard wheel and beaten. Instead he said in a painfully conciliatory voice, "But I'm ordering you to. Why not?"

"Why not. Because it's not a march instrument. Because I can't march and bow at the same time. Because sand will ruin my fiddle. It's everywhere." Simon jammed his tattered Confederate infantry cap down over his nose.

"Well, you had better do something," said the sergeant. "Musically."

Damon had a D whistle and a C and a big low G, but he had great trouble getting a good sound out of the G. So Simon borrowed the G whistle and learned it in a fairly short time. It had six holes and played in two keys. The trick was to cover the bottom hole securely. The dark man showed him how to pour boiling water down it to keep it clear of spit. The man had trouble with it because his right-hand fingers had been injured and he couldn't reach all the holes, even in a piper's grip.

"Caught it in a sheave block," he said. "At one time I was conscripted into the ironclad Yankee navy in New Orleans." But he could be burning hell on the smaller D whistle and once in a while in the evening as the cookfire died down he would sing in a rich bass voice. *These fleeting charms of earth, farewell, your springs of joy are dry* . . . while Simon sat with his arms around his knees and his shirt open to the evening breeze, his fine reddish hair sticking up like twigs, following the complex phrasing of that old song with his mind in a state of timelessness. He saw thin stars rise out of the unseen ocean, out of the distant east, and a world changed, a world burnt down with themselves held harmless from it all. If they were lucky, if they could continue to be lucky. *I'm a long time traveling here below to lay this body down* . . .

At drill they played the usual marches: "When Johnny Comes Marching Home" and "Rose of Alabama." They guarded the trains of cotton bales that came in one wagon after another, crossing over to Mexico to be sold. Simon heard talk that the officers pocketed a good deal of the cotton money. Men gambled, told stories, walked out into the shallows of the river in their drawers or naked to drench themselves. They squashed their shirts and underwear in the thick water, laughing and throwing water at one another, and traded for *chinguirito,* a kind of blistering cane rum, with people from the Mexican side. The sergeant told them that the French were on the other side of the river. Why the French were there the sergeant didn't know. Maybe they were buying the cotton. It was a strange gathering of immobile armies at the end of a world of desert and ocean and a slow brown river.

Simon worried about his hearing; someday this goddamned war and all its insanity would end and he would have to make a living with his music. He was likely to lose part of his hearing, the high tones at any rate, with this perpetual target practice. Jeff Davis had already been captured and was in jail, so what was the army's reasoning on this matter? Lee had cashed it in a month ago at Appomattox. Lincoln was dead at the hands of a demented actor. Why were they all still here?

"Nobody tells us lowlifes," said the bugler.

"Of *course* not," said Damon. "They have forgotten about us. Let us not remind them." They sat sweating in the shade of the cane-and-canvas tent. The mindless talk, the endless talk, wore on Simon's nerve ends. He felt like his brain was being sandpapered.

"Who has got wax?" Simon got to his feet. "Where can I get an apple?"

"Oh, oh, an apple!" cried the bugler. "And a chess pie and a diamond stickpin!" He sat and sawed off the legs of his drawers with a penknife so they would be cooler.

"Do you not know," said Damon, "that people in hell want ice water?"

"I wasn't aware."

Simon stood up and stepped out into the blazing white-hot heat. He sauntered off to the cook's wagon. How he managed to come back with a greasy candle end and a withered apple he never said. He broke off bits of candle for wax balls for his ears, cut up the apple, and shared out all but two slices, which he wrapped in bits of muslin and laid inside his fiddle case, then snapped it carefully shut. The apple slices would give a bit of humidity to the inside of the case and keep the delicate woods of his fiddle from drying out and cracking.

"Well, I'll be damned," said the bugler. "That's clever."

"Stop swearing. You're too young to swear," said Damon in an exhausted voice.

"Be damned if I am you son of a bitch," said the bugler. "I been swearing since I was six months old."

Simon had to save the candle wax for firing practice and so from time to time he wondered if he would go insane. He loved solitude; it was as necessary to him as music and water. He walked away from camp in the evenings when he could to spend an hour or two playing, working through the complexities of slip jigs in 9/8 time. If he played there at the regimental band tent, people came around to listen and sometimes applaud, and often they cried out for their favorite tunes. They wanted "Lorena" or some sea shanty, as if his entire duty in life was to entertain them.

So he went out alone among the saw palmetto and the carrizo cane in his shirt and vest, next to the river, where he practiced double-stopping and hokum bowing two-to-two and two-to-one, over and over. A mindless drone for anyone who came to listen. He stood straight and poised as a candle flame in a vast windless room of imagined silence. His reddish hair flew in the Gulf wind; on his face was a look of blank intensity. Every song had a secret inside. When he was away from shouting drunks and bartenders and sergeants and armies, he could think his way into the secret, note by note. "The Lost Child," "Wayfaring Stranger." He squinted in the low evening light at the few musical scores he possessed. He was teaching himself to read music. He played the scale on the G whistle and then some simple tunes. After an hour or so he replaced the Markneukirche in the plush lining of its case, wiped off the rosin dust, and flicked the hasps, listening for the solid *click* that told him his fiddle was safe inside its hard-shell case.

He knew that he did not play music so much as walk into it, as if into a palace of great riches, with rooms opening into other rooms, which opened into still other rooms, and in these rooms were courtyards and fountains with passageways to yet more mysterious spaces of melody, peculiar intervals, unheard notes.

It was there at the Confederate encampment at the ranch called Los Palmitos that Simon considered his life and how he would survive in the world to come. After the surrender, after the surrender, that time and change arriving any moment. If he were not able to play for a living, he would become restless and fall into contentiousness, ill humor; he would be sharp and impatient and inside a deep nameless distress. He sat alone and ate hoarded jerky meat, so thin it crackled. He had bought it from one of the Mexican women who crossed over holding up her skirts to sell it to him. Pretty wet brown legs. The river was very low.

His first problem was to find a girl who would fall in love with him despite his diminutive stature and his present homelessness. The right girl. He had not been a celibate; nobody growing up in the river-port town of Paducah, Kentucky, on the Ohio or playing saloons in Texas could lay claim to a life of sinless perfection, so perhaps he had no right to make demands, but the girls he had met and courted, briefly, had no comprehension of 9/8 time. They regarded him as a poor choice given his occupation as a traveling musician—always disreputable—and his stubborn, relentless dedication to his fiddle.

Never mind. After he found her, then there had to be land for sale somewhere and this would be his base and his bastion. It would be in a valley with running water and pecan groves and a surrounding of green hills. He would build her a fireplace with a waist-high hearth so she did not have to be bending over all the time at the cooking. And so he constructed an imaginary place of private loyalties and slow impeccable evenings into which he would send reels and hornpipes, furiously played. They would be for each other as much as the world was not. When life was very calm and ordered, only then could he get on with his music. Some of those invisible rooms were ones of anarchy and confusion and a person needed a quiet life to approach them.

This was not an idle fantasy. Whatever Simon determined on, he would not quit until he had it or was dead or incapacitated. Like the fiddle, for instance. It was a very good fiddle and it had cost him years of meticulous saving. People often badly misjudged him. He was, after all, only five foot five and 120 pounds and although he was twenty-three, he looked as if he had barely gotten past his fifteenth birthday. He tried to keep a firm grip on his temper by answering people quietly, to pause before replying. All those sorts of sayings that girls sewed into samplers. Lessons of life.

So the hot days of the beginning of May dragged on. The dark man, Damon, was given to quoting Edgar Allan Poe in a deep terrible voice—*Resignedly beneath the sky the melancholy waters lie*—and the bugler talked endlessly about his relatives in Louisiana, who all apparently did little of interest except lose their tools, get struck by lightning, and develop chronic and inscrutable diseases whose symptoms the bugler described in appalling detail.

Simon sat on his blankets in the choking dead shade of the tent and put his head in his hands, thinking, *Shut up, shut up, shut up.* He waited in steadfast silence for the platoon cook to start hammering at a suspended tire rim to call them to their supper, their mess plates held out like beggars for their increasingly meager fare.

CHAPTER TWO

On the morning of May 12, 1865, when a storm arrived in banks of hard blue clouds straight out of the Gulf, Federal troops decided to row across from Brazos Island and attack them. Nobody knew why. It didn't matter why. Simon was awakened by ear-splitting thunder and lightning, a crashing rattle of rain on the canvas. He sat up in his blankets and called out, "Who moved my hat? Who?"

Somebody had moved his good felt Kentucky hat from his rucksack to his boots. Rain pelted the cane walls of the tent, drummed on the roof. The bugler was playing "Alarm" for troops to fall out under arms, when a ball came through the canvas with a ripping whine. After several frozen seconds, they grabbed their ammunition boxes and their smoothbores and bolted out of the tent.

Two hundred and fifty Federal troops attacked across the sloppy open ground running, splashing, firing. They had come up in the night. Wind and rain tore through the encampment. The pickets had been driven in and one of them yelled, "My God they're all niggers!" The man next to Simon was hit and went down. Somebody else grabbed him and hauled him to his feet and tried to get him to run, but then the rescuing man was hit and went down as well. The drummer hammered out "Retreat" as best he could on a wet skin.

Simon turned back at a run to get his fiddle. It was all he had against a chaotic world and the mindlessness of a losing war, against corruption, thievery, cowardice, incompetence, cactus, gunsmoke, and hominy.

An officer in Confederate butternut rode up and aimed his revolver at Simon. Rain gushed in streams from his hat brim as he stared down from his dancing, nervous horse.

"Where the hell are you going, Private?"

"My fiddle!" Simon shouted. He gripped his wet musket barrel and clenched his eyes against the rain. There was gunfire coming from everywhere. A group of men had taken shelter behind a crate of rifle balls.

"Get back to your unit or I will shoot you!"

Simon turned back and ran with the others; a scattered, shameful retreat past their own stores and wagons and horses, into the flat wastes of the Rio Grande plain in which they were all slashed by palmettos and ocotillo. He turned once with two other men and knelt in the drenched sand, loaded, rammed, and fired, then got up and ran again. He was knocked down by a loose horse, which caused him to lose the Springfield. Damon pulled him up and thrust his revolver grip-first at Simon as if it had become a liability, as if he had stolen it and wanted to be rid of it, as if it were red-hot.

"Take it." He was hunched up against the rain. "I'm a terrible shot. You look like you're prepared to kill people."

"No." Simon shoved it away. "*You* kill people."

"I mean it, take the damn thing!"

So he took it.

That night they lay up in a draw. The storm rumbled on like a celestial caravan loaded with rain, to the west, upriver, and then on to parts unknown. Stars came out intermittently between the low, separating clouds. Simon heard a corporal crawling past them, whispering, *Dawn attack, dawn attack* and saw the watchful, anxious faces around him and men feeling in their pockets for pieces of cornbread or chew or lead balls, groping with wet hands. There were three shots left in the revolver and Simon didn't know where he was supposed to get more ammunition. He turned it over in his hand; it was a big heavy object. He rolled up an empty chamber under the hammer and lay down in the wet dirt, with the revolver clutched under his coat. It stopped raining. Simon lay curled up with his head on his arm, waiting for sleep, and suffered through a peculiar feeling, a kind of interior weeping, because he knew his fiddle was gone—broken or stolen.

At dawn Simon woke up confused, in the orient light of a desert newly washed with rain in which hid men who wanted to kill him. He was dirty and wet. His hands were black with gunpowder residue. Men stirred, made small noises. Damon crawled toward him and tossed him a leather satchel. It had the powder measure and patches and balls in it. Shortly afterward they followed shouted orders to charge and retake their camp, and as he ran he heard the tearing crackle of musket fire. Within seconds black-powder smoke hung over their heads in sliding layers. Simon sprinted straight for the regimental band tent. The cane walls and canvas roof had collapsed and all around it their blankets were scattered like tattered corpses, bundles of nubby wool all sodden. The attacking Federals had stolen whatever was to hand.

Simon cocked the hammer repeatedly until he had a load up, thumbed on a cap, got a running Federal in his sights. With a vast, furious, vengeful joy he pulled the trigger and saw the man go down and hit and roll like a rag doll. *And damn you stay down,* he thought. He found that they were once again in possession of their camp. Confederates ran bent over, ducking rifle fire, looking for their possessions. Simon and his tent mates pulled at the wet canvas of their shelter and there he found his rucksack with his savings inside in a pool of water, and others cried out in joy at finding some few of their possessions.

"Stop mucking around in that, you sons of bitches!" a sergeant yelled at them. Simon dodged a galloping team of artillery horses and sought shelter from further conflict at an abandoned provisions wagon. He sat under the tail of it and considered the revolver—how much it was worth, where he could sell it, and how he could start in again on the long road to contriving and saving for another fiddle. Then a deep discouragement came over him and it was a heavy feeling like he had rarely experienced in his life.

The next day, Colonel Santos Benavides and his Tejano Confederate troops arrived as reinforcements. At ten o'clock Simon heard ear-splitting thunder very close by and threw himself flat on the ground. It was Colonel Rip Ford with French artillery from across the river. Colonel Ford had gone over and borrowed the Frenchmen's cannon. In a screaming tide of men and a thick screening of powder smoke they drove the Federals back to their island. Colonel Ford rode into the surf and sabered a Yankee struggling for a boat so that his head half came off and the next wave rose up marbled with his heart's blood. Then Giddings's regiment stood on the shore of Texas and danced and waved their regimental flag, making rude gestures at the Yankees fleeing across the water.

And then they surrendered.

The day they surrendered was perfectly clear and it had turned hot. Simon and the other men of Giddings's regiment were mustered to march to Fort Brown several miles farther west up the river. This had been the Confederate fort, this was where they would formally surrender. Damon handed Simon his big G whistle, bent over, and blew the spit from his D. The musicians were put behind the colors, dressed right, and started out in a rolling step. With the two pennywhistles and the drummer and bugler doing their best, they played "The Braes of Killiecrankie," that terrible lament of an old Scots battle where the clans had fought against one another and left bodies strewn in pieces all over a rocky battlefield. He and Damon had to fake the low notes but Simon heard many of the men behind him singing the words; they knew it, they had always known it would come to this.

If you had been where I have been
ye would not be so cantie-o,
if you had seen what I have seen
in the braes of Killiecrankie-o.

Simon was drained when they got to Fort Brown. It took a lot of wind to keep playing that big G and he hadn't eaten for some time—he couldn't remember when exactly. Outside the earth walls of the fort, Colonel Giddings and Colonel Benavides turned in their muster rolls and called for the men to unload and stack arms. Somewhere along the way General Kirby Smith had taken the Confederate and Texas colors and crossed over into Mexico and it was said he and his men kept on riding toward Veracruz.

Simon wandered winded and gasping until they were told to form up. He did not have a long gun to stack in the arms pyramids, as did everyone else, but he stood to attention in his shabby trousers and suspenders and butternut forage cap to watch. The Confederates from Giddings's unit and Benavides's infantry pulled themselves once again into a military stance as the sergeants screamed out "Prepare SLINGS!" and then "Stack ARMS!" In groups of four the men stacked arms to make pyramids of four long guns each while the Union soldiers stood at attention to watch, somewhat abashed, as they knew they had not won against these surrendering men.

Simon stood unmoving in the rear rank. People noticed movement. He was determined not to be noticed. He had disassembled the big revolver and hidden it in his rucksack. He was thinking that if they caught him with it, what the hell, life could not get much worse than it was at present.

Then Simon saw a Yankee soldier standing around with a fiddle case under his arm and Simon's hat perched on top of his head because Simon wore a six and three quarters hat size, which was small, and the soldier had a big round head like a pumpkin. Both hope and rage came to him in the same instant. The sun was blinding there on the flat stretch of land before the fort where palm trees lifted their arms restlessly and old smoothed river rocks gleamed. Simon threw off his rucksack and left the ranks at a flat-out run straight for the soldier.

"Get your filthy hands off my fiddle, you son of a bitch!"

The soldier turned to see Simon running at him and threw out a hand. "What? What?"

Simon picked up a fist-sized rock, stood back on his right leg, wound up, and threw. It struck the soldier on the bridge of his nose with the force of solid shot. The hat flew off and the big man sat down in the dirt. Blood burst out of his nose in a spewing gush. Then, since the soldier presented such an easy target, Simon kicked him in the head with the heel of his boot. The man fell flat, making vague movements with one hand. Simon took up his hat and his fiddle case and felt whole again. Then he stood and waited for whatever would happen next.

What happened next was a Federal provost marshal and two

privates took him in an armlock. They had him bent over and stumbling toward the garrison punishment cells.

IT WAS A dignified and amiable surrender as far as the officers were concerned. They were all to have a dinner together at the Fort Brown officers' mess and for a formal dinner, musicians are needed. Simon spent two hours in the punishment cell; a long two hours. He sat with his hands loose between his knees in a dim light and the sweat seemed to jell on his body. He tried to think where it would be, how he could get it back, how long he was going to be left in this hole without food or water. The piss bucket buzzed with flies.

He heard steps and the clank of keys coming down the corridor. He lifted his head but remained expressionless, watching the soldiers' shadows preceding them.

"Well, fiddler."

A private turned the key in the lock and its sharp cry pierced the air.

"That's me."

"You're wanted."

"Good to hear." Simon stayed where he was. "For what?"

The soldier pulled the cell door open. "Get your ass out of there and you'll find out."

He was escorted to the food storage room next to the kitchen, where five others sat with various instruments. They shoved him in the door. After a moment a sergeant arrived and threw down Simon's fiddle case, his hat, and his rucksack. Simon took up the case without a word and instantly sat down, opened it, and in an interior tidal wave of relief that was beyond his ability to describe saw that the Markneukirche was intact, that his extra strings and his tuning fork were there, his rosin, his scores with his scribbled notes all over the staves, his bow in one piece. There were the slices of shriveled apple. He sat for a moment with his head in his hands. *Thank you, God,* he thought. Then he looked up.

They were turning up dippers of water, eyeing one another. They sat on barrels of flour, big tins of meat. A little Union drummer poured a dipper over his head and sat with eyes closed in relief as the water ran down inside his blue collar. He couldn't have been more than thirteen years old. His thatch of dirty yellow hair stuck up in sweaty points.

They had to get quiet. A quiet inside themselves. They had to make up a band. It was the only reason they had let Simon out of that shithole and had given him his fiddle back. They had to think *music.* The heat was that of burning suns, lakes of hellfire. Simon knew somebody had to take charge. He figured that person was himself. He took the dipper from the child drummer, poured water over his own head, and said, "Listen, you all." He hitched his suspenders higher on his shoulders. "Listen. We've got to get paid for this. We've surrendered, well, the Confederates have, so the war's over and we're civilians now and they've got to damn well pay us."

The others stared at him. They were thinking. Simon dried his face on his dirty checkered shirt sleeve, lifted the open fiddle case and blew out all the sand from the plush lining. He turned the screw on the bow to tighten the horsehair. He waited. From outside came the noise of somebody cranking a windlass to bring up another bucket of taupe-colored water from the Fort Brown well.

The musicians were both Yankee and Confederate. They were all filthy. They had recently been trying to kill one another. They smelled of gunpowder and were sweating like animals in the ninety-seven-degree May heat, while outside palm trees made their endless whistling rustle in a Gulf wind. They sat and ate of the food brought to them. Simon took out his knife to spear up as much bread and bacon as he could from the metal platter. They wiped their hands on the hemp sacks of beans. A guitar player with a double-aught guitar from Benavides's Tejanos was there, and a black Federal color sergeant with a five-string banjo, a man in a Zouave uniform who appeared suspiciously French and also had a guitar, the little Yankee drummer who had brought his bones and a bodhran, Damon with his Irish whistles. Damon wore a striped shirt and his top hat. You could tell he and Simon and the Tejano were Confederates; few of them had intact uniforms anymore. But even in his torn trousers Damon sat slim and tall with an air of undefeatable gentility, twirling the C whistle in one hand.

"How do you figure on doing that?" he said.

"We got to clean up," said Simon. "Stands to reason." He threw out both hands, palms up, in an appeal to that rare jewel-like thing called reason. "We got to get out of these uniforms or at least into some white shirts. We got to *look* like civilians."

Another long considering silence.

"Might," said the banjo man. He was still wearing his blue sergeant's uniform coat, buttoned up even in the heat. He began to turn the pegs on the head of the banjo. "You got a tuning fork? Pitch pipe?"

"Tuning fork," said Simon absently. "Officers have got to have some white shirts, don't they?" He got out his tuning fork and struck it on the door frame and said, "It's an A." As he held it humming in the hot air they all began tuning up, and to help out, Damon blew A on his D whistle. The air vibrated with incipient, unformed musical structures and two kitchen helpers and the cook bent around the edge of the kitchen door to stare curiously. Simon said, "Get out, you," and they did.

The banjo man said, "I know the dog robbers. I bet they can get some." He tapped the air with his forefinger, counting. "Six. We need six."

"Eh?" The Zouave ran his thumbnail over a chord, then another. "Dog robbaire?"

"Valets," the banjo man said. "We call them dog robbers. All right. You all figure out what we're playing and tune up. I'll go see what I can do. I'm tuned." He paused at the door. To the Zouave he said, "You're not with them or us either, are you?"

"*Mais non.*" The Zouave waved his forefinger in the air. "I come from other side the river with that French *armee* there. I come across very quietly to see the surrender and I stay for the *fete*." He struck out a series of chords. "Is it well?"

"Yes. Behave yourself." The black color sergeant ducked out of the storage room.

"What about coats?" Damon said. "Playing in shirtsleeves, well, might as well be in our drawers."

"Can't be helped," said Simon.

They scrubbed their faces and hair at the well in the kitchen yard with lumps of gray lye soap, scraped their nails with pocketknives. They went back into the storage room, whose palm-leaf thatching was overrun with rats and various sorts of insect life, and shaved, staring into the bottom of a polished tin plate. They beat the sand out of the knees of their pants. The shirts arrived. A corporal strode into the storage room, threw the shirts down on a stack of molasses kegs, looked around in a theatrical manner, and said, "You get them back to me!"

He turned on his heel to disappear into the dust and noise of the soldiers, wagons, and horses of two armies all sorting themselves out. They could hear the shouts of sergeants, a man repeatedly bellowing for tent stakes. They jettisoned their uniforms, threw their forage caps and shell jackets and uniform frock coats into a corner, blue and gray and butternut all in a heap.

Simon grabbed the whitest shirt before anybody else could get to it and buttoned up the high collar until it appeared his neck was stuck in a cast. His head thrust out in a ragged red-brown mop of hair. The shirt had an immense tail to it. Simon jammed what seemed to be yards and yards of white linen into his britches. The others struggled into whatever seemed to fit and the Zouave was left with one that had ties at the neck and fit him like a cotton pick sack. They all looked at one another.

"*Bien,*" said the Tejano. "*Somos elegantes. Adorables.* And so I think the fiddler leads us."

"Yes, take the lead, fiddler," the color sergeant said this in a voice of indisputable authority.

"All right. Can y'all do anything besides marches?" said Simon.

"Like what?" The boy with the bodhran rattled his tipper across the skin.

"Reels, hornpipes. I say we start hard and fast and then when they're all drunk and declaring eternal friendship, get into 'Lorena' and 'Home Sweet Home' and 'Hard Times.' I want to see them crying into their rum. Anybody know 'Nightingale Waltz'?"

"Of *course,*" said Damon. "For hard and fast, what? 'The Hog-Eye Man,' 'Cumberland Gap,' 'Blarney Pilgrim,' 'Little Liza Jane.' " He blew down the whistle. "I hope my suggestions are not dismissed out of hand. Also 'Mississippi Sawyer.' "

Simon said, " 'Whiskey Before Breakfast'?"

Confusion; silence.

"Some people call it 'The Fiddler's Dram.' "

They shook their heads.

" 'Rye Whiskey'?" Everybody nodded. "All right, then. And listen, everybody gets a turn. Y'all know 'Eighth of January'? Let the sergeant take the break."

Damon said, "Of *course.* Now, on 'Rye Whiskey' let us do a verse a capella. The 'if a tree don't fall on me' verse. I can do the bass on that."

"Me lead tenor," said the banjo player.

"Yes, a verse a capella," said Simon absentmindedly. He rosined his bow with long loving strokes as the sunlight poured through the open door and lit his hair afire. He had drops on his eyelashes and wiped them away on his shoulder. "Me high tenor. I can get above the melody if we're in G."

"I do the hum," said the Zouave. "I do humming *effets*."

"Some officer's wives are coming," said the bone-and-bodhran boy, the Yankee drummer. He tipped his head from one side to the other as he ran through triple clicks with the bones. "From over on the island. Right at first to join them in prayer and cast a glow of femininity and grace on the gathering. Then the women go. Then you can play the dirty ones."

Thus they solidified as a group as musicians do, or perhaps their minds and thoughts precipitated out of the military suspension in which they had been held and so they once again became servants of music and not of the state.

CHAPTER THREE

SHE WAS A SLIGHT person with black hair and dark blue eyes who gazed around herself with a polite and cautious smile. She walked in behind the wife of a Union colonel. She was holding a young girl by the hand. The master of ceremonies was the regimental chaplain who, along with the ladies, would also disappear before they got into the off-color ones like "The Hog-Eye Man" if he knew what was good for his immortal soul.

Simon sat with a solemn, respectful expression while he silently ran over key changes in his mind. But then he saw her.

He instantly abandoned all thoughts of key changes. She filled his entire vision with her pale round face and a little gesture of putting her finger to her lips as she leaned to listen to a major beside her. Simon did not hear the chaplain's courteous words about reconciliation and returning to homes and hearths now that this terrible and fratricidal war was finally over, how Colonel Webb (a lift of the hand toward the Union colonel) had brought the war to a close single-handedly with this victory amid the sands and bitter storms of the Rio Grande, sonorous statements about the dinner being honored by the appearance of Colonel Webb's gracious wife and little daughter, a sign of trust, a sign of civilized customs, behold this innocent child, Josephina, who will grow up in a finer and better world where all men can now behave as brothers. The girl with the black hair was not introduced, and so Simon thought she might be a governess or tutor. He couldn't take his eyes off her.

She wore a dress of black and brown vertical stripes with a perfectly white collar and a wide black belt. She looked intently at the chaplain as he spoke, and then into Colonel Webb's face as he replied. An expression of deep attention, an intelligent face, hair so black it carried blue lights in the late sunlight that poured in through the open windows of the adobe mess hall. Since it was an evening event she wore no hat, and Simon could see the intricate braids and burnished ebony of her hair. He watched as she moved, turned to the child, bent down and spoke to her, smiled at the colonel's wife, looked up overhead in sudden alarm as a rat thrashed its way through the roof thatching. He watched every move, spellbound. Elegant, contained little body under all that vertical striping.

"Fiddler."

Simon jerked his head around. It was the sergeant with the banjo beckoning to him.

"I seen your face," said the sergeant. "Do you want to speak to her?"

"Yes!"

"Go down there and tell the chaplain that you'd like to ask what the ladies wish to hear for the toast. This is what the army calls a dining-in, ladies are introduced. Then the music starts, toast, everybody bows, the ladies leave."

The black color sergeant carefully turned the peg on his fifth string. He spoke in a low voice like the voice of a spirit of temptation or aid in a time of need. Simon put his hand on the sergeant's shoulder and leaned in to listen.

"So slide down there and keep your head low and speak real quiet to the chaplain and say that you'd like to know what the ladies want to hear."

"Thank you," Simon said. "What's his whole name? The colonel?"

"Franklin Webb. You just call him Colonel *sir*."

"Do I salute?"

"Not if you want to look like a civilian."

Simon tucked his fiddle against his left side in the crook of his wrist and the bow in the fingers of his left hand and he slid like a haint from the makeshift stage. He continued silently along the wall and moved past standing officers in both blue and gray with their drinks in their hands. He reached the back of the mess hall in a quick, ghostly, reptilian slide.

The chaplain was talking and smiling at Colonel Webb and the women. He wore the black coat and cloth-covered buttons of a Union Army chaplain, and as Simon came to stand at the man's side he felt her eyes on him. She gracefully turned her entire body to regard him, her skirts swinging. Simon turned to her in what he thought would only be a passing glance but he was held there. Her eyes were a clear, dark blue. After a second or two of paralysis, he inclined his head to her and then had enough sense to turn and address the chaplain.

"Sir, chaplain, sir," said Simon in a low voice.

The chaplain swiveled his head, looked Simon up and down. "Ah? I uh . . ."

"Yes, sir, I just was wondering if the ladies had a song in mind or a song they would prefer to sing, I mean to have played for the toast, or you know, when you, when the dinner begins here . . ."

Just shut up now, he told himself. He kept his eyes resolutely on the chaplain. Colonel Webb turned and with one hand pressed the girl away from him and out of the way as if she were a chair or a door. Then Webb bent his gaze upon Simon with a *What is this going on?* expression on his bearded face.

"Do the ladies have a song they prefer," said the chaplain to Webb by way of explanation. The colonel's wife had a set face and a pair of tightly shut hands in lace mittens. The girl with the black hair was finally able to step away from that hand and bent to the child and spoke to her. Simon watched her graceful movements, noted the ray of sunlight that fell on her hair and danced over the braided crown. Her flushed face. Simon was only a fiddler of a defeated army, but he would have given a great deal to catch this man alone. To have shoved that girl the way he did. He managed to smile at her, a quick bow.

The girl tugged at her mother's lacy sleeve. "Mama," she said.

"Oh well, then, do they?" Webb stared at Simon carefully. "Have a song they prefer?" He had the manner of men who have just come through a hot battle, in fact a losing battle, and Simon knew the colonel would still be strung taut and vigilant. There would be no quiet in his heart. Enemies everywhere. Simon bent from the waist.

"Colonel, sir," he said.

Colonel Webb's wife put her hand on his elaborately braided coat sleeve and said, "My dear, Josephina says her governess would very much like to hear a song from Ireland."

Governess. All right. Irish.

Webb took out a handkerchief and patted his forehead. Like everyone, he was longing for the moment the sun went down. "An Irish song," he said. "Mostly sounds like bawling out of tune. Well, go ahead then." He glanced at the girl with a kind of secret contempt. "What is it? What do you want to hear?"

Simon knew it was rude of the colonel not to use the girl's name, but now he could look her in the eye again, into her beautiful dark blue eyes. She had a broad forehead and a quick manner, a relieved smile now that she was beyond reaching distance.

"I hope I can play whatever you wish," Simon said, with a polite smile. He was grateful to be wearing a clean white shirt instead of the old homespun grimed with gunpowder and bacon grease. So grateful that he felt strangely elevated and different. Her gaze made him different, he could not say how.

She tipped her head back and forth as if trying to decide and then said, "And would you know 'The Minstrel Boy'?" She spoke in a wonderful Irish lilt.

To Simon's enormous relief, he knew it. It was another sign that this was *meant*. This was a meant thing.

"I do! I do indeed," he said and he was afraid his tone was too eager, idiotic, or perhaps on the other hand maybe it was too reserved. He didn't know which. Her round face and little black drop earrings. He could tell she had a narrow rib cage all bounded in a vertical stripe as slim as her waist. And God above she was shorter than he was. She gazed into his face with that intent expression and he felt that he might begin melting or dissolving in some way. He cleared his throat. "I am honored to play it for you, Miss. I am delighted."

And he was even more delighted when nobody corrected him when he said *Miss*.

The colonel turned to Simon; condescending, irritated. He said, "Why are we messing around with this? Play whatever you want." He moved away with one hand on his wife's elbow, and the girl with the black hair and the child fell obediently into his train as he escorted them to their places. She sat down with a whirl of skirts and a straight back, her hands in her lap. Simon would have bet good money that every man in the dining hall had his eye on her but none of them had seen what he had seen and did not realize that here was a creature of great beauty in need of rescue or comfort or a staunch defender, none of which was in his power right now; only music.

Simon slid along the wall, through knots of men in blue uniforms and officer's insignia, most of which he could not read. Around groups of men in butternut or gray. There was an unsettled and brittle feeling in the hall; men who had surrendered to men they had just beaten. He slipped back to the bandstand. Strange how a musical instrument in your hand made you the innocent of the world. He stepped up onto the creaking boards of the bandstand that had been hammered together at the last moment and said, "Listen. They want an opening song called 'The Minstrel Boy,' men, it's an Irish slow air, used to be called 'The Moreen,' four-four time and I'm going to do it in C, are we agreed?"

The black color sergeant nodded to himself. "He has breasted the walls of the fortifications."

"Did I?" Simon paused and then laughed. "Yes, sir, maybe so."

The color sergeant, now a banjo player, regarded the group with a sergeant's critical eye that they all duly recognized. "Ready?"

Simon said, "Wagons ho." And then, "One two, one-two-three . . ." and slid the horsehair down the strings.

He put his heart into it; many knew the melody but few knew the words. It was long, slow, and full of yearning, it lifted all the faces to him and tilted them over into the stream of magic, some long-ago time when the wars had not yet begun, before the first shot and before the first lie and the first burning. When all was summer again and the cattle were safe in a green field. Simon heard the guitars bring off harmonizing chords and they all instinctively turned to Damon and gave him the bridge. He lilted it up into the high octaves and handed it back to them.

As he played, Simon watched Mrs. Webb and the colonel shake hands with other officers, all of them bowing to Mrs. Webb and the little girl and the young woman with the shining black hair, now safely out reach of the colonel's furtive hand. She lifted her head to the musicians, to Simon as his bow flashed and leaped in the long javelins of light that came through the overhead palm-leaf thatching. She watched him play with that same expression of a deep listening.

He brought the tune to its end. There was some applause but after all they were supposed to be background music, this was not a concert. Nevertheless, Simon laid his bow alongside his leg, held his fiddle across his body at the correct angle, and bowed to her. To her, her alone, the black-haired girl with the blue sea-cloud eyes down on the Gulf of Mexico at the end of a terrible war.

Simon saw the women do a sketchy curtsey at the toast—"To the ladies!"—and then they were escorted out. He saw the last flick of her brown-and-black-striped skirt as she disappeared out the door. Wondered where they were staying.

"Fiddler."

"Yes!" he said in a loud, startled voice and then, 'Mississippi Sawyer,' D," gave the opening notes with a double-shuffle and off they went into that reel and then another. Simon could hear the boy picking up low and high notes on the bodhran and then on other fast songs he made the bones clatter in triple clicks and the joy the boy took in it made Simon and the others smile over their instruments. Then Damon and his D whistle on "Blarney Pilgrim," which was a jig. They did "Eighth of January" to give the black banjo player a chance to show off.

Then the sun had set and the Rio Grande Valley began to cool down, the enormous Gulf sent forth sunset clouds in magenta and gold, and the lamps on all the tables were lit.

It was time to be mellow and sentimental. The officers didn't know they were being managed. They never did. If any of them recognized their own shirts on the backs of the band members they were silent about it.

"Lorena" was a good start. Then "Rye Whiskey," slowly, so theatrically mournful the officers leaned back in their chairs and laughed, clapping one another on the shoulder. As agreed, the musicians left off their instruments and sang a verse a capella like a funeral lament over the tree that might fall on a person, who would live 'til he died. Simon could hear Damon's steady bass in harmony and was relieved to know the man knew what he was about. Then "Home Sweet Home," at which everybody joined in except those who were unable to sing because they had choked up. Simon could see several men with their heads bowed; another dashed at his eyes with his coat sleeve. *Good.* Simon would have preferred outright sobbing but that would do.

When they came to the end, men began to stand up and shake hands in preparation for leaving. The Confederate and Union officers toasted one another and made edged jokes that could get lethal if carried too far. Finally, Webb lifted his glass and bid them all good night.

The other players looked at Simon.

"Go on," said the banjo player. "Go now."

"All right," he said, and walked down from the stage, past the tipped-over glasses and remains of beefsteaks on plates.

"Sir," he said. "Could you arrange for our pay?" He stood resolutely in front of Webb, unmoving.

"Pay?"

"Yes, sir."

There was a long silence, a sort of standoff as Webb waited for Simon to explain himself, but Simon remained stubbornly silent. He held his bow in one hand and his fiddle by the neck as if it were a turkey. Somebody dropped a dish in the kitchen.

"Pay," said Colonel Webb. "Well, I don't know." He raised his head to look at the stage, where the rest of them stood in their very civilian white shirts, holding their instruments and looking at him. The lamps were being blown out one by one. "I see," he said. "Well, what you need to do is take up a collection." His faultlessly clean hands drifted about his coat front.

"Yes, sir, that seems like a good solution." Simon turned on his heel and cried out in a loud voice, "Very well boys, the colonel says we are to take up a collection!"

"You do it!" shouted the banjo man.

"All right, I will!"

Instantly they all put down their instruments and smiled expectantly at the officers. Simon took up a soup tureen, wiped it out with somebody's napkin, and held it out to Webb.

"You could encourage the others, sir," he said. *You despicable hound.*

Webb snorted. "Fiddlers. Always greedy. Avaricious. Take it and get the hell out." He dropped in a half-dollar silver piece. "Get yourself home to whatever hole you live in."

Simon did not reply but turned to walk among the officers both in blue and gray with the soup tureen held out and even went out, where others stood talking in groups and did the same. They came up with $17 in coins, and Simon shared it out back in the storage room.

"Not a bad haul." Simon pocketed his coins and his anger. He wondered where the girl was, if she was safe. It was deep into the night and so she must be asleep somewhere, and he would have thought more about this but hunger overtook him. "Where's supper?"

"Here," said the color sergeant, and led them into the kitchen. "Sit down. Y'all are hungry, I know." He held out an invitational hand.

Damon and the Tejano and Simon got their supper from the cooks and ate sitting at one of the long tables in the mess hall like rats arriving in the dark. Roast beef, potatoes, light bread, corn pudding, a jelly made from agarita berries. Not a crumb or a rind remained when they were done. Damon and Simon exchanged glances.

"Where do they get all this food?" said Damon in a low voice.

"If I knew I'd be there," said the Tejano guitar player.

Back in the storage room, Simon snatched up shirts where they lay on barrels and hemp bags. He changed his own and counted; one, two, three, four. He stood in front of Damon with his hand out. "Give me that shirt," he said. "I'm going to take them back to the dog robber." Damon folded it neatly and handed it to him.

"I'll do it," said the banjo man. He stripped off his own white shirt and held it wadded in one hand and looked around for his uniform blouse. "I know him."

Simon opened his mouth, paused, always that hesitation in his speech. Then he said, "But I want to. I need some information from him."

"Ah," said the banjo man. "Persistent aren't you?" He shook his head and smiled. "You have taken a direct hit, my man."

The dog robber had left word with his orderly sergeant about the shirts and had himself gone to bed. Apparently, it was the orderly sergeant who did the books and had to account for money and shirts and pounds of salt. Simon found his way through the hot dark, threading among the adobe buildings, cookfires going out in clouds of ash as cooks doused them with dishwater while the stars floated up out of the sea. The staff sergeant was with Webb's 62nd U.S. Colored Troops, who all had white officers. They had taken over a long barracks made of adobe and roofed with canvas. The sergeant had his own room at one end.

Simon fetched up in his trim, quick walk at the sergeant's

doorway. The man sat with an oil lamp preparing his evening report. He raised his head. He was blond and spare, with half-moon eyeglasses.

"Thank you, sir," said Simon. He handed over the shirts. They were in a stack neatly folded. "Much appreciated." He was once again dressed in his checkered shirt, his vest hanging open and his pants held up by suspenders, with no hat to identify him one way or the other.

The sergeant regarded the shirts on his desk and Simon could see him counting them. "All right. Did you get paid?"

"We did."

The sergeant said, "Good. Remarkable, since you should have been in the cells for assaulting a Union soldier after you had supposedly surrendered." He took off the glasses and looked Simon up and down. "But then you're a fiddler."

"Yes." Simon didn't know where this was going, if anywhere. It didn't seem promising, but he plunged on. "Yes, sir, so, I wanted to ask about the young lady with Colonel Webb's wife and daughter."

"You did, did you? And you a surrendered rebel of no rank. A musician. Asking questions about the colonel's personal household." The sergeant gazed up at Simon as if he had just been offered some very interesting fact.

"That's about the size of it." Simon stood with both hands at his sides as if at attention because he thought that might help. He said, "I don't know any way of sneaking up on the question."

The sergeant carefully lined up his report papers. "You are not the first to ask."

"Well," said Simon. "No, I expect not." He wondered what form of address was proper to a sergeant of the opposing forces, but since he didn't know he just kept on. "Then, I'd just like to ask, sir, are you going to tell me or not?"

"Yes. I will." The thin blond sergeant considered the question. He said, "She is eighteen, Irish, and she's signed a labor contract with the colonel that legally obligates her to three years of service. It's better than starving in Ireland. What do you think?" He leaned back in his chair with a deceptively agreeable expression.

"Yes, sir, much better, of course, an immigrant, Ireland, fortunate to get a good position . . ." Simon was trying to think and could only come up with fragments of sentences. So she was in the colonel's power, somehow. The power of a contract, she an immigrant, away from friends or family to help. "You mean three years before she is allowed to, well, make acquaintances . . ." Simon gestured at random, finally put his hands in his pants pockets.

"Exactly. The contract, as I understand it, means no courting, no visits, no sighing over secret letters or flashing those blue eyes of hers at anybody. *Any. Body.* All her letters are read first by the Webbs. She is the governess and personal servant to an officer's wife, and when young men try to present themselves for her attention we hang them. *Hang. Them.*" The sergeant smiled.

A brief silence. Then Simon asked, "And how many years have expired?"

"Why is this your business? You're lucky you aren't in manacles. Big iron ones."

"Yes, sir."

"It's a crushing disappointment, isn't it? Colonel Webb will take up garrison life in San Antonio as part of the occupation army. *We* are occupying *you*. May you enjoy it. Her name is Miss Doris Dillon. Great playing, by the way. Beautiful. Do you know anything by Handel, by any chance?"

Simon ran the name over and over in his mind and then said, "Not yet."

"That's what I like to hear. Positive thinking. You could possibly have a future in the U.S. Army. Regimental bands. Think about it. Good night."

Simon hesitated. He wanted very much to know how much time had passed since Doris Dillon had signed this contract. He wanted to know if others had seen that dismissive shove, how to approach the subject, if in fact he had misinterpreted a random gesture. He took a breath and held up one finger. The sergeant put on his eyeglasses again and carefully hooked the earpieces around his ears.

"Get. Out."

He picked up his quill pen and turned back to his reports.

CHAPTER FOUR

THE NEXT MORNING AT sunrise Simon bent over a basin of water, wiping sand and dirt from his eyes. When he lifted his dripping, unshaven face he saw a little excursion wagon coming from the gate of Fort Brown, the kind that was well sprung and had side curtains, the kind that rode more comfortably than the heavier freight wagons or buckboards. In it were Webb's wife, littlc Josephina, several other women, and Doris Dillon.

They were all talking and wrestling with the side curtains in a flurry of skirts and petticoats. The Irish girl sat up front beside the driver and had bent back to help with the curtains, her skirts gripped in one hand against the Gulf morning breeze. The big horse in the shafts trotted out smartly. Behind them came the freight wagons bristling with soldiery. It was a long way to San Antonio and attacks from the Lipan Apache or Comanche were not out of the question.

Simon wiped his face with his shirttail and then quickly took his fiddle from his case. Water and soapsuds ran down his neck. They were coming toward him from out of the fortress, crossing the dry resaca. He must send her a message somehow, that the song had been for her and her alone, that he wished her to remember him. He stepped forward to the side of the road, tightened his bowstring, and began to play "Death and the Sinner" without even tuning up. It was a haunting Irish slow air and he sent it out to Doris Dillon note after note, phrase after phrase, out over the river and the deafening silence of a new-made peace.

She turned, squinting out from under a heart-shaped bonnet to see the slight fiddler with his curling mop of reddish hair playing alone under the palm trees, facing her. As they passed close, she leaned out of the driver's seat to listen, with a delighted expression on her face. She lifted her hand to him in a small, shy gesture. Somebody reached out from behind her and pulled her arm down. She turned front again and all her body told of her exasperation, but then she glanced over her shoulder at him, with a very small wave, a fugitive smile. And then they went on to San Antonio. Simon bowed his formal bow and when he lifted his head all he saw were dust and glinting trace chains and men moving slowly past to the equipment stacks.

Simon felt elated, suspended somehow. She had looked at him, waved to him; she had smiled. He sat down under the palms where he had made his small camp, and with a feeling of unmerited joy he began to put together his possessions. He considered them, and what he was to do and where he was to go on his journey to getting his land and acquiring the good regard of Miss Dillon. He had saved exactly thirty dollars in Spanish pesos over the last few years. He kept them in twists of muslin in his rucksack so they would not chink and then the twists rolled in a sock. Mexican pesos were the currency of much of the southwest and Felipe Quinto's haughty Spanish face seemed to give them even more value. Simon was under no illusions that he would receive back pay from the Confederate Army and did not even want to ask in case he had to write his name down somewhere.

He had left Kentucky determined to buy a piece of land in Texas and somehow he would find it. Somebody would mention it, somebody would be lamenting they couldn't sell it, but somewhere he would hear about it and it would be meant for him and the black-haired girl who was from Ireland and indentured to an uncharitable beast of a colonel for three years.

He thought, *That's just fine. She's not promised to somebody else and that gives me time to make money and find someplace, and she can't marry anybody else in the meanwhile. If she can avoid worse from the man.*

He stood for a moment to see the crowd of surrendered Confederates packing their gear, tents coming down, the tent ropes coiled. The war was finally over. A great otherworldly hand had swept across the South and destroyed so much and what now was to happen to others he did not know, but as for himself he flew a private ensign with several imperatives written upon it, one of which concerned music.

He jammed the fiddle case in his rucksack along with the disassembled revolver, his odds and his ends. He rolled his blankets into a long tube and slung it over one shoulder, tied the ends together on the other side. It seemed strange to see the American flag floating over the walls of Fort Brown, over the end of the greatest conflict America or any country had yet endured, all her flags folded now into one. He pulled on the Kentucky hat, no longer a soldier for the Confederacy. He started to walk out of the muster area in front of Fort Brown and was quickly stopped by a Union provost marshal's man.

"Where are you going, son?"

"Galveston," said Simon.

"Yes, but you have to be written down for discharge and you have to have a pass."

"Yes, sir," said Simon. "Where do I go?"

The officer said, in a careful, patient voice, "See that line of men in Confederate uniforms? They are all waiting in front of that tent to have their names checked against the muster rolls. Then they are given a discharge paper and a pass. Go there."

"Yes, sir."

Simon started off for the row of slouching, patient men. As soon as the officer had his attention taken away by a nearby argument Simon ducked out behind several commissary wagons, threaded among the Yankee tents, and found the road going east toward the mouth of the Rio Grande.

HALF A MILE down the road he heard a noise behind him and turned quickly.

It was the Yankee drummer boy, Damon, the black sergeant, the Zouave, and the guitar player from Colonel Benavides's regiment, who lugged his guitar in a case.

"Well, good morning you-all," said Simon. His strongly planed face, now furred with a day's growth of beard, lit up with a pleased expression.

"Hey hey, wait up!" the drummer boy shouted. "Where you off to?"

Simon gestured up the road. He said, "They are going to come and make you all stand in line in the hot sun here before long. As for myself, I am on my way to Galveston."

The banjo player said, "Not me. But I just come to give you a dollar out of my pay from the dinner. You got a long hard road ahead of you."

Simon said, "That is damn kind of you." He took the silver piece and lifted his hat. But the drummer boy, who said his name was Patrick, declared he was coming along with Simon; so did Damon and so did the Tejano guitar player.

"I ain't ready to go home yet," said the boy. "I aim to have some adventures here before long." He was carrying his bodhran in one hand, his rucksack on his back, and the pair of bones in one pocket. He rattled his thumb down the bodhran's head. "I got my discharge and my pass and I aim to see some of this old world before I go back." He did a quick reel step.

"The Federals gave you your discharge just like that?" said Damon. He gazed down at the boy. He had traded his top hat for a Hardee hat with a frayed brim and it shadowed his face.

"Said I never should have been in in the first place." The boy had ears like a carriage with its doors open, big Union-issue boots, a short nose, and a wide slot of a mouth. He kept on dancing as if the percussion of his boots on the road were more than enough, tune or no tune. "That I was a mere child. Glad to get shet of me."

"I cannot go," said the Zouave. "Ze banjo man cannot go and me eye-zer. I must return to my regiment zere in Bagdad across the rivaire. But, please, take zis my dollaire as well for you good leading us last night *et* also you *idees* about ze shirts, very esmart, *et alors, adieu mon vieux et bonne chance."*

So they said farewell to the banjo man and the Zouave. The two of them turned back toward the fort and Simon, Damon, the Tejano, and the boy started out for the Gulf of Mexico one foot after another in the searing heat. They carried with them their meager possessions, their blanket rolls over their shoulders, convinced that in Galveston were saloons and hotels, all in need of musicians, all filled with various sorts of people with money in their pockets. Simon would earn good hard silver there and eventually show up in San Antonio dressed to the nines with land of his own and he would sweep off his hat: *Miss Dillon, I hope you remember me.*

They said their names: Damon Lessing, Doroteo Navarro, Patrick O'Hehir, and Simon Boudlin. They stopped to shake hands all around and then went on.

"I knew Walters wasn't your real name," said Damon. "I have a keen intuition in that regard." They marched forward down the hot and sandy road.

Simon said, "Very well, then, does your intuition tell you how we can get to Galveston?"

"Of *course,*" said Damon. "By water. Walking up the coast all the way to Galveston is for madmen and jackrabbits. We need a boat."

"Yes, but I'm still waiting for a more specific idea," said Simon. They trudged on. "As to how to get a boat."

"We steal a boat from the Yankees there on the island. I know the place well. I worked the coastal ships for a year. The Yankees got me in New Orleans. Conscript labor. So I got away from them. Get away from one, grabbed by the other. The Confederates got me after I escaped the Yankees."

This was more than Simon had heard the dark man say about himself since he had first met him in the regimental band tent. "How do we get across to the island?" The heat of the day increased; the south Texas brush country around them was dense with the ganglia of creosote bush and acacia, all starred with thorns.

"They are ferrying stuff over to the mainland now that they got Fort Brown," said Damon. "Stores from Brazos de Santiago. Their endless cornucopia of food. We could hide on some boat tonight, one going over. We don't want them to see us crossing over. Then when we steal a boat, they won't figure out who did it. That substantial enough for you?"

"It is. I still have your revolver. It's in two pieces in my rucksack."

"Keep it, son. I don't want to get caught with it."

"All right then."

Simon lifted the rucksack higher on his square, bony shoulders.

They came upon various sorts of people traveling back and forth between Brazos de Santiago Island and Fort Brown; provisions and equipment carried in the freight wagons, empty wagons going back for more, Yankee infantry on their way to the fort and people who seemed to have no particular identity or purpose in life slogging along like automatons in the heat. Men without uniforms or wearing parts of uniforms and men clad entirely in rags, who were most likely Confederates.

When they came to the shore Simon glimpsed a long stretch of perfectly white sand and beyond that the white foam of the surf. They did not pause to enjoy the scenery but hid themselves among the dunes in the palmetto and salt grass. They were deadened by the heat. Simon pressed into the shade of a palmetto and undid his vest and shirt, flung his arms out. One inch beyond the shade and the sand was too hot to lay your hand on. By late afternoon they were nearly comatose. Boats and men and supplies were arriving, the boats bouncing on the gentle rollers while men in small lighters carried stuff ashore in a variety of packets and barrels. Others waded in carrying bundles on their heads.

The sun sank into the west, into the great unknown inland stretches of Texas, throwing out long shadows, flooding the coast with dark. Then a wind came up. They all made small hushed noises of relief. Simon crawled to the rim of the dune and parted the sea-grape and grass stems to look out upon the Gulf of Mexico; at a long white band of surf and a blue sea horizon without end. The breakers rolled in according to some great unknown accounting or a score past comprehension and every wave top glittered with red.

Simon had seen many mezzotints of shipwrecked sailors on rafts amid the mighty billows being tossed upon the stormy main, and he had imagined ocean waves as perpetually cone-shaped. It seemed to him the waves would then arrive at a given shore as a collection of triangles. Then they would fall flat on their faces, dissolve, and their place would be taken by yet another rush of water, et cetera. Spiky. He had imagined waves as spiky water. But what he saw were long rolling terraces of blue water that rose and fell into sparkling foam in hushing sounds, over and over. They had no end. He could have watched forever.

He had found his girl, the war was over, he had not gotten killed, and now he was before the great gulf itself. He felt cautiously happy; he felt that life was going to be all right. It was all going to work out for him. Maybe. He laid his hands on his rucksack and the fiddle case. It was going to work out; dreams of the good life in someplace far and secreted from the chaotic world, its wars and imperatives, and it struck him that to live near this body of water would be the right place. Fish. Sea winds. The unrolling surf. He clasped a sea-grape vine in his sand-crusted hand and thought, *Maybe somewhere near here, Galveston maybe, where the ships from England come in now the blockade is off.* A thought-picture of her walking beside him in this air laundered bright with salt wind, new strings in his fiddle case, Colonel Webb's foul designs foiled, and out on the ocean, a ship flying a flag with two sharps; mountain music.

When the Dipper stood overhead, so immense, so distant and brilliant, they waded into the surf and slipped aboard a big forty-foot lugger. Simon shoved his gear over the gunnel and then in the noise of breakers and men shouting at one another, he slid over on the rise of a wave. The others were over as well. They hid among pallets and empty barrels. Simon pulled a piece of canvas over himself. It was a stroke of good luck that, in the dark, an officer came and ordered the crew to sail immediately for Brazos de Santiago. They were way behind schedule, the officer shouted. Listen, even now you can hear the wagons coming down the road from Fort Brown to take on freight.

So in the black night the crew clambered aboard the empty lugger, raised sail, and hauled up the gaff rig. In this dark confusion Simon and the others were not noticed. They rocked across the two miles of salt water to the docks at Brazos de Santiago Island. The watch lights on the docks seemed to float on the water; first as dim sparks and then as warm yellow light throwing deep shadows between the warehouses. Simon and the others managed to slip overboard and crawl ashore in the surf without being seen. Simon carried the fiddle case on top of his head, squashing his Kentucky hat. When he reached the shore, he kneeled for a moment with the white waves breaking around his thighs, distrustful, trying to make out where they were going. The Tejano grabbed him by the collar and whispered to him to get up and run.

They spent a few hours dozing in the lee of a barracks wall, huddled together with their clothes draining salt water. When the tide was sliding out lower with every wave Damon got them to their feet and they crept to the docks. They found a twenty-foot dinghy or catboat, which the Federals were using as a tender. They loaded their gear with great delicacy to avoid making any noise; Simon came aboard last, easing over the gunnel like a wary cat with Damon hissing *hush hush* at them all.

Then Damon sat on the one thwart and took up the oars. He rowed them out into the Gulf for some distance; at last the few sparks of light from the island dwindled and disappeared.

Stepping the mast took some effort even with Damon's instructions, which soon turned to exasperated shouts. Then the sail; it was gaff-rigged and they fell afoul of what seemed to be hundreds of square yards of canvas and limitless amounts of rope. The boy drummer was struck on the head by the boom but his Union Army cap softened the blow even as he shouted in pain and started cursing. The wind stayed steady and Damon put the cutter on a beam reach as they sailed north on the east wind. The height of the waves increased. By dawn they were out of sight of land, plunging up and down on a rolling sea.

"We don't want to be out of sight of land," said Simon. "Turn this thing west."

"Where's that?" said Patrick. "Oh God." His hand went to his mouth and he bent over, turned to the gunnel, and vomited into a wave.

Damon shook his head. "Just don't throw up in the boat, young'un."

"West is opposite the side the sun is coming up," said the Tejano. He sounded discouraged. "*¿Y saben que?* We don't have any water."

"Or a bottle to put it in." The boy had turned a greasy color, like pork fat, and he dipped up water with his forage cap to pour on his head and then lost it into the sea. "Ah shit," he said. "Well, just shit."

"Look around," said Simon. He lay in a heap with his shirt and pants soaked and his rucksack and blanket roll at his back. "May be supplies under the cuddy."

They found two wooden canteens, one full, the other half-empty. The Tejano took over the tiller and turned the catboat to catch the wind on their tail so that they sailed more or less to the west. This made the catboats' motion even worse, bucketing straight up the waves and plunging down again. The sun rose into the sky and became smaller and the waves shot intense heat reflections into their faces. The motion sent the boy doubling over the side again, retching. A gull hung in the air over them, its head bent down to see who they were, what they were doing, and in its still, stiff airborne stasis it turned its head from one side to the other as if searching their faces each in turn.

At least there was a wind. Simon pulled his Kentucky hat over his face and rolled his sleeves down. Having been on the Ohio

River a good many times, he knew what water reflections could do, especially to skin like his. He threw his Confederate cap to Patrick and told the boy to tie his kerchief over his head and let it hang down behind and shade the back of his neck.

"Well hell's bells, what about this?" said the boy. He put on Simon's cap and then over that the bodhran. He clutched it by the crossbar and held it over his head. "This here is like a big Texas hat, idn't it?"

The hours grew hotter and brighter. Simon hung on to the gunnel and watched the strange unstable world of Gulf water rushing past them, a place that was without footing or rest, all the same color and swept by salt wind. He bent over the side, watching shafts of weird light sent into the deep by the white-hot noontime sun.

Sometime in the afternoon his mind turned back to the girl and so he called to Patrick to ask if he knew aught of her. Where Colonel Webb and his family were going. He had heard it from the sergeant but he wanted a second opinion.

"San Antonio, they say," said the boy. They were all speaking loudly against wind and water. "To go into garrison there." He held the bodhran against the sun and squinted. He was trying not to throw up again.

"That's right," said the Tejano. "Everybody was asking because of the girl. And me too, one of these days. Going to San Antonio." He shut his eyes against the glare. "It's Spanish anyway. So far."

Doroteo wore a wide-brimmed hat of palm straw and he was down to his blue-striped shirt. His coat and pants were regulation Confederate gray, but he had cut all the insignia off his jacket. He held the tiller in one hand and his guitar case in the other. He rocked to the motion of the waves, trying to save the case from falling into the water in the bottom of their boat. Damon tipped his hat to the back of his head to protect his neck and stared down at his two different shoes, exhausted.

Young Patrick breathed through his nose and paused to see whether he would vomit. He didn't. "I talked to her once. She is fair kind and I took off my hat to her. I was wanting to pull the head on my drum, you know, loosen the hoop and she said, 'Oh, sit in the shade then and here's a dipper of cold water.' It was going on for two hundred degrees in the shade, on my mother's grave."

Simon listened with drops of sweat draining from under his hatband. "And so she is from Ireland directly, herself." Simon held his rucksack with the fiddle case jammed down in it in both arms. Maybe he was making a fool of himself out here on the hot ocean, in love like it was a taking, going someplace unknown and in what had to be admitted were mere rags.

"Yes. I told her my parents back in Pennsylvania, they had come over too. From near Waterford. She said she was from Tralee, which is where a lot of Dillons come from, the ones that ain't dead or come here."

"Dead of what?"

"Of no food to keep them alive, since the potatoes all went to slush in the Black '47."

"But she's just come over, ain't she?"

"She has. Said she was very happy to find employment in America, even though she did end up in Texas and a battle besides. And I said as God is my witness, I never thought I'd have ended up in Texas either and look at me now."

"But where will she be in San Antonio?"

"They said they were going into garrison at that old Spanish mission where the Mexicans killed everybody." The shade of the sail rolled over him and back again, over and back.

Doroteo nodded. "The Alamo," he said. He smoothed down his mustache with his thumb and forefinger. "Didn't do any good."

"That's it. Alamo." The boy swallowed and then sank back once more against the gunnel. His great ears were bright red on the tips and his large boots were nearly sole to sole as his knees flopped open.

"What do they say about Colonel Webb?"

"Say?" The boy opened his eyes.

"He's her employer isn't he?"

"He didn't have nothing to do with no drummer boy." Then in a cheerful voice, "But he was fair and easy with the men. The men liked him. He made them laugh."

Simon said, "Well, there you go." He doubted, somehow, what he had seen. It was just the vague thrashing about of a man in a state of nerves after a battle. An unquiet mind.

And so the day went on. They talked in a slow desultory way, releasing words as reluctantly as they sipped at the precious water. Patrick roused himself in the heat and glitter of salt water to say that he knew three dances. "I can do the flatfoot, a jig step, and a reel step."

"We are a regular traveling circus." Simon lay back with his hat over his face. "Can you swallow swords?"

"I never tried it," the boy said, "and I ain't about to." The thought made him vomit over the side again. "Ah shit," he said and wiped his mouth on his Union blouse sleeve.

Far away to the west the Gulf coast came into view, so they turned north again. This caused more sail adjustments. The backstays and halyards sagged. The Tejano said that he had once been a fisherman on the Gulf in his former life, and sagging backstays and halyards—these ropes here—were not good. Damon agreed. It was a scandal the way they sagged. Patrick and Simon were told to tighten them and after they figured out how, they did. This put them on a beam reach again, going north. The plunging and bucketing smoothed out somewhat. Then Damon said that Galveston was on a long sand island that lay across the mouth of a deep harbor and the main place was on the inside, the harbor side. That's where the saloons were. That's where the money was.

CHAPTER FIVE

THEY SAILED ALL DAY without seeing another vessel. The sky overhead was clear blue, as if they had left all rain behind and all hope of rain. Damon called up quote after quote from Edgar Allan Poe: *No swellings hint that there may be a far-off happier sea, Nothing save the airs that brood over the magic solitude . . .* And the boy called out for him to leave off, would he? He'd heard enough poetry. And Damon suggested that he go over the side and swim if he didn't like it, ignorant spotted-faced little fiend and could he just stop puking? Simon and Doroteo shouted for them both to shut up.

They glided north past a low and varied coast. They squinted with sun-reddened eyes on miles of white dunes and clumps of vegetation, including a few trees. Once they were close enough to see longhorn cattle grazing, egrets and buffalo birds fluttering about them in the hot and shimmering air.

That night the wind changed and began to blow from the south. Doroteo said he was not sure where they would end up, because he could not see the shore and see there, the skies were clouding over.

"I can't see the North Star." He leaned back and searched the soft rolling black overhead. "*Estrella del norte,* the fisherman's friend."

Simon said, "That's not good. How do we know we're going north?" He pulled his suspenders off his shoulders and let them fall to his elbows. He unbuttoned his shirt and vest to the wind and sat with his eyes closed, feeling the relief of it, the blessed relief. It seemed to blow right through his ribs and into his grateful soul with a power never felt on land. The stars came and went.

Damon said, "We'll stick close to shore. Watch and see if you can see house lights."

There was a good foot of freeboard to protect them from the waves; it was, after all, a haulage vessel, but still the spray struck them when the catboat heeled. They sailed on into the darkness, thirsty and hungry. They had shared out all the water of the full canteen during the day. Patrick managed to keep down his swallow of water. It was oily tasting with tinges of red dirt and horse manure. They had no more than one half canteen now. With the heavy scrim overhead all they saw was the breaking white foam of waves on their starboard side. They silently listened to the sound of the waves and from somewhere on shore a low hooting.

The Tejano stayed at the tiller. He said he would stay within reach of that hooting sound, because it had to be coming from the land. Simon fell asleep on his rucksack. They rose and fell, rose and fell. Simon lay clinging to the gunnel and slid back and forth, back and forth, in the sloshing bilge water.

He woke up in the dark to Damon calling out. "Look yonder! That'll be Indianola." He lifted a hand to indicate a row of dim lights on the shore.

"Let's go there for water," said the boy.

"Hell no, the Yankees got it." Damon stood to stare at the lights. "I never got my discharge papers. I just took off."

"So are we going in the right direction?" Simon asked.

"Yes, yes. We're good. Take the tiller and keep those lights on your left and then astern."

Simon took the tiller so Doroteo could get some sleep on the hard, unforgiving strakes with his pack under his head. It didn't take long for him to get the way of it. He felt the living pull of the tiller in his hand as their sail drew them on northward. The clouds blew away and then he could see the North Star. He kept the masthead in a rolling circle with that dim star in its middle. He wondered why they had not had sense enough to steal more canteens or find some way to fill the ones they had. Too late now. But they were at liberty on the open sea and sailing toward their own futures, precarious as those futures might be. Then Indianola fell astern and was extinguished by the night.

The next day they shared out one good drink each from the last canteen and by the afternoon Simon began to feel the torture of thirst. The waves grew larger and the sail filled until it was hard as a drum head; they heeled to the left and the bluff straight-up-and-down nose of the cutter dug in. The shore was so flat and low it was nearly invisible except for the occasional clump of trees and the airburst frondiness of the native palms.

"Don't drink the salt water," said Damon. "Just don't do it." He took his turn at the tiller.

"Let's go in to shore," said the boy. "I'm so thirsty I can't stand it."

"What makes you think there's water on shore?" said Doroteo. "There isn't any water on shore."

Simon pulled the fiddle case out of his rucksack, opened it, and shared out the two slices of mummified apple, half a piece each. It helped. They crowded into the shade of the sail on the lee side, and wherever the sun touched them it was like hot metal searing their skin.

"Get back on the other side," said Damon. "You sons of bitches are going to capsize us."

The waves flung them up and then down into the next trough and the boy became seasick again. He dry-retched as the bow sidled sideways up the next roller. Then he lay limp and silent and held his bodhran drum over his face like a parasol. Doroteo bent to him and urged him to drink the last drops of water from the canteen. The boy tipped his head back and let the few drops run down his throat and then lay back again. His wet yellow hair stuck out in discouraged tufts, his face was slack in the shadow of the drum head. His dark blue army shirt rattled in the wind over his body and he seemed to have lost ten pounds in the last twenty-four hours.

"There's fish down in there." Doroteo gazed into the depths of the Gulf. They slid down another wave. "But we got no hooks, no tackle, no bait." He dragged one hand in the water. "You cook them over an open fire with achiote, some epazote." He closed his eyes against the glare.

"So what are we doing in Galveston?" said Damon. His face, normally a dismal bluish color, was now seared with bright sunburn.

"We're going to play music and make money." Simon bent his head against the sun as if against a storm of wind. "Everybody agreed?" He ran a hand through his hair and it was sticky with salt and so were his hand, his skin, his clothes.

"I'm in," said Doroteo and Damon. The boy lifted his hand and let it fall back again.

Doroteo took his turn at the tiller once more, and he seemed somehow tireless, endlessly strong, as if made of some indestructible wiring. The sun was finally quenched under a layer of cumulus that came up out of the east and the boy seemed to revive. They all revived. Night came and Simon watched for shore lights but saw none. After some hours he laid himself against the side, curled around his rucksack. Then Patrick woke them up crying out about lights and music.

Simon sat up out of dreams of clear water. "What?" he said, and stared around himself. Damon sat slumped against the thwart in the slopping bilge. The boy was shouting still. Doroteo stood at the tiller, staring.

On the far horizon was a misty, gleaming city. Its light shone on the low cloud cover and in sparkles over the waves as each one lifted in turn. Over the water they could hear disconnected noises of wheels rolling over pavement and a long urban sighing of surf and music. Simon buttoned his shirt and vest and fought out of the confusion of dreams, the pain of thirst.

"Galveston," said the dark man. He smiled and the harbor lights reflected from his black eyes. He was like a devil come home to hell at last. "We made it."

"What's the light from?" said the boy.

"Gaslight," Damon said. "Streets lighted by gaslight."

They approached over the midnight sea. Damon said, in exhausted and disconnected sentences, they would run up long sand island to north end, gap there, get inside harbor, wharves, city all on other side. He then stopped talking, as it was too difficult with his tacky mouth and split lips. He reached over the side and scooped up a handful of seawater, spit it out again. Then he signaled Doro to give him the tiller. Doroteo held it until Damon had his hand on it and they crawled past each another, switching places.

They sailed past the Union works along the seaward side of the island. Timbers had been thrown up for bulwarks and Union soldiers paced along the berms. Faint lights came from barracks, spilling over the long stretch of white sand beach.

They slid over the sea until the barracks were behind them

and came to the passage between Galveston Island and a headland on the other side that Damon said was called Bolivar Point. There they saw a soldier on a high structure like a shot tower. He watched them sail past through a spyglass. He was illuminated by a light inside a bull's-eye lantern, and he turned slowly, mechanically, keeping the spyglass on them. It was very strange. The soldier seemed like a clockwork figure in his precise movements. Simon wondered what kind of music they had here, lying in wait for them. Where the nearest source of water might be.

They came through the gap under Damon's directions and then sailed slowly, in a diminishing breeze, into a harbor where the blue-white illumination on the docks threw stark, harsh patterns of shadow and light. The gas lamps stood like sentinels along the streets. They all listened carefully and did not speak. From somewhere they heard disjointed music. As they came toward the docks they heard the heavy breathing of some kind of steam machine. Galveston lay asleep under the rolling slurry of cloud and the white light of burning coal gas.

Then the breeze died entirely. They unshipped the oars and Simon flailed wildly at the water with them. At last they came upon the wharf, where all the ships were tied up, and there they saw Galveston's long waterfront and its brick warehouses, many of them scarred with cannonball shot, presenting a grim face to the oily water. A sign on two tall poles said KUHN'S WHARF.

They lowered the sail and wadded it up in a sloppy and unseamanlike way and coiled the ropes. Simon grasped at his possessions and finally got his rucksack on his back, his blanket roll over his shoulder, and his hat on his head. They found a place to tie up under the lee of a great cargo ship, a steamer, whose watch leaned over the gunnels and called out to them.

"Don't you tie onto this ship, you sons of bitches. Hear me?"

"Ya ya," called Damon. "We hear you, stow it, tying onto the bollards." Then he asked, "Still a pump around here?"

"There is," said the watch. He peered down at them and seemed to regret his harsh words. "Yes, just up in front of the seaman's employment building."

Simon wondered if he had the strength to climb up the wharf timbers. "Give me the rope," he said. His voice was weak. "I'll go up and tie on."

"*Esperate,*" said Doroteo. He caught up the long tie rope called a painter, carefully rolled it into a large coil, made a hondo and a loop, and began to circle the loop over his head. He threw it with an expert overhand, lassoing the bollard high above.

"Ro-*de*-o!" cried Damon. "Man of unsuspected talents." He climbed up the ladder of timbers and fell down with his rucksack on his back, lost his Hardee hat, regained his feet and his hat, and then stood quietly gathering his strength. Simon reached the dock after several clumsy tries. Doroteo came after. All Simon could think of was that soon he would not be thirsty anymore, he was not going to die of thirst. There was no other thought in his head.

"They'll find this boat." Patrick clutched his drum as he stood unsteadily in the boat and stared down the dark of the waterfront.

"And so?" said Doroteo. "Not got our names written on it." He reached down to help the boy but Patrick first handed up Doroteo's guitar case and then struggled up himself.

Simon said, "We have to find that pump."

"Then we got to find a place. Sleep, lay down," said Damon. He looked to the left and then to the right. "Untie that boat. Let it float off. Then somebody finds it, they'll just take it." His voice was hoarse. "They won't go and try to find out who came in on it. They'll just take it."

"Yes. Good thinking." Doroteo turned back, untied the painter, threw it in a long loop into the boat, and watched for a moment as it began to drift. They stumbled along Galveston's harbor front with their baggage strung about them.

They found the pump set in a concrete housing in front of the Seaman's Employment Bureau and pumped water into one another's hands. They drank and drank, extravagantly. They splashed water over their heads and the handle screeched like a banshee over the silent wharf. They drank again and refilled the canteens and then just sat for a while. They regarded the lights, the great buildings, the many ships tied up at the wharves. Tall canted cranes, black skeletons, stood over the docks and from the ships came the sparks of watchmen's lanterns.

It took half an hour or more to recover, but at last they got to their feet, shouldered their burdens, and went on.

As they walked, they passed the canteens back and forth as if they would never get enough water. They went past brick buildings and empty lots littered with bottles and broken kegs. Flyers advertising various events and services flapped in the sea breeze. One building front had been entirely battered in by cannon fire and glass lay in the street still. Their steps sounded loud on the pavement, the eerie light shone on every street, on the low clouds and a city asleep.

Then Simon saw two figures approaching from far down the docks, two Union soldiers who fell in and out of step with each other as they checked the big warehouse doorways and shone their bull's-eye up onto ship forepeaks. They moved through pools of gas illumination. Simon dodged through stacked bales and barrels with names printed on them: *Pryor, Bailey*. Steamships tugged at their hawsers. The soldiers were coming closer.

"Hey, hey," he called in a low voice and ducked into an alleyway between two warehouses. Rather than go crashing noisily through the trash, he sat down with his back against a wall. The others came after him running low and sat down alongside.

"Patrol," said Simon in a whisper.

"Why are we hiding?" Damon whispered back.

"I don't know," said Simon. "Seems like a good idea." He thought of the revolver. Maybe he wasn't allowed to have a revolver.

"*¿Se pueden callar?*" Doroteo whispered. His head flopped back against the wall and it made the back of his hat brim stand up. Patrick snatched the Confederate cap from his head and jammed it down into his rucksack.

The four sat silently amid unseen garbage and refuse as the patrol went past. The two soldiers murmured between themselves and went on, their footfalls stark and heavy on the stones. Without speaking the same thought occurred to all of them: *They have good boots*. They heard church bells ring out; one. And stop.

After listening for a long time Simon stood up and said, "Let's go."

"Where?"

"I don't know that either. Someplace."

They turned away from the waterfront and into the city. They walked together in a defensive group, Simon leading and Damon bringing up the rear. Doroteo kept the center with his guitar case on his back and the boy Patrick beside him, bareheaded, holding the round drum in front of him by its inner bar like Saint Brendan's shield held out against the devils of the night.

They finally came upon a sort of saloon. A light gleamed out the front window and music could be heard from inside. Simon stood in the street listening to the rich, full sound of a German flute playing a lighthearted shanty.

He stepped forward and pushed the door open a crack. He turned up his head to see what had once been a two-story building; the upper floor had been taken out and now it was a cavernous tall space with broken beams overhead.

A thin man sat on a packing box. A single lantern burned at his feet. The flute was silver, the kind you blew across the mouthpiece, with stops on velvet pads. At several tables men were asleep with their faces on their arms and one on the floor curled up around a seaman's bag, snoring. The man lowered the flute and sang, *Sail away ladies, sail away* . . . Then he noticed the newcomers.

"Well, well," said the thin man. "Come in."

"We're looking for a place to sleep," said Simon. "Where we won't bother the patrols."

"This is the place," said the man. He held out his bony long fingers in a gesture of invitation. "Join the merry crowd. They've drank themselves insensible. From the Liverpool ship called the *Lisa Rose*."

They sat down on the chairs; Damon plucked at one knee of his trousers to straighten a nonexistent pleat and regarded the filthy litter of the floor.

Then the flute player said, "Did you all just come from Brazos de Santiago? There was a big battle down there."

Simon cried out, "No! Was there? What happened?"

The flute player tipped his head to the side and shut one eye. "Sorry I asked. It was the remains of your Confederate uniforms."

"No problem," said Damon.

Simon lifted a hand and then placed his rucksack against the wall, sat on the floor with his legs out straight in front of him, and immediately fell asleep. *Sail away ladies, sail away, live with the angels by and by.*

WHEN DAYLIGHT CAME the flute player was gone. The English sailors still snored. Simon, Damon, Doro, and Patrick stepped out into the street again. They gazed around themselves at a ruined city. Thin horses languished in their harnesses and most windows were broken, but still people bustled down the cavernous streets, ship's boys ran hither and yon clutching bills of lading, men in homburgs walked along reading the latest newspapers from New Orleans, sailors loitered in slanky unobtrusive loiter stances in whatever shade they could find. They bought a sack of broken ship's biscuit from a marine supply store and walked along biting at it, drinking from the canteens.

"We must find a place for renting," said Doroteo. "A room." And then in a discouraged voice, "The verandah, the roof, the gutter. Someplace, anyplace."

"That takes money." Damon had the sack of biscuit by the neck. "We ain't got a pot to piss in or a window to throw it out of, as they say in the vernacular."

"We got our dinner money from the officers," said Patrick. "Ain't we? I do." He wiped crumbs from his mouth. "Whyn't we ask somebody?"

Simon said nothing about his thirty dollars; it was to buy land with and he was going to hang on to every coin until Felipe Quinto screamed for mercy.

They stopped a passerby for information and stood uneasily as the man paused and put his hands in his pockets and looked them over one by one. He noted the way they slung their gear and the remains of butternut uniforms. He was used to returning soldiers, it seemed. Ragged men set loose from a defeated army, trying to find their way back into human life, its fabric, its customs, the long-forgotten uses of civilization.

"Looks like y'all carrying musical instruments there," he said.

"Looks to me like it too," said Damon. "Does it look like it to you fellows?"

The rest of them murmured agreement. Simon said, "We were

wondering about places to rent. Where we could set down our musical instruments, sort of."

"Why hell, boys, just go out there toward the Gulf side, they's all kinds of abandoned go-downs and shacks and shanties and all that." The man gestured toward the east. "People tearing them down for firewood. Tore up about half the wood buildings in Galveston for firewood. Deserted out there. Shantytown, about deserted. Magruder came in, chased the Yankees out, and then half the city was told to leave. Blockade. Union came back again and blew us all to hell. No blockade now! Get yourself a house, boys."

They walked off in the direction he indicated. The better part of Galveston was inside the island, facing the harbor, where the wharves and warehouses were and a long elegant street called the Strand. They passed a big building called the Hendley Hotel, whose facade was missing cannon ball–sized chunks of masonry. They could see some of the grand houses, mansions built on cotton money and shipping money before the war and still elegant. But they were not going there. They trudged out toward the seaside. Soon they were slogging through sand in a kind of shacktown.

They came upon an empty house that seemed suitably abandoned. It stood somewhat slanted among other single-story cottages and shacks, the unpaved streets floury with white sand. They slung their baggage onto a splintered floor. Simon could hear the roar of the surf in the distance, could see the blue glint of the Gulf of Mexico. The house had lost many of its cypress shingles, the chimney was about to collapse, there was only one window that still had its shutters, and the front door never quite closed.

In the next few days Simon shored up the chimney with stones robbed from other chimneys nearby, Patrick carved at the door with his knife until it would shut, Damon hung hemp sacks from the waterfront over the windows, and Doroteo made an excursion to the wharf and brought in two sacks of cotton from a busted cotton bale sitting unsold in Bailey's Exports warehouse. They made themselves beds by stuffing the cotton into yet more hemp sacks. They set up a kitchen table with shaky legs by bracing it into a corner, found a pail and a dipper, located the nearest pump, and they were in business.

CHAPTER SIX

DAMON SAID THEY WERE all going to starve if they did not eat more than hardtack and so they made their way to the northern pass, where the fishing boats came in. There Doroteo bought five redfish from a black man with a Jamaican accent for five cents apiece. He called them *huachinangos* and regretted his lack of achiote. Nonetheless, he built a fire in the fireplace and said, "Leave this to me. Get away." He placed several pieces of iron strapping over it, and he soon had them crisp as winter leaves on the outside and snowy white within.

Simon picked up large pieces with his knife and told them it would all get better as they went along, they would find jobs in the saloons if they worked at their music, he was sure of it.

"All right with me," said Damon. "'*They had gone unto the wars, trusting to the mild-eyed stars*' . . ." He stretched out his legs; his shoes were coming apart. One was a brogan with two-hole laces and the other was an ankle boot that laced up his shin.

"Whoa," said Patrick. "Not more dead cities and stuff." He was trying to throw pieces of fish in the air and catch them in his mouth.

Doroteo said, "I am finish with the dead cities, Damon."

"That's not 'The City of Sin.'" Damon lifted his chin in an offended gesture. "It's another one. Patrick stop that, Jesus Christ."

"There's no end to them." Patrick wiped his mouth with his blue shirt cuff. "Dead cities, talking ravens, spirits in the outhouse just waiting to bite your butt. We got any lard?"

Doroteo handed him a small packet and the boy began to lightly smear the lard over the skin of the bodhran. They had each taken one corner of the shack as their own. Simon had settled on the corner to one side of the fireplace, where he laid out all his possessions as neatly as he always had, as he had been taught to do by the old man. He reassembled the revolver, carefully, after cleaning it with a stick and a rag, loaded five charges, rolled up the empty chamber under the hammer. He leaned back against the wall, listening to the fluting noise of the wind in all the cracks of the abandoned house. He was very tired. He was still hungry. But *Sail away ladies* kept running through his head and he fell into the song and the sleep it brought with it. Images of ladies sailing away in their big hoop skirts, moving toward a sea horizon like hot-air balloons of many colors, Doris Dillon among them. His mother young and pretty and dead. Revolving great rays of sunset and beyond that sunset a presence so vast it struck terror in his heart and he jerked awake.

Evening. He was still thirsty. He got to his feet and thought, *I need water, that's why I am dreaming so much. So strangely.* He took up the dipper from the bucket, swallowed one dipperful, two. The water was cloudy and tasted of bog pools and salty rain. He poured a third dipper over his head. There was a great deal to do, much facing him in this new peacetime. If it was a peace, if military occupation was a peace, then it was all right with Simon as long as he could make music happen, as long as his girl did not float away into some windy unattainable sky, as long as he could make a living. He wiped his face with both hands.

Long dark shadows came up out of the continent to the west of them, crawled over the harbor, and block by block the lamplighters set fire to the streetlights. In Shacktown there were no streetlights. Simon built up the fire in the fireplace for some illumination. The other three smoked, rested, were talkative, but Simon sat on his pallet and leaned against the wall and returned slowly to the present world.

He had to get them all into a passable band and make enough money for clothes; his were in tatters. Only the old checkered homespun shirt had not broken its seams. Eventually he would need a horse. Then he could get to San Antonio and find some way to present himself to Doris Dillon. To see if she was the same as the person in his imagination and if she was, then to tell her he would wait for her, for three long years if he had to. Maybe he didn't have to, but that would take more information than he had or knew how to get.

His future was all there like a three-draw spyglass shut up and compact and he would draw it out cylinder by cylinder. Behind him were the flames of a burning barn in Kentucky and a childhood of bastardy. The worst was knowing all the time he was a good fiddler, even a superb fiddler, but long before this time and surely now many a good man had gone down to ruin or death unrecognized and probably drunk into the bargain. Simon sank into sleep and once again into dreams, but these he could not recall the next morning.

They woke up sticky with heat and the salt air. Then they went out to the local pump to pour water over their heads and then to the beach to gather driftwood for the fire.

"Well now," said Damon. He stood shirtless and barefoot with water running down his narrow chest. "Let's figure out what we all know in common and start practicing."

"There you go," said Simon.

"Take the lead, fiddler."

"All right."

They returned to the derelict house to clean up as best they could. Simon stood in front of a piece of mirror to shave, carefully stropping his straight razor on his boot sole. Since they had no scissors to trim beards, Damon did the same, waiting for his turn in front of the broken mirror. His beard was heavy and blue. The boy Patrick regarded him with a critical squint and then held out a wad of gray soap.

"Here, Mr. Damon," he said. "I been a-saving of it. If you got lice it'll kill them dead and if you got sunburn it'll take your skin off."

"Well, bless your little Irish heart," said Damon and grabbed it before Doroteo could get his hands on it. "Simon is afflicted with pale peach fuzz and you Mexicans don't have face hair to speak of."

"Yes," said Doroteo. "I thank God every day He did not give me that hog hair you got on your face, man."

They went over a list of tunes and ran through them until late afternoon. First tune was "Ailen Aroon," because it was simplest, and then several of the tunes they had played at the officer's dinner. They all looked up at the same time when they heard some church bells ring out five o'clock. Then they walked out with their clothes too loose on their thin bodies, lugging their instruments. The fine sand poured into Simon's broken boots. He ran his thumbs under his suspenders and hoisted them higher on his shoulders. The lowering sun glowed red hot and hostile, but they struck out with determined step, music cases in hand.

The center of Galveston on the harbor side was composed of brick buildings two and three stories tall. They gave only a glance down the broad street called the Strand to take in its houses of several stories with turrets and cupolas, shaded by palms, those houses far away and guarded by money, by their air of a coastal nobility. Their task on this first evening was to find the places where they might be hired. They found at least five saloons, four dining establishments, three hotel bars, and several places that could only be called low dives on the harbor front.

At each place they stopped to listen to the competition. At the first they paid for plates of bread and butter with coins from the officer's dinner and devoured every crumb. The boy licked his fingers until Doroteo elbowed him.

Simon gazed around at the other men sitting slumped back in their chairs to listen and knew they all shared memories of the chaos of the Civil War, of death and destruction, poverty, dislocation. But he had his music. He could lift them out of all that for a few moments. Music is clean, clear, its rules are forever, another country for the mind to go to, and so this search for employment among the drinking places of Galveston did not bother him. To Simon, the world of musical structures was far more real than the shoddy saloons in which he had to play. Nothing could match it, nothing in this day-to-day world could ever come up to it. It existed outside him. It was better than he was. He was always on foot in that world, an explorer in busted shoes.

They listened to a badly tuned banjo and a concertina, not great but the duo had volume. They walked on.

One dining room had a piano, a cheap one; they stood quietly back against the wall and left as soon as they saw a waiter coming toward them with a determined expression on his face. One of the saloons had a group of three players on guitar, fiddle, and banjo, churning out jigs and shanties. They came upon the thin flute player in a place called the Windjammer. He nodded to them and then finished his piece and came to sit with them.

His name was Peter Hendrick and he was hired here and there to provide music for the pleasure and enjoyment of not only the patrons of saloons but dancing parties, garden parties, and the various thrills and delights of the small theater on C Street. But he was moving on to Houston, where there were more places, more money. Unlike Galveston, that town had not been fought over twice, blockaded and shot up, and half the population evacuated.

Damon was relieved of care and worry by this information. He sat back in his chair and pushed his hat off his brow. There was no way he could compete with that German flute, not with a six-hole pennywhistle. The silver flute had sixteen holes and could cover three octaves.

"Well, *bon voyage,*" said Damon and smiled like a villain.

Hendrick told them two other facts about Galveston that they should know; that often great storms would come, storms called hurricanes with winds that could pick up a grown man and deposit him five miles inland without a stitch of clothes on his body, on my mother's grave. And then there was the yellow fever, which turned a person the color of a pumpkin while at the same time he vomited black stuff. So if one of the storms came, they needed to dig in low somewhere.

"What about the yellow fever?" Simon asked. With water, good sleep on solid land, and some food, Simon had regained his strength and his living, tight verve, his low-spoken intensity. He had lived through a battle, had been shot at and shot back, survived the Gulf of Mexico in a small boat, and knew what lay ahead: work, music, land, a girl. Surely he could survive the fever and a hurricane. He wiped his reddish hair from his face and in front of his taut and famished body he held the Markneukirche in its case.

Hendrick paused and then lifted a hand palm up in a helpless gesture. "Well, just kiss your behind goodbye, boys, and leave some money for your funeral."

They shook hands all around and wished him luck.

And so they began their rounds, giving saloon owners and proprietors of low dives what they had for a repertoire. They played while the owner sat in judgment, men with dirty aprons, men listening with their heads bowed and their hands between their knees. They were raw and uncoordinated and had to keep glancing at one another to stay together. One after another the owners said no. They said, I could use that fiddle but not the rest of you and merely shrugged when Simon shook his head. They said, Well, we already got somebody this week. They said, I was looking for a group that had brass—trombone, cornet. We need somebody that can play piano.

They kept on trying. Galveston seemed a city of darkness and the sea since they only walked out after dark and slept most of the day. They became creatures of gaslight and shadows. Soon they were out of ready money and very hungry.

They finally got their first employment in a saloon alongside the Hendley Hotel but within two nights were ousted by another group with a much sharper sound. This other group was composed mostly of sailors without a ship, a scratch band like themselves, but they had all been on the same crew and had sung sailor's shanties together, so they were coordinated like gears in a machine.

"No, no, sorry boys, this sailor group is better. Patrons like them better. If your fiddler won't play with them then your boy there with the bones and that drum, he's good, they could use him."

"No, sir," said Patrick. "I am faithful to my friends and you can go to hell and shovel ashes."

"He didn't mean that." Simon stepped up behind Patrick and gave him a quick, secretive punch in the kidneys. "He was raised in an engine room by a coal slinger. He doesn't know what he's saying."

They hustled out, quickly.

As soon as they were on the street Simon cried out, "Did you *have* to? Did you just have to?"

"What?" said Patrick. His jug ears were bright red. He seemed on the verge of tears. In the gaslight they sparkled on his lashes, a look of distress on his young face.

"Insult the owner. That was a great idea. Insult the owner. Yes, that's it. That's how we get work."

"I never was in a band before, I never learned." Patrick clutched his bodhran in front of himself, a shield held out against Simon's anger.

"Learn now or get the hell out."

"Simon," said Damon.

Simon marched on half a block in silence and finally got hold of himself. Then he said in a taut voice that they had to practice five songs and get them down perfect. Note perfect. If they had those faultless, then they could fake the rest until they learned them. As it was, they were sloppy and uncoordinated and the more he thought about it the madder he got. They tore at pieces of old bread as they walked along, biting it as if it were some stubborn foe. It tasted terrible.

In their shack with half a candle to light their slovenly existence Simon jerked the suspenders from his shoulders and unbuttoned his shirt in the deadly oceanic heat, put both hands on his hips, and said, "Goddammit, we have got to *start* all at the same time and *stop* all at the same time." He turned on Patrick. "And if I hear you start that damn drum one beat ahead of us one more time I am going to jerk a knot in your tail, do you hear me?"

The boy sank back on the tar keg he was using for a seat, lowered his head, flushed red.

"Simon, Simon," said Doroteo. "*Es joven.*"

"Yes, well, so was I at one time too and nobody cut me any slack."

Which was not true and Simon knew it. The old man had cut him all kinds of slack. He looked out the window in search of a distraction. He had resolved to keep his temper in hand, because as his old man had told him over and over again, great trials and tribulations awaited him if he did not. Across the sand-filled street in the moonlight, a cat crept out of a dislocated house wall and trotted down the street with a kitten in her mouth. "Very well. I have not lost my temper. I have myself firmly in hand. Patrick. Here. It's not when I bring the bow *up,* it's when I bring it *down*. Got it? When I bring it up it's 'get ready' and when I bring it down to the strings and nod to you it's 'haul away.'"

"We're a scratch band," said the Tejano. "We just got together. The fault is not with us."

"Yes, you're right. Now let's get at it."

They needed a week of practice and how would they eat in the meantime? They had no choice. This was when the boy took up Damon's G whistle and every morning he silently marched out to the lonesome seaside and there amid the sea grape and vermilion morning glory taught himself to play it, trying over and over again with a desperate resolution. He came to Damon, confused about a certain phrase, holding it with his fingers over the holes.

"Here, you half-hole it," said Damon. "Then you can get that sharp. Listen."

When he had learned where the music lay in it, where the songs and the hidden melodies were, he played "The Minstrel Boy" in a way that left Simon silent and listening in silence and regretful that he had been hard on the boy.

"That's wonderful," Simon said. He gripped Patrick's shoulder and gave him a friendly shake. "That's very good." The boy twirled the big G whistle between his fingers and smiled, did a little skip. Outside the shack the fans of the sabal palms thrashed and made harsh sounds in the hot wind, the Gulf waves ran up in polished sheets and drew back again as they sweated and played. They went over five fast songs—"Glendy Burke," "Blarney Pilgrim," "Cotton-Eye Joe," "Leather Britches," and "Mississippi Sawyer"—until they had them precise and sharp and all together. Then they fooled around with six slower ones, starting with "St. Anne's Reel," and on to "The Nightingale Waltz," "Rye Whiskey," "Hard Times," and finally "Lorena," which they could all have played upside down and underwater.

Damon said, "Let's try 'We're Bound for the Rio Grande.' It's a capstan shanty. Sad, slow. We could do one chorus *a capella*. Here, I'll write down the words for you. Try it in G."

Damon swiftly wrote out the verses on the back of a handbill. They tried it. It needed work. They worked. Then they went over each one of the fast ones in turn, over and over. On the fast ones especially they had to start out precisely together and with volume.

And that's when the other people in Galveston's shantytown paused in what they were doing and listened to four voices harmonizing on *Waaaay Rio! We're bound for the Rio Grande.* And those people often thought, *I wish I could sing* . . . They heard the satiny low notes of the G whistle and the ripping, blistering pace of the D, the crisp rhythm of the bones, the immeasurably ardent phrases from the fiddle on "MacPherson's Lament" and thought, *I wish I could play an instrument* . . . and the great Gulf poured out its long waters upon the white beaches and took them away and came back again. Sometimes small boys gathered at the open windows to watch them as if they were onstage in a play.

With the last of their pennies and nickels they bought salt junk and old bread, bait shrimp from the fishermen, condemned ship's biscuit, and sometimes turnips from a farmer's cart. Doroteo took charge of all the food that came to hand; he diced the turnips, boiled the salt junk to tenderness, toasted the tiny shrimp on palm-leaf spines.

They got work, finally. First at the Jamaica and then at the Windjammer. They played the lively tunes at the beginnings of the evenings and then slid into nostalgia as the lanterns in front of them burned up their oil and the late hours wore on. It always worked, it worked like a charm, the sailors and harbor-front workers and off-duty soldiers sang along and banged their glasses on the tables in time to the fast tunes when the four flung themselves into the splendid crackling excitement of "Mississippi Sawyer" like a steam engine in sawdust hell. Damon, with his unlikely air of refinement, poured out cascades of notes and often the boy would dance a reel step or a flatfoot and made the bones rattle in his hand as he rolled through triple clicks.

Then as the men at the tables got drunker they were lulled to sleep or unconsciousness by the slow tunes. Simon and his group gathered up the audience and took them out of the bitter air of a harbor-front dive. Even in their ragged clothes and broken shoes they bore the drunk and the lonely along far sea currents, drifting up unknown forelands, into lost battles, defeats, unto the missing, the loved ones gone astray or unfaithful. Deep in the night they sang "I'm Bound for the Rio Grande" with the boy on the G whistle.

"One more," said the boy. He looked up at them from where he sat on the edge of the stage. "'Death and the Sinner.'" And Simon gave a slight one-sided smile; then the complex haunting tune of that Irish slow air threaded out into the dark streets. Finally, they would pack up their instruments, wake up the owner, collect their money, and walk through the dark streets home. Soon they were starting to make good money, both from the owners and from tips. They were able to buy meat to put on the fire and soap for a good foaming scrub at the pump. Simon slit the plush in the fiddle case and slipped all his coins inside.

There were the occasional fights. Once at the Sailor's Rest, a drunk called out Damon, said he could not play a single melody without flubbing a note, a man with a crippled hand shouldn't be playing an Irish tin whistle anyway, get off the stage and let the boy do it. The drunk stood up and made shooing motions with his arms.

Patrick paused in the middle of a flatfoot dance that was so limber it looked as if he were walking backward over glass. He held up the bones.

"Shut up," said the boy, "you fart-faced old wreck, you useless piece of shit, get your butt hole out of this saloon."

"Patrick!" Doroteo shouted. "*¡Por Dios!*"

The drunk charged up onstage in search of an exciting evening.

Simon threw open his fiddle case. They were living in a world of returned soldiers who had fought, had seen death and destruction, suffered hunger and want, and were not afraid of Satan himself. Fights could start up with amazing speed. Simon shoved the fiddle in its case and threw in the bow. Damon was dancing around like a bare-knuckle fighter, windmilling his fists, one of which would not quite close because of the old injury.

Then Damon turned and came face-to-face with the drunk. He drew back in pretended maidenly alarm with his Irish whistle clutched close to his chest. The drunk reached toward him and Damon's hand shot out fast as a striking snake and he rammed the end of his whistle into the man's eye, hard and fast. The man screamed and clutched his bloody eye, Patrick and Damon grabbed him, turned him around, and Simon planted a boot in his rear end and kicked him offstage. The drunk sank down like an emptied poke sack. He was going to have somebody reading the evening news to him for quite some time. Doroteo stood and watched it all. He stood the guitar on its tail pin, placed his hand on top of the pegboard, and spun it, smoothing down his mustache.

It was suddenly quiet. The locus of the trouble lay flat on the floor, moaning with a hand over his eye.

"Anybody else?" Simon shrugged his suspenders higher on his shoulders and turned to look all the men in the eye.

"Yeah," said the boy. He danced like a spring toy on his busted shoes and made an invitational gesture with the two bones. "Come at me, you sluts."

Overhead the beams of the saloon's low ceiling threw long shadows and the Galveston rats stared down from the rafters with their eyes like stars in the lamplight. Damon regarded the men gathered around the stunned and groaning drunk and stepped to the front of the stage. His face was flushed. He stood with his two feet planted firm and with a defiant glare at the audience launched into a beautiful rendition of "Neil Gow's Lament," a Scottish slow air.

Simon took his fiddle and bow out of the case and joined in. Doroteo struck out light chords, the boy started in on the bodhran and outdid himself, running the tone of it from high to low, slowly, from the rim to the center, a march for the funeral cortege carrying poor Neil Gow's second wife to the graveyard. At the end there was a moment of complete silence and then the applause began and went on for a long time.

CHAPTER SEVEN

THE LONG BATTLE CRIES of the war had faded and now life settled down the way a bombed building settles down, extinguishing all the lamps as the walls fold in and it was every man for himself, a kind of societal darkness or twilight that would take a long time to lift. A different world was coming after the surrender, along with the news that ran down the telegraph wire and the journals and newspapers that arrived on the train from Houston, its steam whistle sounding out over Galveston Bay.

Simon calculated that the military convoy should have reached San Antonio long since. The colonel with Mrs. Webb, the daughter, and the lovely Doris Dillon in his ponderous wake, should have found a house. He asked around about the mail and the bar manager at the Hendley Hotel said it was moving now, between Houston and San Antonio, sometimes by freight convoys and sometimes by private courier. Might take a couple of weeks or so.

For a two-cent copper he bought some clean paper from Englehardt's Print Shop on C Street, which was just gearing up to get back in business. For an additional twenty cents he bought a bottle of ink and a steel pen with two extra nibs. He noted that the owner also had pages of sheet music. He flipped through them and although he would not allow himself the luxury of buying any of them, he saw scores for the latest Stephen Foster, piano scores for bits and pieces of symphonies by long-dead composers. *Some other time,* he thought and laid the scores down again.

He sat at the rickety table with one clean sheet of paper and the pen. He had to get a letter to her somehow. To let her know he was alive, that he was thinking of her. He had no idea how to go about it. It was around five in the afternoon; a short while before they had heard the bells of St. Mary's and Patrick and Doroteo had just come back from Mass. The window with the shutters faced west and the sun sent bars of light through them and onto the paper. He wiped off his sweaty hand on his pants.

"Don't say you admire her from afar or any of that estuff," said Doroteo. "What about you say if she wants news about Ireland? That you met somebody from Ireland." Doroteo lifted a shinbone onto the table, sharpened his knife on a stone, and then set to work expertly peeling off flesh.

"Yes, but that's a lie. She would find out after a while." He pondered the empty sheet of paper in a long painful stare. He had lost a suspender button and so had taken them off, parted them at the cross behind and used one as a belt, tying it in a knot in front. He thought and hitched up his pants, moved both feet, thought again.

Doro said, "Well, think of something not a lie but not a love letter. Do not say 'I love you passionately. I love you when I see you, *al instante.*' Everybody says that."

Simon tried to think of some neutral, ordinary reason for her to receive a letter. He was curious about Ireland and did she know any Alexanders there . . . no, that was no good. Alexanders were Scots. He thought, *It can't be from me. It has to be from somebody else with news of me.* He peeled off his shirt and threw it in a corner. It was rank, really rank.

He swiveled around on the tar-bucket seat and said, "Now listen, Patrick, you're Irish. You will write to Miss Dillon."

"I can't hardly read nor write." The boy raised one hand in alarm. He had been marking out a checkers board on the floor and Damon was shaping the checker men with his penknife.

"You can now. I'll write it for you."

"No, me," said Damon. "I can do the punctuation correctly and add some phrases." He laid down his work. The rolling boom and wash of the incoming tide in the distance sounded very good. Doro sat before the fire and flipped the strips of meat from one side to the other.

Simon lifted both hands. "God, you'll say stuff about falling towers and Death riding in on the tide or who knows what?"

"I will not," said Damon. "Trust me."

"I never was going to write her," said Patrick.

"Sure you are. And it will have news of me. Think about it. The Webbs will let her have the letter if it's just from a fellow Irisher and got news of the old country."

Patrick thought about it. "Maybe. I guess. My people there in Pennsylvania, there's a Dillon aunt. One of my mother's sisters married a Dillon. He came over in '48. Well, hell's bells then, go ahead then, say it's from me. Colonel Webb knows me, he knows I am too young to pay court to her. Just go ahead and lie."

"Good!" cried Simon. "Tell me about your uncle, the man she married."

"Well," said the boy. "I'm thinking." He thought. "You been to Pennsylvania?"

"Pittsburgh," Simon said.

"Well, I hope you enjoyed our fair state."

"I did. Now, your uncle."

They all bent over the letter. Patrick supplied the details, Damon contributed the modestly elegant language and correct punctuation, and Simon wrote it out in his best hand. He sat in his sawed-off drawers in the midday heat with the Gulf wind peppering their shack with sand grains. He wiped his hand on his trousers again and poised the pen.

September 15, 1865
General Delivery, Galveston, Texas

Dear Miss Dillon; I entertain hopes that you might remember me, I am the snare drummer that was with Colonel Webb's unit in the regimental band. I shall always recall your kindness to me at Brazos de Santiago.

"That's S-A-N-T-I-A-G-O," said Doroteo.

"How would the boy know how to spell it?" said Damon. "He don't know it from a hole in the ground. Misspell it."

"Damon?" said Simon.

"All right, all right."

I take the liberty of sending you this missive as one immigrant to another as a means of conveying to you news of our country there across the sea.

"I never came across the sea," said the boy. "My mother and father did, that's a bald-faced lie."

"Who's to know?" Simon blew dust and sand from the paper and dipped the pen in the inkwell again with great care. "So just hush up."

It is said you came from Ireland directly and because my family also is from Ireland then I thought I would send you what News I have of that unfortunate Country as you might be homesick for News of it, as we Irish must help one another as best we can. I am doing well with the help of the very kind fiddler named Simon Boudlin, who played at the dinner at Fort Brown, and also have the friendship of Doroteo Navarro, guitarist, and Damon Lessing, flautist, so I am not alone in this world.

Now, my mother's sister married a Dillon and he came over some ("be vague," said Damon) *years ago from Kerry and settled in Pennsylvania in Allentown, where I am from, and he is doing very well working on the Lehigh and Susquehanna Railroad. His name is Brandon Casey Dillon. He came over on the* Jeannie Johnston. *He might be a relative of yours. Also that the family of Peter O'Dougal Dillon in the village of Ballyroe has gone over to Scotland to work in the Shipyards there, I don't know which ones, but all say this is Excellent. I know that the priest of Ballyroe sends Letters directly to all of us in that part of Pennsylvania and he kindly includes news of the people of Tralee and all of County Kerry as best he can to be read aloud and indeed his Letters are sent from place to place and all delight in them.*

This is to give you good cheer and greetings and news of the old Country and indeed I am hoping you are well with this excellent family with whom you are so fortunately situated. This is being written for me by a Friend who writes a good Hand and swears he will write down exactly what I say in all respects, to whom I am quite grateful, since I have joined with him in a small scratch band in Galveston, where we play in various refined places and we are doing well, he is the Fiddler named Simon Boudlin and he plays "Death and the Sinner" so that it brings tears to the eyes.

Simon laid the pen down and read what he had written. "Ahhh, I don't know." He ran both hands through his curling hair. "Is that too obvious?"

"Dealer's choice," said Damon.

"Well, then leave it." Simon looked around and realized they had eaten all the fried beef while he wrote.

And so I come to the close of my Letter to you and hope this has helped to bring you news of the old Country and if I hear of more news I will send it on, for my parents receive news regularly and I meet many Irish here and there. I remain yours truly in deepest respect, Patrick Matthew O'Hehir

"Not 'scratch band,'" Damon said. "'String ensemble' appeals to the ear."

"She's not going to believe that Patrick plays in any ensemble," said Simon.

"But 'scratch band' sounds like musical chickens."

"It's my letter," said Simon. "My name is mentioned in it."

"It's mine, indeed," said the boy. "Is it not?"

Simon made motions of tearing at his hair. "I'll put 'musical group' or somebody gets thrown out the window."

When it was done, he blew on the ink until it was dry and then folded the letter carefully as he had been taught. He pressed down the crease with the hilt of his knife, tucked in the ends, and wrote what he thought might be her address.

Miss Doris Dillon
In care of Colonel Franklin Webb 62nd USCT
U. S. Army Garrison at the Alamo, San Antonio, Texas

After that they walked to the seashore, happy with their small conspiracy, then farther down the beach, where some sabal palms grew in a mop-headed cluster, surrounded by sea grape and buckthorn, and with a quick glance around to see if there were any people nearby, stripped naked. They ran shouting into the surf. It lifted them in its blood-warm surging and foam and dropped them and lifted them again. They paid for it with sunburns and salty hair, but when the wind blew on their wet bodies it was so cool it gave them the unusual and startling feeling of shivering.

THE LAMPS IN the saloons burned coal oil or whale oil, the beams overhead creaked in the wind off the Gulf, the streets were incandescent under the gas lamps. Sometimes bats streaked through the white light, moths danced in a city of seagulls and scarred buildings.

Once as they walked home a midsummer storm broke over them, and for the next few days it rained and blew through the cracks of their small house in torrents. Simon and Doroteo moved their instrument cases here and there until they found leakless places. Simon took his hat in hand and said they had a job at the Jamaica and he was going, they could stay if they wanted. They wearily clapped on their hats, put their instruments under their coats. They followed him out the door, toward the city center once again, where the Jamaica's patrons were so deeply grateful that anybody had showed up to play on a stormy evening that they made twenty dollars. Simon put yet another five-dollar gold piece and two Federal bills for ten dollars each in his fiddle case.

When Simon lay down at night he slept as if he were in a coma. People tired him; always had, always would. He wished there were a roof he could go and sleep on but since he got his sleep during the day, he would have been roasted by the summertime Galveston sun or rained on. He was tired of the talking and disheartened by the thought that he was the odd one and the fault did not lie with his companions but himself. When he could, he took his fiddle and went off alone in the early evenings to Fort Point and its sandbagged fortifications now so dusty and unwarlike where the one solitary Union sentry stood on the tower, behind him that extraterrestrial landscape of sky and cloud being assembled in places unknown and sailing eastward. On the headland there was always a wind to blow away the mosquitoes and so he played for himself in blessed solitude those songs he loved that nobody cared to hear. He explored the strange modal scale of "Down in the Tennessee Valley," which some called "A Man of Constant Sorrow" or "The Farewell Song." It could lead you astray. It could abandon you in a thicket of sharps and flats, far from the major scales and utterly lost. He retuned from the standard GDAE to a cross-tuning in GGAD that gave him a drone. He paused, a redheaded fiddler poised with his bow on the strings but taut and still. Thinking. When he found the note, it would be perfect. He stood outlined against a falling sun at the edge of what was once again the United States and the sentry stopped his pacing to listen, transfixed.

At one or two in the morning when they had come home and Damon had perhaps bought half a bottle of cheap liquor to pass around, Simon sometimes talked about his land, and what he would grow on it and the house he would build. Simon did not remember ever living in a house but only himself and the old man in the three rooms in back of the livery barn and so the one he imagined was odd and impractical, but none of the others had the heart to point this out.

Patrick listened with a deep interest. His mother had been born in the middle of the Atlantic Ocean, he said, on an immigrant ship from Ireland, and his father came over not long after with his own parents and they had all gone to work for the Susquehanna railroad. They had hopes of being able to buy an entire ten acres to themselves and they were in a state of perpetual astonishment that around them the native Americans owned twenty, fifty, a hundred acres. They had come to live among the northern Yankees in Pennsylvania, he said, and all those people hated people in the South like burning hell, they despised them, you should hear them talk. Said you all were animals.

"We are," said the dark man. "We are beasts of prey, we are slave masters every one, we gorge ourselves on jelled blood and the meat of corpses." He held the bottle by the neck and turned it up. "*Lo, death hath reared himself a throne in a strange city all alone, far down within the dim west . . .*"

Their food had improved as well as their music; Doro spread lard on the hard bread and toasted it, then added a sprinkle of sugar. He often came up with a fruit called guava and more huachinango, oxtails, and shin meat. They cried out their appreciation; he had assigned himself cook's duties and they wanted to encourage him in this. Then they wiped their mouths on their cuffs and went out into the nighttime city.

They walked past women in patched frocks whose faces were drawn with hunger creases and cheeks artificially red, calling to them in hopeless voices, past heaps of lumber and glass where repairs were going on. They came to the Bayside Saloon or the Sailor's Rest or the Jamaica or the What Cheer; they searched out the patrons and the appearance of the place to see what might be awaiting them—a fight or the possibility of good tips. They borrowed bar rags from the bartenders to stick in the bands of their trousers to wipe their hands so they could grasp their instruments. Simon used one as a chin rest. The sweat ran from their faces in a lantern-lit sheen.

There was also the possibility of yellow fever in the dank miasmas of the gin houses and the funeral processions that trundled down the waterfront toward the island cemetery. Like everyone else on the street, they removed their hats as a hearse went by.

Now that they were making money Simon's concern settled on the matter of white shirts. They looked as ragged and filthy as if they had been lost in the woods for some time. If they wanted to garner what money there was to be had here in this city they had to look good, then they would be paid for playing at weddings and receptions and garden parties (if there were any gardens left after the bombardments, if there were heart enough left in the wealthier citizens of Galveston for parties of any kind).

Simon walked through the waves of heat to the warehouses and shebangs down on the waterfront, searching for a washerwoman. He carried all the clothes they had except what they had on their backs.

There in a little plank shack that had not yet been torn down for firewood a woman dumped loads of laundry into wooden tubs. Water simmered in two great fifty-gallon washpots on outdoor fireplaces. She was thin and young and wore shoes made of leather nailed onto wooden soles. She shoved back a frayed rag she wore over her hair; it promptly fell forward again.

"Ma'am," he said. "Yo, ma'am."

"Shirts two cents apiece," she said. "Bleach and ironing extra, and we can talk about how much for repair if you got shirts all torn up." She pressed two small slivers of soap together, trying to make one lump of them. "And if you're looking for good-time girls, they ain't here." She squinted at him, probably thinking he looked too thin and hungry to be disporting himself amongst the ladies.

Simon paused in that almost imperceptible hesitation that always fronted his words as if he were waiting, wanting to be sure he would speak into a listening silence.

"No," he said. "Not at all." Then he explained that he had a bundle of clothes for her and also, Did she have any shirts for sale? That people might have left behind?

"I got shirts from the nun's hospital that were left behind, after the battle when the Union came back. Their owners gone forever into the dark beyond. You mind bullet holes? Take a look," she said and threw a tumbled wad of fabric on her plank counter. Simon took up one in his hand; it looked like linen and cotton in a heavy weave. They would do.

"Confederates, Yankees, who knows?" she said. And then a quote she had most likely heard at the little theater on C Street: "All probably weltering in their gore."

He paid out fifty cents in Federal silver and came away with four shirts of a dim whitish color in various stages of repair. Back at the shack he spread the shirts out on the table. No need to tell them they would be wearing dead men's clothes. "Now here, see what I did for you. No no, don't thank me, don't thank me. See here, they've all been repaired."

They eyed the shirts with suspicion. Patrick muttered about bullet holes.

"No, they're just, sort of, random tears and piercings there. Now, we need to put up a notice." Simon sat on the tar bucket and leaned forward on his elbows. "There are better places than the saloons. We could try, 'Music provided for weddings, funerals, and garden parties.'"

"Nah," said Damon. He held out his shirt and regarded it with a critical expression. "Churches do wedding and funeral music. They, like all of humanity, prefer their own people."

"All right, all right." Simon never had a quick answer for Damon's depressing observations. "But *garden* parties."

"In this day and time? Ha. Galveston wallows in its self-imposed poverty. What garden parties?"

Simon's face grew smooth and cool. After a pause he said, "You wait. You'll see."

MUSIC FOR CONVIVIAL GATHERINGS!

Musial group lately come from the mainland offers songs and dance tunes of the most refined character! Airs, waltzes, and quick-steps for your evening or afternoon festivity at a reasonable price! Band consists of violin, flute, guitar, and rhythm instruments. Contact S. Boudlin in care of the post office.

He carefully wrote five copies in his best hand. He put them up in the better parts of town and also on a Hendley building colonnade post on the Strand.

He took to trudging up the steps of the Customs House every day at two in the afternoon, interrupting his hot, sweating sleep to do so. He came all the way from their collapsing shack out on the seaward side, past other shanties in which all sorts of people had squatted, had strung out their laundry, had built sheds for their pigs and chickens if they had them. They said, Hello fiddler, where you been so long? Hello fiddler, play me 'Wayfaring Stranger.' He lifted a hand and went on.

On the street in front of the post office he looked up; it had been four years since Simon had seen the United States flag on a government building. It flew from the roof of the Customs House against the pure white clouds that sailed up out of the Gulf, against the blue air, with its thirty-five stars and the extravagant stripes. Then he walked gratefully between the shady columns, into the cool building, on to the post office on the first floor, hoping to find some notice that they were wanted.

This is how they ended up in the garden of one of the great houses on the Strand. It was the Pryor House, an edifice of wealth and pure white walls and the wonders of mowed grass. A note had arrived in General Delivery that they might be needed for an afternoon gathering. Simon raced back to the shack and shouted them all awake and read it aloud.

CHAPTER EIGHT

He said, "get up boys, we got to go meet one of them, they want to look us over and be sure we don't have lice. Get to the pump, would you? Comb your hair."

They met with a stern old man named Heidemann who was a majordomo of sorts for the family. They met him at the fortifications and played several pieces for him, pieces that they judged to be elegant and refined. They sang "Bound for the Rio Grande"; Patrick was so nervous he flubbed it repeatedly on the G whistle, but the majordomo couldn't tell because they were oversinging the boy as loudly as they could, they were in the outdoors near the slapping dirty waves of the harbor, and most people didn't have a good ear anyway. Heidemann listened with his hands clasped behind his back and asked, "Have you left the Confederate forces? Do you have your discharges and your passes?"

The boy spun the G whistle between his fingers, sitting in the sand. He said in a nervous, unsteady voice, "Yes, sir, I mean no, sir, we didn't need any, I was a drummer with Webb, sir, we were with Webb, regimental band, they just released us and said go home."

Simon and Damon and Doroteo murmured, *With Webb, yes*.

"Trying to make money for our passage home," said Simon. He knew the man could hear his accent, which was Ohio Valley, but Doroteo sounded Hispanic and Damon's speech was Southern but as to place indefinable. The boy spoke like Irish immigrants one generation removed speak; a hard *r* and a lilt.

"Webb," said the old man. "Yes, he was down at Brazos de Santiago."

"Yes, he was. We were."

"But he was in command of colored troops. The Sixty-second. You don't look colored."

"Well. No, they have white officers."

"You don't look like officers either."

"Regimental band," said Simon, and then he became resolutely silent.

Despite Heidemann's suspicions they came to an agreement for twenty-five dollars for the evening. He nodded smartly and then he told them,

"You will do well here if you aspire to more refined music. I tell you, Texas will never be developed except on the coasts. Houston, Galveston, Indianola. It will never be anything inland. There's no semblance of civilization there. No place to play your music. Lacking in refinement and rainfall, therefore neither crops nor symphonies, no, not ever. Perhaps crude approximations; Indian corn and back-country fiddling but no more, no, not ever."

"Thank you for your advice," said Simon, and then they turned to walk back to their wretched shack on the sea, dodging the wagon traffic, a loose donkey galloping down the street with a man running after it.

"Oh Jesus Mary and Joseph," cried the boy. "I'm sorry, I can get it better, I can! I mean 'Rio Grande.'" He was terrified of another outburst from Simon.

That sense called Better Judgment came to Simon in a rush and he said, "Sure you can. Don't worry." He beat the boy on the shoulder in a comradely way. "You're good, you can do it."

Then a scramble to cut hair, shave, and press down the white shirts. Doroteo borrowed a skillet from the house half a block down, heated it on the fire, and then threw a thin rag over the damp shirts and ironed them down; he fried the rag but the shirts were pressed and unscorched.

They managed to borrow cravats and jackets from the waiters at the Hendley Hotel dining room with extravagant promises to bring them back, and a dime apiece to the barber of the ship *Orion* recently in from Jamaica and docked at the Kuhn wharf, therefore wanting for coins to spend onshore. The barber cut hair like he was harvesting hay; Damon sat on a coil of rope and the barber made his dark hair fall in hanks. Simon wrote down the titles of songs on the back of a handbill he had torn off a wall. The handbill advertised passenger train fares for Buffalo Bayou and Houston. He scribbled the titles down with a carpenter's pencil.

"'Robin Adair'!" cried Damon. "That's it! I had forgot the title. It's English, it will sound reasonably elegant."

Patrick whizzed up and down the scale of the G whistle. "Sing it," he said.

Damon said, "The first four measures are the same as 'Ailen Aroon.' He cleared his throat and sang, "*What's this dull town to me? Robin's not near; He whom I wished to see, Wished for to hear?*"

"Goddamn, sounds like somebody went and drowned," said the barber. "Ain't that a downer." Barefoot sailors stopped their work with ropes and mops and tools and paused to listen to them. In the intense heat tar dripped in black bullets from the rigging overhead. All up and down the wharf were the ringing sounds of metal ships' tackle banging against other metal parts and voices from the engine rooms far below. Cries of men loading and unloading from lighters and at the ships' side the little salt-water waves said *wash wash wash.*

"Well, we're not singing your dirty sailor songs for *this* job," said the boy Patrick. The sailors turned to him, surprised at what seemed like a wild outburst from a mere child. Simon started laughing.

"Oh God," he said. "He's turning into a critic!"

"Well, bugger me," said one of the sailors. "Your soul to the devil."

"He's gone mad," said Damon. "He has a religious mania. And you, barber, just cut my hair, would you? Here's the bridge: *Where's all the joy and mirth, made this town heaven on earth, O they've all fled with thee, Robin Adair.* Yeah, so, it's weepy and woeful and they'll all fall to bawling over their dead relatives killed in the recent unpleasantness. Moldering in the grave."

"After they weltered in their gore," said Simon. "Give it a go in G, Patrick, and the rest of us will sing it." He lifted his chin to Damon. "Take the melody."

"Why should I?" Damon said. "You have a good voice."

Simon got a grip on himself. After a pause he said in a reasonable voice, "No. I'll do high harmony."

After six tries they got it right; crisp and sharp. By that time, they had their hair cut and the sailors were asking where they would be performing.

"Nowheres they're going to let you lot in," said Patrick, and they quickly climbed down the ship's boarding ladder to the wharf, ragging on Patrick all the way back to the shack.

Simon tore off his patched checkered shirt, now with clips of red hair scattered all over it, and fanned himself with the handbill that had the words to "Robin Adair" written on its backside.

He said, "Listen, Damon, next time I tell you to try a song, do it. Do you hear me?"

"No," said Damon and threw his hat across their cluttered room. "No, I am fucking deaf, Simon."

"Stop!" Doroteo shouted. He who so rarely spoke, the quiet one, cut the tension with a hard, precise shout. Then he began to polish his boots with a combination of axle grease and stove blacking. He said, "We must play the varsoviana. I will eshow you." He finished with his boots, wiped his hands, and then plucked at his guitar strings carefully. Chord after chord, striking out the tune with his thumb.

Simon calmed himself, made himself listen. Suddenly he raised his head. "Why hell, that's 'Put Your Little Foot.'"

"I have no idea what you call it up here in English, but it is a dance of dignity and gracefulness and there is no putting little feet."

"They'll fall to dancing," said Damon. "Grandmothers will cry out, despairingly. '*Dance O maiden feet along the strand so cool and sweet . . .*'"

Simon suddenly needed to get out of the stifling shack and the talking. It hit him as if a heavy weight had fallen on his head. He went out the door for the pump. He walked in the burning sun of late September stripped to the waist, with the checkered shirt dragging in his hand.

He knew this poem would go on to describe the maiden feet rotting in the grave and worms crawling out of jewel-like eyes and towers falling into a sullen sea. He poured dipper after dipper of cool water over his head. As he walked back past sun-bleached, unpainted wooden dwellings, some abandoned, some being lived in, he fought to get his hands into the shirt armholes and with gratitude heard Patrick tell Damon to give it a rest, just give it a rest.

They walked down the Strand in the heat of the day, managed to find the three-story house. It was embellished with gables and Palladian windows and quoins. There was a wall around the front lawn. A black servant in a white coat opened the cast-iron gate for them and they were then rushed in a body to the rear garden.

Simon looked around at the astonishingly level grass, the spindly chairs and overhead palm trees, the tables being set out. They all felt stiff and unnatural in their borrowed coats and borrowed cravats, their new-ironed white shirts with repaired bullet holes. They were cautious in this place and among these people; they were fresh from nights in low dives and fending off drunken sailors who wanted to buy them drinks, or fight them, or stagger up and demand to play their instruments. And three of them had been in the Confederate forces.

There were a number of early arrivers in Union blue; officers with a lot of ornamentation on their sleeves. Simon walked smartly to the majordomo to ask him in a confident voice about someplace private to tune their instruments and rehearse. With luck they would be told to go someplace near the kitchen. The old majordomo, with his face of worn stonework, lifted a hand to indicate a separate building behind a stand of laurel trees and said,

"Pump. Kitchen. Woodshed. Facilities." Then he turned on his heel and began to pursue a boy who stumbled along carrying wreaths of paper flowers, crying out, "You will ruin them, you little fiend!"

They laid down their instruments on the stage, shoved through the hedge of laurel, and ducked into the kitchen. The smell of good cooking made them faint.

There were four women in there: a black cook who was very thin, her head in a snow-white cloth, eyeing them distrustfully, and another black girl rolling out dough with a bottle in lieu of a rolling pin while two young white women loaded hors d'oeuvres on trays.

"Hey hey, we're the music this evening," said Simon and then they bore down on the food like Comanches. They ate a good third of the appetizers—bone marrow on toast, tiny meatballs swimming in a red sauce, herring in a peppered cream, tubes of rolled ham and the German Harzer cheese on toasted rye bread—in the space of fifteen minutes while the cook looked on in astonishment. Doroteo picked up a marrow on toast and inspected it carefully, as if searching for recipe guidance. The boy Patrick swallowed miniature sandwiches entire; Damon delicately lifted a pig-in-a-blanket, regarded it, and then ate it. He put another one in the pocket of his borrowed coat. Simon saw the cook turn to snatch up three bottles of wine and drop them into the water butt.

"My lord!" cried one of the serving girls.

"Starved," said Damon.

Simon devoured another meatball. "Living on our wits," he said. "Starving. Stove up with heat and insufficient food. Now, tell me, what song would you like to hear?" Simon smiled at the girl who had said My lord. "We will play it for you." He leaned forward from the waist. "And that is just between us."

The girl flushed. She was dark, with bright red cheeks like the Creoles of New Orleans. She rolled her black eyes to one side in a fit of thinking, wiped the flour from her hands, and said,

"Ummmm . . . I bet you don't know 'La Savane'?"

Simon saw her lift a hopeful face to him and then she laughed a small laugh and looked down. She took out a pale blue handkerchief and fanned herself with it to cover her shyness, her embarrassment.

"That I do," Simon said. He paused with a meatball in the air.

"My own version. I will play it for you if you keep the food coming. It's in G-flat major." Then his face grew abstract with inner musical calculations.

"*T'inquiete pas!*" she cried. "It's for me, homesick." She lifted a floury hand. "For somebody that, so, he and me, we love that song together. He is in New Orleans. He is not here. Play it for me and I would bring you all the food you like."

"Jesus," said Damon. "Can you play it in another key besides G-flat major? That's six flats."

"Do you know it?"

"No, but I could hit harmony notes once I hear the first part, if you play it in D."

"I know it," said Doroteo. "Do not fear, Simon, I will back you up."

"Good. No," said Simon. "I'm sticking with the G-flat major, that girl wants to hear it so bad, and I ain't going to mess it up trying to change keys on it. You do the best you can with your G whistle."

Simon sat on a keg to eat Harzer cheese with chopped bacon and fresh spinach, bent over, thinking of the intricate geography of "La Savane." It was an old Creole song. Simple, but you could do variations on it until the cows came home. The others regarded him with some anxiety as they ate. He had earned them a full meal of mouth-watering food, and even though the food was all somehow very miniature, their bodies were responding like sea anemones in a current, the flavors new and delectable.

They were finally evicted from the kitchen and hustled to the bandstand. The stage had been thrown together with pallets and covered with a tarpaulin. Fortunately, it was in the shade of several live oaks. They unshipped their instruments. Simon made sure his bridge was straight and got out his A fork and rapped it against the hard-shell fiddle case. They all listened intently, as if hearing a voice from a distant star. They then made droning, plucking noises; Doroteo quickly tuned one string against another all the way down E-A-D-G-B-E with a final triumphant *ping* on the high E, and then ran his forefinger to the twelfth fret and struck out the harmonics. Simon worked his tuning pegs, tuning off his A string. He tightened the hair of his bow and rosined it, glancing covertly at every face, every uniform in the crowd. The habit of years.

As they stood carefully poised, listening to one another's instruments, a young man who said he was Mr. Albert Pryor Jr. came upon them in a rush. He stopped and gazed at them with suspicion. Then a young woman with light-brown hair, in a swinging flare of pale green hoopskirts, walked slowly to stand at his side. Junior did not introduce the young woman but he turned to her and said, "Hello, Sis, is it all going all right?"

Apparently everything was going all right.

"Now what are you playing?" He turned back to the musicians. "We want nothing low."

"Low?" cried Damon. "Us? Are you referring to sailors' verses or those frenetic Southern mountain jigs so beloved of the poor whites? Of *course* not." He did a little toss of his head and smoothed down his greasy waiter's cravat.

"Well," said young Pryor, and then stopped. He blinked. Damon did not.

Simon said, "Yes. Well, we thought 'Lorena' and 'Robin Adair' and then some Steven Foster. Maybe 'Jeanie with the Light Brown Hair' and 'Beautiful Dreamer' and then a varsoviana, leading with the guitar." He half-turned and opened up one hand to the Tejano.

Doroteo bowed.

"And then some light airs, maybe 'The Parting Glass' . . ."

"Is that Irish?"

Simon paused and then said in a positive voice, "No, it is not. It is Scottish, as a matter of fact. I know my music, sir."

"Maybe a tune that is a little livelier?"

"'The Glendy Burke.'"

"Well, that will do, I suppose."

"It all sounds very nice." The sister turned on them a gracious, hesitant smile. They all bowed. Then she lifted an admonitory forefinger. "There's a new song, come down from the North. They're playing it in Omaha and St. Louis. Very pretty, it's called 'Red River Valley.' Do you know it?"

"I'm sorry, I don't," said Simon.

"It's very popular with the cavalry. Oh, I should play it for you . . ." She looked around distractedly. "It would be so lovely on the violin. This is our winter house and we've just come back and we wanted a song that was new and special." Then she said, "I'll sing it."

"You will not," said her brother. "Singing some cavalry song here at our garden party! Stop it."

He took his sister's arm and they strolled away. The musicians tugged at their coat hems, snatched down their cuffs, and started out with the modestly lively tune called "The Glendy Burke."

The back lawn filled up. Where had people hidden these light dresses and fashionable small hats, how had the men come by unworn suits of black and waistcoats in worked silk during the blockade and the two battles of Galveston? The listeners put down their cups of tea or glasses of lemonade and clapped for a moment and then went back to talking and gliding across the leveled grasses.

They went through all their modestly lively tunes very quickly and Simon said, "Let's do them all again."

That got them through the first hour and a half. By this time, they were wet with sweat and Damon wiped it from his brow with his sleeve; Simon opened his vest and shirt as far as he dared. The boy laid down his drum and disappeared into the crowd and came back with clean bar rags and handed them around. Doroteo wiped down his frets. It came on evening and the sea light was low and the grateful wind picked up off the Gulf to come rushing across the island and into the broad, elegant Strand. Much stronger beverages were being added to the men's drinks and so nobody was leaving. Damon ate the pig-in-a-blanket from his coat pocket. The junior Pryor wandered up.

"Excellent, you are doing very well. Will you have a drink?"

"Thank you, no," said Damon. He wiped his hands on a bar rag. "What can I do for you?"

Simon thought, *Keep those Union officers away from us,* but he said, "We're doing fine, much appreciated." Then he said to the others, "I am going to play 'La Savane' in G-flat major, follow if you can."

And he sailed out upon that particular sea with his bow leaping like a dolphin in the bow wave of a fast ship, into the four parts that he had learned at the cost of fifteen cents from a man named LaPlante there in Paducah, nearly two years ago, when Nathan Bedford Forrest stole all their horses and burned down their barn.

Everyone stopped to listen. Even in their excited, urgent talking, their news of the occupation, gossip of the sudden new alignments of loyalties and prestige, new sources of wealth, still they listened to the phrases of melody that somehow fitted together as constellations fit together far away in the deeps of space, shining over the Gulf.

Simon at last lowered his bow and when he looked up, he saw the Creole girl holding a tray of smoking brisket, staring at him enraptured. The tune had been for her and her lover far away in New Orleans, and in the garden cressets he could see that her eyes shone with wet. He smiled at her, laid his bow alongside his leg, and bent in a very slight bow.

CHAPTER NINE

WITH THE ONSET OF night, the moon rose out of the Gulf as if spying covertly on the world of ocean. People were scattering. The musicians began to open their instrument cases, take a small drink. As Simon returned from the facilities behind the kitchen building, buckling his belt, the thin cook stood in front of the kitchen water butt as if still guarding the wine she had dropped into it and said, "She wants to see you." She nodded slowly, knowingly, at Simon's surprise.

"Sorry, who?"

"Miss Pryor. She said she wants to show you that song."

Simon straightened his coat. "What song?"

"She said 'Red River Valley.' In there." The cook gestured toward a rear entrance to the house. Simon picked up his fiddle and bow and walked to it; the entrance way was, like the rest of the house, elegant. It was arched over with rustic-cut stone and a set of steps led upward, into an empty hall. One gaslight burned. Down at the end of the hall a doorway was open.

HE WATCHED HER slow, reasoning gesture, a light tap at the air.

"No, he was right. I shouldn't be singing cavalry songs."

Miss Pryor put one hand on the keys but did not press them. Simon stood at the left side of the piano in a loose slant with his bow held straight down his leg. The fiddle was under his arm and the atmosphere in the drawing room was immobile as a lantern slide. The Gulf air seemed to have come to a halt at the tall open window. An oil lamp burned under a milky shade.

"Maybe not," he said and waited. He had followed her invitation; it seemed this was a secret escapade that he might hear her sing "Red River Valley" after all but now this. She'd sent the message by the cook. *The cook; take note.* In his walk down the hall he felt the silence of the house, not as if it were empty, but as if someone stood silently behind one of the many doors, listening. He said, "You don't have to sing it, Miss Pryor. You might single-note it on the keys."

She lifted her bare shoulders. "I don't really know where to start. I suppose . . ." She struck F. "No. Not there." Her hair was a bright, clear brown. She sat at the piano bench and lifted her face to him. "What do you play, usually? You are very good."

"What do I play." Simon watched her tap her fingers on the keys, making no sound. "Why do you want to know?"

"Oh!" She snatched her hands down into her silk lap. "Well. Because you're so accomplished and—that was rude."

He bent his head briefly and said, "Yes, it was. Still."

"Because there are so many places you could perform." *She doesn't want to know what I usually play.* "Or teach." She gave him a broad smile and lifted one hand and shook down a bracelet. "You could, say, travel to cities other than this one. St. Louis? And teach."

He moved his head against the constriction of the cravat and let several seconds pass like a bright wire hand on his personal clock that ticked away in silence. "Teach who?"

"Me." She said it almost defiantly. He had been rude once and might be so again; with his thin refined face and pale damp skin and the deep eyes so guarded that he might have just been turned out of the spirit world for transgressions unknown. She had had contacts with the spirits and they had given her various permissions, certain promises. "We have to return to St. Louis shortly."

"What is shortly?"

"Oh, I don't know, I don't know, just fairly soon I suppose." She waved away dates, times, the hard data of the world. "We do chemicals." Once again a lengthy consideration. "Pryor Chemical Company."

And you want a pet violinist to play . . .

"To play some of the modern pieces. The ones that express lightness of heart, the finer emotions, perhaps yearning, such as those by the Italian composers. I like those. Do you know them?"

She was soft as down and he had not touched a woman in a long time, especially not one this delicate. Someone who took pains and care to attend to herself and her hands, carefully choose the right color of dress and have it made with a very low bodice. Off the shoulders.

"Which ones? For instance." Simon touched the fiddle strings with his thumb, as if to silence them, as if they might be resonating to something in his body without his permission. "I'm in the dark here." *Not really.*

"No, I don't really know them. I should work at it more. I'm incurably lazy."

He saw her bend forward to the sheet music on the piano and look at the notes searchingly and then sit back. All her movements were slow and her interest in music was minimal and her skin pink with the heat—her arms and her throat and the crease of her breasts in the low bodice. He turned away for a moment to settle himself, to feel the relief of being inside a house finely appointed with little note of war. All the windows unbroken and the walls unscarred. How had they managed it? One lonely bullet mark on the wood framing of a fanlight. Carpet somewhat worn. Candies bright as toys in dishes. Her dress new and fresh and so was she, so slow, slow as an infant with the same deep impenetrable self-absorption. He stood in the middle of rich textures and clean scents and polished wood flooring, white unstained walls and unbroken glassware. He tipped his head as if he were interested in what she was saying.

She was speaking of her brother and her father, her influence with them. How she could obtain a position for him as a music master. He listened to her spin one fantasy after another; he to take ship with them on the return to New Orleans and then upriver. They would stand together on the rail to watch the great river pass by.

Simon had been proofed against these kinds of offers since he was seventeen and of a mind for any sort of adventure that came his way. An elegant woman on board the *Cumberland Star;* the steamboat was tied up in Paducah for six days because of low water, himself on the outer edge of full grown and a wizard with an ancient fiddle locally made. Her husband far away in Pittsburgh. There were so many opportunities for a young man like him and she would see to it, she had advantageous connections in Pittsburgh, theater, private groups. He made her head spin. Her cabin was far to the rear and very private. He was lost in her for seven days upriver.

Then there were fantasies that fell apart piece by piece into sly, unanswerable mutations and a rising scale of hysteria. By the time they were fifteen miles from Pittsburgh, it was clear she didn't know anybody in the theater world there or about music at all and was terrified of her husband. But seven nights in bed with her almost made it worth it, almost. At the landing she sent him off to find a hired coach and then she disappeared. What did he know? He was seventeen. By the time he got back to Paducah he knew quite a lot. It took him a month to work his way home.

He said, in a cool, light voice, "You seem to think I have no life of my own that is not worth abandoning on the instant."

She shrugged her white shoulders. She got up in a slack, untidy shifting of green silk and hoops, ignoring her hem caught on a corner of the piano bench. Simon waited with an increasing sense of danger until she started to turn and then lay down his fiddle and bow, lifted the bottom hoop free, opened his hand, and let the silk fall.

"Oh, that's just me," she said. "Always catching on furniture. There's too much skirt in this skirt. But St. Louis."

He said, "You have no influence with your brother or father, Miss Pryor."

"Oh. Now how would you know one way or the other?" She went to the window where it looked out over the street wall, onto the decorative short palms, and onto the Strand. House windows stared back at them with lantern eyes from across the street. "Come stand beside me."

He did.

"Why are you in Galveston?" She tucked her arm into his, pulled a ribboned decoration from her hair, and tossed it on the windowsill. "Why are you so rude?"

She was as tall as he was and he could feel her bare arm against the coarse wool of his coat, his ribs. "It's my invincible will. I crush all before me."

Her heat touched him and drew unwilled sparks and he listened to her slow laughter. She withdrew her arm, stepped away, back again. A dance. She took up the ribbon curled on its pin and tucked it into his lapel. He caught her hand and closed his own on it and then let go.

"But I do have influence with them! Why would you ignore an offer like that? Are you married? You have children?"

"Not married," Simon said. "No children. Not that I know of."

He watched her face as that sank in, watching with his hooded gray-green eyes and only the trace of a smile. She seemed taken aback at first and then made a short, derisive noise that was unbecoming to a young woman in a new silk dress. She waved it away. There was about her an innocent confidence in her own attractiveness in that she did not make flirtatious appeals or give him any of those glances many women relied upon. She didn't bother.

"You don't want a life like that. Those women. You play on the waterfront? I think the music is repetitive? Simple and repetitive?"

"A kind of howling," said Simon.

"Would you not want a better life? It must be painful to be so talented and reduced to, well, howling." She put her hand on the back of her neck and regarded a brilliant blue-white star that had roamed into the frame of the window.

"I just suffer." He took a deep breath and blew it out as a person would blow out cigarette smoke. "Miss Pryor, you are inventive. You have any number of music masters to teach you any number of songs. There is no offer. Your brother and your father are not going to arrange any teaching position for me." She frowned, stiffened. "I hate teaching. I love howling. The evening has been beautiful and so are you. Your friends in St. Louis will be captivated by stories of your adventures in Galveston. This will be at least one of them I would imagine."

She put a hand to her mouth and wheeled away in a revolving motion of hoops.

"I wanted to help," she cried. She was near tears. "You are capable of so much more!"

"We are playing at intrigues," he said. "Or you are."

He took the ribbon and its pin from his lapel. Wondered how many others she had invited to St. Louis, how many times she had had confrontations with her brother and father over situations exactly like this one. He took one step to close the space between them and pinned it on the deep V of her bodice, put his hand along her bare neck, and kissed her small pink mouth. At first gently and then repeatedly and with more urgency, as a thick sweet fire moved through him without hindrance. His lips parted from hers very slowly, slowly. He sighed out a long breath and pressed his cheek to her hair. Then he drew away. Despising himself for a fraud, he said, "I will regret this the rest of my days. What I could have had. But instead given over to an abandoned life. Good night, Miss Pryor."

He walked down the hall, past whoever might be invisibly listening, back to the bandstand. Saw they stood waiting, Doroteo with an open case and his guitar still in his hands.

"Sorry. Miss Pryor wanted a private lesson."

Damon said, "Those private lessons." He blew a high, piercing C and slid it down into a half note.

Doroteo single-noted a sweet and sentimental melody and batted his eyelids. The boy looked both confused and suspicious.

"What then?" said Patrick.

"On your next birthday," said Doro, "I am to tell you all. *All.*"

The boy flushed at their quiet laughter. They got out before some officer in blue demanded their passes or their discharge papers simply because he was drunk and he could. The moon was nearly full and stood over the mineral glitter of the sea, sending out a path across the water, and Venus glowed with white fire. All the palms and live oaks of Galveston ran the sea wind through their fingers and it dried the sweat on their faces. As they packed up, the majordomo came over with their pay. Not only the agreed-upon price of twenty-five dollars but a pale blue handkerchief in which was wrapped a fifty-cent piece.

CHAPTER TEN

WHAT A WEALTH OF animals.

Doris Dillon is traveling across a new world that seems to have no end and every lift of the land delights her. It keeps on rolling beneath their wheels hour after hour and day after day and there are new, strange things every mile, some that dart away and others standing crowded together, holding up flat hands like dark green banditti in a play. They are called cactus and she has been told not to touch them.

There are remnant spirits in this country from another time. She watches for them in the trembling heat waves of the noontime and she listens carefully during the hot nights with the fernlike leaves of the mesquite overhead and the cook fire dying down. She might as well be on the moon. She is prepared to be astonished; she is eighteen and not long out of County Kerry. A fine thrill runs through her heart when large white birds sailing on a Gulf wind follow them out of the Rio Grande Valley. They seem to take turns as escorts and on their heads a crown of star-white feathers. She realizes that they are the feathers that the Denny's women put on their hats back home in Ireland, the shameless thieves.

"Those are called snowy egrets," says the driver. "They are great fliers, only bird better for staying in the air is a buzzard."

The birds sail away in a high-atmosphere blur of white. *They are making sure we leave,* she thinks. *They will tell the others.* Trees become fewer and fewer, and far ahead Doris can see black shapes. Large animals, alert, moving away. She thinks this must be what enchantment is like, when a person is taken into the other world. Her spirits are effervescent now they are away from the colonel; joy comes back to her and unwraps itself gift by gift.

She has always loved animals. She has always been mystified by them, pulling carriages, dragging a plow, the heedful dogs guarding the sheep on the hillsides, her striped cat stalking a rat behind the grain bin. They fascinate her for reasons she does not know, but she knows we owe them for their trust, the ones that have come to live with us. Her father had acquired ten acres of land and a cow that had a calf every year and a sow and an ox to pull the plow and the harrow and the stoneboat and their small cart. He had done it by working himself to the bone, and now she is fairly stunned by these thousands of acres that it seems nobody owns and by the wild animals that live on them.

Since she was small she had been on her feet in the dark early-morning hours, desperately pulling on her boots to go with her father to bring oats and fodder to their ox and to the milk cow. A person says *Yosh, yosh* to greet them, to ask them to move over. She watched them eat with the candlelight shining in their deep eyes, wept when the calf was sold away, learned to milk and listened to the men talk of remedies for the colic and what to put on a wound. She stood to watch the carriages of the great, like the Dennys for instance, with their four-in-hands, the horses' hides gleaming like silk trotting past on the road in front of their cottage.

And here they were running free. Long manes and tails floating behind them as they fled the train of commissary wagons heading to San Antonio. Whoever would have thought she would ride in a convoy of wagons like this? Each wagon pulled by four and even six shining horses with rays of light glancing off the hame balls and all the metal parts.

She sits up beside the driver. He is a wide man with a springing dark beard and an old-fashioned courtesy. He is almost shy with this sprightly dark-haired girl and he answers her politely.

"No miss, nobody owns them. Hard to catch, hard to break, but then again, the price is right."

They were free to *anyone*. All her life she had known how costly it was to buy a horse, to keep one. So few had them, either to ride or to pull a carriage. A kind of low greed almost overcomes her and for a moment she imagines herself owning one of them, and it would somehow (she was not quite sure how) become tame and carry her over this landscape in a floating gait. The wild horses disappear into the distance in a cloud of dust; faerie enticements.

Her parents had contrived and saved to send her to the nuns and what she loved most about her education at the convent was going to the beehives with Sister Angela, watching the bees dance before the gates of their hive like David before the tabernacle, and the hours of learning music. She was taught on the pianoforte, all the strange arithmetical conclusions of the scales. Once she slipped away down the street to see the farrier place shoes on the feet of a mad, fighting saddle horse, a sight she would never forget. She knew that in the horse's big muscular soul there were inharmonious clashing notes of broken music. Sister Angela had been very patient with her. *A girl mustn't go alone to a blacksmith shop, my dear.*

And a girl perhaps had not ought to go alone into a new world, but she had stepped aboard ship with the wind in her face. Into trouble. She had known she would need allies the moment she understood the sort of man Colonel Webb was. They first journeyed to Camp Thomas in Ohio, and the army wives, who she had met in Ohio and who also had come with their husbands to Texas, had been fair kind to her and so she had made them small gifts; a small personal gift would always earn a person good regard. She knew they were all Protestant and so she made them bookmarks for their Bibles, which she assumed they all read devotedly. She crocheted the edges of the bookmarks and embroidered them with a cross, holding them close to her face to get every stitch perfect. *How clever, how kind!* they said. So they would remember the colonel's governess then, and if help was needed someday, it might be theirs to give.

She hears the girl behind, complaining as usual, and it makes her nerves light up like hot wires. *Patience, the child is only fourteen and this is an unhappy family. Patience.*

"Josephina, my dear, give me your bonnet and I will fix it," says Doris Dillon. *I am to pray for a quiet heart at times like this, but I never remember to remember.* She reaches back into the interior, opens her hand. "Give it to me and don't cause me to fall to cursing in Irish."

"Oh, you must *not,*" says Josephina. Her voice is prim and censorious.

"And how would you know, then?"

"I would just be able to *tell.*"

"What if it were a recipe for fish?" Doris keeps smiling.

"Jo, stop fussing with it," says Mrs. Webb. The mother and daughter stay in the shade of the awnings. They are not interested in these uninhabited stretches of Texas; they are weary and irritable. "Give it to Doris."

Doris takes the bonnet, fetches out her kit, and clips the ties loose. She turns them inside out and turns to the girl with what she hopes is a happy expression. "You see, Josephina, this is a needle," she says. "This is a thread."

"Oh, ha ha."

The needle winks bright in the Texas sun and her fine black hair is coming out of its chignon. She manages to restitch the tie even as the wagon crashes over humps of grass and alarming little municipalities of red dirt that the driver says were made by ants.

She is still trying to understand the people here and what a girl can do and what a girl can't do. For instance, the maid Mercedes, who is from the Spanish people but how the Spanish people got here she doesn't know nor does she know if she will be allowed to make a friend of Mercedes or not. She has been reprimanded so often.

Colonel Webb has gone on ahead to San Antonio, to rent a house. May a cat eat him and may the devil eat the cat.

All she can think of now is how many horses all these people have, and the wild ones, running across the great bald world in this hot month of June. Running perfectly free. The driver points things out to her: the nests of those snowy egrets, a desert willow heavy with blossom. Who do the cattle belong to? Nobody. Catch them if you can. They have enormous horns, they are in all colors, they are speckled and brindled, black and red, there are white ones with black spots over their eyes like a highwayman's mask. They are fey and dangerous, she thinks. Those ones would take a horse out from under you before you knew it, Jesus, the horns on them. The wild cattle gallop away into mirages of gilt and silver and screaming dark birds.

Their little excursion wagon, followed by six big commissary freighters, comes over the top of a rise, and she stands to see all the tilting earth go on for miles. Only once before in her life has she seen wild deer, and there just ahead are five of them! All so alike as to be quarter notes on the waving staves of grass.

"Hang on, miss," says the driver. "We don't want to lose you."

"No such luck," she says with a laugh, but she sits down again and shades her eyes.

Doris is in a state of delight with it all, even in the heat and the sun hot enough to be splitting stones. She has always known that the animals live between ourselves and the rest of Creation. How like us they are and how unlike. All people are only people, but there are a great plenty of animals of all kinds and they are each one named in the Book of Life.

"And do you often go back and forth?" she asks the driver. "Are there not Red Indians?"

He smiles down at her. "Yes, miss," he says. "But this road is safe. I go to Galveston next trip." His attention is taken by his off leader, he calls to her, she tosses her head in irritation. "Galveston, there's many immigrant ships coming in there, coming and going."

He clearly wants her to tell him where she's from, how she got here, but she says, "And do you take people there? As passengers?"

"Sometimes. But they mostly go on Santleben's stagecoach, service to the coast just started up, getting fancy around here now."

Santleben's. Ships leaving for England or the Continent, just in case. She tucks this away as she would her bedding, something to rest upon.

They camp out like Gypsies right in the middle of all this uninhabited land. She braids her thick black hair out of the way and falls asleep listening to distant wolf howls, a weird clacking chitter of long birds soaring overhead. Sometimes she lies on her stomach, lifted up on her elbows in a tumble of blankets and chemise to listen to the night. She wakes up to the smell of smoke and horses. They come to Floresville and then they are only twenty-five miles from San Antonio. She doesn't want this journey to end.

Mrs. Webb tells her in an absentminded way to keep her bonnet down over her face against the sun. Doris wants to lift her face to it, to flood herself with sunlight. She wants to walk out into the land and reach out to the vigilant deer as they thrash their tails from side to side in alarm. Their tails are as long as her forearm and all white and suddenly, with the sun sinking low, their huge ears glow red as the evening light shines through them.

"Jo, look!" she says. The girl wearily gets up from her trunk in the wagon's interior and comes to stand at her back.

"What?"

"The sun is shining through their ears, like a red lantern, you see?"

Josephine turns away without answering and says, "Mama, she says the sun is shining on the deer's ears."

A long pause. "The deer's ears? Yes. Well. I am at a loss for words."

"So are they! Um . . ." Doris's laugh trails off.

"I don't know how long I am to endure this endless gushing over every cactus and every bird, Doris. You are a governess, not an entertainer."

"Yes, ma'am."

"She was just destroyed over the Pangborns' puppies," says Josephina to her mother. "Remember that? They were 'wee.' Everything was wee, wee, wee."

Doris is caught flatfooted with this astonishing rudeness and is silent. The driver glances down at her and shakes his head. She busies herself folding up her kit and putting it away. *They never laugh,* she thinks. *They do not understand jokes and joy to them is as foreign as the bottom of the sea.* She looks down at her hands. *Patience.* Quail skitter up in short flights, fall to earth, explode into the sky again trailing their cries behind them and Doris's face is red with the humiliation of the child's words, to which she cannot reply.

And alongside rides the sergeant with his little round eyeglasses and blond hair, a spare man with his band collar undone in the heat. He lifts his cap to her with a smile.

"This country amazes me too, Miss Dillon," the young sergeant says. "I am from Connecticut, with a village every ten miles and a great deal of stony ground."

"Are you then?" She manages a polite smile. "And there is no danger?"

"No. Not so far. We have scouts out. Be reassured."

"I will indeed."

She thinks of the fiddler; her thoughts go back to him repeatedly, as if he too were part of this landscape, with his dusty red hair and his worn clothes all the color of earth, but he stood in them with careless ease and so he outshone them. It was a private place to go with her thoughts, with her mind. His taut, poised body and the fine lines of his face, it was "Death and the Sinner," his bow to her. He was ragged, a man of a defeated army and at the dinner he had played his heart out in a borrowed shirt. In short, very like the Irish. She tried to ask about him discreetly, got a few answers. He had taken on a man twice his size to get his stolen fiddle back again, they said, knocked him flat with a stone and he had got away with it, standing there asking what song she would like to hear and not a mark on him. A ginger man. A man for this new world and its wild animals that run ceaselessly through her dreams. She had asked for "The Minstrel Boy," an Irish song of rebellion and surrender so that he might know from whence she came.

There at Fort Brown they had set up tents for the women behind the earthen walls with a separate tent for herself and Josephine and Mercedes. Doris was delighted with the tent, the light glowing through the fabric walls, but she knew better than to say so. She was safely away from the colonel. Jo and Mercedes complained of the hard army cots, but she stood holding back the flaps until late, listening to the music of his fiddle as it tore through fast reels and jigs and it made her move her slippers in a quick step. *Here I am dancing in my nightgown, Doris Dillon get hold of yourself.* Then he played softer music and she listened until the candle burnt to a pool of tallow guttering in the dish. The night settled in; silence.

The maid leans forward to tap her on the shoulder. In the rear of the wagon Mrs. Webb and the girl Josephine are sleeping.

"The fiddler," whispers Mercedes. "You bewitched him."

"Oh tish," she says, and laughs and puts one hand to her mouth. "Away with you."

"I have two eyes in my head," says Mercedes. "And a man of my own and I know when they get bewitched."

Mrs. Webb calls up, "Doris, you are giggling again. Must it go on all day long?" She lies back, faint with the heat. "Do leave off."

Doris almost says *Oh ha ha* but stops herself in time. Mercedes rolls her eyes and they both suddenly bow their heads and clap hands over their mouths.

Mercedes was from San Antonio. She had been down in Brownsville visiting relatives and now hired on with the Webbs to return. She had taken on the care of Doris Dillon with the instincts of someone who adopts the abandoned of the world to be their guide and their loyal if somewhat insistent shadow.

They go on; Doris knows she will be in this New World a long time, perhaps for all her life, and she must be mindful of every step she takes. She does not yet know how to judge these Americans. All she has known of America has been its military, its ranks and rules. But the people outside the military do not seem to have social classes or an aristocracy either, and in Ohio people wearing dusty, worn clothing could be masters of a hundred acres. She must take care every second it seems but then she falls into remembering the fiddler's spare body, his upright stance. His lean, refined face and his low-spoken courtesy stay with her across the sea of grass. His music. He had called to her. The blond sergeant was attentive to her and kind, made sure the ladies were as comfortable as possible, but she could tell one thing about him: he disliked his own horse.

There was much to come to grips with. Maybe *endure* was the word. Not the least were Colonel Webb's footsteps at her closed door once in the silent late hours, in the attic there at the house in Ohio. Slow steps, a pause, a waiting. She with a chair against the door and her mouth dry as a threshing floor and her heart pounding, also waiting. *Go away, please dear Lord make him go away.*

She shut her eyes. She must take great care. Trust in God, her mother said, but never dance in a small boat.

A HEAVY STORM came in after days of scudding clouds and soaked the piecework shack in which they lived, cleared the air and refreshed the sand-blasted buildings. They made good money at the Wanderer's Rest. They were asked to play discreet background music at the dining room in the Hendley Hotel, a first for them. They once again borrowed coats, scoured and skillet-ironed their shirts, and came back with twenty-five dollars in silver and banknotes.

"We will be ruined by wealth and pleasures if this keeps up," said Damon. "We will throw away our bread crusts, buy special cakes of perfumed soap for shaving."

"Dear God save us," said Simon.

"An awful fate," said the boy. He lay on his back on the splintered flooring with his legs up in the air. He was trying to juggle his rucksack on the soles of his feet. It landed on their rickety table and knocked over the fragment of mirror. Doro barely saved it.

"Stop, Patrick," said Doro. "Quit it."

"I'm trying to juggle with my feet!"

"*Mi hijo,* do it outside!"

In early October the postmaster in the Customs House handed Simon the letter. It was a hot day even that late in the year, even at nine in the morning. Simon held the letter in his hand in a fixed, silent way, as if he were afflicted with lockjaw. It was addressed to Patrick Matthew O'Hehir in care of Simon Boudlin and it was from San Antonio.

Simon said thank you sir and turned to walk back in long strides through the heat like an engine, and then as he began to enter the world of shacks and sagging houses he slowed down. They were all asleep inside their little house, where hemp sacks over the windows kept the sun out and flies sailed in and out without hindrance. Doroteo, Patrick, and Damon were in a comalike sleep in their drawers. Like everybody in this hot climate they had sawed them off above the knee. They had been playing last night at the Little Bermuda until they had heard the bells of St. Mary's ring out two in the morning. Even though they had entered the month of September, there were still mosquitoes and still they heard of the death toll of the yellow fever.

"Patrick," said Simon. "Patrick, wake up."

The boy sat up, ran his hands through his spiky hair, and looked around.

"What? What's happened?" He heard the urgency in Simon's voice.

"A letter came for you." Simon held it out and then saw it trembling in the early light and so moved it back and forth, from hand to hand, to conceal the nervous shaking. "It's from Miss Dillon."

"Oh then!" The boy smiled with his great wide mouth. "You open it, Simon. You go on and read it. It's for you. Read it to me later."

Simon settled his Kentucky hat on his head and took off at a fast walk for the sea. By the time he was out the door the other two had sat up, looked at each other, and then lay back down without saying a word.

Simon walked among the rows of shacks. He was alone at last under a hot and cloudy sky. He touched his hat to women at their housework, flying clean sheets in the wind, roosters calling one to another, dodged a running piglet, and then the beach stretched out before him. It was astonishing to have a private life and it lay in this letter; maybe a rejection, maybe a request that he not write her again, but whatever it might be it was his business, his alone. He was weary of spending his every moment with three other men and their incessant talk, but that's the way it always was. Simon had come to know that he was the odd one, not them. He was the only person on the beach and his lone dark figure walked on beside the roar and receding draw of the waves.

At last he couldn't stand waiting any longer and in the windshadow of some unnamed bush with the noise of the patient Gulf before him, he pulled out his knife and slit the folded envelope.

Before he read the first sentence he made himself think about it. For the last hour he had actually been thinking that it would be a letter to him. But it could not possibly be a letter to Simon Boudlin, because she was writing in answer to Patrick. Mrs. Webb or that detestable Colonel Webb would have read it and approved of it. Whatever she had to say had to be disguised and filtered through those two conditions.

August the 10th, The Alamo Garrison
San Antonio, Texas

Dear Patrick O'Hehir,
I received your letter of July the 15th with much interest and so I write to thank you for sending me what news you had of those from

Tralee and Ballyroe as it brings a great deal of comfort to hear of occurrences in Ireland. I am writing this letter with apologies for my poor hand at the pen.

He bent over the paper. The gray light glared on it, and close at hand the Gulf rolled in with long flat waves; the tide was going out.

It delights me to hear that you are with a respectable music troupe and are able to play in the best establishments. Patrick, I hope you are able to see some part of this wild Texas and its delightful yet strange open country as we have none of this like it in our Ireland, it left me amazed as we traveled to this town and I was much taken with the sight of deer and horses running free as if it were the beginning of the world.

He read this over several times. She was not a creature of display and stratagems, the natural world delighted her! She was not avid for social events and the endless striving of towns! He came to this conclusion on the strength of that one sentence. He scattered mental exclamation marks throughout his own thoughts! He blew sand from the glittering pages.

Please give my greetings to the Dillon family as indeed I am related to Brandon Casey Dillon, for he is the first cousin of my father and married an Aherne from Waterford. If you hear from them please do convey the news to me as we shall be here in San Antonio for more than two years, for that is the colonel's tour of duty. Forgive my long delay in replying as there was so much to be done upon arrival and the colonel does not approve of my writing many letters. It was a matter of several months altogether what with getting his approval with the weather quare warm and mail not moving.

I include here in a separate page the news from my parents if that would be of interest. As for myself I am very happy and my little charge Josephina is a dear delight to me. To him who writes for you please convey my plentiful thanks. Remember our good Irish airs such as I heard played there after the battle, a scene to wring the heart. Let us say our thanks to God and His Angels that this war is over and in hope that no more dreadful occurrences come upon this country. If you were to be in San Antonio I am sure that the colonel will remember you and would welcome a visit, for you played your drum most bravely, and so I remain respectfully yours in friendship,

Miss Doris Dillon
c/o Mrs. Franklin Webb
In Garrison at the Alamo
San Antonio, Bexar County, Texas

On the separate page were the doings and mishaps of the little town of Ballyroe, with twins born to the Ahernes, milk prices, who had emigrated, who decided not to at the last moment, who fell in the shuck in her good dress, the roads between Bally and Tralee claggy with mud, and the milkman's cart all banjacked and lacking his best wheel.

Desperate and irrational thoughts came to him: to leave now for San Antonio on foot. Join the Union Army and hope to be sent to the Alamo garrison. Rob a Western Union telegraph office and buy a new pair of boots, trousers, and a sack coat and show up under her balcony, if she had a balcony, playing "The Minstrel Boy."

But behind these wild imaginings was a certain saving caution. Maybe she was not the person he seemed to see on first acquaintance. She could be a person who was self-seeking or vain or silly or an unstoppable talker who would make his life hell whether she needed help or no.

And what are you then, Simon?

Not worth a crying dime at the present moment. A bastard out of Kentucky with no way to make a living but playing in cheap dives and at the occasional garden party. All he had to his name was a good fiddle and a decent hat, neither of which would overwhelm a young lady of any standing.

And a Dance and Brothers revolver. He had forgotten the revolver.

Simon held the letter in both hands and looked down at the clean grain of it, the good paper, her clear-cut handwriting. The sun splintered off the outgoing tide and half-blinded him, and he was suspended between these two different worlds, the windy Gulf and on this paper her voice, as real as anything. She had a pretty hand of writing. He smiled as he read it. She had written, "To him who writes for you please convey my plentiful thanks" and "free as the beginning of the world."

He lay back against the rise of the sand dune and made himself remember the times before the war, to think his way back into it. Before he left Kentucky. He used to laugh a lot; he and Stand MacFarland. They went for days back in the heavy woods toward Stiles Crossing to hunt and sit up by a fire and talk half the night. The old man allowed him to take his good Pennsylvania rifle, fourteen pounds and forty-four inches in the barrel. MacFarland could imitate people; he used to make Simon laugh until he was paralytic. He told stories about his grandfather and the Shawnee wars and they were always somehow funny. It was different then. The air was different and the long remote crying of the steamboat whistles as they came down from the Monongahela and Pittsburgh seemed to tell a story of a great nation and a great people with adventure and the look of distance in their eyes, and now it was somehow soiled with the stench of the dead. MacFarland was dead. Lincoln was dead. Neighbors had shot one another dead.

It was not the same country.

It occurred to him that he rarely laughed anymore. Maybe laughter would come back, but it was a dark sun that had come over the country and a plague of crows. But here in his hands was a lifting of the heart when he came upon this delicate handwriting and the hope of making her love him despite his poverty and an unmarried mother and a father disappeared into Louisiana, despite it all. Simon sat up, folded the letter carefully, and got to his feet. When he walked back into the house he said, "I'll read it to you, Patrick. She sends greetings, and thanks to me."

Patrick looked up into his face and said, "Another time, Simon. It's yours for now. Another time."

CHAPTER ELEVEN

HE HAD NOW SAVED fifty dollars.

It was near the waterfront one afternoon after a late night at the Jamaica that he saw an advertisement: LAND FOR SALE. It was a new sign, painted on a board on the front of a wooden structure. The door was difficult to open. Simon shoved hard and it gave way and he nearly fell inside.

"Yes?" A man looked up. "Did you bring the corn pudding?"

"No," said Simon. He ran his hand through his gnarled hair to make it lie flat and tucked a packet of new strings into his pants pocket. "I'm not from the cook shop. I've come to see about buying land."

"I see." The man wore a derby hat and a shirt with an open band collar. His beard was streaked with white. He looked at Simon carefully. "Well, we all have our little fantasies."

"Yes, sir, that's probably true." A small hesitation like an indrawn breath. "But maybe you could start me out here, and tell me what land is for sale. And how you go about paying for it, and who you pay." Simon pulled up a rickety chair without being asked and sat down. "And how you go about all the legal stuff to buy it."

The man nodded. He poised one hand flat over the desk and slammed it down in an attempt to kill a fly. He missed.

"You? Buy land?"

"I'm just asking." Simon looked around at the stacks of documents and leather-bound legal tomes. And then, "Why not?"

The man tipped his head from one side to the other. "I should be frank with you. Disasters abound everywhere. I no longer sell land, it seems. I sell hurricanes and war and military occupation and Indian attacks. I am a vendor of droughts and tornadoes. Which do you prefer?"

Simon had his entire life stretching ahead of him and to be making plans to order it all ahead of time, as it were, especially since he was only a musician, seemed foolish. But he did it anyway, with a brief shrug and the hope that the man had nothing else in particular to do today.

Without thinking he said, "Tornadoes. Did you ever see one?"

"God is merciful," said the land man. "No." He shuffled through a stack of papers. "Here. One hundred and fifty acres on the Colorado River, near Austin, a spring reportedly, a structure reportedly, unfenced, undefended, and subject to miasmas. Here is another—taken by the Confederate government for taxes. It's on the Guadalupe, abandoned, since the family was all killed in a Kiowa raid. This is near a town called, horribly, Comfort. They probably left their skillets and bedding, all things considered."

"I see," Simon said. He put a finger on the top paper and turned it toward him, but he could not read the legal language and so turned it back.

"And what are you doing in Galveston, young man?"

"I play fiddle," he said, hesitantly. "And we have a group. Currently playing at the Jamaica."

"Ah." A knowing silence and then the land-sales man recovered himself. "And here . . ." He drew out a deed from under a stack of badly printed maps. "This is an interesting one. The attempt to get a clear title should take you the rest of your life. It's a section of the old Peters Colony land grant, far away in the interior of our great state, where an English consortium attempted to set up a colonizing scheme and tried to run it like a lord's estate back in old England. The settlers came after his manager with loaded pistols. Then the settlers ran off with all the deeds and records to the Dallas County Courthouse. The Texas Republic and then the State of Texas passed some laws regarding this situation as to titles and deeds, to what end I do not know. But here you have four hundred acres, unimproved, unfenced, no structures, situated just south of the Red River. Indian country. Five dollars an acre. All yours for two thousand, in what currency is a question. I assume you know how to load and shoot a weapon? Because you would have need of one, if not several."

"Yes," said Simon, and took the paper. He was silent for a measure, two measures. He looked at the other papers pertinent to the deed. It was all very legal and confusing: deeds, grants, maps with great white spaces, reports by the Texas Rangers. He leaned back in his chair and drummed his fingers on his thigh. "Do you have some kind of land for sale that is . . . *simple*?"

"Land titles are never simple. Never. Not here. Maybe back in . . . where are you from?" The man gave him a narrow glance as if the better to understand Simon's provenance, his background, his finances.

"Paducah, Kentucky."

"Ah. Who are your people?"

"Alexanders. Boudlins."

"I'm from Little Egypt. I knew some Alexanders in Paducah. They owned the big livery stable, the one Forrest raided."

"Right," said Simon. "That's my mother's people."

The man raised a grizzled eyebrow and seemed to perk up; maybe this fiddler had money after all. "Well. Your mother's people. But I'm afraid I don't know any Boudlins."

"They're from around Baton Rouge," Simon answered. He hoped the man would not continue to ask impertinent questions. This was about money, about finding a piece of land and somehow making a deal on it, and not an inquiry as to his antecedents. Simon was not quite sure how these deals happened but he would find out. "So what does that mean, a clear title?"

The man considered; a mosquito circled relentlessly and the smell of the office was of damp leather-bound volumes earthy with unclaimed acres. "It means that nobody else has a claim on it, that claim being hidden away in some obscure land office or government office having to do with legislation passed by either the Republic of Texas or the State of Texas or the Confederacy or all three. Some claim you don't even know about. You pay your money down on a mortgage and then at some time somebody else comes along and says, 'Wait a minute, that's mine!' And they got a paper says they paid down on it. "

"All right," said Simon.

"And Texas land titles are a dog's breakfast. Because first it was under Spain. To register a land title you had to travel all the way to Mexico City. So hardly anybody did. Then it was under Mexico. Same deal. Nobody had a secure title to land or buildings. Then it was the Republic of Texas, and their files are moldering yet in the dankest corners of the capitol in Austin. The State of Texas added a whole new pile. Then the Confederacy, which is now in its death throes and didn't do squat about land titles anyway, and soon we will be under some other government, who knows what, and so there you are."

And Simon thought, *I don't care. I'll buy land somewhere, somehow. There has to be a way.*

He said, "But lots of people own land. Here in Galveston. They own town lots and businesses and so on."

"Yes, well, we just cripple along."

"What about this place on the Red River? The old land grant place?"

The man shuffled out the papers. He read from the title description. "Four hundred acres approximately fifteen miles south of the Red River, straight south of Preston's Bend—survey marks here indicated—unfenced and unimproved, no structures." He ran his finger down the pages. "Here's the latitude and longitude. Latitude thirty-three degrees and four minutes north, longitude ninety-six degrees fifty minutes west. Here, I'll write it down for you. Also the various survey markings, blazed trees, bluffs and so on and the fact that there is a spring of water flowing into Big Mineral Creek, hardwood trees meaning live oaks and Spanish oaks, so on and so on, about two hundred acres of open meadow, or so they say. Plus a noxious sink of rock oil where your milk cow can sink in up to her hocks and die. Price is five dollars an acre, that's two thousand dollars in case you don't want to be seen counting on your fingers. Owner, Solomon G. Bradford."

"I want it," said Simon, and suddenly smiled. "That's it. I want it." It seemed that the papers had been waiting for him in this untidy little office, waiting for his appearance with fiddle strings in his pocket. It came to him sure as guns.

"Subject to Indian raids. Also I warn you, white people up there are lunatics. They hung a lot of people up there because they weren't loyal to the Confederacy. It was a hanging spree of unparalleled dimensions."

"I want it. Who do I pay?"

The man raised his head to look into Simon's face. He took off his low-crowned black hat and wiped his bald skull and put the hat back on.

"Well," he said. "I swan."

Simon waited.

"Son, you need a down payment of about two hundred dollars as ten percent of the price, but I am going to make that two hundred fifty as times are so unsure. Then you need a lawyer to draw up a deed of sale, and you have to pay him because he has to go look up stuff in whatever records are available. Let's say you just give the down payment to me. Makes it all simpler. Then you have to also pay me for title research and to record the deed. Then you have to go there and survive. Now, what else?"

Simon lowered his head as he counted up the costs. He had to find the man who owned it. If he were dead or alive. He needed a hundred dollars down payment because he was sure he could get the person to come down. Then more for title research and recording the deed. This was his land and he knew it.

"So where is this Solomon Bradford?"

"No idea. Don't know anything about him; old, young, killed in the war, died of yellow fever, living a life of luxury in Austin as a clerk to some politician, who knows?"

Simon got up out of the chair. He was not about to hand a penny over to this man. He had been born into a world of horse traders and was well acquainted with deception and the need for caution at every step when it came to buying and selling. He casually pressed aside the top paper, read the second, the longitude and the latitude of this land up in the Red River Valley, then bent his head down to regard his hands with all the music in them and a brief thought of how rare it was to have your heart stirred like this out of an ordinary day in the ordinary sunshine. He needed to find Solomon Bradford. That was the first job.

"Well, thank you, much appreciated." His land and his girl almost within reach. It was going to take some doing. And himself yet young and inexperienced in many ways. But that's why God made people young at first, to get the doing done. He smiled politely, pulled the sticky door open, and said, "Looks like I'll just have to wait a few years to go looking."

"That would be wise."

ANOTHER POLITE LETTER from Patrick to Miss Dillon, full of inventive half-truths, gossip about Ireland that Patrick dredged up from hearing his parents talk, incidents that had occurred more than twenty years ago, assurances of his desire to join the army again before long (this zinger was directed straight at the Webbs, who would no doubt read and approve of the letter before handing it to Miss Dillon), a careful mention of the very kind violinist Simon Boudlin, who was teaching him to read music. Sealed and stamped, handed over to the man behind the post office counter at the Customs House and the long wait began again. Letters seemed to walk of their own accord down the road from San Antonio, to get lost, wander, camp out for a while beside some pleasant river, finally to amble unconcernedly into Galveston.

Then her reply came back. She wrote about the demands that army life made on a person and chances of promotion in case Patrick wished to make the military a career, news of Indian depredations in the north, a wagon accidentally driven off the Losoya Bridge. She wrote of things that were often funny, lively, and completely impersonal. A letter went back up the road from Patrick, full of bland, boring news of Galveston and the interminable gossip about imaginary Dillons. Simon wanted to tell her about the garden party (some of it), and the shack they had fixed up (no details about the latrine), about the pennywhistle fight (omit blood and hollering), and about the land he wanted near the Red River. About himself, his thoughts, the voices he heard singing in slow perfect harmony on the ships tied up in the harbor. How much he wanted to meet her. To put out his hand and touch her. He began to despair of ever writing to her directly, of learning the ways of her heart through these censored pages, or revealing his own, such as it was.

In the next letter he decided he would say Patrick was coming to San Antonio, but then he thought, *Wait, wait.* He wanted to be able to say he was a landowner, a horse owner, a man with two suits and a watch. He wondered if this would matter to her. He very much hoped it would not.

So the letter was about four men making do with household chores, the songs they played and in what key, the names of ships coming from all over the world to dock in Galveston, and speculations as to who might emigrate from Ballyroe this year. Safe enough. Painfully safe. It came to the month of November and still the yellow fever persisted. There had not been a hard freeze and mosquitoes hummed and bred in the rain pools.

They played at a wedding one early afternoon. It was a gathering of people who had returned to the island from inland after having been run out in Magruder's forced evacuation in '63. They came by boat and over the railroad bridge with their possessions much diminished and their tools in disrepair. Two of these people decided to get married despite the unsettled conditions of the times, in spite of their poverty. At the two-story wooden house on Twenty-seventh Street near St. Mary's the dancing went on until late. The celebrants were regaled with whiskey and fish. It was a cold evening. The gulls flew over crying to one another like the lonesome thieves of the air that they were and the evening train from Houston came over the bridge under a thin moon with steam billowing from between its great driver wheels.

Simon laughed at a little girl trying to dance in front of their improvised bandstand as he bowed out the final notes of "Angelina Baker" and gave the one-two hard and sharp to signify the ending. At the edge of the stand the boy Patrick sat down suddenly. He carefully slid his two polished bones into his coat pocket and sat the bodhran in his lap. His head dropped forward until his forehead rested on the rim of the drum.

"I've taken a fever," he said.

They got him home by half-carrying him. He kept saying he didn't feel well but that he would be better in the morning. Simon was up and down with him the rest of the night, helping him to the outdoor latrine, then back again. Toward dawn Damon took over as clouds were building out on the Gulf.

He did not feel better in the morning. Doroteo quickly made up the fire with driftwood and heated water, held a cup to the boy's mouth. The morning dragged on and they sat with the boy as the chills and then the fever struck him. It seemed some invisible devil had taken hold of the boy and would not let go.

"We should to take him to the Ursuline nuns," said Doroteo. "They have the hospital there."

"No," said Patrick. "I'm good. I'll get over it. It's just the malaria that we had there from the fish." He rolled back and forth on his cotton-sack bed. He was restless and in pain. "You go to the hospital to die. I am not going to die because of everything I already said."

Doroteo leaned on the doorframe. He said, "He is not making right sense. It is not good."

They pooled their money and Simon and Damon went to find

a doctor. An Ursuline at the wooden house that served as their convent gave them the address of one of the city's three doctors. It was a substantial house with verandas on both stories and sago palms in front. The doctor was not at home. Yellow fever was pacing up and down the streets and the back bayous of Galveston in long unseen steps, touching a child here and a strong man there and a sailor panting in his hammock belowdecks on a tied-up ship that was soon flying the yellow flag. Damon and Simon sat on the curb and spoke in short sentences. There was little to say. Finally, at sunset, the man arrived in an open carriage pulled by a thin horse.

He leaned out over the door. "Where?" he asked.

Simon stood up and pulled off his hat. "Back near Lost Bayou."

The doctor was shrunken and weary inside his black suit. After a moment he said, "Who is it? You're the band that come up after Los Palmitos, aren't you? You're the fiddler."

"Yes, sir," said Simon. He put his hat back on. Damon stood with his face stricken with anxiety and he did not seem to be able to change his expression. He turned the pennywhistle over and over in his hand. Simon gestured toward the Gulf. "We live back there. It's our bodhran boy. The one with the bones."

"Get in," said the doctor.

CHAPTER TWELVE

THEY CROWDED IN AND felt between themselves fleeting moments of hope that came and went as if they were passing them back and forth. They clattered along Broadway and then turned into Shacktown, into the leaning wooden single-story houses where women looked out over yard railings as they passed, saw it was the doctor, and shook their heads.

The doctor pulled up his tired horse in front of their shack when Simon said, "Here we are."

"Yes, here we are in Mosquito Flats," said the doctor. He got down and Doroteo ran out to take the hitching rein and lay it gently and carefully over the yard railing, and then Damon went inside for the bucket and hurried to the pump. He soon came back with water and stood outside holding the bucket for the horse to drink as if he could not bear to come inside and hear the words.

"Yellow fever," said the doctor. "That's what I think. He may get through this first phase and live. If it comes back a second time he may not. If it comes back a second time it is almost always fatal. Is he throwing up?" He kneeled down beside the boy.

The boy lay on the bed they had made for him on the floor. They had piled up their own beds one on top of the other for him. He was in the fever stage and so he had thrown off the blankets. The blankets were threadbare brown wool stamped CSA. His eyes were glittering.

"I throw up all the time," said the boy. "On the sea, on land, in the street, at the governor's ball in Harrisburg."

"Open your mouth," the doctor said, and Patrick opened his wide mouth and stuck out his tongue. Then he shut it. His yellow hair lay flat and wet.

"Take a look at that," he said, "I bet you never seen anything like it."

The doctor smiled and held the boy's wrist to note the pulse rate, listened to his chest with a stethoscope, and then reached into his bag.

"What I have might do very little," he said. "But this is laudanum, this is willow bark." He set out a paper packet and a large bottle of liquid. "The willow bark is for fever, make a tea of it. The other is for pain. Give three spoonfuls of the laudanum. He may get a restful sleep."

"Mama, it's good you're here," the boy said, and then his hands grew restless together as if he had suddenly begun to count on his fingers.

They stood around with deep attention. Then they gathered their coins and Simon held them out.

"That will be a dollar." The doctor got to his feet. He selected two half-dollar pieces from Simon's hand, said God be with the lad, and went out to his carriage.

As soon as the doctor was gone Damon heated water to infuse the willow bark. Simon poured some water into a canteen, then three tablespoons of the laudanum, shook it, and held it to the boy's mouth. He watched him drink it until he had taken every drop. After that the boy slept heavily. A cold wind came rushing up from the water and it played mindlessly with the sand all around the house while Doroteo carefully arranged the boy's blankets, his hand resting for a moment on the sweaty hair of his head.

The next night, Doroteo and Simon went out to play at the bars and earn money for medicines while Damon stayed with the boy and then they switched off. For twenty-four hours he seemed improved and sat up and drank the beef broth Doroteo made for him and thanked each of them by name, holding out his hand to clasp theirs one by one, but then the fever and chills came back worse than before. He could not eat. In five days he had become skeletal, his teeth bared as he struggled for breath.

"Listen," he said. His voice was thin.

Simon sat cross-legged beside him and said, "I'm listening, Patrick."

The boy fell silent for a moment and turned his head as if he were trying to hear some distant sound. His eyes stood out in his head, his cheeks had sunk into his face. He seemed attentive to the sound of gulls sailing in over Shacktown, searching out scraps and garbage, and from far to the east over the water came the sound of rumbling thunder. Finally he said, "Simon, it was beautiful. All of us in ranks. An army is so beautiful. The cannon was beautiful. Angels of fire out of the mouths of them. I remember it in my mind. Us drummers did 'Hell on the Wabash' and everything and now everything I remember will be gone."

"No," said Simon. He could not think of what more to say. He clasped his hand on the boy's arm and was surprised to find tears running down his face, into his mouth. He wiped his mouth on his sleeve.

"Yes. Will all run off to the sea."

"Don't go," whispered Simon. "Don't go, Patrick." Then he

dropped his chin to his chest and pressed his clenched fists against his eyes to stop his crying.

The boy became quiet, settled his thrashing limbs, and then began to weep. He sobbed in short gasps, and the rush of tears was stained some strange color. "It's not right," he wept. "I'm too young. If I could just be home with Mama and Papa. Take me home."

Simon's throat felt as tight as a wrung cloth. He stroked the boy's brow. "You'll get better, then we'll see that you get home. People live through this, Patrick. They get well."

There was a long silence as if the boy had not heard him. He said at last, "Yes, God lives in the Gulf and he is coming for me."

On the sixth day the storm trundled in and rain hissed at their leaking roof. Doroteo said they should take him to the hospital but in a hot whisper Patrick said no, you could catch the indecent diseases there and he would not die and go meet God with an indecent disease in his body.

All of a sudden he got to his feet with wild, angular movements. He stood up and vomited a great purge of black blood all over the floor. He wandered from wall to wall erupting with the black vomit and crying out between retches. He puked all over Simon. All over Simon's hands. The boy had sunk into his bones and his skin was yellow as a finch. Finally they got him to lie down on the soiled bedding, and with a feeling of horror Simon saw that the boy was bleeding from the eyes and ears. His gray eyes swam in a puddling of red blood.

"Oh my God," Simon said in a low hoarse whisper. He wiped the boy's face with a wrung cloth already stained brown.

"We have to get him to the hospital," said Damon.

"There's too many people there already," said Simon and then, suddenly, put both bloody hands over his face and wept in a tearing harsh noise. "God*damn*!" Jerking sobs overwhelmed him. He sat on the floor, bent into his hands, and it was some long terrible minutes before he got hold of himself.

Doroteo touched the boy's wolfish face and said, "There will be a priest there. He needs a priest." Then he too palmed away tears, wiped his cheeks on his shirtsleeve.

They tore the shutter off its hinges, loaded Patrick onto it, and covered him with blankets. They set off on foot through the rain. They came to the convent and hospital. Lights shone from all the windows, one after the other in a luminous row with the rain running in long strings from the roof edges.

Simon sat with him in the noise and hum of the men's ward, taking his turn, while Doro and Damon caught a brief moment of sleep in the hall. In the middle of the night the boy cried out, "Mother!"

An Ursuline knelt beside him with her skirts out in a broad carpet around her. "Your mother is Holy Mary and she is right here."

The boy said, in a tiny thin cry, "I'm sinking. I'm sinking."

"Let go and you will float, dear child," she said. "You are invincible."

Simon sat with his hands over the boy's hands where they clasped a rosary and listened to the nun recite the prayers. He listened to the steps of the priest coming down the hall and into the ward as he arrived to administer the sacrament of extreme unction and bent to the drawn face, the open mouth, and said the words. He crossed the boy's forehead with oil. Simon sat without speaking until the child had grown cold.

THE YELLOW FEVER was an invisible being restlessly searching up and down the coast. It wanted to live on its own but everybody it inhabited died, and so it kept on searching. It stared out over the glittering flat water of the Back Bayou, peered into the houses, buzzed above the water pails. And in answer to it what did they have except music? Simon played "Death and the Sinner" at the muddy graveside, where so many others were buried and more were coming even now. Damon laid the G whistle in the boy's sunken and inhuman hands as he lay there in his coffin, so he could play before the angels. The nuns said they were to fumigate their house and get rid of all their blankets and bedding and clothes. Take only what you wear and boil that. Your cooking utensils are suspect. Abandon what you can. Best of all would be to leave the place altogether.

But first Simon would have to write a letter. It would be in his own name. It would pass the censorious gaze of Colonel Webb because it was news of the boy's death.

Simon sat with his rucksack at his feet as the wind spattered Gulf spray on the little house. The others waited patiently. He stared at the paper, then wrote,

Dear Miss Dillon.

And stopped. He was not good at this and never had been, but he bore down on it as if approaching a previously unknown melody in a mysterious key. Doroteo and Damon sat against the wall, blank and disconsolate.

I take pen in hand.

He would have to write to the boy's parents as well. Your son survived the battle of Los Palmitos and fell victim to the yellow fever in his attempts to return home to Allentown. We his companions found him cheerful and ever ready to help his fellows. I am sending his bones.

No, I am sending his rhythmical instruments and his bodhran.

Simon held out the last sheet of paper.

"Damon," he said, "you do it. Write to the boy's parents."

"I will. Just finish your letter to Miss Dillon."

I take pen in hand to acquaint you with the sad event of Patrick Matthew O'Hehir's passing this Saturday last, the 27th of November, 1865, in Galveston, Texas, at one o'clock in the morning. It was a fever and he endured it for six days without complaint, but it turned to the worse and neither medicines nor doctors were to any avail. The priest was there with him at the last as was I and one of the Ursuline nuns.

Simon's hand threatened to string other words together whether he willed it or not. He could write *I very much want to meet you again in order to convey to you my feelings.*

He wrote on and on in his mind, words he might never use. Are you safe from that man? Are any of us safe from the yellow fever and its terrors? Is it possible that you might look favorably on an invitation from myself to an event (any event) in which I might hold your hand, a dance might occur, I might put my arm around your waist and we move down the center in the steps of the Virginia reel and leave death far behind us? May I sit at the door to your bedroom and speak with you? Tell me the story of Tralee and the tales of the Dillon ancestors, here is a carriage, I lift the reins, we step smartly into the future on the Red River away from coastal fevers and the impending horrors of those fevers. It was terrible. I have seen death now several times, I fear it.

Miss Dillon, I regret his passing extremely. He was loved by all. He wished you to have a medallion of Our Lady that he treasured. You may reply to this letter at General Delivery Houston, as I and the others in my musical ensemble have been invited to that city to perform musical offerings at several private homes. It is possible your letter may be delivered there at the Houston General Post Office although there is no guarantee. With sorrow in having to convey this news, I remain in deepest respect yours truly, Simon A. Boudlin.

And so he wrote in his own name and voice to Doris Dillon to tell her that Patrick was dead, a burden too serious and heavy for subterfuge. Now they must pack up what they had left and get away from this fever coast. Somewhere they would have to play happy jigs and reels to purchase their food and shelter whether they personally felt happy or not. He placed the letter in the hand of a freighter going to San Antonio who said he would deliver it for ten cents, admired Simon's hat, tried to buy it, and then gave up when Simon showed him the size, lifted his reins, and was off into the distant interior.

And so they left behind almost all of what they had garnered in their time in Galveston as the nun had told them to; their bedding and their cooking gear and the furniture they had knocked together, the white shirts that had proved after all unlucky. Who knew what contaminations resided in the weave of the cloth or the grain of the wood? They were all too young to die and always would be.

They journeyed on, the three of them together. Simon wore the old Confederate shell jacket and his Kentucky hat. He took out the Dance revolver, put the cylinder and frame together, loaded and capped five loads, and left the empty chamber under the hammer as always. They walked down to the train station of the Houston and Texas Central Railway on the waterfront.

They could not afford seats in the passenger cars, but in the loading yards there was a thin young man with only one hand and a dancing, elusive manner who told them they could sneak aboard some of the freight cars. He showed them how to lie hidden in the brush and weeds just outside the main part of the city. The trains ran south down the island and then they slowed to take a right turn to get onto the bridge going over the bay to the mainland. When the train slowed, you ran alongside and pulled yourself up. Be careful be careful, cinders from the smoke stack can set you afire, you can fall under the wheels and they will chop you up like stew meat, hook your fingers in the ladder and fall and you'll be dragged, it will tear your fingers off. The young man's eyes darted and shone.

They carried their soldier's rucksacks and their instruments down the railway as it snaked along the island. Just before the tracks made a hard right turn they sank into the palmetto and cranky stiff cordgrass.

"Laudanum," said Damon, looking back. "That youngin's become an opium slave. Probably when he lost his hand."

They waited through the evening and finally in the dark they saw, far back on the loading docks at the harbor front, a sudden leaping of red light that meant an engine was being fired up. It came toward them with its bull's-eye headlight, steam roared out from between the drivers in clouds, and the tall inverted cone of the chimney chugged out woodsmoke. The bell never stopped ringing. They rose out of the weeds and ran alongside and Simon was first up. He turned to help Damon and Doroteo and soon they were all crowded into a tiny space among stacked barrels.

"What happens if they find us?" Simon had to shout over the noise.

"I don't know," said Damon. "Dear God, look at how fast we're going!" He was shouting as well. He peered out the door. "They say it can do ten, fifteen miles an hour!"

Doroteo stood by the open freight-car door and held on to its edge to lean out. "We're going over the water!"

The miracle of speed and effortless movement stunned them into silence. Simon had no words for it other than it was somewhat like the steamboats on the Ohio, but now they had gained the land and were trundling along to Houston, fifty miles away, in a kind of land-boat. The steam drifted back and at last they sat down in the midst of their rucksacks and instruments and fell asleep.

CHAPTER THIRTEEN

SIMON WOKE UP WITH Damon shaking his shoulder.

"We've got to get off before they find us," Damon said.

When the train slowed down they saw, here and there, a few men from other cars jump off into the thick tangle of vegetation at the edge of Buffalo Bayou. The Texas Central was only a mere fifty miles of track, and already it was carrying freeloaders, discharged soldiers who would never get their pay.

Houston was strung out along a muddy bank of wharves and warehouses much like Galveston except here there was no clear seawater, only the heavy green bayou. Landing stages and steam vessels nosed into the bank, men loaded cotton and hemp, unloaded salted fish in barrels, train oil, shoes, and crates of patent medicines. Along the waterfront were warehouses and leaning shacks where men ran in and out like figures in a cuckoo clock. They went up the slope toward the city itself. They passed a brick-making factory and the unspeakable stink of a tannery, which discharged its waste into the bayou in a foaming dark rapid. Two- and three-story brick buildings loomed at the top of the slope, all close together like a wall. BEER, they said. COTTON

BROKER. BOOTS AND USED CLOTHING PLOWS SHARPENED WAGONS REPAIRED COTTON WAGONS FOR SALE SEE J. FARTHINGHAM FOR THE BEST IN HARNESS.

Once again they were in a new town and this time there were more Union troops than before. The soldiers walked in twos and threes along the streets. Now that the war was over, cotton was moving again; four-hundred-pound bales were trundling toward the waterfront, one to a wagon. Not only cotton, but lumber and hides and salt and corn. They hoisted their rucksacks and instrument cases and started out in search of a place to stay. Simon hoped they had outrun the yellow fever.

"We got to get further away from the downtown," said Damon. "*Down, down this town shall settle hence, and all Hades from a thousand thrones shall do it reverence.*"

A city of eighty thousand on the unstable flooding ground of coastal Texas, threaded with bayous and their tangled drainages, sidewalks of cypress blocks, and the landslide of horses' hooves pouring down every street. Union soldiers passed one another in groups. Simon carried his fiddle case in his hand, where he could see it in this kaleidoscope of people and wagons. A man in a bowler darted across the street and nearly ran into him. Simon gave the man a flat stare.

"Get the hell out of my way," he said.

Damon watched amazed as the man touched his hat and stood aside, but then this was the way of it when somebody carried a musical instrument, who knows why but they treat you like a woman carrying a baby. That plus a threatening glare would clear the way. Soldiers and others watched them pass with interested looks because they carried instruments and there is not a human being on earth who does not have a favorite song, lacking only somebody to play it.

Then they heard shouting and murmuring ahead, the sound of

a crowd. They came around a corner and there saw a large gathering of black people in front of a building. A sign on the building said FREEDMAN'S BUREAU.

"What is that?" Simon stopped.

He smelled danger. He was looking at chaos. A great crowd filled the street and the sound it made was comprised of longing and bitterness and confusion. A white man shoved his way among the crowd handing out tickets of some kind. A black woman suddenly jumped up into a wagon bed and began calling out for everyone to hand the tickets to her, and when they did she read from them, called to one person and then another, and handed the tickets out a second time. She was taking charge. She shouted for silence.

"We should go," said Doroteo. "Who knows what is happening here?"

"I say get to the edge of town," said Damon. "Find a place to stay and then come back in and look for work."

They started walking west, away from the center of town, away from the crowd. They walked through an unsettled city swarming with wanderers and soldiers and the soiled doves of the streets who called to them, the smell of flooded privies, and the tall thin pines that stood over their heads like falling threads from heaven.

After an hour of making their way down a street called Preston they cleared the main town. Now they trudged through an area where houses were scattered out among the pines and after another half mile they came upon a lumber yard. They stood regarding the heaps of sawdust, two-wheeled plank carts parked with both shafts down, mules in a large corral, canvas spread over the sawpit and between trees to make a shelter where workmen had settled down for the night. The smell of fresh-cut pine and meat frying.

A group of men were playing cards on a box. Damon bent to

look; they were playing seven-up for a dollar a corner and five on the rubber. A fellow with sawdust all over him laid down his cards, stood up, and regarded them with a questioning look.

"We'd like to stay here the night," said Simon. "Just bunk down somewhere."

"Y'all got a fiddle and a guitar, I see," said the man. "You're good, throw your stuff under that canvas there, where the saws are. Some fiddling is always welcome." He made an expansive welcoming gesture.

Simon shrugged out of his rucksack. "We get paid to do that," he said. The look on his fine-drawn face was that of a kind of casual arrogance or perhaps just weariness. He pulled off his blanket roll. The man said, "Well excuse *me,*" and turned away. It started to rain.

Simon lay on his blankets under the tarpaulin alongside the great toothy pit saws. He listened to Damon and Doroteo talking about the merits of flour versus cornmeal—aid to digestion, salutary effects of one or the other—listened to the sound of rain battering on the canvas over their heads. Mules steadily ground corn kernels between their square heavy teeth and somebody tried to make sense of a concertina. That person started a tune and then stopped, started again, trying to find a way into the melody, off-notes, flat notes, then back again into the only phrases the player knew for sure, over and over.

Simon pressed both hands over his ears. Here they were in the wet lowlands and piney woods of mainland East Texas, the smoke of Houston, and all he wanted was to get married to that Irish lass and settle down so that he could play fiddle and live in the world of music. *Why is that so hard?* His worrying kept him awake. The country was in chaos, there were no rules, law was a matter of speculation, nobody knew how to buy land or put savings in a bank since there were so few banks, how to get a loan, register a title to land, or legalize a marriage, everybody was dubious about the new federal paper money, there was little mail service, and nobody seemed to know where the roads led.

Sometime in the night he fell asleep.

The next morning they went on down Preston Street and after a while it became merely a sandy dirt road cut through the pines. The road was being churned up by two-wheeled freight carts as well as buckboards and freight wagons. Buffalo Bayou wandered on to the west as well and the street or road called Preston brought them once again to its banks. There Simon found what looked like an abandoned flatboat, tied up under a dock. Simon regarded it from under his hat. He thought it would do if they could get possession of it.

They asked around. A freighter told them that the flatboat had been abandoned because the man who owned it had been arrested by the Union for selling stolen rum.

Doro stepped on board and bounced up and down on the decking; it was solid. Damon stood with his hand on his chin looking at it. "They usually bust up those flatboats for lumber," he said.

"Yep, abandoned." The man leaned his forearms on the wagon gunnel and said it was quite a story if you have time to listen. The coonasses had been using it to carry ammunition to Terry's Rangers in salt hogsheads until a deckhand was shot out of the stern, sweep in hand. So the owner quit that business. He sold it to a steamboat man and that steamboat had towed the flatboat all the way from the Atchafalaya to Galveston. Then after the surrender, one of the hands bought it from the steamboat owner and stole a load of rum and come up the bayou. And there's more.

But Simon declined to sit and listen to the story. It was starting to rain again and he thought it was possible he would never be dry and that the man would never shut up. He worried about his fiddle, he worried about the man to whom he had handed the letter to Doris getting bogged down on the roads in the fall rains.

The man had apparently not run out of story yet. The steamboat hand who owned the flatboat was arrested and taken somewhere unknown. He could have been sent to prison but there was only one prison in Texas, and that was in Huntsville, but it was a place for hardened criminals and those who had used firearms to deprive others of their goods and savings, who had shot somebody in a political argument, had chopped up other people into tiny bits, that's the kind of people they send to Huntsville. Likely he had escaped the Yankees and run for the lawless Nueces Strip. Nobody was looking for him.

"We don't look for him either," said Doro, and lugged his guitar case and pack onto the deck with a decided air, and then the other two followed. So they took up residence on it. It was forty feet by twelve, it was decked, apparently had no leaks, and it had a good-sized deckhouse in the middle tall enough to stand up in, where they could get in out of the rain, which they did frequently. The deckhouse even had a table in it. They scavenged wood from the bank, had a sandbox for their hearth, dipped up bayou water in their only pot. Buffalo Bayou here was narrow and tangled with brush and thorn thickets, its roving green surface overshadowed by the pines. Every pine needle dripped, every stretch of open water was speckled with raindrops, and even at this time of year mosquitoes danced and bit.

In the deckhouse Simon found his corner and set out his possessions carefully. Damon sat pouring hot water through his whistles and Doroteo cleaned his boot welts with a stick. Simon laid out his small stock of paper, his bottle of ink, his pens, then his musical scores, his soap and razor and his hat. As the day dimmed down to evening, Doroteo set out a line of hooks over the side and Damon got up to heat more water for what remained of their coffee.

The next day they set out into the city center, if it could be called a city, and played for a couple of saloons and waterfront go-downs without getting paid, to show what they could do.

The manager of a gambling house and saloon on Fannin Street told them, "Boys, I hate to say it, but the owner here don't want no raggedy-assed performers up in front of everybody here in this place, you know, the war's over, everybody tired of being poor or looking like skillet-lickin' dogs, people want to see players looking *prosperous,* cotton's moving, things are better, you know, no offense. Y'all play good. People are looking for *tone,* you know. The owner's looking for *tone.*"

They walked back to the flatboat.

"Well, kiss my ass," said Damon.

"There's work," said Doro. "I can work. We can earn enough to buy soap, anyhow. Then pretty soon get fixed up and try again." He walked along slamming one fist into the other palm, lightly, persistently, his face expressionless but his cheeks were red with a bright and angry flush. He carried his guitar case on his back. "*Pendejo,*" he said.

"Yeah, we need to get *squared away,* as they say in the maritime professions." Damon nodded to himself.

"All right," said Simon.

They looked for work at the loading docks and they fished for whatever they could get out of the bayou. The mosquitoes lifted from water surfaces, buzzing and hungry, and the coastal fevers kept the church bells ringing for funerals.

Simon got a job shoveling coal on a steam vessel, banging up his hands deep in a greasy engine room. He and the other coal heavers hung their shirts over the boat's rail and went shirtless down into the hole. The others called him Moonshine, on account of his coloring and his pale skin marked by streaks of coal grime. He was not as muscled as the others—they were big men with bulky arms—but he could hold his own. He had the dense, wiry musculature of those who had worked hard from an early age; carrying buckets of feed down the fairway, helping the old man cut and stack wood, riding out the crazier horses, hefting the thick harnesses at age seven, nine, ten. He fell into the rhythm of shoveling the shattered lignite coal alongside the others for hours without a break, throwing it from the roaring chute and into the bins.

Damon and Doro found work loading hides and hefting wheelbarrows of rubble. They took any work available to earn their keep. Simon came back to the flatboat and fell down on his bedding without even bothering to wash. Damon and Doro returned exhausted and silent. They barely made enough to feed themselves. They were out of coffee but did not buy more; any extra coins went to a cobbler to keep their shoes together, for squares of canvas to cover their heads against the rain in the walk to town, and for lucifer matches and candles.

Two weeks passed; they watched Christmas come and go, and Doro went to find a Catholic church to go to confession and attend midnight Mass. They said "Happy New Year" to one another in glum voices and passed around a bottle of cheap Barbados rum. Guns were fired all over the city, people shooting up the chimney as was the custom. Simon took up the Dance revolver to stand on the prow and join in, firing off three rounds to thin cries of celebration from the other two, while 1866 rolled in like a freight train full of bad luck and poverty.

Mail was moving better going east, and so Simon wrote the old man, his guardian, who was called Walking David, a long letter full of jokes, a sketch of himself fishing from the flatboat prow, assurances of his good health, the words to "The Lost Child," and his love. Somebody would read it to him. The place where people got their mail from inland Texas was at MacHinney's Freight Office. He stopped in almost every other day, with coal dust masking his face and his nails black with it.

On a chill, humid day the clerk handed Simon an envelope with a knowing smile. "Well, son, finally," he said.

Dear Mr. Boudlin;
I find myself with pen in hand but without words to describe the sorrow I feel over the passing of my young relative and friend Patrick O'Hehir. I write in deepest gratitude that he had with him friends at the last to offer him aid and comfort and to see that he was attended by a priest who could offer extreme unction for the good of his soul, which is now in Heaven as God is merciful and good to those who have served their Country in its need. I shall write the priest at Ballyroe to forward the news to the Dillons there and acknowledge your condescension in writing to his parents in Allentown Pinnsilvania (I do not know how to spell it) to inform them as to his passing and to his burial place and also the other Dillons of Pinnsilvania, namely Brandon Casey Dillon and in Tralee itself Peter O'Dougal Dillon, if indeed Uncle Peter is returned from the shipyards in Scotland. My mother and father will be sad to learn that another Dillon is gone to the Beyond when I write them next post to Galveston to be carried by ship to our unfortunate country over the sea. Ever will the blessed sisters of St. Ursula be in my prayers. Were you to find the opportunity to deliver the medallion of Our Lady that Patrick wished me to have I would be most moved by his thinking of me under such dire circumstances.

Simon noted his own black fingermarks on the paper and so laid it carefully on his bedding and tried to scrub away the grime in bayou water, came back, and took up the letter again.

I remain quite well and find much joy in my young charge and indeed the lovely gardens of San Antonio. From time to time we make excursions into the countryside to see the great cypresses and it seems to me a land of faerie both beautiful and dangerous in which I wish I could live instead of this loud and busy town. At least I am allowed to go to Mass, where the walls keep out the city for an hour. I practice pieces on the neighbor's pianoforte, which is an upright, and it and I make noises out of tune but joyful. Please believe me most grateful for the effort and selfless care you have expended on a young friend here in these unsettled conditions as we all find our way to a new era of peace and prosperity. I remain yours truly, Doris Dillon

He sat at the stern of the flatboat and read it over three times. The letter bothered him deeply with its hints at poor treatment.

She had invented brilliantly, however. Patrick was not her relative. Peter Dillon was not her uncle. Texas was not finding its way to a new era of peace and prosperity. He regretted the lie about the medallion. He would either have to buy one or confess.

Anyway, she managed to convey something of herself; the town life was not one she loved, and what was a bit ominous was "At least I am allowed to go to Mass." What, was she held in chains in a root cellar? Fed on turnip rinds? And that slithering reptile who backhanded her at the dinner, in front of everybody. Simon bit his lower lip and fumed. A running anxiety made him get up and walk out into the small breeze that moved his shirt upon his body and he watched a boat come down the bayou with a pair of oars clawing at its surface. He pulled on the tattered old shell jacket.

But she had written to him; she had written of herself, her thoughts. "In which I could live instead of this loud and busy town." And then he wondered how she could have been impressed with him as her last sight of Simon Boudlin was a dusty ragged person standing by the side of the road in a desert with a fiddle in his hands.

He held the letter tightly, as if it might be taken away by some random happening; the yellow fever or a stray bullet or a fight in a saloon or a runaway horse. Some accident, some flood.

He sat out on deck until late and looked overhead, hoping for stars. There was no place to go and be alone; houses were spotted everywhere here at the edge of a city of eighty thousand people and the men in the wagon yard up on the bank were loud and contentious with one another. If he were to practice his fiddle, to try to perfect "La Savane," they would all come to the edge of the brown bayou and cry out to him their favorite songs, they would yell, "Hey, there's a fellow playing a fiddle down here!" and he would not have as moment's peace. On the other hand, he was not of a mind to go walking up the edge of the bayou to get away from everybody, since he might be carried off by a giant snake, be bitten by a water moccasin, or eaten by an alligator. So late in the dark he leaned on the gunnel with the letter in his hand and listened to the bayou, its faint, sinister sounds, thinking of the music in his mind.

Then he heard somebody singing in a low, clear baritone:

Motherless children have a hard time when their mother is dead
Motherless children have a hard time
All that weepin' all that cryin' . . .

It was like a gift dropped into his hand by a stranger. He followed the eccentric journey of the melody, its difficult changes, the flats and sharps, how the singer returned to the beginning note, and Simon knew he would have never found his way back there. It was a riddle as well as a deep mourning, and Simon was acquainted with both of these things, and so in the chill night, winter on the bayou, it was as if only he and the unknown singer lived in the same universe for the brief time that the song was sent out into the dark.

CHAPTER FOURTEEN

THE HARDTACK AND FISH and salt pork were not enough for them to stay ahead of the demands on their strength and by the second week they were very hungry. So was the alligator slicing through the water, a long rippling V in its wake. It was watching them.

Doroteo dragged a string of fish out of the water—four catfish, one of them over five pounds by the feel of him. He strung the rest by the gills and dropped them back in the water to keep them alive and fresh. Damon sat on a box with his hat down over his nose against a drizzle, eating ship's biscuit, waiting for Doroteo to boil the fish. They would draw out bits with their knives as soon as the fish were done.

Damon looked across the bayou. He lifted his chin.

"Yonder," he said.

There was a moment of silence as Simon and Doro searched the water.

"What *is* that?" said Simon.

"It's a log," said Doroteo. Then after a pause, "No. It comes against the current."

"It's a Goddamned *alligator,*" said Damon. The creature slid closer with a slight weaving of its long head back and forth. Damon jumped to his feet. "It wants your fish, Doro, just give it the fish!"

"Be damned if I will," said the Tejano. "These are my fish. *Hombre,* look at it. I never seen an alligator before." He threw the catfish he had in his hand into a bucket, picked up a coil of rope, and began to build a loop, first tying a hondo and feeding the other end through, then tossing out a coil to test the weight of the rope. He bounced on his toes, overhanding the lasso, calling out, "Hey, hey!"

Simon watched it with a sort of doomed fascination and wiped his knife on his pants leg in slow strokes. The alligator turned toward them in a seething wave. By some means it lifted its entire front third out of the muddy water and slammed down on the string of fish that hung in the water. It looked as if it were about to come aboard and Damon flung down his biscuit and actually screamed.

"They'll take your hand off!" Damon jumped up into the prow and clung to the gunnels. "Shoot it!"

Simon came alive, ran to the little deckhouse, and pulled the Dance revolver out of his rucksack, scattering socks. He spun the cylinder, jammed in four prepared cartridges, and seated them with the rammer. He ducked out of the shelter again, clambered on top. He got to his knees and held out the revolver in one thin hand. He remembered that the Dance had no recoil shield. He cocked the hammer back with two clicks and then sighted down the barrel with one eye squinted shut as the sudden ferocity of a hunter overtook him.

"Don't let it get away, Doro!" Simon shouted. "Throw it a fish!"

"No, no, don't throw it anything!" Damon waved both hands in the air. "No!"

Simon aimed between the creature's eyes and pulled the trigger.

There was a great exhilarating explosion and the gun barrel kicked up into the air while fire and gasses and bits of wadding flamed out of the rear of the cylinder. He was instantly enveloped in a cloud of powder smoke. Simon watched with intense interest as the alligator thrashed wildly in the water and gunsmoke drifted downstream in fire-lit clouds. By this time a couple of wagon men had come to the shore.

"Shoot it again!" called Doroteo, and he tossed the coiled rope up and down in his hand. Simon got to his feet there on the roof, leaned forward, cocked the hammer, and pulled the trigger once more. A dead click. Misfire. "Again!" A second hammer strike set off the cap and the .44 bucked up in Simon's hands; another explosion and flash of light, more gunpowder smoke and a roaring from the alligator. It rolled over and over, its white belly appearing and then its leathery corrugated backside, and finally, in the foam, flaunting streams of red appeared. Simon pulled the trigger again and with a lucky shot the big .44 slug hit the spine.

One of the freighters shouted, "Grab him, he'll sink!"

The last shot made the alligator curve itself backward, its head lifted and its white mouth wide open and fish falling out. Doroteo threw a perfect overhand loop and roped it around the jaws. "*Hiiiiiiijo!*" he screamed in triumph. It began to sink. Doroteo reached hand over hand, pulling the alligator to the surface.

A teamster on the bank shouted, "Jesus me Lord it's a whale!"

Doroteo jumped onto the dock and then ashore with the rope in his hand. Simon looked down at the revolver and lowered the hammer carefully on an empty chamber. "By God this thing kicks," he said, laying it down, then he jumped out with Damon to help haul it to the bank. But even with three of them it was too heavy to pull it all the way onto the land. The alligator had no neck and its front feet were star-shaped and scaled. It looked like an afterthought God had come up with on the eighth day when all

He had to hand was black rock and pure evil. It probably weighed three hundred pounds.

Simon stood in amazement, watching it, oblivious of anything but that he had shot an alligator. All the dogs in the wagon yard were howling and barking in a demonic chorus.

"What'll you take for it?" said a man with a clean-shaven face. "I can sell it to the undertaker, he'll stuff it."

Another man said, "Hell no, man, that hide is valuable. They make boots out of them."

The three musicians looked at one another.

"Ten dollars and trade," said Doroteo. He was still holding the rope and the dead alligator had turned on its back, half out of the water. Its belly was blue-white and its open mouth was bloody. The enormous thick tail was still moving. It was weltering in its gore.

"That's an idea." Simon raised his head and squinted through the drifting gunpowder smoke at the freighter. "Yes, sir, we need ten dollars and stuff in trade."

Damon said, "A good tarp, a metal bucket and dipper, a skillet, soap. Two, three bars of soap."

"A mirror," said Simon.

"Three forks and three plates," said Doroteo. He worried the rope off over the corrugated head and smiled up at the gathering of staring teamsters. "*De acuerdo* then, hey?"

The man said, "Done," and turned back to his wagon. In half an hour they had gotten all that in trade for the enormous shot-up alligator, plus ten dollars in pesos. It took four men from the wagon yard to drag it up the bank and into the camp, where the skinning and butchering went on into the dark hours and the dogs made merry over the entrails.

The next day the three of them washed in turn with a bucket of hot water, they fried their hard-won fish in a skillet with lard, ate it with forks and plates, shaved using the mirror, and made an awning with the tarp. They went at their hands with soap and a rough cloth and Doro used the tip of his knife for a careful manicure.

Damon held his hands out in front of himself. "Beautiful," he said. "Behold, fair ones, the piper's hands are marvels of cleanliness and elegance. He never worked in his life but to run a cran on a D whistle."

"Mine are wrecked," said Simon.

"Use sand on those calluses. People notice."

"Hmm. Sand. I never thought of it." Simon inspected his palms.

"You should have. This is what we mean by *tone,* my dear boy. An indication of worklessness. Doro, front and center."

"*Quisquilloso que seas,*" said Doro. "No lady has hands like mine." He blew on his fingertips.

"Splendid," said Damon. "Like an upper-class layabout. I congratulate you."

They walked into town and bought, for the first time, shirts that were not previously owned from a seamstress on Bayou Street. No bullet holes. The newest kind that buttoned all the way down the front. They found black frock coats secondhand; Damon was delighted with one with a velvet collar. They had their boots shined and their hair cut. Doroteo bought a cake of wax for his mustache-ends and twirled them into points. For everyday, Simon found an old military coat with a stand collar from the Mexican War era. It was dark blue, thick, and warm. He gave the woman the Confederate shell jacket; she said she could dye it and then get a good price for it. Damon bought a pair of shoes that matched each other and gaily threw the old ones away.

Their improved appearance made their music better in the eyes of the saloon owners. They now had tone. They were hired by the Slippery Jack and by the beginning of March they had permanent employment at two different establishments. Simon pushed the other two into hard and fast mountain music. He wanted the relentless drive of Ohio River reels and jigs, because he wanted to exhaust these crowds and wear them out. He wanted to make them tip the musicians and then go to whatever home they had. It was exhausting, but by the second week they started to make good money, they began to bring in customers. Damon looked as if he had come upon the correct attire at last; he was tall, narrow and refined. They were black-clothed and formidable; they sent the music sailing out into the saloons and hotel dining rooms with a precise zest, not one missed note, starting and stopping together on a dime.

Simon's fiddle case became heavy with silver.

He wrote his reply to Miss Dillon. He sat up late when the other two were asleep. Since they were making money, they had all the candles they wanted, could burn them half the night if they wished. He dipped his pen. Always he reminded himself that Mrs. or Colonel Webb would demand to read the letter first. They, the menacing censors of her world. So he said that a member of his musical group had indeed written to the boy's parents in Allentown, Pennsylvania, and had sent on to them his effects, including the bodhran.

Simon knew he had to keep up the connection with Patrick as an excuse to write, but he was increasingly unsure of how to do that. Patrick was still his voice, his mask; then the memory of the boy's bloody eyes came to him unbidden. He got up and walked back and forth on the flatboat from stern to prow and after a while he returned to his letter.

He wrote that the boy had been learning to read music and had become adept on the Irish tin whistle in the key of G, and had attempted "La Savane." Did she know it? Also "The Last Rose of Summer." Did she know that the tune to "The Last Rose" was originally called "A Young Man's Dream"? He would like to ask her advice; should he send the musical scores on to the Dillons in Ohio or would she care to have them as a memento of her young relative?

He wrote of the tragedy of a young life cut short, and that Patrick had spoken often of someday buying land in Texas, in particular a site near the Red River where that river ran very clear, it was said, where oak forests covered the hills and the very bones of the low hills were a steel-colored sandstone. It was said that the soil and the climate were conducive to fruit trees of all kinds. Patrick had confided to him that a good life might be had there, were he ever to grow to a man's estate and find someone who would welcome his company.

The tragedy of his passing affects me deeply, and as I have turned twenty-four I feel almost an old man. I wish to bring to you the medallion, and will do so when I come to San Antonio in the beginning of the coming fall if that would be suitable and if you have the permission of your kind guardians.

Meaning: *I am now twenty-four years old and wish to arrive at man's estate, I am looking for land to buy, am sober and industrious. I very much want to meet with you and walk and talk and make gentle, cautious jokes, hand each other food, a glass of wine, be courteous and also passionate, is that possible? If we can somehow evade those fiends who hold you captive in their dungeon.*

And instead of a medallion he bought a ring, his heart lurching in small unsteady thuds. It was at a little shop that sold the latest sheet music; strings for both guitar and violin; collar stays; cuff links; pocket knives; secondhand spectacles with wire rims, gold rims, or no rims; little books teaching you how to speak French adjusted to the meanest understanding; and little round boxes of rosin. The good kind, the rosin that was the color of honey. He took up a ring on his forefinger and wondered about her ring size. Her hand seemed small; she was small, so would her hand be likewise.

"Size six," the man said. He dredged up a thin ring with a garnet set in the band. "Women are partial to garnets."

Simon, betraying his nerves, grasped the leather of his new belt in one hand and stood at a hopefully casual slant. "Are they now? You wouldn't be making that up would you?"

"Lord, no. Ask my wife. She's not here at present but will be later. The one you have there, the peridot, is for people born in August. When is her birthday?"

Simon didn't know. He didn't want to admit he didn't know and so he said, "Just give me the price."

The peridot ring was twelve dollars and he paid it, peso by peso; he also bought the good rosin and walked out feeling as if he had stepped over a cliff.

Once the bartender at the Harbor Light asked them if they did not have some slower tunes. He appeared anxious, making this request. He twisted the bar cloth in his hand.

Simon placed the Markneukirche carefully in its case and the bow in its groove. "People tip more when it's the fast music. When it's slow they just cry in their rum and go to sleep on the table." He had a cool expression on his face. It was because the slow airs would remind him of Patrick, and his death, because his eyes would begin to fill and he would not be able to stop it.

Doro's eyebrows flicked upward and he nodded and said nothing. Damon gave him a sympathetic look. "Simon, that's not always so."

Simon clicked the clasps shut. "I don't want to play 'The Minstrel Boy' here," he said in a low voice. "I can't do it."

"Then let me do 'Gow's Lament' and back me up."

"All right."

So Damon and Doroteo took the slow ones, with Simon bouncing his bow on the strings with a light touch, making a soft harmony.

By two in the morning they were tired and facing a mile walk home. Simon fell into the habit of ordering a whiskey for the three of them. The bartender brought the glasses willingly, smiled, and set them down and said it had been a good evening. He said he could barely keep from dancing behind the bar, then stood and watched as they took up the thick bar glasses in their hands.

Simon lifted his and said, "To Patrick."

The boy's restless and lamenting ghost followed them all the way home.

CHAPTER FIFTEEN

IN LATE APRIL ANOTHER letter came for Simon. It was in the possession of a Union soldier.

They were playing at a saloon called the Bayou Belle one block back from the landing and the docks and warehouses. The Bayou Belle had pretensions. The flooring was very good. The bar was of some kind of rich wood with a long mirror behind, reflecting all the bottles. There was a stuffed armadillo and women in low bodices, short skirts, and no pantalettes, so that their bare ankles showed. A sign said drinks were 15 cents.

It was murky and humid. Every surface was wet to the touch. Their strings would not hold pitch. Doroteo churned out the chords mechanically—D, A, D, G, G7, D7—pausing between tunes to lift a cigarillo to his lips or to take a short drink from a glass on the floor beside him. Simon's upper lip glittered with sweat, his eyes shadowed by the Kentucky hat. Damon lowered his whistle on "Cotton-Eye Joe" and sang,

I'd have been married a long time ago
If it hadn't been for Cotton-Eye Joe

The clientele was, in the main, wagon masters and steamship captains, cotton dealers. They all had money now that cotton was moving again. It was a Saturday night and the crowd was ardent with the good feeling that comes from handing out pay to the crews; much was left over to spend at the Belle.

Three off-duty soldiers from the occupation forces walked in. Their blue uniform tunics were unbuttoned and their forage caps were pushed back on their heads. When the three musicians swung into "Angelina Baker," a man near the stage shouted at Simon and Damon and Doroteo to play "The Bonnie Blue Flag." He stood up and bellowed his request as if they were waiters.

Damon took his whistle from his mouth and said to Simon, "Ignore him." He could see the soldiers in the back. "He's looking for trouble."

Simon said, "Right. 'Waiting for the Federals,'" and laid his bow on the strings. This tune usually brought a round of applause because almost every man here had waited for them at one time or another under various circumstances and in various armies.

"'Bonnie Blue Flag!'" the man called out again. "Damn those sons of bitches! Play it!" and he threw a silver dollar onto the platform. Simon stepped forward and kicked it off. The man shouted, "Well, who do you think you are, you son of a bitch!"

Simon yelled back, "Simon Boudlin!"

The off-duty soldiers in the back stood up. Simon and Damon and Doroteo then flew into "Whiskey Before Breakfast" at an outrageous speed and with as much volume as possible. A glass was thrown, a cuspidor knocked over.

"If you won't play it I will!" The man had a great flouncing yellow beard, a white shirt front, and kid boots. He got to his feet and came toward Simon. They always went for the fiddler. Simon stepped backward and kept on playing and Doroteo moved forward with his guitar at his side and a dangerous look on his face.

"Quit it, quit it! Gimme that fiddle! Here! I'll play it! 'Bonnie Blue Flag!'" The man was still yelling when all three soldiers from the back table came forward in a rush, knocking over furniture and shoving other men aside. There then commenced a general fistfight. One of the soldiers got onto the stage and cried out to Simon to play "Marching Through Georgia" but Simon stopped playing, tucked his bow into his armpit, braced both feet, and said,

"Get out of my face. Do you hear me? Get out of my face."

Simon quickly put the fiddle and bow into the case. He clicked it shut and grabbed his hat.

"Let's go," said Doroteo. "Go, go." He had already put up his guitar. A man came up beside him and without turning his head Doro gave him a hard, powerful punch with his elbow. They grabbed their instrument cases, but when Simon stepped the four inches down off the stage area somebody slammed into him and tripped him. He fell on his back, clenched up around his fiddle case as he rolled over and then got up and found himself face-on with one of the soldiers who was drawing back for a blow. Simon ducked. Then some other large person was in front of him, and this person had his hands clenched in somebody else's lapels. Then truly loud shouting came from the door as the provost marshal's men bullied their way into the room.

They simply snatched up people whether they had been fighting or not. They hauled in Damon and Doroteo and Simon and the man with the great yellow beard and one of the off-duty soldiers. They were shoved out the front door: there Damon carefully removed his arm from a soldier's grasp and daintily brushed off his shirtsleeve where the man had laid hands on him. Then they were marched up Main Street with one guard in front and another behind, both carrying their rifles at port arms. The group straggled toward Fannin Street and the provost marshal's office, passing by other saloons from which came music and laughter and cigar smoke.

Simon hated cities. He hated towns. As they trudged through the humid cold streets of Houston he thought of the property near the Red River and it gave him comfort. It was as if he already owned it and this incident was only a temporary setback. There would be a spring of clear water and around it great pecan trees, deer would bed down in the post-oak mottes at night. Wild horses would tread the smoking earth in dimly seen caravans, the breath of the great brown buffalo drifting white in the winter air.

They marched on through dark shadows of business establishments jammed up one against the other. Somewhere a dog howled. It was overcast and all the windows were beaded with the damp. Dark streets, unlit, unpaved. Every building with a veranda and every veranda with a cat staring.

Simon sang words he made up to the tune of "Jeanie with the Light Brown Hair":

I dream of the Red River where some kind of flowers grow . . .

Damon pulled out his C whistle with the ribbon on it and played the melody. *Ta dum ta dum-dum . . .* and Doroteo sang a harmony.

"Should have stuck to your music, you dim-witted hill-jacks," said the guard ahead of them.

They came to a confectioner's shop. It was now the office of the provost marshal. The provost marshal was a fat man with a receding chin and Simon could see burnt-looking pale hairs on the backs of his hands as he wrote down their names and particulars by the light of a railroad lamp. Simon could tell he was some kind of an officer because he had bars on his shoulders, but he was

Union and so Simon wasn't sure what they meant. He stood the fiddle case on one end and kept a hand on it and turned to the others, who widened their eyes innocently; Doro gave a small shrug.

All around them candies glistened behind glass; taffies, ribbon candy, lozenges, lemon drops. Simon wondered where the candy man had gone. The man with the fuzzy yellow beard sat down on the floor with his legs straight out and a sullen expression. The provost marshal told him to get up and he did, reluctantly.

"Names," said the provost marshal. He leveled his pencil at Simon. "You."

"Simon Boudlin," said Simon. He had claimed to be Simon Walters when he was conscripted, so it was safest to go back to his real name and hope he was not on paper anywhere. "I never started that fight and I never hit anybody." He pulled up the neck of the white shirt against the cold and his reddish hair was curling outrageously in the wet atmosphere.

"Nevertheless, you're charged with disorderly conduct unbecoming. Where is your pass?"

"What pass?"

"Pass to travel," said the provost marshal. "Pass to keep breathing."

"I don't have one." Simon spread one hand. "Nobody ever said I had to have one. What is it?"

"Never mind then, fiddler, where are your discharge papers?"

"Me?" Simon took on an alarmed expression. "Discharged from what?"

"The Confederate Army."

"I was never in it."

"How did you manage that?"

"Hiding."

"Me too," said Damon and Doroteo chimed in, "I also." Damon groped in his pocket and came out with the D whistle.

"Then where did you get that vest?" he said to Simon.

Simon was about to become very angry. Why did he have to answer to somebody as to where he got his damn vest? So what if it was Confederate issue? "At the gettin' place," he said.

The fat officer stared resolutely at his papers; then said again, "Names."

"Private George Farley," said the soldier.

"Nepomuceno Policarpo Yturri y Contreras," said Doro, and he spelled it for him, slowly, relentlessly.

"To hell with that," said the officer. "Give me the short version."

"Doroteo Navarro," said Doro and then instantly regretted it.

"Angus Oppenheimer." Damon blew out his whistle.

"Stop that." The officer sat at the confectioner's counter with papers in front of him and clearly felt that it was all getting out of hand and his detentions and arrests were unraveling at an alarming speed. He stared at Damon, who was running through the D scale. "Just stop it."

Damon lowered his whistle. He said, "Are we under arrest?"

"I haven't made up my mind yet," said the officer. "I will in a minute."

Doroteo said, "There has to be a sheriff to do that. I know this."

"Wrong. You're under martial law. We're the law." The fat man kept on writing. "We'll have military tribunals here before long and you are lucky they ain't convened yet."

"All I was doing," said the off-duty soldier, "was looking to deliver a letter to Simon Boudlin. A fiddler, they said. Him."

"Letter," said Simon. His head snapped up. "A letter? Give it to me." He put out his hand.

The provost marshal got up and quickly shoved his way in between Simon and the soldier. He said, "Give it here."

Damon grabbed Simon's arm and said, "Don't."

"That's mine," said Simon. He tried to wrest his arm away from Damon and keep hold of his fiddle case with the other. "It's either from Miss Doris Dillon or David Alexander. See here, it is from Miss Dillon. You cannot open a lady's mail. You cannot."

The fat officer took the letter and regarded it in the light of the oil lamp while in the mild winter air his breath clouded the lamp glass. "Well," he said. "It's from Miss Doris Dillon. How do I know you are Simon Boudlin?"

Simon stood stiff and furious, barely able to contain himself. "Come with me back to our flatboat and I will show you an envelope with the return address on it from that same Miss Dillon, and my name is on it."

The off-duty soldier said, "Sir, I got a description of him from a freighter in San Antonio when we were leaving out for Houston and he asked me to deliver this letter to a fiddler of that name with reddish hair, short, size six and three quarters hat."

Simon whipped off his hat and held it out. There in the inner band was his hat size. There was a hot, high flush along his cheekbones.

"Well," said the provost marshal. "I suppose."

He was one of those people who, if he had something you wanted, would try to hang on to it until the trumpets blew for the Last Judgment. He dithered and in an increasing rage Simon saw him clutching the letter between his two damp fat hands.

The man with the yellow beard cried out, "Well, now I've seen everything. I have seen it all. A Yankee opening a lady's mail in a candy store. This beats all. This is the sick and bitter end of it." He sat down on the floor again and his head flopped back against the wall. "Might as well go to sleep."

The provost marshal let them go but he had written down their names on some kind of register. Their real names. Their real descriptions. Only Damon had escaped. The musicians and the soldier were released. The man with the yellow beard was taken away to the city jail. He was charged with seditious conduct for yelling about "The Bonnie Blue Flag." Testimony of the soldier.

April 11th, 1866, San Antonio

Dear Simon if I may call you so,
You must not write to me any longer. Colonel Webb has forbidden me any letters except those direct from Ireland, he says it is quite enough that we have communicated over Patrick's death and now that is all settled and so any more from you breaks his rule that I may not enter into what he calls "deceptions" and "sneaking about" and more that I am reluctant to tell you here. I am sending this by a soldier through Mercedes, who works for the Webbs and is a friend to me. Mercedes Bethancourt took it to a freighter who delivered your last, and the freighter will give it to a soldier so there is no chance of the colonel finding out. Now I may write you the truth, this is an unhappy house. I volunteer to go with Mercedes to oversee the laundry done in the great blue San Antonio river spring called the Blue Hole merely to get away and be where the Good God intended me to be, that is in the world beyond cities, and all the noise of city life here, for I was raised in a green land and the sea never far from us.

Colonel Webb never speaks but what is blame and anger out of his mouth, to me and Josephina and his poor wife, always an unkind disparaging word. You would not know that the army came near to making a trial of Colonel Webb, what they call a courts-martial, for the attack he made at Los Palmitos, as it was unnecessary and he did it for mere glory, as he had never been in combat before and the war had ended and he wanted a decoration for bravery before all was disbanded and thus he threw away the lives of good men. I tell you this because I may never see you again.

Simon, I am sorry to tell you my troubles and indeed to have any troubles to tell, God means us to be happy. He does indeed. He means us to be happy and to sing and He gave us each musical note that lives in all the songs struck clean in our hearts. Stay well and God keep you safe from bandits and Comanches and the fevers, I do not know if I will ever see you. If you do not hear from me again it is not because I do not wish to write but because I cannot, please accept the dearest wishes and lasting regards of Doris Mary Dillon.

He instantly sat down with pen and paper. *Calm down,* he told himself. *Tell her the funny happenings, like "we are living on a flatboat surrounded by alligators." They may end up taking her letters from her.* So he skimmed over the alarming news about Webb's behavior at Palmitos, his forbidding her letters at all. He would find a way to get letters to her. Then he wrote of the tunes and songs they played and where they came from. He wrote of his intention to buy land far from the cities and the coast, where fevers seemed to rise out of the wet ground. He described a particularly fuzzy waggoner's dog that wore a leather collar with a bell and could sit up and beg, looking very like a person. He told her of his first sight of her and remembered her dark blue eyes. He wished the colonel in the hot place and dancing in everlasting flames.

She would certainly see him. He wrote of his concern for her well-being and his true and faithful friendship, that thoughts of her had made pleasant many long hours of work in various establishments, and that every slow air he played brought her face to him and the graces of her letters had brought a desire to be with her. If she would but give some indication that his presence would be welcome he would journey to San Antonio. How he hoped she would receive this letter in the spirit it was meant, that of friendship, concern, loyalty, and a desire to make her laugh. He had seen her laughing. He wished to do so again. I remain yours in steadfast friendship, Simon Boudlin.

"You need to suborn the maid," said Damon. "That's what they do in all the plays." Damon picked at the keys of a soot-stained upright piano in the dim tobacco fog of the Jolly Tar saloon while the rain roared down outside in the most aggressive way. The melody sounded like that dismal piece called "The Old Oaken Bucket." They had come early to rehearse and the place was mostly empty. "The theater as a guide to life."

"Suborn?"

"Of *course*. That means bribe. The maids run messages for languishing swains. It was done in *Lorena and the Brigand of Algiers* and Shakespeare and all of them that imitate Shakespeare. Find the maid, cross her palm with silver."

"And she does what?" Simon hovered anxiously at his elbow.

"She delivers messages, provides comic relief with lighthearted songs in dialect, helps you to get around the dragons that guard the princess—the cruel wife, who spies on her, the angry upstanding senatorial father who roars and threatens."

So this was a way to answer her, through Mercedes. Her misery and unhappiness were there in every sentence. He felt like tearing his hair. Where could she go, what could she do about it? She was in a strange country she knew little about and was legally bound for some unknown number of years to a man who was a blowhard and a coward and who was reading every one of these letters.

Simon didn't want any trouble with authorities like Webb, he wanted a clean clear road in front of him and her with him. He addressed the envelope to Señora Mercedes Bethancourt and for a return address he drew a stave and on this stave the first ten notes of "The Minstrel Boy." Then he gave it over to a man going to San Antonio aboard a dark, stout mare, a man whose saddlebags were full of letters and business correspondence so that he might well have called himself a mailman. To him Simon handed the letter and fifty cents and hope and an unanswerable desire.

May 9th . . . Dear Simon, I must tell you that Mercedes slipped the letter into my basket of sewing scraps. Then several quick measures with answering notes from "Slieve Na Mawn," she wasn't sure how to spell it. *She is indeed a friend. And so, Simon, you see that I am dependent on the novel* John Halifax, Gentleman *for intelligent conversation although the main character is a stuffed English shirt and I am dependent also on Mercedes for news of you. How grateful I am that you write of a fight in a drinking place, since it has enlivened my entire week, but take care for someday when I see you, no matter what happens to either you or me, I wish to see you with two good eyes and an unbroken nose. Jesus, Mary, and the Wayne! You should have seen me laughing.*

The clerk at MacHinney's now reached up to a certain shelf the moment he saw Simon walk in the door, his appearance much improved since he was often in his performing coat and shirt, still smoky from a night's playing.

May 16th. Doris, dear friend. If you found that amusing I have many more but will wait until I see you. I will fill your hours with comical tales of how we nearly perished of thirst sailing up the coast after Palmitos, and do you know what a raccoon is? Let me describe the one that ran off with Doroteo's socks . . .

May 30th. Dear Simon, having received your last I must ask why did this raccoon animal want Doroteo's socks? . . .

June 10th . . . They are depraved, my dear Doris, and I wish them all in perdition. May I visit? Should I prepare for a trip to San Antonio? . . .

June 22nd . . . I am at sixes and sevens with this family, Simon. Mrs. Webb is slothful so I manage the house myself entirely which is interesting and I have learned to drive the trap and pony, but I am only one and they are three, they seem to make trouble enough for a fully staffed madhouse . . . remember I have signed a legal contract . . .

July 15th . . . Read over your contract, Miss Dillon, if you would, and you might even take it to somebody with knowledge of the law although for now with Texas under occupation and the old state constitution suspended, I have heard, we don't know what contracts can be honored, it is all confusion. But I am but a mere fiddler and not acquainted with the law. Better I should tell you about the score I bought yesterday of "Beautiful Dreamer" and which now has Doro's tobacco crumbs all over it and Damon trying to call a crane with his whistle, making crane noises . . .

Early August: a tropical storm had been born in the Gulf and it had traveled to Houston, gaining strength as it came. They stood out in it and soaped up, flinging spray. Then he and Doroteo and Damon lay up in the deckhouse, Doroteo carefully pulling apart his tuning pegs and sanding down the peg ends. Simon dried his hair with his old checkered shirt and then sat down to reread Doris's last letter. Damon had brought home half a bottle and now, clean and fresh from a rainwater shower, lay asleep in his drawers. They were hungry but they had not yet decided on how to cook the cut of beef Doro had splurged on with his tips from the Bayou Belle. It was a section of loin from the butcher's on Fannin Street.

"Let's get out of here," Doro said. He began to restring the double-aught. It had inlaid designs around the edge made of mother-of-pearl and ebony and the patterns glistened in the candlelight.

"That's what I'm thinking," said Simon. He folded the letter carefully and put it in the fiddle case. The case was heavy with nearly seventy-five dollars in banknotes and silver; money for the property up on the Red. He took up the tenderloin in both hands.

"Sear that first. Then you must scatter the fire a little, not so hot, then put it on."

Simon did so; he seared it and then raked most of the fire to one side and put it on a rack over the glowing coals. Pale smoke rolled up and flowed out from under the awning even as rain poured down from every edge. Simon came back into the shelter and wiped his hands on a rag. "It's yellow feverish here. I heard of three cases now in just the past four days. And the provost marshal has got our descriptions written down."

"I'm thinking about this. He can find my name on Colonel Benavides's muster rolls if he was look."

"Did you get a discharge?"

"Yes. But that proves more trouble. I threw it away from me. So I can say 'Hey, I am just Messcan. Donkey, big hat, serape, I don't espeak English."

Simon pinched the top of his nose between thumb and middle finger and leaned his head on that hand. "Yes. Let's get out of here. I am going to San Antonio as soon as I have a hundred and fifty dollars."

"In the meantime where to?" Doroteo rolled two cigarettes in newspaper and handed one to Simon. They lit up from the candle and filled the deckhouse with tobacco smoke. "As for me I think Brownsville but they are going to want songs more *Mexicano,* bailes, dancing."

"Also it's going to be full of Yankee soldiers," said Simon. "They're going to want passes, there ain't no way around it. They also will have Benavides's muster rolls."

"Hmm." Doroteo began to turn the pegs and pluck one string

after another. "Where is your A fork?" Simon opened the fiddle case and handed it to him; Doroteo struck it and tuned up his A string. "Yes, they will have my name. We could go on down into Mexico but they are fighting down there. Everybody is shooting everybody else. The French, Benito Juárez's people, bandits, women, children, dogs. Belgians."

Simon finished his smoke, went out to throw the butt in the bayou, and came back in with the tenderloin. They cut it in half and shared it between them while Damon snored. It was tender and crisp with fat; they ate it with hard ship's biscuit and jalapeños in a twist of newspaper.

After a silence Simon said, casually, "So Doro, do you believe in signs?"

Doroteo lifted both black, winged eyebrows. He thought and chewed. Then he said, "Yes. Generally. But more when I am scared or drunk." He laughed to himself and stabbed up meat crumbs with his forefinger. "But tell me your signs. You have it on the mind."

Simon regarded the planking for a moment. Then he said, "At first when we came up from Los Palmitos and I seen the Gulf I wanted to buy land someday around the coast. But then this land salesman in Galveston showed me a paper, land for sale, up on the Red River." He paused, then stopped.

"I see," said Doro. "Then the young woman tells you she knows a song called 'Red River Valley.'" He tipped his head back and forth. "Private lesson."

"Yes."

"Then we lost Patrick. So the coast isn't that great."

"That's about it."

"Yes, I believe in signs. They come and go. I miss to see them, I don't pay attention, life is busy, hungry, hard. But I believe in signs." He rubbed at his eyes as sleep nearly overcame him. "I wish I had some," he said. "I would pay attention this time."

Simon nodded. "Something will turn up." Two in the morning and the water of the bayou moving past, its surface hammered with firelit rain. No noise, no saloon full of yammering men. Somewhere a bittern made a deep boom like a ship's horn and then fell into a series of gulping clicks. The stillness astounded him for a moment. He had forgotten that there was silence in the world. "Let's wait. Like the alligator. Something will turn up."

CHAPTER SIXTEEN

ONE EVENING AT SUNDOWN, in late August, a man came to the edge of the wagon yard to call to them, saying something about a job waiting for them down in the south. They were going about their business and then suddenly there he was on the bank just above them, looking down.

"Ho there, sir, I hear you in town, you are a good fiddler!"

Simon stood at the prow wringing out his white shirt, which was becoming less and less white the more he soaped it in bayou water. As he twisted it he scanned the dimpled surface of the water for alligators.

"You did, did you?" Simon slapped the wet shirt against the side and then laid it on the roof of the little deckhouse. "Well, there's three of us players, you know."

"Pardon, yes yes, you are good players all," said the drover. "I hear you in town. You all play good. There is a job for you to play at a wedding. Very festive time."

Simon stood with his hands on his hips and squinted up at him against the midmorning light. The man was in rancher's clothes. He wore a broad hat, knee-high boots, and a neckerchief as big as a tablecloth in a bright patterned red that seemed to cover most of his upper torso. He was very fair and Simon could see his freckles and at the same time his eyes seemed like those of an Apache, and it sounded like English was not his native language.

Simon held out his hand toward Doroteo and Damon. "Here they are; the Irish whistle player and that's the guitar man."

"Oh yes, *excelente, excelente,* both!" The man on the bank lifted his hat.

Doroteo and Damon and Simon all looked at one another. Simon tipped his head. Doroteo put his hands on his hips and said, "*¿Y de donde es usted?*"

"Ah," said the redheaded drover. "*Bueno, hablamos español! Bien bien. ¿De donde vengo? Pues, pues . . .*"

"*Y digame quien es.*"

Simon listened, catching a few words here and there. The smoke of morning cookfires curled out of the wagon yard and down to the surface of the bayou. Damon sat in a careful silence, listening, as he broke up a ship's biscuit to put into their bag of salt against the humid air.

There was a big wedding coming up, the man said. A *baile* for three days of festivities. Dancing? Hooo. Good whiskey? The answer was yes. The man who sent him was offering them $25 in gold each.

The drover saw the surprised expression on Simon's face and he chuckled inside his springy pale-red beard. Doroteo sat in stunned silence with his paper cigarillo in his hand and his eyes fixed on the man onshore.

Damon said, "Did I hear twenty-five dollars *each*? In gold?"

Simon sat with a still face, thinking. Considering. Wondering why so much.

The man's name was Rosillo, he said, and to Doroteo, *Pelirrojo soy. Un hombre pelirrojo, y mi papa lo mismo, un caporal por Don Ricardo de los Kinges. Soy kineño.*

"Where?" said Simon. "Where is this wedding?"

"Banquete. Down in the area they call the Nueces Strip."

"They call it a lot of different names," said Doroteo. He drew on the cigarillo and released the smoke slowly. "My home place. It is why I am here and not there."

"Good Lord," said Damon. "The Nueces Strip? 'Tis the ghoul-haunted woodland of weir."

"You stick with me," the man said. "I guard you. No trouble."

"No deal," said Doroteo.

"There's easier ways to earn that much," said Damon, and tied up the salt bag with a firm snatch at the strings. "A lot easier."

Doroteo shook his head. "We could possibly not get out of there with our skins much less a twenty-five-dollar gold piece."

"You'll have a great time of dancing!" The drover waved his hands in the air. "It's old man Solomon Bradford's daughter! Wants to send her off right before he falls into the great beyond place. Which is going to be any time now."

Simon became stock-still. "Solomon Bradford?"

"You know him?" The red-headed Hispanic man smiled inside his wad of red beard.

"No, no, I just heard the name, I heard he had filed on land up on the Red River."

"Yes, he's got land up there, he says. Yes. Got land everywhere. He said, 'Go up to Houston, find the best fiddler in town. Bring him back.'"

Simon turned to the other two as their flatboat nudged with a gentle knock at the bank and the red-bearded man stood squishing and anxious on the muddy path they had made going ashore and into town each night. "Listen," he said. "I'm going. I have to. I have to see this Bradford."

"Why?" Doroteo took his hat off and slapped it back on. "Why, why? Just a lot of trouble there."

"There's three of us," said Simon. "And I can shoot alligators." He pulled his undershirt on over his pale torso and then the old butternut vest, buttoned it. "So, what if we got another revolver? Doro?"

Doro thought about it. Then to the man on the bank he said, "We want the money ahead of time. Now. We want it now."

"I give it to you." The red-headed man gave one solemn nod and then lifted his right hand palm out as if swearing. "I heard you play and this is fair money. Big wedding. Bradford's only daughter. Old man Bradford, yes. He lives at W6 Wright's place. W6 Wright's place is at Banquete. Banquete is there on the south bank of the Nueces. Let me know. You think about it today. Then you let me know."

When they turned to one another to consider this, he was suddenly gone. They looked up at the bank and he was gone.

SO THE FOUR of them started off in a buckboard toward the Nueces Strip the first week of September. Simon sent a last letter to Doris, in which he rather exultantly said he was going into the south grasslands below the Nueces to find a man who had a parcel of land he wanted. That sounded mature, businesslike, substantial, and as if he were a man of standing. He said from there he would make his way to San Antonio by November. If she wished to write him in the meantime, Goliad or Victoria would be the place to send the letter. He said his regard for her was very deep and the thought of seeing her again brought him great joy. Yours with believe me fondest regards, Simon Boudlin.

They left the fevered coast and the piney woods of East Texas for the interior, in the buckboard piled with supplies and their instrument cases, all their senses standing on end and at the same time astonished by the beauty of it. They had these rivers to cross, Rosillo said: the Brazos, the San Bernard, the Colorado, the Guadalupe, and the San Antonio. Then they would come to the Nueces, and on the far side of that river would be Banquete.

On this first day of September the sun burnt its way through a thick atmosphere of cloud that left the distances hazy. Water collected on their hat brims, the horses shook it from their heads. They rode into the glassy shine of flooded grasslands, abandoning the sounds of rivermen's calls and the steam whistles of Houston's docks and the wandering intricate bayous. Every mile they rode southwest they could see the rains following them in wandering columns. They also rode away from the occupying Union Army and the sight of soldiers on street corners, the noise of riots in front of the Freedman's Bureau offices, away from martial law and into no law at all. This was the notorious Nueces Strip and the entertainment was never-ending.

Doroteo rode on the tailgate looking backward. Rosillo had lent him a weapon; a twenty-gauge shotgun with ready-made cartridges of solid shot.

"Just watching," he said. "It is best to watch both ways."

"There," said Damon. He gestured with his D whistle. "That was the last pine tree."

There was that day a big wind; it was indeed the last pine tree they saw, dwarfed, with little clenched pine cones the size of thumbs. The wagon moved on the Taylor trail to the southwest, across open land with grass heads in waves of light brown pouring downwind. They rumbled into the timbered valley of the Brazos. This they crossed by putting their baggage and supplies on a ferry while Rosillo drove the wagon and horses across in a foaming, churning fifteen minutes of hair-raising pandemonium.

Then through the river-valley forests on the far side and once again up onto grassland, where groups of feral cattle with great lyre-shaped horns stared at them from a distance. Deer shot up in surprise out of the tall grass and sprang away in all directions like mechanical toys. With the recent rains the cenizo was flowering in clouds of magenta and the yucca sent up its white silky candelabras. This was the interior of south Texas, where all the maps faded away, the murky rivers came from unknown sources, and the world's authority lay in firepower and the loyalty of those who rode with you.

"And so this is your sign, here," said Doroteo. "Old man Bradford."

Simon thought about it. "Could be." He jumped over the warped boards of the wagon-side and walked to relieve his bones from the jolting. "You reckon?"

Doro lifted a hand. "Ask me anything, I am the expert."

"As for me," said Damon, "I have in my rucksack a sign of imminent prosperity in the shape of a coin in gold, ninety-nine percent purity."

"If you can keep it," said Doro, and smiled.

All was prairie and grass until they came to the gallery forests of the river valleys. Simon stood in the jolting wagon, and he could see the curving strand of trees from miles away. In one of these river bottoms they became entangled in a canebrake and had a hard time getting out. They seized hold of the spokes and shoved, and beneath them they crushed the cane, water squdged up out of the ground, while over their ankles unseen creatures bolted away on either side.

"Earning our money," said Damon. He wiped the mud from his face with his shirtsleeve. "I for one was not hired to unstick stuck wagons."

"Just push," said Doroteo, and started laughing at the sight of Damon with his Hardee hat and whistles in his pocket, dotted with buttons of sludge, shoving at the spokes.

During the day Rosillo stood several times to search the horizon and once he saw skylighted to the west the silhouettes of four men on horseback, ambling slowly, dark against the late and misty light. He pulled up. Simon got the Dance revolver out of his rucksack and made sure he had five loads and a cap on every nipple, sat down behind their baggage, and tracked them with the barrel. So did Doroteo. They all watched until the men rode on, Rosillo observing them with a deep interest. At night the red-bearded man went out to picket his team and they could hear him talking to them. Then suddenly he was standing at the fire, turning the skillet to warm his bread, silent as if he had materialized out of the dark.

Often Simon saw bands of wild horses running away from their wagon noise. He pulled the Kentucky hat down over his face against the sun and kept the fiddle case at his feet, Doro never let the shotgun out of his hands, and Damon tried to call up birds with high notes on a whistle. After five days in this country, with crossings of the San Bernard, the Colorado, the Guadalupe, and the San Antonio Rivers, they came at last to the Nueces.

The banks of that river were thick with short, wiry mesquite and the bouquet stems of the guajillo trees that shot up out of the ground in long rods, every branch bristling with little thorns. The country here was completely flat. The road led them straight into the dark water. Simon crossed holding his fiddle case over his head, wading against the current. It seemed to him the river was about to swallow him. He fell once at the far bank, stepping on a writhing object underwater. Above them caracara eagles sailed searching for the dead, for the remains of kills, for whatever bloated and wet might be floating downriver.

Doroteo carried the shotgun high over his head in one hand with the other arm clutching his guitar case to himself like a big hard baby. Damon fought clear of the glutinous water and cried out, "What do people drink around here? This? This shit?"

"Makes the hair grow on your chest," said Doroteo.

"Hog hair," said Simon. "Oink."

"Stop laughing at me. I am your elder." Damon squished up the bank.

Rosillo pulled up the weary horses and let them drink. They plunged in their soft noses and sucked up water in a long gulping run of their throats.

"Not far," he said. "Drink it and be glad."

And so at last, early one morning, they came to Banquete, where a light wind scoured them of their smell of scuffed leather and woodsmoke, the look of tired men and tired horses, where voices came out of the evening, singing a song of celebration: *Los pajarillos cantan y la luna ya se metió.*

SOLOMON BRADFORD ROSE to shake their hands. Simon watched him cross the warped board floor of the adobe house with one hand out, looking vaguely in their direction. His eyes were glazed with casts.

"The fiddler!" he cried in a hoarse voice. "A fiddler graces our festivities!"

Doroteo said in a whisper, "Simon, be patient, he is not of right mind from his old age. *Um besito mas quesito.*"

Simon nodded and dropped his rucksack on the floor. They had been on the road now for an eternity it seemed, from Los Palmitos to Galveston to Houston, and then to the dry country here below the Nueces. He had a two-day beard that sparkled with sweat and his dusty old checkered shirt was open to the waist.

The first consideration on Simon's mind was where they were to stay, he and Doroteo and Damon, and so he asked immediately.

"All the way from Houston!" the old man said. It was a jolly welcoming bellow.

"Yes, sir," said Simon. "So we've had a long journey and if you'll show us where we can bed down I would be grateful."

Doroteo stood at the door, watching both inside and out. He carried the shotgun in the bend of his elbow. People came up to him and greeted him gravely, offered a hand. Doroteo's gaze was restless and seeking, never still.

"They said you were the *best*." Solomon Bradford shook Simon's hand at last. "My wife, Estela, will be very happy, very happy you have made it."

"Well, sir, that's very kind, but we need to know where we can put our gear." Simon rolled his weary shoulders and held his hat in one hand, then stood straight to appear a man of address despite his two-day beard, smelling of horses and cookfires.

"I hope you've got stamina, young man, because there's going to be dancing and carrying-on for several days here!" Solomon Bradford roared out his sentences in a loud voice.

"Glad to hear it, but it's coming on evening and we'd like to find where we can bed down."

"You'll be wanting some refreshment! And so where are you going from here?"

"San Antonio."

"Be damned. That's a wild town."

This was going nowhere. Simon needed rest and food and then he could think of how to deal with the senile Mr. Bradford. At last he turned to the door and said,

"Mr. Bradford, they are calling us to come unload and so we have to go for now."

"Make yourself to home, make yourself to home!"

Doroteo said, "Let's go find somebody."

Doroteo's gaze roved over the small adobe houses scattered at random, the outdoor ovens and the guinea fowl rushing about with cocky pecking gestures, the running children. He searched out the pens where Rosillo peeled off the harness from his sweating horses. A tiny chapel the size of a chicken house stood in a space by itself, guarded by saints. White plastered walls written upon by mesquite-leaf shadows in a delicate calligraphy. Women in bright clothes hurried from place to place. The little settlement resounded with talk and loud calls, the bumping noise of arriving carretas, horses snorting, the endless slapping of women making tortillas.

They picked up their baggage, walked out into the village.

Doro said, "About twenty horses in the pens. Saddles in the tack shed. Every saddle has a scabbard on it."

"Who lives here?" Simon hooked both thumbs in his belt and looked around.

Rosillo was suddenly standing beside them. He said, "Used to be a remount station for the stagecoach from San Antonio to Fort Brown. But everybody steal the horses. And they stole the feed too." He began to strip off his shirt; a thick gray cake of soap was in his hand.

"Isn't there anybody to stop them?" asked Damon. "You would *think*."

"Not down here. You send a guard of troops, you got to send food for them too. After a while you run out of supplies."

"Go get more," said Damon. "A simple but elegant solution."

"Corpus Christi is twenty-three miles away. Maybe you won't make it back with what you bought." Rosillo smiled. His thin-skinned pale face was deeply weathered and when he smiled, creases like knife scars formed around his mouth. He strolled away to the river to join other men in the water, behind the grapevines, soaping themselves, shaving, their rifles leaning against the trees.

A girl carrying an overflowing basket of shelled corn walked out of the shade of a storage building. Doroteo swept off his hat and bowed to her. She refused to look at him. She stalked past without speaking and went on to an encampment of one carreta and an awning; a pleasant encampment by the river, under sabal palms, two old people laughing together in the shade. Doroteo spoke to her but she did not turn.

CHAPTER SEVENTEEN

SOLOMON BRADFORD WALKED UP and down the little one-room adobe. Outside the window his daughter and three other girls shook out tablecloths, laughing, talking, greeting new arrivals. Fires were building, great heaps of burning mesquite that would soon become firebeds of coals for roasting. In the pens a calf shrieked and then was silent. Men in worn leather chaps made jokes about its agony. The children imitated it. Everywhere there were people gossiping and working among the scattered mesquites and sabal palms, setting up tables in the shade of adobe buildings in the bare bones of a country where rivers came to slow down and turn greasy and snake uneasily through dry brush country toward the Gulf. And now in this unaccountably rainy year there were coneflowers and Indian blanket in orange and yellow, the verbena bloomed purple, people seemed hale, quick, shiny with water and fruit.

"Yes, yes, I have a great deal of land here and there," the old man said. "But there's people that want it and they want to make off with my only daughter. This is why they are carrying on so out there." The old man gestured toward the window. There was no glass in it. The wooden frame was silvery gray and around it small pieces of adobe had fallen out and from one of these holes a scorpion crawled out with its tail in a high hook. It saw there was company and so it darted in again. "And you, fiddler, you're going around the world walking up and down in it looking for a gal, too. You are. You have the look of a man like that."

"Yes, sir, that may be," said Simon. "But I was asking about the land up on the Red River. The old Peters Colony." He had brought his fiddle in its case for no other reason than he felt it was safer in his hand.

"Music is devilment. It makes you believe things you wouldn't ordinarily believe. You're a sorry lot, you and that whistle player and that guitar man. What's his name? He's from around here."

"Is he?"

"I said so, didn't I?" Solomon Bradford swung around to stare at him. "Listen once in a while. What did you have to offer the world anyhow? You just went and learned a fiddle. That's a lazy way of making a living."

Simon wondered who it was the old man had confused him with. But it made no difference. He watched Bradford's eyes turn from himself, Simon, to the window and then to the open door, as if seeking a clear place in which to rest his gaze and he found none. He waited for the old man's mind to turn some other way as well, also seeking a clear place. When he fell into silence for a moment Simon said,

"I've been told that you might sell that land up on the Red."

"I sell a lot of land. I buy a lot of land. I can't even see what land I sell and buy anymore. It's all light, light, blazing at me from the morning until the sun goes down. I'll never see that land up there again, even if they haul me there in an excursion wagon. What do I want it for? Son, you are useless as tits on a boar but if you would listen here for a bit I'll tell you about some land I have for sale up on Mineral Creek in the Red River Valley."

There was a blanket hanging at the open door of the adobe building but it didn't go all the way to the floor and under its fringed edge a chicken appeared and made a slow, drawn-out inquisitive sound, creepily lifting one foot, setting it down, lifting the other foot.

"I'd like to hear about it," Simon said. He wondered how long the old man was going to be able to hold a thought in his mind and then also remember that he held it. Or what the thought was. "Tell me about it."

"Is that a Goddamned chicken?"

"Yes, sir."

"Well, for the love of God throw something at it."

Simon saw a corn cob near his chair, picked it up, and threw it. The chicken squawked and fled.

"They shit everywhere," the old man said. "And here I am getting my Lisia married tomorrow. You had better be prepared to play a decent varsoviana, young man, polkas, jigs. Fiddlers are thieves."

Simon flushed; he could feel it in his face and neck. He said, with determination and in a thin voice, "I would like to hear about the land up near the Red River."

"Goddammit, is that all you can talk about? As soon as you walked in here it was Grayson County, Grayson County, shit man, that's four hundred miles from here!"

Simon looked down at the warped and splintered floor boards. This house and the chapel were probably the only places in this entire little settlement that had wooden floors. He tried to think his way out of the situation. They had already gotten their money. There was that. Getting to San Antonio was more problematic.

Even more problematic was any sort of financial conclusion concerning the piece of land in the old Peters Colony. If any agreement he made would stand scrutiny. Signed by a madman, paid by a thieving fiddler. The words burned in his head. He was furious. He had never stolen anything in his life. The old man was demented with age but still. Simon paused in a few seconds of silence, drew it around himself.

Finally he said into the gleaming-hot September air, into the noise outside and the yelling men, the chattering girls,

"Mr. Bradford, where are you from?"

The old man stopped in the middle of the floor and lifted one hand palm open in front of his face. He inspected the palm and then said, "Well, now it's called West Virginia." His voice became lower and less harsh. "That's what they are calling it now. I was born there in 1784. We finally came down the Ohio after much aggravation from neighbors. We just left them to their own devices. There's some people you just can't get along with. Tighter than the bark on a tree and wouldn't pay a farthin' to see a piss-ant eat a stook of hay. Then I come here and bought a lot of land before Texas became a state and it's still good, every bit of paper I hold is good." He lifted his hand again and regarded it. "I can see my hand very well. In 1799 I turned fifteen years of age and I left Virginia for the world out there, whatever it might be. I could see whatever I looked at then."

Simon took out the fiddle and stood it on his knee the way a mother holds a toddling child. He tuned one string against another and did not bother with the tuning fork; G as the hold note and then D, A, E. He lifted it to his shoulder carefully, as if in fear of breaking some delicate web being spun in Solomon Bradford's mind. Then he stood and began to play "Shenandoah."

He made the Markneukirche sing. After the first phrase he double-stopped and the melody seemed to cry out of its own accord in several voices. It was a song that came to people as sadness, as memory, as longing. It was a kind of spirit unto itself, reflections of a mountain river that carried with it the souls of the ancient people who had lived there long before the white man came; the blue Shenandoah River, fifty-five miles long and clear as air. *I love your daughter.* A remote place of memory and recall now far away from this arid land.

The old man turned and watched him play and stood as still as the sun seemed to stand without moving in the sky. Beyond the window the girls' chatter stopped, the laughing and talking of the men came to an end, and along with the phrases of the short-haul shanty known as "Shenandoah" the wind in the leafless wires of the mesquite slowed to a hush. Beside the Nueces River all the horses watering lifted their heads and drops fell from their mouths into the dark green water; another river, another time, another century.

At last Simon stopped and lowered the fiddle and the bow.

"Well," said Solomon Bradford. A long silence. Then, "You was wanting to buy land from me, up there in Grayson County. Did you know that's part of the old Peters Colony?"

LATER THAT EVENING, with Doroteo and Damon as witnesses, Simon signed an agreement to buy four hundred and fifteen acres. The old man wrote out the agreement by copying another of the same kind, drawn out from a sheaf of papers tied up in agave-fiber string. Sold, to Simon Boudlin, the following described tracts of land belonging to Solomon Bradford the same being parts of land originally titled to the Peters Colony as their headright situated on Mineral Creek in the northern portion of Grayson County, State of Texas, to wit: Block Number 5 (Five) lying in the northeast corner of the league lying north of and adjoining Block Number

Six (6) the total containing 415 acres. Terms of sale five years on credit on notes with one hundred dollars paid outright and mortgage on the land . . .

His hand was that of another age, with every noun capitalized and all his *s*'s were *ſ*s. The paper stipulated fifty cents an acre with a hundred dollars down. Simon emptied his fiddle case onto the floor where the money so hard-earned rang on the boards. They counted it out, including the twenty-five-dollar gold eagle. This left him four dollars and seventy cents. He watched the old man sign as well and sat in a poised and fearful silence wondering what he had done. What he had just bought. If he had bought it.

"And may you hold it," said the old man. "And may you stay alive holding it."

"How am I to pay you the rest?"

"Put it in Twohig's bank in San Antonio. He'll handle it for me. He handles my business. Twohig. Irishman."

"You're trusting me to pay it?"

"Son, I know a lot of people in San Antonio. They would come to pay you their respects if you did not pay up." He stood up and laid his hand on the paper as if to swear by it. "Well, we better find you a place to unload."

They were led to the loafing sheds inside the horse pens and there they slung their gear and baggage. They cleaned it up and made camp. It was near the river, and Doroteo was watchful and unsettled all night with the shotgun laid near him on a cotton sack to keep the dust and litter out of the works. It was loaded. On the clear skin of his face the moon shone like a bright celestial polish. He got up once to take a piss and said *vete* to a horse that had come to mumble around in their baggage. *Vete pendejo.*

Simon woke up in the dark and saw Doroteo standing in the moonlight. Then it occurred to him that Doroteo was watching for the girl they had seen earlier, the one that did not return his greeting. Doro leaned over the rails with his face toward a fire by the river. After a while the occasional lights died down and Doro came back fully dressed and finally slept.

The next day, after cleaning up in the river and changing into white shirts, they went to the main house with their instruments to say good morning to the old man. Solomon Bradford patted Damon on the shoulder and said, "Well, let's get that girl married."

So Simon played his fiddle there in a land without law, without notaries public or agents of justice or jails or judges or justices of the peace to record either marriages or land titles. Like everybody else, he took his chances. He was now a landowner and it made him feel strangely heavy and also committed in a way he was not sure he liked. He spun the screw on his bow between his fingers so that the horsehair was taut and then drew the rosin down the stream of white hair, this device for calling up both grief and joy from naught, from the vacuum that surrounds life and celebration. A breezy morning, his hair wet.

Lisia, short for Felicia, was led to the tiny chapel as if it were a long journey, and perhaps it was. Her mother, Estela, on one side, a thin woman with thick black hair in intricate braids, her father on the other side, tears running down his cheeks unregarded. Behind them came girl cousins in their best skirts and blouses. Young men trailed along in buttoned leggings and silvered spur straps, their wide-brimmed hats turned up behind. It was a long voyage from girlhood to young matron, from her father's house to that of her groom.

Inside the chapel the groom and a priest stood with clasped and sweating hands. It was ten in the morning on a Saturday and the heat of September in the Nueces country was already building into the high eighties. In the shade of the small chapel the bride's white tunic gleamed. It started at the neck and ended mid-thigh, embroidered and looped with lace. Under it she wore several skirts in madder and yellow. She had ten strands of beads around her neck. She wore small slippers that slapped as she walked. Somebody nudged Simon.

"Wagons ho," said Damon.

They began to play; it was to be waltzes at the ceremony and varsovianas at the feast afterward. So they launched into "Mockingbird Waltz" and then "Ma Petite Marie" and then "La Savane" which was not a waltz but at least they knew it. When it came time to say the vows, Rosillo patted the air and they stopped.

Volo, said the groom, and *volo* said the bride.

The girl who had passed them by with her basket of corn was stiff and unmoved by any of it. When Simon dropped his fiddle to his side and could take surreptitious glances at her, he recognized her by her round face and the tilt of her eyes. She also wore a long white tunic, edged by lace and embroidered in very fine purple and red thread. Her skirt beneath was full, probably several skirts, and in colors of dark blue and vermilion. Then he realized her clothing was nearly the same as the bride's: a wedding costume.

He saw she was resolutely not looking at Doro. Doro, with equal resolution, was not looking at her. *Weddings are dangerous times,* thought Simon. It was the first time this had occurred to him. He saw people fall into memories of their own weddings and both jealousy and undiluted joy flowered like the Spanish Dagger. Doro bent over his guitar until the final words were said by the priest. Votives flickered beneath the faces of saints, a whitewing sat on the mesquite outside and called out long melodic moon sounds, and a little girl clutched the bell rope in a state of round-eyed anxiety, waiting to be told to ring it.

Suscipe, quaesimus, Domine, pro sacra conubii, lege munus oblatum . . . per omnia saecula . . .

Everybody straightened up at the amen, threw their arms in the air, and began shouting. It was over. Gunfire from just outside the chapel as long guns and pistols were fired into the air; the penetrating small crack of revolvers and the bigger deep thuds of Sharps and smoothbores. The little girl pulled the rope with all her might and was lifted onto her toes as the headstock tipped and the chapel bell rang out. The young woman in the tunic with purple and red embroidery turned and hurried from the chapel with two girlfriends behind her.

The shouting crowd carried them out into the hot air, where cabrito roasted slowly and tecomates with tamarind water were set out. Doroteo hurried to sit at an outdoor table and began to work his way through the dishes on offer: pulled pork, tamales, *carne guisada* and *arrachera, salsa verde,* a cake of *tres leches.*

"This is real food," he said. "Real food at last. Come, come, Damon, Simon, eat. *Mira,* these tortillas just now from the comal, fresh masa made this morning. Gold." He closed his eyes as he ate. "*Al fin,*" he said. "*Volvi a la vida.*" He handed around the dishes. "Just in a while I will get out the guitar. Then it is one varsoviana after another." His smile was enormous over his pointed mustache and he had the shotgun leaning against the bench where he sat. "Eat, sit down, eat this."

Damon and Doro and Simon barely had time to wrap food into tortillas and eat it before they found themselves onstage. The dancing seemed endless. Simon knew they were earning their pay. The tiny settlement was filled with people now, people from every other settlement and ranch outpost within thirty miles. Hispanic and Anglo, Mexican and American. There were men pointed out to him who came from Camargo, far down across the Rio Grande, near to where he had been involved in a battle. Who would miss out on old man Bradford's daughter getting married to a bandit from Espantosa?

A racetrack of 440 *varas* had been cleared out in the brush and the races went on into the evening. The little horses spewed clods of dirt and horse manure in their blazing quick sprints, there was more firing into the air and yells, and the tables were covered with barbecue, huge square tamales with fillings of pork and chocolate.

They took a quick break to pour down a cup of the tart tamarind water. Doroteo stood with a pottery cup in his hand, watching the crowd.

"Come, here." A young woman came to take Simon by the hand.

"My dear," he said, smiling. "I am but putty in your hands."

She led him to a skillet full of Spanish Dagger flowers, thick and creamy, being scrambled up with eggs. She took up a broad leaf from the wild grapevine and filled it and handed it to him. Simon ate it all with his fingers. Eating flowers. He walked away with his hand full of another grape leaf and a trembling yellow mound of flowers and egg that smoked in the cool evening air. The air was full of celebration, color, and noise. Men who had ridden in dusty and worn, their ammunition belts frayed and pistols shiny with use, had made themselves spanking clean and wore embroidered sashes in many colors.

When the musicians began their music again somebody broached the first keg of rum. Doro grounded his guitar and tossed down a glass, then started playing again, having missed only three measures. Then that keg was gone and another opened.

Over the noise Damon shouted, "A polka!"

Simon called out "Fire away!," charged on into the finish of a reel, and then picked up the polka. The hair of his bow was becoming more and more ragged and as he played loose horsehair flew up in a wave. The dancers spun like tops, combining and parting and coming together again. They would dance all night.

Then he and Damon watched with astonishment as Doroteo laid down his guitar in its case, snapped it shut, stepped off the stand, and walked up to the girl with the tilted eyes. He swept off his hat and bowed to her.

She turned away.

All around people glanced at them. Doro placed one hand on her shoulder, turned her to face him, and began to speak. She lifted the hem of her long tunic and pretended to wipe off a stain—barbecue, meat drippings, a fleck of tamal. Doro spoke again, bending low to her.

Then after a moment he took her elbow. She resisted but he did not let go. Then they walked off, avoiding spinning couples and staring grandmothers, into the dusk.

A DAY LATER they left without him. He had gone, they said, to her people's settlement west of the King Ranch headquarters, a place called San Diego. He went to make arrangements, they said. It involved another person, but when Damon pressed for details he was told not to ask or they got vague stories, one piled on another, with much contradiction. But Doroteo was not coming back.

Finally an elderly woman said, in perfect English, fanning herself, it was the girl's fault. All hers. She had flirted with another man and out of a jealous rage Doroteo had joined Benavides's Tejanos and ended up in the Battle of Palmito Hill. So there. Simon and Damon realized they had lost their guitar player into the hot and brushy country of the Nueces Strip, where he was at home, where his own drama would be played out and would come to its own end, an end they might never hear of. Rosillo harnessed his horses and gave them a ride to what was still known as the Cotton Road, at an hour of the early morning when it was yet dark.

So then it was just Simon and the dark man with his pennywhistle, on foot to San Antonio.

CHAPTER EIGHTEEN

THEY STARTED OFF GOING northwest. The road led them through small draws holding spreads of mesquite trees and a few live oaks, which came for water to these natural drainages like animals, filling every hollow with tangled branches and wicked greenbrier. The sky was clear almost every day now; the rains had fallen away and as the sun came up the sky was streaked with long clouds that stretched thin and fell apart.

As they walked Simon spoke of his determination to meet Doris Dillon, to present himself to her as a friend and a lover. A man who would take his place in her life for all the time to come. And San Antonio was nigh on a city, there would be work for them there. Damon listened, all his irony and cynicism laid aside, and said he would come along to just see what happened. *In the greenest of our valleys, by good angels tenanted . . .*

The road was a braided series of tracks where wagons had gone to one side or another during the rainy season to avoid holes and sinks, then coalesced again. Every once in a while they could see drifts of cotton that had fallen from the big bales during the war and had snagged up against thickets of prickly pear or Spanish

Dagger. It was gray and webby now and birds had used it for nests, mice for their burrow linings.

Simon had the deed in his rucksack and the mortgage papers, signed and witnessed. They were going west and upriver, so the Nueces would become more and more clear as they traveled. He felt, despite the long slog on foot ahead of them, that he was getting somewhere. It seemed very precarious, true. The deal was only as good as his ability to enforce it. The girl was his if he could present his case and himself to advantage.

Damon said, "I'm too old for this."

Simon slapped him on the shoulder. "My friend, you better not be too old for it, since this is the only way we're getting to San Antonio."

"What about horses?"

"What about them?"

"Wild horses are all over the place."

"Even if we did catch some, how are we going to talk them into letting us ride them?"

"Music soothes the savage breast."

"Who said that?"

"I have no idea. Let me try something else: '*Within the heart do springs upstart . . . and strange, sweet dreams like silent streams that from new fountains overflow . . .*' What's the first town we come to?"

"Now take note how I am not complaining about all these poetry quotes." Simon bent forward against the weight of his pack with fine dusty little puffs surrounding his boots at every step. He knew that soon in the heat of the day his belt buckle would burn his stomach every time he bent over, but the slosh of his water bottle was like a voice telling him they would make it to the Nueces without falling on the wayside from thirst.

"I have," said Damon. "I have taken note. What's the first town?"

"Rosillo said we cross the Nueces and then we come to San Patricio. Maybe there'll be some fountains overflowing there. Maybe a wagon convoy heading west, if we're lucky."

That night they secreted themselves in a motte of mesquite, bashing into the low limbs in search of some shelter at the heart of it, maybe a live oak, maybe a seeping *chupadera* spring. They were happy with what they found: a thick live oak with umbrella limbs. They sat beneath the branches and lit a small fire. It was enough to boil water for the last of their coffee. Simon lay back and listened to the galloping rhythms of Poe. There were dying gladiators and the Conqueror Worm, in human blood imbued. Then Damon picked up his C whistle and played a series of phrases that seemed beyond melodic structure or perhaps it was a thought he spun out note by note.

The next day they came to the Nueces River and camped there in the early afternoon. It was the *vado* of San Patricio, the crossing place. Whatever town there might be was several miles away on the other side. Simon watched their fire die down to coals and their food reduced to broken, dried-out tortillas and goat cheese. It was another hundred or so miles to San Antonio. Without the weight of all those coins in silver and gold his fiddle case seemed very light, almost weightless. From time to time doubts came to him; what if the old man died and then his daughter said the paper was not good? Or demanded more money? He told himself, *Don't think about it now.* Damon laid out their cooking gear, reflecting to himself that Simon was so guarded about his thoughts but at the same time was so transparent, his lean face abstracted with worry, plucking absentmindedly at his forelock of auburn hair.

At this *vado* they were very likely to run into people, men crossing over the Nueces with stolen cattle or cotton buyers up from Mexico on their way to San Antonio or, what was least likely, a Union patrol sent to police the area. Here, miles farther northwest, the Nueces was blue as turquoise and beached on this side with pale sand. On its banks were tall trees: sycamore and live oak. The Nueces was a through-way for birds, trees, animal life. The wind picked up from the Gulf, fanning their cookfire flames out flat.

They watched for a while, but since no one came, Simon scrambled down the bank, stripped, and fell backward into the water. Far upriver a bird cried out and was answered. He had not been in swimming water for a long time. It was miraculous. He floundered out deeper, for the feeling of floating, of being free of gravity. He blew water from his mouth, spouting like a whale, and watched the darkening sky reveal star after star. The surface of the river was like silk and trembling with star reflections. It quieted his mind and finally he waded back to shore, water streaming from his naked body as he stood with his arms thrown wide to the evening breeze. Then, at last, he reluctantly pulled on his clothes.

Simon collapsed on his blanket. "Why is the Nueces Strip like some other country or something? Isn't it part of Texas?"

Damon boiled water for his whistles. "Mexico says it's part of Mexico. Says the border of Mexico is the Nueces. Texas says it's theirs, says the border is the Rio Grande. It was some agreement or nonagreement they came to in settling the border after the Mexican War. Neither side will give way. And neither side will police it. Texas got caught up in sending everybody to the east to fight in the war and Mexico got caught up in fighting the French. So it's dog eat dog and Devil take the hindmost. So it has been in human memory, wild places where the only law is the strength of your good right arm." He lifted his arm and made a bony fist. "That's how it is in all of human memory. 'Vastness! and Age! and Memories of Eld!' "

"So they haven't come to an agreement yet? The Mexican War was twenty years ago."

"Oh! Oh! I see! You expect the government and the diplomatic corps to proceed at some foolish breakneck pace! There are substatutes to argy over and rewrite! And meantime the politicians must be paid their stipends and their travel expenses. Become wise, young man, and cynical, and life will be far more understandable."

The night drifted on. The river sparkled, it was a light-bearing streak through the level country. A black-crowned heron waded with high steps in the dark shallows, intent on fish. An elf owl slid in a long trajectory over its surface. From far out in the brush they heard a water creature call out *rum-jug, rum-jug* in a low conspiratorial cry.

Damon said, "'A midnight vigil holds the swarthy bat!'"

"I wish we had some more coffee," said Simon.

"I miss Doroteo. A boon companion. He roped that alligator."

"Yes. I miss him too. And Patrick."

It was a dreaming time; the long blue Nueces curving through this grassy country with a secret life of its own, and on both sides of it herds of wild horses stood together quietly grazing or sleeping. Wild cattle lifted their heads down in the brush alongside the river to hear the noise of the loping, scenting wolves, who ran with their noses to the ground searching for the smell of something newly born, something wounded, something old, something sick. The river fed the darting Guadalupe bass and its own gallery forest on either side.

In the morning they crossed waist-deep, holding their rucksacks on top of their heads and their boots tied by the laces around their necks.

SAN PATRICIO WAS a village of adobe houses and horse pens. The fencing was made of two uprights with limbs jammed between them. Chickens sat on the top rails being nervous and twitchy.

There were trees: mesquites and a few treasured live oaks. A man who sat in front of the little store, switching away flies with a cow's tail, told them there might be a convoy forming up at Goliad, in the old Spanish mission just outside of town. So they bought that day's provisions, tortillas and a sheaf of jerky, and kept on walking toward Goliad, nearly running out of food, water, and strength before they got there.

They joined up with a freight convoy at Espíritu Santo mission and got a ride on one of the fifteen wagons. It was a combination of three trains come from harbors on the coast, Corpus and Lavaca and Copano, all heading to San Antonio. Damon and Simon paid two dollars apiece with the agreement that they would lend a hand when needed, eat whatever the teamsters ate, and would sleep wherever they found it convenient.

In the cool of the morning the teamsters apportioned out the freight; they arranged and reloaded barrels of oranges, crates of picture frames, bolts of machine-made cloth from England, sacks of pecans and beans and horse-shoe blanks, nails and smooth wire, staples and ladies' slippers, cured leather in rolls as big as tree trunks; all of these articles were tagged with their owners' names in a neat secretarial hand.

A pack of dogs trotted alongside with their tails wagging in half-circles of joy at all the noise and movement, barking to one another in a conversational way in their happiness in being part of a big caravan heading to parts unknown. The weather had turned rainy again as slate-colored clouds with spilling blue fronts rolled toward them out of the Gulf.

The interior of wagon number four was not as crowded as the others and Simon found himself a space between crates of crockery packed in straw. When they started up the river trail there were cries and shouts of farewell from the people of Goliad, sitting on fence rails to watch them pull out. The drivers called their teams by name and the big axles roared as the wheel hubs turned on their bearings, harnesses jingled, and the vehicles started west on the trail to San Antonio.

Before they left the head teamster had handed Simon a letter from Miss Dillon. It had gone to Houston, where many people knew the young red-headed fiddler, and the news there was that he had gone down to the Nueces Strip to play for Old Man Bradford, and so it had been sent along with a singing master who had been hired by the Goliad infant school in hopes that the fiddler might be found there, and so he was.

Simon sat down with it amid all the noise and shouting, his hat down over his face. A volcanic explosion would not have moved him. This letter, with her cherished, familiar handwriting, was full of the sights and sounds of the old city, the names of the bells (*La Perla, La Golondrina*). Did he have a horse? There was an orange cat that came to her window and she saved scraps for it by dropping them in her napkin at dinner so that the Colonel or Mrs. Webb did not see. She and the cat sat together at the open window to listen to people down on the river talking and laughing, she supposed they were fishing. If she heard the colonel's steps she had to shoo the cat away and close the window. He had kicked it downstairs once, poxbottle that he is. Little Jo wanted a dog but Mrs. Webb said it was better not and herself in agreement lest he wring the head off some orphan pup. Then, brightly, they had had a gadhar at her home in County Kerry, a sweet dog with a brindled coat and a cold nose that woke her every morning. And then: he must not write in care of the maid anymore. The colonel had taken to going to the post office and asking for any letters to Mercedes Bethancourt to be delivered to himself. And he paid the man to do so. And the man took the money.

I am in a foreign land, she said, *and I end this letter with gratitude to have a friend and for your kind concern and must answer your question that I am now eighteen years old and every year a gift.*

He lay on his back inside wagon number four with the letter on his chest and his hands folded behind his head. He stared at the wagon sheet above him. Heard the slow sighs of mules as they ate their evening hay, snorted, shook their heads against the increasing wet wind. He thought of her listening at the window; she would be like a lady in a play, he supposed, one of the three plays he had seen in Paducah with outrageously painted actresses leaning at flimsy artificial windows. This was a dangerous image. Possibilities of lies, false representations.

But then a life of unease and silent speechless anxiety must somehow erode the spirit when you were under the thumb of somebody who would kick a cat down the stairs. Her captive there, a guardian never speaking but what there is blame and anger out of his mouth.

He felt he was approaching San Antonio as if it were an enemy city to be taken by stealth, at its heart a young woman who had been promised to him by some unknown means. He meant to have her. He had land now and real men owned land. So it had always been. Then a dangerous feeling that he might come to think of himself as bigger than he really was, invincible, that he could in some way go back to all the mistakes his parents had fallen into, that he could make it all right.

But why should he not? He and Doris would be married as his parents never had been, they would be parents to their own children. They would not allow their house and barn to be burnt down by marauding armies. You could work like a mule and all you had could be destroyed, wrecked in a night of flames and burning horses. He shut his eyes against the memory. But this would not happen to them, not while he lived and had the Dance revolver to hand. *Let me live.*

The old man had been there for him when his mother took the cholera and when she died he had rocked Simon in a rocking chair for hours. The floors of their rooms behind the main barn were badly planked and the rockers made a strange rhythm of repetitive knocks. He was five or maybe six years old. He cried himself to sleep and woke up and began crying again and still the old man rocked him back and forth, back and forth, all night long and into a motherless dawn.

They called the old man Walking David to distinguish him from the many other David Alexanders in that part of the country and because in his youth he had walked all the way down from Pittsburgh to Kentucky along the Shawnee Trace and had emerged from the forest primeval somewhere east of Paducah. He was nearly without clothes, his trousers worn off to the knees and only one shirt on his back, but he carried a good Pennsylvania rifle and never spoke of the savage encounters with the Shawnee or the murderers of Cave-In-Rock or the hunger that had happened to him between here and there and said not one word about that journey and probably would not until the day he died.

In Paducah he found other Alexanders preceding him, successful in the horse business, and there he took charge of the big Paducah livery stable when his niece, Simon's mother, Mary Beaton Alexander, was found to be with child by a traveling fiddler. It was her barn by inheritance. It had shedrows with stalls for fifty horses, twenty-five to a side, and a center roofbeam forty foot overhead. The floor and fairway were planked with squared oak logs and the haylofts could store hay for an entire winter for every horse in the barn. The harness room was a wonder to behold.

Why Henri Boudlin did not remain and marry her and become a horse lord of western Kentucky no one knew. Maybe it was the call of steam whistles on the broad Ohio, or the thought of New Orleans, or perhaps his family in Baton Rouge. Maybe he went and meant to come back. Perhaps he went down to that city and died. Simon always knew in his heart his father meant to come back with presents for his mother, for their marriage: laces and perfumed powders, yards of taffeta in the color called Alice blue.

Simon often told people his mother and father were married by a Justice of the Peace because his father was Catholic and they differed and so compromised. But this was a lie and he tired of it and soon he stopped repeating it. When people came to know that Henri Boudlin had not married his mother at all they cried in false voices, "Oh, *that* don't matter!" They said, "Character matters!" But Simon in his cool withdrawn way knew it did matter. It mattered terribly.

When, at age seven or eight, he understood that his mother and father had not married his despair was bottomless and without remedy because now she was dead they could never marry and make it right. Why did he not marry her? What was wrong with her? He had fleeting, disconnected memories of his mother: pretty, charming, singing, clean hands that smelled of hard soap and her thick reddish brown hair and her earrings, black and silver drops; himself standing on a chair to help with the bread dough; her laughter. What was wrong with her? This thought tore at him and would all his life. Why was she not good enough to marry?

So in his mind, in the manner of the extravagant theatrical presentations of the day (*The Bandit Lord of the Dolomites, Innocence Betrayed*) his father became the rich inheritor of a great fortune, son of a Louisiana sugar baron, with a thousand slaves and five thousand acres of land, Copperbottom horses, plantation houses, and his mother the beautiful girl of the western Ohio, a wilderness child, torn from Henri Boudlin's arms by the aristocratic fiends of Louisiana who said she was not good enough.

The old man was the only parent Simon had ever known since the age of five or six, when the rocking chair and the arms of

Walking David held him relentlessly, indefatigably, faithfully, and without cease, singing *If you had seen what I have seen, ye would not be so cantie-o . . .* So Simon had grown up in a world of men who, however kind and patient, were not women after all, and the thought of having a woman of his own to marry and love forever made him pause in wonder. Especially one like Doris Dillon, with her blue eyes and that glimmering black hair, slender as a ramrod. His own. He felt almost avaricious, heavy with desire.

He would make everything right. This time it would be right. As the wagons lumbered on he fell to imagining that Henri Boudlin would stray into some elegant garden party where Simon was playing "La Savane" and his father would be struck speechless by his grown redhaired son, by his touch with the Queen of Instruments, and Simon would take Doris Dillon Boudlin by the elbow and say,

"Allow me to introduce my wife. I hear you never had one. I recommend it."

Walking David had made sure Simon's last name was duly registered in his father's name and spelled correctly. He had put him down on the 1850 census in that name, on the county corvee muster list in that name, and finally as part owner of Alexander's Livery in that name, but then came the war and Forrest burnt it all down and stole the horses to deny them to the Union Army. Walking David retired to MacLean's old cabin and Simon left for Texas to escape impressment.

And now he was approaching San Antonio as one might a fortress with the intent of taking it and carrying away the princess. One had to assess the strength of the walls, the occupational habits of the princess, one had to understand the cunning or the stupidity of her captors.

The wagons crawled up the San Antonio River trail toward the hill country, slowly, slowly, going inland where the earth rose with every mile and the rain came at them in segmented clouds like a building surf. Simon helped pull out the wagon covers into awnings and on his face was a look of provisional happiness, quick jokes flying back and forth between him and Damon, and they heard overhead the chirring clatter of the sandhill cranes as they made their way south to some unknown place along the Gulf Coast with the late sun glittering on the undersides of their wings. One night he at last heard the haunting melody of "Red River Valley." One of the freighters stood to sing it before the fire. He had a good voice and was clearly much in demand. Someone played a mandolin to accompany him and Damon tried out both his whistles and finally found the key. The freighter had, by ear, opted for the key of C, which suited his low voice.

"I know it," said Damon. "It's called 'The Bright Mohawk Valley,' the one that I know."

Simon turned back to the wagon and got out his fiddle, and he and Damon nodded to each other and Simon launched into the tune. The freighter stopped singing, waiting for them to find the notes.

"Go on, go on," said Simon. So the man started up again and in a short time they had all found their way into the melody and the man's strong voice blended well with the fiddle. *Come and sit by my side if you love me . . .* It was a cavalry song, a freighter's song, drifting low and sad like the wind in the branches overhead. It had many verses and it was late before they quit playing.

CHAPTER NINETEEN

THE RIVER HAD MADE its way down the elevations from San Antonio in a series of easy falls. The teamsters said that town sat at the foot of the hill country and you could see the sawtooth rim of the hills behind it. All the rivers came down from there. The Medina, the Guadalupe, the Colorado, the Brazos, the Nueces, and the Trinity, sliding down southeastward to the Gulf. In the summertime it was cool up there in the hill country, they said, but dangerous because of the Red Indians, who ruled the earth and all that walked up and down upon it.

The teamsters said San Antonio was growing now, it was the only city inland, in all those blank places on the map of Texas. Since Santleben and Twohig and the Mavericks, Dullnig and Guenther moved in, why it's a hummer. Seems like there's a fandango or a cockfight or a gunfight every night.

The cook sang, *They say I drink whiskey but my money's my own and if you don't like it you can leave me alone . . .* The river led them to the west, along the galleria of river trees and no other trees anywhere. Banquete and the old horse pens were far behind. A new world lay in front of them. Not even the Spaniards in all their armor could keep San Antonio but now the German merchants have moved in, why the world is different. They were traveling straight into the wind and it bit at Simon's bare face. He wrapped a sock around his neck against it. *If a tree don't fall on me I'll live 'til I die.*

Simon sat with the driver of number four, bundled in his old Mexican War coat made of blue wool and patches, mismatched buttons. He was surprised to learn the driver was from Kentucky. They talked for hours about Paducah and the war, how the driver had been raised in Bowling Green or near there, had known Walking David as a great horseman and a good trader. How the big Alexander's Livery stable had been burnt down during the war and the horses stolen, what a shame it was. If there was aught left of it.

"No," said Simon. "Flat burned down. Who was you with?"

"Tenth Kentucky, under Harlan." And then he added, "Union. I was commissary. Driving wagons. Looks like I'll never stop driving wagons and I don't care if I don't, it's a good life. Who was your old man?"

"David, Walking David."

"I mean your pa."

"A fiddler," said Simon. "He went his way."

The driver nodded and asked no more questions. Simon sat and listened to his talk, his reflections. Mile after mile they bumped over the old Mission Road, and they camped where others had camped before them, in places near the river and under great live oaks so that their fires lit the undersides of the leaves all the way to the crown. Then there was a great bustling of mules and horses being unharnessed, men walking backward from tree to tree uncoiling ropes from their cold, wet hands for overhead tie-lines where others had strung lines before them. Somebody sang, *Shady Grove, my little love, I'm going back to Harlan . . .*

Sometimes the noise bore down on him and he had to briefly

put his hands over his ears. At the first gray light of dawn the wagon master banged on a metal basin to roust out the scouts and send them forward into the bitter wet morning. The scouts stood around a fire eating what there was to eat and pouring down cups of black coffee. *All right boys get on top of 'em!* Bang bang bang. *Get your asses in the middle and a leg down each side!* When they galloped out, every horse and mule in the place set up a racket. Then men ran down the rows with nosebags of corn and the mules made shrieking noises of great volume when they saw them coming. The horses called and pawed holes in the ground. The cooks dropped tailgates for working surfaces and there was a great clashing of crockery and tin. Simon split and carried wood for their fire and helped repair harness while Damon was set to kneading dough with his sleeves rolled up past his elbows. Every night big skillets turned out frybread and bacon, a man walked past tossing apples at people, one box of oranges was broken open by agreement with the owner. Freight payment.

If they sat up late they could hear the night hunters singing wolf to wolf or the low hushed sweep of an owl. An arrow or bullet out of the dark was a possibility. Instinctively Simon sat with his hands between his knees, to be protected at all costs.

The first mission they came to was Espada, barely recognizable in a clustering of hackberry and cedar elm trees. Its facade stood alone among overgrown rubble. Then San Juan and then San José. All with purposes unknown. To Simon they were ruins ancient and lost that he did not understand and as he walked through the roofless nave of San José he wondered about their music, what it was they sang, how they sang it. What instruments they played and to whose glory. On the remains of the plaster, men of three different armies and two languages had carved their names. He thought of the acoustics and so, since it had stopped raining, took out his fiddle, stood on a great fallen beam of cypress, and played

"Neil Gow's Lament" to hear the echoes from the high standing walls in which once had sounded plain chant or the songs of the Indians of the mission.

Back in wagon number six Damon sat on a heap of harness to be repaired and as the wagon groaned past on its shrieking wheels he heard Simon playing as if in a great cathedral and knew he had sought out isolation as always, and as always needed to be left alone. He tapped the end of his pennywhistle against his lower lip and wondered what woman would be happy with a man whose need for solitude was so great, if Simon was headed for marital disaster. He thought of his own. Who among us is ever spared?

Then San Antonio was ahead of them, tucked into the knees of the hills, a layer of mauve woodsmoke sliding overhead in misty layers. The sound of the bells of San Fernando Cathedral rang out, rain crows sailing through the air.

THERE WAS RAIN when they left the wagon train and its triumphant arrival in the wagon yard south of town. It was the first week of November 1866. It was a year and a half since he had last seen her, riding past in the little wagon with its side curtains, in a sweet heart-shaped bonnet thrown back on her shoulders and her hair shining. Simon and Damon walked up Flores Street with their rucksacks on their backs, past little houses of wattle and daub. Women hurried by with their rebozos over their faces against the fine mist. A rooster with flagrant black and red tail-feathers stalked a roof spine.

"Remember we're under military rule," said Damon. "A person tends to forget. Keep it in mind, Simon." He glanced at Simon's still, attentive face and knew the thoughts behind it.

Simon looked at him with a vague expression. "Yes, I will," he said.

They took note of the old adobe and stone buildings now being replaced by modern constructions. There was rain when they stood under the veranda of Cassiano's Feed and Supply on Dolorosa. They stared out at the cathedral with its one tower and a small, walled graveyard, the two plazas on either side of it, both unpaved and rutted, the collapsing facade of the old Spanish governor's house, the *comandancia*. He noted an adobe building painted in great high letters—INTELLIGENCE OFFICE—on Soledad and Commerce as those streets emptied into the wide plaza, which meant it was the place to get your letters and telegrams. Despite the fine drizzle, they saw housewives and girls coming for their morning supplies in Military Plaza. In that wide-open space gardeners and farmers and bird-sellers offered their wares from under awnings. They heard the shouts of men and horses and hay wagons.

Damon said, "Let's try there." He gestured toward the Plaza House Hotel, which fronted Main Plaza. They dodged puddles and melon wagons and ducked in. Inside were several musicians laying out the evening's work: scores, instruments, music stands.

God, they're playing off scores, Simon thought. *Music stands!* They stood against the back wall in their wet coats and rucksacks. Simon needed to know more about the audiences and so they sat drinking coffee as the waiters cleared the tables and the musicians began to play.

They were doing elegant stuff. He felt the restlessness of the men gathered to drink and gamble at the tables with a great deal of satisfaction. They wanted jigs, reels, hornpipes, and all those tunes that he and Damon could supply. But he and Damon needed a guitar player and somebody on rhythm.

Damon regarded the players carefully. "My guess is that they also teach ballroom dancing," he said. "They probably don't have any body hair."

"You are a cruel man," said Simon, and elbowed him. "Bitter. Envious."

"We all suffer from some deficiency and must bear our sinful natures with patience."

The rain slackened. They finished their coffee and slipped out to walk east on the street called Paseo and crossed the river at Losoya to see the remains of the Alamo Mission. All around it were heaps of rubble from the walls, various indefinable collapsed structures, and open land beyond where small fields backed up onto Salado Creek.

The old Alamo Mission chapel was now the U.S. Army's Quartermaster depot and the long barracks beside it housed the Quartermaster company. Simon and Damon stood gazing at it in a fine mist. Damon said that it had been their last holdout, that chapel.

"Dramatic," said Damon. He held on to the brim of his Hardee hat. "Holding out to the last man in a chapel. Statues of saints falling face-first into debris, cannon smoke, shrieks of the wounded and dying . . ."

"You boys looking for somebody?" A man with sergeant's stripes came up to them.

"No, sir. Just came to see the old battle site."

"This is it."

"Just this?" Simon tried to imagine 2,000 Mexican soldiers and 187 Texans all fighting in the small chapel.

"Oh hell no, they fought all over the place. There was a big mission compound. Crockett was killed here on this spot where I'm standing. I found his coat button the other day. That's the truth."

"No," said Simon and laughed. "I bet it had 'Crockett' written on it."

"Yes, son, on my mother's grave, and you can find those old .65 caliber balls everywhere. Stuck in the plaster and the mortar."

Simon said, "So I guess Colonel Webb lives here. He commanded the 62nd Colored."

"Hmm." The quartermaster regarded Simon carefully: his dripping broad-brimmed hat and his boots, his rucksack and the fiddle carried there carefully jammed down and covered against the wet. "And was you with him? Now discharged?"

Simon opened his mouth and gestured with one hand as a kind of split-second delaying tactic while his mind ran with plausible and implausible lies. Saved by Damon.

"Yes," said Damon. "Actually, to be quite frank, we were at Los Palmitos and we played for him and the officers at a dining-in after the surrender. It was a most joyous occasion. The end of all the conflict. A scratch band. A colored color sergeant played banjo. And we've made our way here hoping to find engagements, these unsettled times, et cetera, but music always in demand, not so?" Damon pulled his beribboned C whistle out of an inside pocket and ran through the first few measures of "Blarney Pilgrim."

"Yes, indeed." The quartermaster smiled as the lilting flute tune took over his mind. Then he lifted his head to stare out the chapel doors. Another freight wagon had arrived. The driver bellowed Ho! and threw the brake lever and got down. The sergeant turned back to the two musicians. "Why no, Colonel Webb has his family here, got a fine house up near North St. Mary's, new houses on Richmond, on the river, can't ask a family to live in that wreck." He tipped his head toward the Long Barracks. "Me and the staff sergeant who does the accounting, we got to live there."

"The accounting fellow?" said Simon. He wanted to know if the spare blond orderly sergeant was here. He could identify Simon as a Confederate soldier, he would remember the red-headed fiddler who had asked about the girl. "I remember him. I guess he's come up as well."

"Come up from where?"

"The Rio Grande?" Simon gestured toward where he thought south was. "After Los Palmitos?"

"That skinny blond fellow, yes, ain't no numbers getting past him."

North St. Mary's. On the river.

They ducked out of the drizzle and into the chapel to see the remains of the great wooden doors that lay leaning against the wall. They had been the front doors of the mission and were beautifully carved but were missing two panels which had been knocked in by rifle butts. A saint stared with stone eyes from between barrels of salted pork. Where men had struggled and died under cannon fire and bayonet there were cans of beef, wrapped bundles of candles, lamp oil, horseshoes, tack, ranked tools, shelves of blankets, tarpaulins, boxes of grommets and clamps. The unending wealth of the industrial North.

They left before somebody started wondering aloud about their passes or discharge papers.

THE STREETS WERE narrow and confining, following the old street pattern of the original Spanish town. Small houses of stone with long verandas stood wall to wall with adobe houses flat-roofed with protruding beams. On Commerce Street were new three-story commercial buildings of brick. The streets themselves were now a geography of red clay and mud. There seemed to be saloons and bars on every corner and in every hotel. The inhabitants of the old houses sat on the verandas and gazed in quiet and wordless alarm at all that was new and loud. But in Main Plaza and Military Plaza still the ancient rhythms of market and trading went on. Hay came in stacked high as cumulus clouds, oxen and horses and mules stood in their traces in front of Cassiano's feed store and the long shaded fronts of the merchants' establishments looked out on the daily market.

Simon thought he saw the woman named Mercedes; he had seen her face in the spring wagon with Doris when they left Fort Brown. He was sure he saw her at a hardware store, but then she disappeared into the crowded streets with flaunting bright skirts.

They slept for the last time with the wagoners on South Flores Street. The next morning they pulled on their good black coats and played for a Mr. Pressley in the empty Plaza House Hotel saloon. Behind them the doors were thrown wide to the cold air and the crashing, volatile scene of Main Plaza and all its vendors. They went through several jigs, reels, and two slow airs; waiters and cooks moved past them with supplies for the day.

"You need a banjo player," said Mr. Pressley. "Those fast tunes are all right but you need a banjo."

"We're looking for one."

"And a rhythm man."

"That too."

"You need some new songs. What do you have? Everybody's tired of 'Lorena'; that's the war, that's old. Nobody wants to hear wartime songs anymore. Don't play 'Hard Times' either. Nobody wants to hear no more about hard times. "

Simon tipped his head from side to side. "There's a new one— 'Red River Valley.'"

"Let's hear it."

Simon played it, sweet and slow. Damon came in on the harmony with his D whistle.

"You're all right. Play for two dollars a night and whatever gratuities are on offer."

Pressley was a fat, pale man with slow movements and protruding eyes. He had a very deep voice that seemed to issue from him as if it had first been cast into him from somewhere else.

"We're going to pick up other jobs if we can get them," said Simon.

"Let me know. You can have a room upstairs. Attic. It's where the help stay if they ain't got nowhere else."

Simon said, "Yes, well then, what will you charge us?"

"Forty cents a day and found. You can eat whatever they have left over in the kitchen. There's plenty. Cook will save you supper. Be ready to play at seven every evening by the bell." He tipped his head toward the door and by implication at the cathedral across the square, San Fernando with its one tower and its campanile.

"We'll be here," said Damon. He and Simon glanced covertly at each other; hotel cooking would be the best food they had had since Banquete, even if it was what was left over.

"And also," said Pressley, "I do magic tricks."

Damon and Simon fell silent. After a moment Simon said, "When do you do these magic tricks?"

"When you all get a night someplace else. Everybody just loves them, just loves them."

THEY ATE EXTRAVAGANTLY that night, shoveling in the roast beef, boiled potatoes with butter, white bread, pan-fried squash, and an entire melon for dessert. Kitchen cleanup went on noisily all around them. The cook watched them eat, shook his head, and filled their plates again.

The room up in the attic had three beds and each of their legs stood in glass casters filled with some noxious liquid to keep bedbugs and insects at bay. They shoved the extra bed up against a wall and used it as a place to put their gear. Simon laid out his possessions carefully, his clothes neatly folded: coat first, shirt on top of that, then his cut-off drawers and socks, hat to one side. The Plaza House offered baths; Simon sank into hot water and nearly fell asleep. They sent their shirts to be laundered and their black coats and trousers to be cleaned with turpentine and vinegar. Simon had himself shaved and left his razor with the barber to be sharpened. He once again broke down the Dance revolver and hid it away in the rucksack; they were in a town, military everywhere, best to keep it hidden.

Then he stood at the tiny window in his old checkered homespun shirt that had come all the way from Kentucky and was apparently indestructible no matter how much abuse it took. He could see over rooftops, and here and there an occasional light shone out onto muddied streets, and to the north in the dark hills he could see a fire burning. This was the city where all the stories would come true. Fortresses stormed, princesses rescued, innocence defended, a city of bells and bright shawls and the cool Spanish courtyards beside a river.

Simon pressed his forehead against the glass, watching the rain come and go. From somewhere he heard a concertina playing a tune he did not know, and a woman's laughter.

THE NEXT DAY a black waiter told them that the ladies and their maids came to the market every day for the daily shopping.

"Yes, sir, the ladies come every morning for they daily food, they eggs, fresh, they tortillas if that's what you eat, whatever fresh on offer, which in November now is the first of the winter gardens if they have them, some tomatoes, some eggplant or rat-tail peppers, yes, sir, every morning behind the cathedral."

Simon went early in the morning to search for Doris and if not her, then Mercedes. The wagons opened their sideboards to stack melons and bottle gourds carved into dippers, candles and eggs, goat milk and hard cheeses and jerky. He did not know how to get a message to her safely; if it were found it would land her in serious trouble. He walked around the two plazas and then stood disconsolate, anxious. Maybe he should try to find Mercedes's family; her last name was Bethancourt. He heard Damon inside the plaza, running through "Whiskey Before Breakfast" again and again and so turned to join him.

The next day a hailstorm drove down the narrow streets. Pressley said it was the rainiest year anybody ever remembered. Mud was splashed halfway up the sides of the buildings. On that day Simon walked across town toward the Alamo, then up Fourth Street.

The house was in the northern suburbs of the town. It was where the San Antonio River turned to the northeast. A man passing by, his head down against the rain, indicated the house to him. It was on the other side and it faced the river, so he found his way across the flooding San Antonio River by a small and shaky wooden bridge. He walked up Richmond Street in the rain because everyone would be inside and not notice him in his old Mexican War coat and his pulled-down rain-streaming hat. The lights of Colonel Webb's house shone out into the downpour. He was spying on them. He must not be caught doing this. Webb, under martial law, as far as Simon knew, had the power to ask for his papers and to charge him with whatever he pleased.

Such a long way to come on the strength of having seen her twice, and of eight letters, half of them to a boy now dead. On the strength of his imagined home and an imagined wife. Of lying down in bed with her every night and waking up in the morning with her beside him. The Webb house was a two-story stone building with tall windows, a half-circle drive, a porte cochere. Sago palms and wisteria in front and a massive live oak, all vague in the dark rain. The colonel must be renting it; the rent must be high. Only the best for the executive officer of the Quartermaster Department. A covered buggy came across the bridge with a wet noise and a halo of rainwater springing up from each wheel. The little horse trotted doggedly. Simon stepped into a workman's shed on the opposite side of the street. The rain thundered on the plank roof. The buggy stopped. The occupants came out, Doris Dillon in a dark cloak. She reached back and helped the girl down. Then came Mrs. Webb and then the colonel. They hurried up under the square porte cochere, where a woman threw the door open for them and Simon watched as Doris pulled off her bonnet to shake the water from it.

He felt an enormous relief and a weight lifted off his heart. It was as if she might not have been real or only a personage in a story he had heard tell of. But there she was, beating the raindrops from her bonnet, as present on this earth as himself. He stood in the dark rear of the shed. He felt like a beggar and a spy. He waited in the drumming noise until the rainstorm bled away and turned to drizzle, then started for Main Plaza.

MR. PRESSLEY ASKED them to take on a friend of his and said with anxious waving hand gestures that the man could play fiddle just fine. Could tap on a drum! Was trying the learn banjo! He had been thrown out of another outfit for drinking and general uncontrolled behavior, but he regretted his actions and was now looking for work.

"You related?" Damon squinted one eye at the manager.

"No, but he's from where I'm from and anyhow he just needs a second chance at life. Now, another fiddle along with you two and we got some *volume*. You can hear y'all above all the carryings-on."

"Where y'all from?"

"Pocahontas, Arkansas. Life has dealt badly with him. He just needs another chance. His daddy was hung by the neck until dead."

Damon nodded. "Must have been on the wrong side. Whatever side that was."

"No, his daddy killed a man with a rock for making off with a toolbox. He was judged guilty of homicide. So his mother took him off to Illinois to raise and she never said the word no to him in all his life."

After listening to the man play in the empty saloon, Simon and Damon shook their heads. Lester Pruitt could play only one song on the fiddle with any facility. It was called "The Moonlight Waltz." Then he promptly fell apart, with shrieking strings, on even the simplest jig. But he was decent with the bones and a bodhran, which he had learned from some Irishman, and they were desperate for rhythm. He was astonishingly profane in his speech, and in addition, downright filthy. His loud yellow-and-purple striped shirt was dotted with food. He had a brooding way about him, searching for trouble.

"Rhythm or nothing," said Simon. "And clean up."

By dark the two plazas were often crowded with freighters and visiting vaqueros from the ranches nearby. Often enough they heard gunfire, whether out of high spirits or serious conflict they did not know nor did they wish to inquire. Simon saw a man stumble out of the Old Stand Saloon next to the Plaza House, when he had come outside for a smoke and a moment of quiet. The man stepped in a bucket, fell down, and got up trying to pull a revolver out of his waistband, intent on shooting at somebody. A deputy knocked him down and he and a waiter sat on the man until he could be convinced that he had not been tripped but merely stepped in a bucket.

And so they rolled through their list of songs for three nights and they collected enough in tips for Simon to take five dollars to Mr. Twohig's bank for his mortgage payment. It was in the French building at Soledad and Dolorosa. He watched carefully as the clerk wrote out the receipt for five dollars to Solomon Bradford's account in payment on note for property.

The clerk gazed down at his signature and then blew on it.

"Well, Mr. Boudlin, we have had a communication from the Boatmen's Bank in Paducah as to a possible settlement by the State of Kentucky concerning the destruction of Alexander property. Your guardian, David Alexander, asked that the monies from this settlement, if any, be directed to his nephew, Simon Boudlin. Mr. Twohig or I could, with your signature, put it straight into this land transaction."

"I don't reckon there will be a settlement," said Simon. "Thank you anyway. Kentucky is broke, the South is broke. What's done is done." He went to the door and placed his hat on top of one fist and with the edge of the other hand he tapped the crease back into it.

The man smiled and lifted one hand. "You never know."

"That's the trouble, never knowing. But, ah, sir, I was wondering if would you know any people named Bethancourt?"

The man thought. "I think there's a carpenter by that name up on Obraje Street, you could try there."

That day he and Damon took the rest of their earnings and crossed to the secondhand clothing store that somebody had set up in the old Spanish governor's palace. They held their money in their fists, their fists jammed in their pants pockets, gazing around carefully. Simon bought a pair of black lace-up boots, nearly new, that fit him well. Then he and Damon found cravats and a second shirt for each of them. Damon's cravat was a shining plaid taffeta and after he wrapped it around his neck, he twirled his D whistle and knocked his hat up in back.

"'*Bring the bowl of which you boast,*'" he said. "'*Fill it to the brim.*'"

"Why were they always drinking from bowls?" said Simon. "Was that all they had?" He regarded the shining black toes of his boots. "Didn't they have any cups at all?"

"I always wondered that myself," said Damon. "I have no earthly idea."

In the kitchen at the Plaza House Simon watched as Pruitt and Damon struggled into their performance clothes. He straightened Damon's bright plaid cravat for him.

"Ready we are," said Damon.

CHAPTER TWENTY

On the following day, he saw her in the market. Or he thought it was her or he wished it were her. She and a maid walked among the wagons stacked with fruit and vegetables, where patient horses stared at the dirt in front of them and the vendors searched the crowds with indifferent eyes. Simon found her pausing in front of a wagon full of birdcages and the great single bell of San Fernando rang out eight in the morning. Its name was La Perla.

He circled around and ducked between a hay wagon and a little excursion wagon, the kind they called an ambulance, so that he could approach her from the front. He was very conscious that he was wearing his good white shirt under his coat and that he probably smelled of cigar smoke and whiskey from the night before at the Bull's Head Saloon. He came straight to her without hesitating. He took off his hat and bowed.

"Miss Dillon," he said.

"Oh!" She became still, a figure halted and upright. A short silence. "You are *Simon*! God above!" Her eyes were round as dollars and one of the men lifting a birdcage turned in surprise at the tone of her voice.

"I am indeed." He looked into her eyes and was moved almost beyond speech. "I am so glad to see your face again, my dear." For a moment he couldn't think of more to say but only gazed into her startled face and stretched out one hand to her, one empty hand balanced on the noisy air.

"You've come!"

"Yes, yes."

She wore that same black-and-brown striped dress, a straw bonnet close set around her face and the tie ribbons loose down her shoulders. Such blue eyes. In all the noise and bustle of the market, in the drifting smoke, she took his hand.

He said, "I'm sorry to surprise you like this. It's terrible, I know. I didn't know how to get word to you that I was here. I have been looking for you every day."

"You have?"

"Every day. Here." He could not stop smiling and his delight was so intense he felt airborne. He did not let go of her hand.

"Oh, dear Simon," she said. "At last I see you again."

He bent down to kiss her on one cheek very carefully. "Miss Dillon, your letters have meant a great deal to me. A great deal. And the memory of you."

He let go of her hand reluctantly. People called out what it was they had to sell. *¡Tamales de puerco!* they yelled. *¡Nopales! ¡Los mejores melones!* She took in a breath and was suspended and then in a kind of smiling desperation said, "And look! Here is Mercedes, who carried your letters."

Mercedes clasped her hands in front with a solemn expression. "I did it," she said. "*Culpable.*" She and Simon shook hands over a job well done.

"All my thanks," he said in a happy voice. "You are very good."

"Oh *de nada,*" she said. "You have come at last!"

Doris said, "Put your hat on, Simon! You will catch cold or be burnt up by the sun." And she took it from his hand and as he bent obediently she placed it on his head. "There. Simon, tell me of your journey here, and about Galveston and the raccoons and all." She too was helplessly smiling, and laughed, and said, "You are here!"

"My dear," he said, and fell silent. He could not take his eyes from her face. "So much has happened."

"Simon, you will tell me all that has happened. You took care of the boy Patrick." She laid her hand on his arm, lightly, as people moved past them and paused to glance back at them. "You did not desert him."

"Of course not."

"Simon, you have a good heart." The wind took her bonnet ribbons and wisps of her black hair. "You have a good heart."

"I wish it were true."

"It is true. And your music took hold of me, it was like songs from home." She paused, caught up in confusion. "Listen, Simon, I must tell you my sight is not terribly good. I had some eyeglasses but lost them aboard ship coming to America."

"Ah." Simon put his hand over hers, regarded her large dark blue eyes, the little bonnet surrounding her face like a portrait frame. He liked every bit of her. He liked her intent expression, her way of searching faces, her wide eyes, and now he knew why. He released her hand and held up his own. "How many fingers am I holding up?"

"Oh, *twenty.*" She laughed and then tied and untied her bonnet strings. "Twenty and a half!"

"What color are my eyes?"

"Green. No gray. No, a sort of greenish gray. Are they?"

"My dear Irish person," he said, and then, at a loss for conversation, "I am so relieved to see you again finally, finally, even here in the market. Right in front of God and everybody."

"Oh yes, yes, even though we are both surprised out of ourselves and can hardly think of a word to say, are we not then?" She laughed in a nervous burst and said, "Do you have work? Are you well? Tell me."

"I have work. We are at the Plaza House, we play at other places too. I am well. I'm here in San Antonio because you are here. Because you are being held a prisoner in a castle by an evil troll and I alone am the man to rescue you. You are not being courted by somebody else I hope?" He bent to hear her answer. San Fernando's bell rang eight and a quarter; someone pulled a rope and so the great bell tilted and poured out its deep tones like coins.

"They sit outside on the steps for hours," she said. "At least ten at a time. They all have *enormous* mustaches." She glanced up at him when he laughed. "I tell you, Simon, I knew you would arrive here, with that music in your head, God's gift, if not the spirits."

"I'm here," he said.

"Oh, how I would love to talk all day and hear about your adventures coming here. And . . ." She paused. "About you." They could not stop looking at each other, this strange public disclosure of themselves after the privacy of letters, the privacy of imaginings, hopes misplaced or not. No masks. He found himself studying her; for all her dark hair she had thin eyebrows, she had an admirable little nose, a rounded mouth. So here they were in the town plaza like creatures in a public drama without a script.

"I would love to tell you about anything. Name it. Cats, horses, fiddles, and the journey to here."

"Anything," she said, smiling, in a kind of hypnotic repetition. "Music then."

He held his palm out flat. "I have here a great many tunes and every one of them is for us. 'Shenandoah,' 'A Young Man's Dream.'" He saw her smile. "And 'Red River Valley.'"

"I must learn them." She took his hand and folded up his fingers as if to guard the songs there, against public view or damage or disappearance. "And I will, then."

The maid turned away to a man selling pecan candies on a tray, then cleared her throat and searched for something else to do before the man sold her one.

"Tell me how many years you have left in your contract with the Webbs. Come with me, this way."

They walked together to a fruit stand, where a sideboard had been let down. All the apples and melons were artistically arranged with twigs of live oak leaves stuffed in between. Her skirts swung as she turned, her fine hands clutching a shopping list.

"Maybe half a year, now." She ticked the numbers off on her fingers. "Yes, and Simon, those are the *days* I am counting." They both laughed. Her gaze seemed to dismantle him, he felt loose in all his joints. "Simon, I am not allowed to meet anyone," she said in a low voice. "I must live like a Carmelite. You'd think I had taken Holy Orders and gotten bricked up in a tower."

"We could meet here at the market. Do you not come every day?"

"Yes. But often Mrs. Webb comes with me, or Josephina." They now stood carefully apart from each other in the midst of people coming and going in the broad open plaza, among men calling out to other men from the hay wagons, waiters arguing with vendors, the women with baskets on their arms. They were seen and probably known. Simon the fiddler from the Plaza, the maid herself waving to her friends.

"I had no idea how to get a note to you, you being bricked up in a tower. Could you not invite me there where you live?" His eyes in the shade of the hat brim were dark with an intent sort of trouble. "Can you not have any visitors? None?"

"Oh no. No. Colonel Webb swears if I meet with young men he will put me out of the house and I will starve on the streets."

"Is he serious?"

A different look came over her face. "Yes," she said.

Simon was silent for a long measure and then said, "Not while I live."

Mercedes said, "Dorita, soldiers are coming."

Doris Dillon turned her head and fear came into her face. She put her hands on her skirt front as if she were prepared to hike up her skirts and run and her slim figure was poised taut as a wild animal. "It's the colonel's dog robber." She turned to Simon. "They'll tell. I have to go. Or *you* go." She then shut her hands together in a distracted gesture. "There is going to be trouble."

Simon said, "I will not."

He ducked around the end of the fruit stand, came behind it, grabbed an apron off the wagon wheel and tied it around himself. He bent over the melons. "Yes, miss? Would one of these do?" He thwacked one with a knuckle. "Hear that? The sound of a happy melon. It's calling your name."

The fruit vendor stared at Simon in astonishment, but Mercedes spoke to him in Spanish, a fast ripping explanation so quick that Simon could not understand, but the vendor raised his eyebrows, then laughed, then handed Simon an apple and tipped his hand toward Doris.

Simon offered her the apple with a triumphant and slightly wicked smile.

The dog robber, a corporal, and another private marched past, their eyes sweeping over the crowd, alert for civic unrest. The corporal lighted upon Doris. They all lifted their caps. "Miss Dillon. Good day to you."

"Yes, good day," she said and waved with a merry smile. Then in a lower voice, "And may you fall in a cistern." Simon tossed the apple from one hand to the other. They did not fall into a cistern after all but lingered with the candy seller and his pecan taffies while Doris lifted up an unwanted melon and expressed astonishment at its succulent goodness. At last they went on.

Simon threw up the apple again, caught it, let it roll down the inside of his forearm, and then straightened his arm quickly so that he tossed it into the air with the inside of his elbow. He caught it neatly.

"You're afraid," he said.

She took a deep breath and held it a second and then said, "Yes. The colonel."

"I'm listening."

"When he is in the house I dare not be alone."

Simon became very still. The smile drained out of his face. She lifted her head and he saw tears glistening in her eyes. She lowered her head again, ashamed of the tears, and pressed the backs of her hands against her cheeks. "I am just nervous," she said. Then she quickly turned from him once again to look around the market for people who might be observing them. The maid was busily going through a heap of tomatoes from a winter garden, inspecting each one with studious care.

"This is outrageous," said Simon. "You, a girl alone come from Ireland, and no place to find help." Another silence. "This is terrible. There has to be a way to get you out of this." He put the apple in his pocket and quickly offered the vendor a handful of change to choose from. The man took a two-cent piece and nodded.

"I don't know, I don't know, I signed the contract with my own hand."

They could stand fooling about with the piled fruit for only so long. In a few quick, halting sentences she told him that she kept away from Colonel Webb as much as possible, although both the colonel and is wife insisted she eat breakfast with them and dinner as well. They did not like each other it seemed and they needed her there to talk to or talk at, forks clattering on plates, big silences, then outbursts of mindless chatter, and it was all false as counterfeit money and enough to drive a sane person into lunacy.

They leaned toward each other over the melons. She said in a low voice, "As God is my witness, Simon, they despise each other and the poor girl Jo, caught between. She is becoming a mean-spirited child with a wicked tongue and a breaking heart to see her parents so."

"Come into the church," said Mercedes. "We cannot stand here forever."

"I could," said Simon.

"No, come."

Simon untied the borrowed apron and returned it to the fruit vendor. They wove through the crowd, dodged a huddle of sheep being urged on by a boy, mashed through the gate in the low wall surrounding the cathedral, and went through the broad carved doors into the dim interior. A Mass was in progress. Simon took off his hat and stood while both Mercedes and Doris tapped their fingers in the holy water fount, crossed themselves, and dropped a knee. Mercedes went forward toward the altar and Simon and Doris stood together at the back of the pews. In the echoing spaces she told him that the colonel would seek her out if she were alone anywhere and so when she heard his carriage arrive and the front door open, or his dreaded steps on the floorboards, she hurried to find the girl, Josephina, or to be near Mrs. Webb or Mercedes.

"Or what?" he said.

"Or, well, he has stood very near me and tried to take the pins out of my hair, he has asked me to come to their bedroom when she was gone to the neighbors for vinegar-making. Oh God, how

I wish I had not come to America!" She put both hands over her eyes but then took a deep breath and straightened. "So."

Simon stood silent. He felt a prickling crawl of rage rising and for a moment it seemed it would flood through him completely. He tipped his head to look up at the dome of the sanctuary overhead, to slow himself down. Be calm. She was in a state of continual and relentless emotional terror as it was. She did not need his own outrage pouring out upon her. Steady and cool, that was what was needed at present, if he could manage it. All about them the statues of saints and Mary herself either looked to heaven or gazed down upon the suffering; the laces were sooty from candle smoke. Overhead the bells sang out nine o'clock.

He stood with his hat in his hands and his head still turned up to the distant ceiling. "What to do? Come away with me."

"No, I will not. Not until I have saved my passage home." There was a tremor in her voice she could not subdue but she kept on anyway. "When I have the price of my passage home I will feel safe, I will know I can make my own choices." She pressed her lips shut as if this helped her think what to say, how to put it. "Of course you see this is the advisable thing to do. Quite sensible. I am trying to be practical."

Simon looked down into her face. "Yes. Of course. But how can you? You are not allowed to meet anyone."

"Am I not?" She tipped her head and then pulled a handkerchief from her sleeve and wiped her nose. "I shall give piano lessons here and there among the Irish and English people and you will meet me when I go and play the waltzes. I am arranging it." He saw that her hands were trembling as she pressed them together. "I asked the other army wives to suggest it to him, not myself. They are very good, they all said 'Certainly, certainly.' They understand he is strict, but they think it is only to guard me from this new country. I have made them all small gifts, you see, so they think well of me and they know I had to act by indirection. Their husbands all came with us from Ohio, we were all deployed together. And so he could hardly say no without looking very unfair."

"Yes, good thinking, that was smart." His estimation of her rose even higher.

"But we must not act as if we were meeting. I know that is very shabby, 'tis very mean and low, but indeed I don't know what else to do."

Simon hoped he had a calm and pleasant expression. It was not a sure bet. "No, it's all right. And so you will say, 'And now we need someone to play the waltzes. Aha! I know somebody! Just come from Houston!'"

"Yes! Then I can perhaps make a little money and we can come to know each other a bit, then? With care. People talk, someone might run to the colonel telling tales."

"You are fearless," he said. "As well as beautiful. And inventive and resourceful. I want you to marry me."

"We have written but now, Simon, we have only just met." And then in a shy voice, "I must be sure of myself."

He said, "I am sure of you."

Tears came into her eyes again. "Thank you," she said. "I am not seen as inventive and resourceful. I am seen as a rebellious, sneaking chit. That is the word he used."

"And has he laid hands on you?"

A pause. "Once. He took me by the upper arm, there was nobody in the house, I broke loose, went out into the street. He said behind my back, 'You'll give in.'"

Before he could stop himself Simon said in a low voice, as if it were a sudden, saving thought, "I am going to kill him."

"Oh my God," she whispered. "What have I done? I exaggerated, Simon!" She raised her hand with the palm out as if to stop him. His eyes had changed. There was a flat look to them, stony.

"Wait, listen, I didn't . . ." She put both hands to her cheeks. "Why did I say that?"

"No. It's all right." He knew there was a spurious, false tone to his voice, so he then tried for a reassuring smile. Reached out and tugged at her bonnet ribbon. "I am straightening your bonnet for you. It's come all si-gogglin."

"I talk too much." She dropped her head and then raised it again as if it were a great intolerable weight. "Simon, I didn't mean to cause you to think like that." She was groping for words. "You can't mean that, I couldn't see you again if it were so."

"Doris, it's all right. I am a peace-loving man, I promise you. That's a promise."

She laid her hand on his arm. "Is it a promise for sure then?"

"Yes. Yes. You have enough trouble and I have just added to it. It is a promise with all my heart. On my mother's grave, on my soul." He closed his eyes for a moment. *Please, God, kill that man with a fever, his horse falling over backward with him, a Comanche arrow in the eye.* And then because he was in a church he added, *In the name of our Lord and Savior, Jesus Christ amen. Thanks in advance.*

They stood for a moment listening to the Latin of the nine o'clock Mass, the responses. She started to speak and then paused, her thoughts leaping from one precipice to another. The pure cold fury in his eyes had frightened her. To distract him she said, "And would you know that tune, 'The Peacock's Feathers'?"

"Yes." The look in his eyes had gone away, it seemed with some effort. "It's tricky."

She smiled up at him. "There's two, you know. One is in the minor."

He stood with his hat held behind himself in his two hands and several conflicting emotions lit him up inside like fireworks. His happiness to be with her, to have touched her, that music mattered to her, that it lived in some secret place in her heart. She was brave. She was in danger. She was astonishingly pretty. He thought of Webb, nearly two years ago at Fort Brown, of how tall he was, whether he had been wearing his sword. If he was any good with a pistol. Then Simon blew out a long breath and reached out to brush away a stray bit of coastal hay stem from her sleeve; it had flown on the wind from a nearby hay wagon as if wanting her attention. He could not stop touching her.

"It's a sweet tune." He made himself clasp his hands behind his back again.

"It is, so." And then, "If only."

"If only what?"

"We had an entire afternoon to ourselves to work on it together."

"We will." Simon smiled reassuringly. "Miss Dillon," he said. "You have already thought it all out, as to how we could meet. You amaze me."

She flushed bright red. "Simon, I am ashamed of myself having done all this beforehand. I am very forward. I am bold, unprincipled, and conniving."

"Good. Good."

The Mass was over. They could see Mercedes rising from the pew and her jaunty, swinging walk as she came back to join them.

"Now as for messages, can you meet Mercedes here in the market, and give her a note for me?"

The maid, a tall woman with light skin and red cheeks, turned to them and then flipped up the end of her black braid under her nose and twirled it in the manner of stage villains, full of mystery.

She said, "I hide it in the vegetables. Notes in the potatoes, letters in the cabbages."

Doris laughed aloud. A merry laugh with a quick shake of her head. "I am so nervous," she said. "'Tis hard indeed to tell you what is going on." Another pause. "I hardly know myself."

THAT NIGHT AT one in the morning, when the Plaza House had finally run out of its need for music, Simon stood at the attic window looking out at the bell tower, smiling. Damon had been cautiously congratulatory about Simon's news that he had found Miss Dillon at last, had endured his somewhat incoherent description of her beauty and charms, and said in a grave voice that he wished them both a smooth road ahead. Any chance of that happening?

Simon turned, walked up and down the floor twice, and said, "She made me promise not to get in a fight with Colonel Webb."

"Why would you do that?"

Again a hesitation; then, "The man is a villain."

"No. I am astonished. Could it be true?" Damon pulled off his boots. "Well, my man, stick to it. But you know that."

Damon ate the half of the apple that Simon shared with him, drank off half a tumbler of rum, and then he slept.

Simon thought about the girls in Marshall, where he had hidden in the icehouse. How they were vivacious and flirting at the barbecue, how they must have been meeting young men for talk, for a dance, for rides in carriages. Those girls made visits to one another's houses. Their parents helped them with clothes and advice and probably sometimes furious arguments. But there was a steadiness, or at least he imagined this. This was how they got to know one another, men and women, and made momentous life decisions. And Doris was being denied this, and her far from home, from her own people and customs, from parents who might be of aid. Living in helpless terror of that villain. How alone she was. Images came to him: the colonel stalking her from one room to another.

Not for long. Simon was having heroic thoughts. Rescuer's thoughts. Savage thoughts.

CHAPTER TWENTY-ONE

THE OLD SPANISH CITY was being devoured by new enterprise—by stage services and freighting companies, by land speculators like the Mavericks and the Mengers, by German and Anglo-American and Irish businessmen named Dullnig and Twohig, Cassiano, Horde and Frost. It was a city of markets and transport whose domination had been secured by gunfire. It had fallen easily into no one's hands. But it had been conquered now by businesses in transportation, vendors to the Union Army, mule yards, wagon makers, ranch supply, hardware, and sewing machines. Now the Menger Hotel offered French wines and sheets edged with lace and a new contraption called a shower-bath. The Irish had arrived and were hungry, used to hardship, worked with roughened hands, and moved from digging new house foundations to poring over account books and finally to afternoon teas.

Mr. Twohig had a house on the bank of the river opposite St. Mary's and there Mrs. Twohig—she had been a Calvert from Seguin—held an afternoon musical event. It was a big house and there were guest houses all around it, shaded by tall trees. The immense cypresses were bare and stark in the brief winter of south

Texas. Robert E. Lee had been a guest before the war when he was stationed in San Antonio, so had Sam Houston, Phil Kearney, John Bankhead Magruder. Simon was made nervous by the ghostly presence of the great and the near great; dangerous people. They could draft you into armies. He palmed up a cinnamon twist the size of a doorknob and devoured it. He had not had breakfast.

Mrs. Twohig looked kindly upon the young Irish girl who sat hesitantly at the piano. Old Mr. Twohig was Irish and charitable, and he had seen Ben Milam shot dead at the Veramendi House during the Battle of Bexar. When Woll took San Antonio again for Mexico in '42, Twohig gave away everything in his store and then blew it up to prevent the Mexican general from getting the gunpowder, was taken prisoner and dragged to Mexico like a beast of burden. He escaped Fortaleza San Carlos along with twelve others. They had tunneled out with stolen ax heads and pieces of broken tile. Now he was a banker and Simon's small account lay in his adventurer's hands, somewhat twisted and hard as sole leather. In another room, old man Twohig and Captain Jefferson Kyle Kidd were in serious conversation in front of a fireplace.

"Oh, it is out of tune," said Mrs. Twohig. Simon stood close to the table with the tea and the food. Doris Dillon ran her hand down the keyboard in a scale, struck chords, and flinched when several keys responded with dull flat sounds as if they were discouraged and had stopped trying.

"Aye. 'Tis fair glundie that." She stared at the keyboard. "You'd think it had been rained on."

"And you?" Mrs. Twohig turned her broad body to Simon. People were circulating in their long drawing room. Cypress shadows danced on the walls. The walls were painted in the newest fashion: scalding white.

"I am only semirespectable, Mrs. Twohig," said Simon. "But

a musician takes work where he can find it." He wiped cinnamon frosting from his hand with a napkin and then picked up his bow and his fiddle.

She closed one eye. "Such as where?"

"The Plaza House, the Horde, the Century, the Bull's Head. For a traveling circus if I had to."

She nodded and did not smile. Finally she said, "You love your music."

He inclined his head. "I do."

"So it is. I will do what I can to advise people of your availability. There are Christmas parties and there is to be a gathering when Commissioner Edmund Davis comes to visit. An evening event. They will need music." She took the napkin from him. "This is not yet a world with much use for the refined arts, young man. It is still a world of fighting men." He started to say that much of his art was not at all refined and he had been in a few fights himself, but he thought better of it. She put her hand on his arm, lightly, and moved away.

Simon watched Doris for a moment, across the main room, seated at the square piano. She was in front of one of the tall windows and in the pouring winter light she ran her hands down the five octaves, with a cocked head, listening. He lifted the fiddle to his shoulder and walked over to her and said, "Miss Dillon?"

She raised her head to him. "Ah, I think I know you!"

"Do you, now?"

Once again he was heart-stopped by those wide blue eyes, at present with a wicked glint as she said, "Yes, yes, it's quite odd, but I do think we have met. You commented on the way I speak, faith and begorrah and blarney and Jesus and Mary and Joseph."

"Girl, stop." They were both laughing. And then they ran out of laughter for the moment and looked into each other's eyes in the clarifying light from the window, suspended in it, in the sound of a honeysuckle trailer tapping against the glass in a slight breeze, the smell of old wood and cloth and the voices of other people that now seemed so distant.

Then she put one hand on the sheet music in front of her. "This is 'Madame Bonaparte's Waltz.' Are you ready, Mr. Boudlin?"

"Hit it, Miss Dillon," he said, and laid his bow on the strings.

They listened to each other through the notes. They were allowed here to be absorbed with each other, to speak together in low tones, to look into each other's eyes. It was almost sexual in its intimacy. He lifted his eyebrows and inclined his head and led her into the bridge once again.

Then Mrs. Twohig came to ask Simon if he would teach somebody how to tune their guitar and Doris cried out in vexation,

"Mrs. Twohig, I have just found a violinist to play these pieces with me and you want to rob me of him! Now leave him alone, I swear, really." Mrs. Twohig sighed and went away.

They tried a schottische; Doris played it very slowly as Simon had never heard this one before and it led to much bending over the score with their faces close together, with Simon murmuring *I see, I see*, as if he had never seen $^2/_4$ time before in his life, as if the simple key signature of two sharps was completely beyond him. He said in a low voice, "And so can you see me?"

She whispered, "You are holding up twenty sort of pink objects. I can't tell what." And they laughed again in subdued gasps.

He thought of how she was different, her confidence returned now that she was seated in front of a keyboard with music before her. In the pale light coming through the windowpanes his red-brown hair took fire and the good bones of his face stood out in a hard architecture, his eyes deep and half-shut against the glare, his skin so fair and vulnerable in this treacherous world that Doris wanted to reach up to him and pull his stock higher around his throat, as if that might protect him against bar fights and bad weather. As if he needed protection. He did not. She bent her head to the keyboard again and then between them they picked up the thumping oompah rhythm of the "Palmyra Schottische." Doris made exaggerated predatory motions striking the chords and their laughter threatened to get out of hand.

And then some other girl wanted to play piano and someone had, against all reason, brought a concertina and made the afternoon hideous with its noise, and so the moment passed.

Simon could not find an excuse to be beside her any longer and supposed he should leave, and so stood turning the screw on his fiddle bow to loosen the horsehair, wavering, hesitant, standing near her without looking at her as she spoke politely to some lady named Maverick. Finally he said his goodbyes, thanked Miss Dillon for her music, put the fiddle in its case, snapped the bow into the groove, and closed the case.

But then Mrs. Twohig came to him and said he should join the men in the book room, warm himself at the fireplace, have something to drink before he left.

"Sir." Simon gave a slight, quick bow when he saw he was to join Twohig and Captain Kidd, both men with white hair. Elders, the experienced ones, the judicious ones with years of hard experience carved into their faces. Captain Kidd wore a worn and faded tailcoat so it was clear he had come on horseback. Old man Twohig was in a thick wool frock coat that was frayed at the cuffs. Simon said, "I was told there would be something to keep a man warm here."

"There is, fiddler." Captain Kidd stood up and poured him a tot from a decanter. Both men gave him that swift, appraising glance that occurred between men in these times, looking for indication of a wound or an insignia in a buttonhole, the unspoken question, *Who were you with?* Kidd handed the thick glass to Simon and sat down again, gestured toward a chair.

Simon sat. He laid his fiddle case down beside the chair and was somewhat shy in such company. They asked him polite questions about his employment, if Pressley paid fairly, what the road was like coming up from Goliad. They already knew he had come up from Goliad on the San Antonio river trail. They were too wise to ask him if he knew this or that tune or to cry out about their favorites. Or to ask him who he had been with.

"I was with Giddings," Simon said. "Down at Los Palmitos."

"Ah." They both nodded. Twohig said, "When Webb decided to attack. For some reason unknown."

"That he did," said Simon. *And now I am in love with a young woman of his household, who is sitting outside this room pretending to be entranced by a Goddamned concertina.* "The reason remains unknown."

"Speculation rife," said Twohig. "Now he's CO of the quartermasters here."

Captain Kidd said, "Battle honors."

Quiet laughter from the two old men.

"And now they are setting up those tribunals," said Twohig. His Irish accent was still with him after all these years.

"Yes," said Kidd. "We're under martial law so you've got to have a way to try people for stealing a hog or passing counterfeit money. Homicide, breach of promise, making rude noises on a Sunday."

Twohig said, "Thus it ever is. It was a hard time, we move forward at a snail's pace. And so, Captain, you are on your way north."

Simon lowered his drink. "North?"

"I have taken up giving news readings," said Captain Kidd. "Recently lost my wife. I am at loose ends. Thus I will make my living, like you, fiddler, going from place to place." He smiled and his face creased like old paper, like parchment. "I have just returned from Dallas, Wichita Falls, Spanish Fort, and I'm going back. Maybe in a month. People are hungry for entertainment up there, even if it is just month-old news from the *Philadelphia Enquirer*. Keep it in mind."

"Yes, sir," said Simon. "You feel it's safe?"

"No, I don't, but I long for excitement in my declining years. From your question I assume you've considered the same."

"I have." Simon tipped up the glass for the last of the whiskey and then held his hand over it to prevent Twohig from pouring him another. "I have to start work here pretty soon," he said. "Yes, sir, I have put some money on some land up there. From the old Peters Colony land grant."

They were both silent for a moment and then shook their heads.

"Never heard of it," said Kidd.

"It's south of Preston's Bend. I never saw it, never been there."

"Preston's Bend on the Red?"

"Yes, sir."

Captain Kidd considered. "Wait, I know it, it's at one of the crossings of the Red. A *vado*. They are moving cattle across at an alarming rate. Apparently the teeming north has an endless appetite for western beef. And the people who supply them are going to have as great an appetite for entertainment. If you keep your hair then you would do well there."

Simon stood up. "Thank you, I am much encouraged." He took up his fiddle case and shook their hands. "Good day to you both."

He said goodbye to Miss Dillon as if they were mere acquaintances, thanked Mrs. Twohig, and walked out into the chill air of a Southern winter. His mind was lighter now, as if he had shed a great burden of worry. He and Doris had picked up the strains of a waltz between them and carried it away together in a private moment, a peerless moment. He had learned there was a way to make a living up north and he felt a great deal better about his land there on that mysterious river called the Red that seemed to have no beginning and its end falling into the Mississippi somewhere in sugarcane country. He put his fiddle case in his rucksack, tucked both hands into the pockets of his black frock coat, and walked in a jaunty step all the way back to the Plaza House.

AT HOME, AFTER talking to the cook and seeing to supper preparations, Doris ran up the stairs to her room. She washed her hands and face in the basin and sat to rest a moment. There was much to do. Mrs. Webb seemed to find household economy beyond her, so Doris had made up the lists for shopping since Ohio while Mrs. Webb and young Jo languished. Here in San Antonio she had arranged storage spaces in the kitchen for the scarce wheat flour, learned from the young maids how to make a *salsa verde* with tomatillos, mixed the pony's feed and bound the forage into stooks, caught the dog robber making off with two bags of corn and threatened to report him, made a list of texts that Josephina needed for her schooling, gathered all the worn shoes together, found a cobbler on the other side of the Commerce Street bridge, and made him sign an itemized list and a date to return them. She had learned a great deal out of necessity.

Now, in the silence of her own room, she laid out her fabric scraps, needles, and threads. An embroidered bread cloth to go over the breadbasket would be right. A thank-you gift for Mrs. Twohig. Not too extravagant but thoughtful. Mrs. Twohig would remember her for her playing and for her considerate gift. Allies were vital, especially now, and Doris Dillon was determined to make as many allies as was humanly possible against the trouble to come.

THEY MET AT the Guenther home near the mill; in a moment of privacy at the pastry-laden table they spoke in short sentences about Ireland and her people there. They had only so much time. Every second counted. She spoke about her fall on board the *Brighton Rose,* thrown against a windlass in a great storm and her eyeglasses knocked completely off her head and into the Atlantic. Down, down, to spy on the fishes. How whatever she saw now had a glow, especially Simon, with his spiky, unruly hair.

Simon said, "Where can we find you another pair?"

"Never mind." She said it with a quick little shake of her head. "Spectacles are so *severe* and grim and off-putting." She wore a different dress that day—or it wasn't a dress, he decided, it was a roundabout jacket in the same material as her skirts. A dark slate gray, and under it a snow-white collar. She had left her hat on top of the Guenthers' piano. "I can see very well up close. Here, I'll show you." They walked over to the piano and she shook out the score. "I can see this perfectly well." She gazed up at him from the piano bench. "And who are you, then?"

He smiled. "Affectionately yours, I remain, Simon Boudlin." He pressed the tip of his bow against the first page of the score to keep it from turning. "Sweetheart, listen. I know there are young officers who come to visit the Webbs on the slightest pretext. Among them a quartermaster sergeant. Meager, a meager man, blond. Not that I care." He tipped his head from one side to the other. "You have to meet others so you can make comparisons and realize that I am a shining example of the perfect husband."

"Who told you this?" She ran through a melody with her right hand; it was a song he had never heard before.

"Mercedes. We ran into each other at the cathedral. Early Mass. I waylaid her. What's his name?"

"Oh. Him. He's a lieutenant now. Jacob Whittaker. And he's going over Colonel Webb's accounts with a flea comb."

"Really. Tell me more."

"There's money requisitioned for forage for horses and mules that do not exist. You'd think the colonel had taken lessons from the Irish, the black thief."

"I am glad to hear this. It makes my heart skip with delight. Maybe he'll be cashiered. Or hung."

"And I know you shot an alligator." She suddenly struck out a chord. A deep, dramatic one. "An alligator!"

"How do you know that?"

"Damon Lessing, the dark man. He met me by chance in the market with his whistles sticking out of his pocket and I said, 'Tell me about Simon, that he's not an ax murderer or a womanizer or he makes counterfeit money.' Oh how he spoke of you, Simon. And him a teacher in a university."

"He was?"

"Indeed. And Simon, I did not get born aboard ship, you know. In Tralee we have social lives, the young people go about and there were sings and dances . . . but I was taken by the thought of coming to America." She paused to think. "Even with a war. But it seemed there weren't any particular battles going on in Texas. So I signed the work contract. And the animals you have! All wild in the earth." She looked up to him. "I came to the New World and here I have met you."

He thought about this, about her mental leap from wild animals to himself and the odd haphazard chance of their coming across each other. "We are having the most random conversation here," he said. He wanted to take her by both shoulders and kiss her forehead and then each cheek and then on the mouth. Then on her white throat. And so on. A person could get seized at the most inopportune moments by sheer animal desire. She ran her finger down the notes and stopped, pretended to find some difficulty.

"There is a key change here," she said. "And moreover you must not miss this quarter rest."

He said in a low voice, "Let us be married and go. To the north of Texas."

She flushed. "I would never be good as a spy," she said. "I think my face is red. Do hush. And how then would we get there and how would we live? Tell me that."

He watched her hands on the keys. She would be leaving a known place, even if it was filled with trouble. Still it was a home, still there was the little girl, Jo, that she cared for and was concerned about. Into the great empty spaces of Texas. It might as well have been into the wilds of India or Africa or the great polar sea.

"I own some land. I have four hundred acres on a river called the Red, far to the north of here and . . ."

"Four *hundred* acres?" Her hands lifted from the wrists with fingers spread in astonishment. "What would you *do* with it all?"

"Sell some of it for the money to build a house. There's a seep of rock oil there and cattle get bogged in it and I would sell that section to buy lumber and windows with glass panes. And we will make a home there. A place to come back to. Our place. Our land, our kingdom. Our music."

Before he could become even more eloquent and convincing, a thin chatty girl in dark green came up to them talking at a great rate and spilled out a long—excuse me excuse me I just have to talk to Miss Dillon for a moment—very long monologue concerning the sale of a German flute.

He left early with his thanks and no differences in how he said goodbye to anyone. A brief bow to Miss Dillon. Mrs. Guenther cried out over his rendition of the Scots slow airs, would recommend him to anyone, and slipped an envelope into his pocket, the contents of which would go into Twohig's bank in short order. She clasped her hands in delight that Doris Dillon would come to give lessons on piano at her house, a piano tuner must exist somewhere, she would find him if she had to track him down herself!

Christmas came and went, cards were exchanged, New Year's Eve brought a fusillade of gunfire over the roofs of the town that went on for hours. Simon often found himself exhausted from playing at the Bull's Head, the Old Stand Saloon, one after another and the Plaza besides, always in search of new strings, rosin, his head ringing from the noise of men shouting and hallooing in close-confined walls, lamp smoke burning his eyes. He found his fiddle case growing heavy with coins once again; much of it went to the bank.

At the Maverick house, a week later, Miss Dillon brought her small charge, Josephina. The girl shook Simon's hand with a rigid smile and then turned away quickly in a dramatic whirl of skirts. He turned to Doris and she gave him one quick warning glance and then followed the child. Mercedes looked out of the kitchen and hurried after them both.

All around him he heard exclamations about how San Antonio was becoming cultured, as if there were no culture in the city beforehand. No Spanish. Neither fandangos nor watermelon races nor Day of the Dead processions, and he stood unclasping the fiddle case and thought about it but not for long. Doris came back to stand beside him at the buffet and put sweet rolls on a plate.

He downed coffee to listen to her quick, fragmented sentences, about her time with the Little Sisters of the Poor in Waterford learning geography and math and music, to read a score and to play it on the pianoforte. Her parents were not rich, but neither were they penniless, having ten acres with a good title to them all to themselves and privileges of the wood. They intended her for an education, saved every penny to send her to Waterford, and cried in front of the entire population of Tralee when she sailed away. Never did they or the sisters imagine her going to Texas, and in a battle besides. Now, speaking of battles, was he shot or was anybody he knew shot or pierced in some way?

"Not at all," he said. "Thank you for asking."

"You're welcome. Come and hear 'The Peacock's Feathers.'" She laid her hand on his arm for a moment. "The one in the minor key."

And again those moments when they drew out the complex Celtic hornpipe together, missed a phrase, went back and started over, a quick glance into each other's eyes, a lift of the chin and a fling into the lively melody once again and nods when they got it right. Her breathless laugh, the long note at the end. A smile between the two of them like a deep secret unshared with any other alive on earth.

Later he stood by the little horse's head, adjusting the bridle. He had become very daring. He had walked out with her to her carriage and helped her and Josephina and Mercedes into it. The driver, a private with the Quartermaster Department, regarded him with a long, slow sober look.

"Leave it alone, would you?" the driver said.

And his people? Simon left the bridle alone and came to stand at the low door of the surrey. He told her they had once owned a great livery stable with many horses, with fifty acres of land, but it had been burnt down in the war and the horses taken by a Confederate officer. All gone. That he stood as inheritor to a burned building and fifty acres with the fences destroyed, that he had been raised an orphan, that three generations ago his people had come from a place called Stranraer in Scotland, of which he had never heard any stories.

"Oh, but that is only across a bit of the sea from Ireland!" she said. "We are almost cousins!" She thought a moment and then said, "They are the most shameless smugglers there, and thieves."

The driver drew his hat down over his face and stared at the ruins of the Alamo.

Simon laughed. "Well, I guess we came to America and took up honest work. And so I suppose I must say goodbye. Until next time." Simon put on his hat, stood back when the driver lifted the reins. Touched his hat brim. But then he said, stepping forward again, "And so, your father wept when you left."

The driver rolled his eyes and lowered the reins again. He searched in his pockets for tobacco, stuffed a pipe, and lit it.

Yes he had, he was not a man afraid to cry, and her mother beside him waving. Like the rest she crowded the stern to see her father and mother and Ireland fading away into a faint blue shadow on the sea and then gone. Her employment with the Webbs was arranged beforehand with an agent in Waterford. She had sailed to New York City and then went with the family on a far journey into the enormity of the United States, to Ohio, a city called Columbus, full of astonishing wealth, farmers owning seven, eight cows and a hundred acres, two hundred! Webb was stationed there at Camp Thomas to be the man of administration for the 18th U.S. Infantry. A man of paperwork and account books. A year and a half there and she had only begun to learn her way about and then he was sent to Texas. She herself had had a night of very fearful thoughts, visions of Red Indians and bloody scalping, but in some way it was stirring, like an old epic, and the land open, in a way it was like those large final chords that came at the end of a piece. In this country there seemed to be no grand people, no making always the diminutives at the end of every word.

And then, there Simon was at the military dinner asking what song she would like to hear, and there he was again, playing "Death and the Sinner" as they drove away.

"I remember you," said Josephina. She stared at Simon with a cold, impersonal look. "They said you went around collecting money afterward. I remember your face."

Simon didn't smile but stared back. "That's right," he said. "You have a good memory."

The girl said, "Oh, men find Miss Dillon very attractive, don't they?"

Simon said nothing. The girl shrugged and sank back into her shawl. Doris and Mercedes glanced at each other because of this sudden dissonance and were unsure how to smooth it over.

The driver lifted his reins and said, "Welp . . ."

Simon quickly wished the ladies good evening, bowed, and hurried inside to collect his money and put his fiddle in the case.

He and Damon were engaged to play at seven at the Horde Hotel. He barely made it in time. Pruitt showed up with a bleeding ear dripping onto his yellow-and-purple-striped shirt. He had again been in some kind of fight in an alleyway, in a dive on San Saba Street with bad whiskey and bad lighting, sinister people. He slumped into a chair just inside the doorway with his face lowered. It chilled Simon, the way he looked upward from his light eyes.

"Get on your feet," he called to him. "We've got work to do."

Pruitt glanced behind himself at the door, at some imaginary enemy, and got up and rolled the bodhran in front of him, down the floor to the stage with expert kicks. Damon shook his head slowly, shoved out a chair, and said to him,

"Sit down, tighten up. Your drum head's slack. Jesus."

Simon lay that night in his attic bed up above the Plaza Hotel and a vision of open grasslands took him by force as he lay naked in the warmth, his eyes closed, drifting into sleep. The sky over these grasslands was streaked with the fire of blue lightning. Rain coming. Beasts with horns and piebald sides strolled over the world of grass with untroubled strides as if at home, as if they had each one been made there by God Himself out of red clay and shining silicate dust and had been given minds that were constructed of unknown songs telling them of every decline and every waterhole. On a planet meant for them and those who loved them. It was here that he and Doris Dillon seemed to have made a house of red stone, far away from the intrigues of cities. Far from dissonances and the chaos human beings could create in their own lives. He would wake up now every morning of the world with her beside him. The wind entered this house through the open windows, where they stood together, and it circled every room to sweep away all misery and all doubt. Her long hair lifted and fell and was resonant with harmonics like an instrument of a million strings.

CHAPTER TWENTY-TWO

WHEN SHE GAVE LESSONS at the Duerler home at San Pedro Springs, he was asked to come once again. It was a long walk to the north side of the city. It was a house of tall windows and white walls, Swiss landscapes in ornate frames, an old square Bechstein piano of only four octaves. He stood at her left shoulder and watched her small hands stretch to cover six notes, seven, failed on eight.

"Simon?" she said. "Are we ready then?"

"Yes, yes."

He lifted his bow to the strings for "Beautiful Dreamer" and could barely follow it. Three or four young girls still in pigtails, including Josephina, ran screaming and laughing through the room, calling to one another while the older women sat with coffee cups and tried to follow the syrupy romantic strains of the music. The girls' voices trailed away outside with more screams concerning the ducks of the lake waddling toward them with glittering duck eyes, intent on violence and muggery.

Simon and Doris looked around for Mrs. Webb, saw she was not within sight, and then they dared to walk off by themselves among the tall pecan trees, telling each other of their likes and dislikes, of their favorite songs, of what they did all day, what they thought of at night when they could not sleep ("You." "You.") and of the chaotic household of the Webbs. He held her hand, turned it over in his, saw the several small pricks of a needle in her fingertips, knew she had been sewing, wondered what.

The Duerlers had made gardens and pools alongside the springs. They walked on, down the course of the creek and the miracle of a spring-fed stream in an arid country, among tall pecan trees now leafless. Smoke drifted through the branches from a nearby charcoal-burner's kiln. They climbed up a shoulder of limestone and down the other side. He watched while she came down sideways. He saw she wore no hoops. Good. She finally stood and beat the leaves and dirt from her hems.

"You are making yourself a traveling dress," Simon said, and lifted the bits of thread from her sleeve. "And you are wearing patterned stockings. I like them."

"Oh hush!" She took off her hat and batted at a droning deer fly.

"When we are married you'll have a riding suit. We'll have to find you a sidesaddle."

She smiled at him and tipped her head. "Tell me, what do people do to get married in Texas?"

"What I've just done this morning." He opened his coat and drew a folded paper from his shirt pocket. "They take out a marriage license at the courthouse, also known as the Bat Cave, you see here." He held it out to her. "And it has our names on it and then we take this and go before a Justice of the Peace at first and then later we'll figure it out about the priest."

She took the paper and read it. "Oh my God, Simon!"

"And then we leave for the Red River Valley."

"Simon, this is . . . well faith, you've . . . this is my name here!"

"I know, it's shocking. Sudden. This was in case you still

doubted me." He bent forward and kissed her on the lips. Kissed her again.

A small hesitation and then she kissed him back, on the lips, a soft, light kiss, and laughed at herself, at her own boldness. In a way the kiss astonished him so that he was blank-faced and suspended for an instant, then placed his hand alongside her cheek, drew her to him.

She said, into his coat lapels, "It would be breaking a contract. I have another half year to go. I signed. What would happen to me?"

"He broke the contract, Doris." Simon tried to think. The military had its own justice system he knew, but what their rules and laws were he had no idea. "Surely he has broken it, with his behavior, pursuing you, laying his *hand* on you, it can't be ethical to hold you to a contract, it can't be."

"No, but . . ."

"Once we are married there is nothing he can do."

He sat down on an outcropping of the sandy-colored limestone and drew her down to sit before him, between his knees. He watched the shimmering surface of the clear round spring, rested his chin on the crown of her head.

"And I will be the best man I can be within my power. You are all I want. I have not been a perfect saint. Someday I will make my confessions to you."

He put his arms around her and she held his hands in her own. She said, "Oh, confess. Tell me now. Everything."

"Everything," he repeated, buying time, and was glad she could not see his face. "Well. Some losses, some gains." He fought for words. He was a musician not a storyteller, not eloquent. After a long hesitation he said, "I never started a fight. I have not. But I've finished a lot of them. This comes from playing in saloons and waterfront dives." He felt her body between his knees, her narrow shoulders. "They always seem to go for the fiddler."

"Aye, they do."

Well, he had got that out of the way. He saw the faint winter wind move the loose wisps of her hair, her black drop earrings. She smelled of citrus and starch and girl. "Needs," he said. He paused again. "Desires. Also called lust. It can drive a man." He took several deep breaths through his nostrils. "But from the time I saw you I put this aside, because I knew you would ask me. Because I wanted you."

"Yes," she said, and then was silent again.

"I saw people with a mother and a father both when I was growing up and I always wondered, I don't know, what it would be like. My mother died when I was five, maybe just turned six. My father was a fiddler too and he left my mother before I was born. I was raised by my great-uncle, who is a man I love very much, I respect him very much. He took me in as easy as if I had been born to him. We had the big horse business in Paducah and it was burned down in the war. I think maybe I still own it, what's left of it. I doubt if even the fences are standing. I was raised with horses and men." He bent his head down and laid his cheek on her head. "Horses and horsemen and Ohio Valley fiddlers."

She was silent, holding his hands in a loose and gentle grip. All around them the pecan forest rang with the sound of birds that always flock to water in an arid country, the chirring sound of some animal calling to another of its kind. The spring pool smoked and steamed in the cold.

Finally she said, "You come from good people, Simon."

"We have done our damnedest. Over time. And so I want to make it up . . . I mean, what I never had. I mean what my mother and father never had. Between them. I want two people to be in love and stay in love and never desert each other. I want this to happen." He closed his eyes. "I love you. I want you to be with me always."

He felt near tears.

Then she said quietly, "Simon."

He said, "I don't quit."

"Yes. I know."

He lifted her hand on the palm of his right one, saw the tiny gold ring on her little finger. "There are of course all the details. But you don't want to know all the details. If we all knew one another's lives in all the details nobody would marry anybody."

She laughed, bending forward. "Nay, 'tis true, all so true." She leaned back against him. "Someday you will tell me the details. Are there a lot?"

"Yes. There are. And you?"

"Oh dear, yes. We stole Sister Angela's whiskey and drank it all. Us girls."

"Doris, you are going to hell."

"We already did! The next morning I wished I could die. I have rarely touched a drop since then, Simon, it was horrible."

"What were nuns doing with whiskey?"

He felt her laughter. "They were Irish."

And then they were simply silent together, thinking of all that had been said, watching the impudent titmice with their dark pointy heads glide down to the water. She had not answered. He knew he must wait, be quiet and wait.

Then she turned to him and laid her warm hand on his thigh without the least idea of the effect it had on him.

"He is coming in the surrey to take us home. We have to get back."

He stood up, quickly, and her hand slid away.

"And is it better at home?" They made their way along the bank of the spring and then on the return path.

"No, no, I am at my wit's end. It's worse than a play at the theater, people flouncing in, flouncing out, screeching. "

"Tell me the rest of it. The details."

And she told him more, and worse; that she now locked herself in her room, pushed a chair against the doorknob, was never without the company of the girl or Mrs. Webb or Mercedes. She told him about the colonel's winks and whispers. They well knew what was going on, they did indeed. Simon kept his peace; one more word about doing violence to Webb would silence her on the matter once and for all. And so in revenge the colonel was beginning to cry out in irritation at Doris's going here and going there to give lessons, to play at receptions, garden parties, musical events, taking Josephina along. That Mrs. Webb had shouted back at him that the girl needed some culture, some education, would he send her to the Catholic nuns, the Papists, at St. Mary's?

"I could tell you about their arguments, if you like, word for word. I hear them from every place in the house." She suddenly put a hand over her face, then straightened and wiped her palm on her skirt. "Oh, look at me. I don't have a handkerchief. I gave it to Jo."

He took out his own, recently purchased, perfectly clean, and held it out to her. She wiped at her eyes and calmed down, turned her bonnet over and over in her hands. "Maybe it would be best if I went back to Ireland."

"No," he said. "God, no."

"I almost have my fare home. From Galveston to Portsmouth. I would be away from the unhappiness every day, every day." She put the bonnet on her head and let the ribbons fall untied on her shoulders. Then she was taken up in a struggle not to cry, and she actually wrung her hands together. Simon was so moved by her distress that he could barely speak.

"You have to leave that house." He put his hand on her cheek. "To somewhere. Even if not with me. What about Mercedes?"

"Yes. I know." She made that nervous little nod of her head.

"She and her husband would take me in if it came to the worst of it."

"And I have the four hundred acres if I can hold it, and my fiddle and my two hands."

"If you can hold it?"

"It is in Comanche raiding territory. But it will change. The army is patrolling there now."

She said, "I am not afraid, Simon. You have no idea what it was like in Ireland." She made a shooting motion with one hand. "The secret societies shooting the landlord's men from behind the sheep walls." She pulled a spiny twig from her skirt. "The landlord's men are probably worse by far than the Comanches or the Webb household." She shook out his handkerchief and then tucked it into his coat pocket.

He smiled. "Maybe."

"At least you are allowed to fight back."

"I want you safe," he said. "You will be safe."

It suddenly occurred to him that traveling by wagon would be a pleasant life, for a while, going from town to town, always a new place to play his fiddle. In his imagination he was riding at the head of two or three wagons, filled with people who could play various instruments. But when the land was paid off, when he had bought a vehicle of some kind and a horse, he would be penniless again and dependent on his music. He was asking her to marry poverty and homeless wandering, at least for the first while and that on a remote frontier. The contrast with these fine homes in San Antonio would be stark.

He looked down in momentary discouragement. Then he remembered that nobody in any of these fine homes had started life with ease. None of them. He lifted his head and reached out to lay his hand along her neck and ran his thumb along the line of her jaw. "Be with me. Stay with me."

"Simon." She lifted one hand and placed it on his cheek. "I have never met anyone like you."

They stood at the base of an enormous cypress whose root system flowed like lava over the stone layers and into the water of San Pedro Springs.

"Make a life with me." He closed his hand around her wrist.

She took a great long breath of air that sounded as if she were about to plunge headfirst into a pool of cold water. She raised her head to him. "I will, then, Simon."

He stood with her hands between his, bent to press his forehead against hers, his eyes closed, listening to the whitewings call, listening to them as they fell out of the air and to the water's edge. Now the trouble would begin.

ALL THE WAY home in the surrey Colonel Webb was silent and so were they—herself and Mrs. Webb. Josephina was singing some song to herself. By this time Doris knew that the colonel was turning every event of the day over and over in his unstable brain. Perhaps it was cunning or perhaps merely demented. Merely. Her mouth was dry and her hands jerked with involuntary movements in the fear somebody had seen her and Simon walking together among the pecan trees and the ravens floating above, spying. In hopeless tones Mrs. Webb tried to talk about the afternoon at San Pedro Springs, very refined, how lovely it was, how everyone had admired Doris's playing and how Mr. Duerler was certainly, *certainly* impressed. She was met with an ominous silence.

The colonel wanted a tirade to please the devil that possessed him and so he would have it. The Webb house was shut up with closed windows and lamps turned low. He gathered them all in the long parlor for a lecture on decorum, on loyalty, on respect. He strode back and forth. He never stopped, even when he lifted up a short thick glass of amber whiskey, sipped at it, and returned to his obsessive accusations.

"Josephina has told me many things, Doris, many interesting things about your behavior. She has been embarrassed to be seen with you. She is humiliated by your conduct." He turned a cold face to her. Mrs. Webb tossed her head in a theatrical gesture of contempt. Josephina twirled her braid over her shoulder and wound the tail of it around her finger and stared at Doris with wide blank eyes.

Doris sat in confused silence. She was seated on a low stool with her skirts crumpled around her. They were in the parlor off the long room, that room which was for receptions, for display, and nearly empty because the Webbs did not have enough furniture for it, so it rang with echoes like a barn. This was the most beautiful house Doris had ever lived in, but she would have given every cent she had and the hair on her head besides to get out of it and be free of the Webbs, who were all worse than Lord Dennys himself for haughtiness and drink.

"She says you have been sneaking out at night to go to the Mexican fandangos in the houses along Camaron Street, you have been dancing with the Mexican men in the most abandoned ways."

Doris's mouth dropped open. She said, "Excuse me?"

"Yes, yes." He smiled. It was a grim smile. "She has told me that you go about with some traveling musician whose name nobody seems to know, you sneak off to commit indiscretions in the woods. You are seen with Lieutenant Whittaker talking and chatting in Military Plaza when you go to the market with Mercedes. You lay your hand on his arm, you go into saloons with him. That you drink whiskey there and come out in an embarrassing condition. *This* is what you are doing with that money you earn. From now on, you will turn your earnings over to me."

Josephina stared off into the distance of the hallway and

shrugged. And then she turned and smirked at Doris Dillon of Ireland, holding in her child's heart a sordid treasury of secret thoughts.

Doris sat in a stunned and empty silence for a long moment. "You can't believe that."

"Not believe my own *daughter*?"

He is truly mad. Lunatic. And now apparently Josephina has taken it from him like a disease.

"You have the right of it," she said. "Not believe your own daughter."

"Doris!" Mrs. Webb was in a state of shock.

"Be quiet!" Webb paced up and down again in front of his captive audience. He addressed some cohort of spectators not present but both knowing and eager, moving restlessly at the edge of his mind. "She has brought *shame* on this family, *shamed* us in front of everybody, just bold as brass, impudent, what insolence, never have I! Right in front of the whole town!"

Mrs. Webb regarded Doris with a lofty distaste but behind it was dread of more of the same in years to come and for a second Doris was sorry for her and her precarious existence, but she had other matters to deal with. She glanced over at Josephina, who had dropped her braid and turned to running her hems through her fingers as if searching for a loose place and then the girl turned a contemptuous face to her. Doris ignored the pain this caused her; she put it away quickly.

"You should apologize for your behavior," said Mrs. Webb. Hoping that he would accept it and they could all get away from him and go to their rooms. Except poor Mrs. Webb had to sleep in the same bed with him. *Enjoy your bed of thorns.*

But for now they were siding with him, with whatever his mood might be, and this was out of fear, perhaps. No, certainly out of fear. *That's the thanks I get,* Doris thought. *Seeing to the cooking and the meals, I should have poisoned you all.* The lamplight glittered on the cut-glass tumblers and the decanter that Mrs. Webb had cherished and wrapped in muslin, shipped from one army post to another, guarded against breakage to be placed on white linen as signs and signals of their station in life. Upstairs creaking noises; Mercedes creeping to the landing to listen down the stairwell.

Doris looked down demurely, thinking of her choices. Another one of these evenings of great raving tirades she would not be able to endure, not one more. Especially this one; Josephina's imaginative lies had broken through some border of decency, even rational thought. It had been bad enough in Ohio, but since then the colonel's drinking had increased, month by month, glass by glass, and bottle by bottle.

"An apology wouldn't be good enough, Miss Dillon! Not good enough! Every family in this town is most likely thinking that we are harboring some abandoned hussy straight out of an immigrant ship and didn't we give you a roof and clothes and food? Did we not? Did we not?"

He turned around to regard the windows and then at the door to the hall. Again he seemed to be stepping about in a kind of dance, a strut, looking for the invisible audience and its applause and the cause of this was the drink and its rivers carving their way through the brain. His heavy, uncharitable face.

She wanted to say *And so?* Or *The more fool you.* But she said, "Indeed." It was dark outside. Despite her insubordinate thoughts she was tattering in some way because of Josephina. This time she felt like crying. She must not cry in front of this maniac.

"Oh indeed, she says, indeed!" He paused to drink and to gather his wits. He filled his glass again and looked at the three females as if to be sure he was the absolute center of attention, like a dark sun and them all moving around him in captive orbits.

"Yes, sir, and I shall say more, because . . ."

"Oh no you will not. You just stepped right out to go for a carriage ride with that insubordinate Lieutenant Whittaker. By yourselves! Everybody saw this, this display, and then some local musician, a redheaded fiddler, flaunting yourself with some low-class clown! And now, and now, we have to give an evening dance for Commissioner Davis, he's on the Constitutional Committee itself, I am being asked to be his host, an honor, an honor, it will be costly and I have allowed Mrs. Webb a sufficient amount and I am telling you, if you make an exhibit of yourself at that occasion you will regret it to your dying day."

He jerked his chin and stared about again at his unseen spectators. Ghosts and admirers.

He picked up the decanter and poured the last of the whiskey. "We'll have music for Commissioner Davis's reception because Mrs. Webb has asked to find the musicians, a dance, she wanted a dance, very well, she has asked in the most graceful and polite ways, you see. She must get them at a low price and she will. And now I tell you, you will conduct yourself with propriety at this event, no dancing, not with Lieutenant Whittaker or anyone, one moment of impudence out of you and you are out on the street."

Doris stared down at her clasped hands. She was relieved that his suspicions had lighted for the most part on Whittaker. She knew it was not about the lieutenant or fandangos, it was some terrible pleasure it gave him that they were forced to sit and listen, turn on one another, appease. The devil was on him and making him dance in rage. She had a wordless vision of freedom, she and Simon standing on the bank of some river. A wide sky with cirrus like horses' manes.

"You will not see any young men, not now and not as long as you are under my roof. You will not go about dancing in fandangos or dancing anywhere, you will not be seen in any of the saloons and drinking establishments, you will not humiliate this family further by your vile behavior, or you will be out on the street in short order."

Doris said, "Colonel Webb, she made it up. Surely you don't believe that."

Josephina dropped both hands into her lap, hung her head, and burst into tears. She said, "Oh, the girls are all talking about you!" She wiped the tears away. "I can't stand it. They're laughing about you!"

From this she understood it was Josephina herself who had been talking about her, spinning these wild tales of her dancing in fandangos and sporting about in saloons. She looked over at the child she had cared so much for and knew that fourteen-year-old girls will believe whatever they hear as long as it is scandalous and saw Jo's slyness, her abandoned knowledge. The colonel would believe it as well, as by now his brains were fixed in whiskey like some scientific specimen preserved in a bottle of spirits.

But he meant it about throwing her out and he could do it. Doris felt her heart fail, briefly, start up again. Then she did the unthinkable. For this family it was unthinkable. She stood up and said, "Very well, I have heard enough. I am going to my room."

"What?" Mrs. Webb and Josephina looked up, staring at her. Webb cried out, "I'll be Goddamned if you will!" He slammed his glass down on the sideboard.

Doris gathered her skirts. "I shall not spend another moment listening while you drink and rant. I was raised with kind and loving parents. I know what is right and good." She knew this sounded schoolmarmish but she had no other words; she turned and moved toward the door with her skirts in both hands.

"Just stop right there young woman!" he cried, and Mrs. Webb said, "How dare you! Speak like that to your employer!" And Josephina cried out, "Ha ha!"

She hurried down the hall, toward the steep stairs. Another set of stairs up to the little attic where she lived. Up there Mercedes had made her pallet to spend the night. House-cleaning was tomorrow early. She had likely been listening to every word. Colonel Webb darted down the hall behind Doris, crying in a low voice, "You just stop right there, Miss Dillon, I am not finished. I am not finished. You are going to sit and listen to what I have to say."

Doris turned with her back to the stairwell.

"Don't you lay a hand on me," she said. "I will fight you."

Mrs. Webb came behind him and had begun to cry. "Oh Franklin, please, please let it go!"

Doris had been through these scenes now at least a thousand times. They were witless and without end. They were predictable and they always had the same progression. He drinks and then he rants, he threatens. Mrs. Webb cries and blames either Doris or Josephina for "setting him off." Then he sets off; drunk on his performance. Then somebody gets up to leave. Then Mrs. Webb breaks into tears. Over and over. They were dimwitted wights, all three of them.

Colonel Webb turned on his wife and this gave Doris one or two seconds to turn and run up the stairs, shoot into her room, and slam the door behind her.

SIMON BOUGHT AN ancient surrey from old man Cassiano, who had it sitting behind the feed store. Cats had taken it over and were comfortable on the plush seats and were living well on the scraps from the neighboring Central Hotel saloon. Simon lay down on his back, wriggled beneath the surrey and checked the undercarriage, the tie-rods, the bolsters, the hounds. It seemed all the parts were good and it would not fall apart on the way to the Red River.

That took a hundred dollars, and then he paid down thirty dollars on a harness, twenty-five owed.

He had not wanted Doris to simply escape, leave, bolt, flee. But the thought of being with her out in the wide world, free to speak and go where they would, had taken over him entirely. They would find the Justice of the Peace in Helotes within the day—there was time for a priest later.

Later, later, it seemed later would never come. Every hour was like pig iron. He bought a hardy little pony that had been stabled at Corrigan's. When he ran his hands over the small horse the livery owner said he might be a little troubled with his eyesight in the right eye. Simon made several feints with one hand toward that side of his head and said,

"No, sir, he's totally blind in that eye."

"Well, that could be true. But now he's a strong fellow, I guarantee you. Sound as a dollar."

Simon led him out with a halter into Main Plaza and the little horse bounced from hoof to hoof in his happiness to be out of the stall, anxious to show he could work, that he was strong and didn't miss that eye in the least, not in the least. He had a brave small toss of his head as if in hope that he would be released from his stinking horse yard, his uncleaned stall that smelled of old horse piss. That someone might buy him, that they might go to far places and walk out into grass and clean water. Simon vaulted onto his back and returned to Corrigan's bareback with only a halter and was pleased with him. Because of his blind right eye Simon paid only eighty dollars for him.

She would want to know his name and so he asked. It was Tupelo and Tupelo the little brassy bay stared after him with his one eye in despair as Simon paid his money and walked away. There is no way you can tell them you will be back, that it was all going to be all right, and so the little horse slowly returned to his hay, his ears flopped down in discouragement. Between paying his money to Twohig's on the mortgage and buying the horse, buggy, and harness he was down to a few dollars and still owed twenty-five on the harness, but that's how his life had always been and he had made it this far hadn't he?

He would meet her on the Losoya Street bridge within a week, no longer, and they would elope, that exciting, romantic, and dashing course of action they would tell their grandchildren about. Tales of valor and undying love.

CHAPTER TWENTY-THREE

THE NEXT AFTERNOON AN invitation was handed to Simon by a black corporal. The man touched his hat to Simon and then left the saloon, stepping over the mop bucket.

Simon broke the seal open. It was from the Webb residence; he tried to shut down his heart rate but then saw it was not from Doris Dillon but from Colonel Webb. Then his heart started hammering again.

Having heard of your excellent music, sir, this is a request for your group to play for a tea-dance at the residence of Colonel Webb on February 24th at seven in the evening held in honor of Commissioner Davis's visit to San Antonio. Colonel Webb is prepared to pay the equivalent amount that your group would earn in one night at the Plaza House Hotel. Please reply if this is satisfactory. Mrs. Franklin Webb.

Damon took it from Simon and read it. The bell in the cathedral tower rang out five o'clock and a man drove along the alleyway singing *When first into this country, a stranger I came, I courted a fair maid, Nancy was her name . . .*

Damon said, "An invitation to disaster."

"No," said Simon in an abstracted voice. "She's invited us because we're the popular players of the moment, she probably doesn't remember me from Fort Brown. Never knew my name. Sure as hell doesn't know about me and Doris." He folded the message carefully. "We've got to get clothes cleaned." He smiled and a sly, calculating happiness shone in his face. "In two more days."

"Commissioner *Davis,*" said Damon. "The feckless scoundrel." Then after a pause, "She'll be there. Catastrophes await."

"Nah." Simon wafted across the saloon floor toward the rear, thinking about a hot bath, a haircut, the names of waltzes.

THE NOISES OF town were now beginning to jar Simon's thoughts like tinning hammers. It was time to go. Time to pull on his Kentucky hat and shake out the old checkered shirt. On the Plaza House stage he tacked up the set list on a music stand and set it to one side, where Damon could glance at it. Then shouts came from the kitchen. Both of them ran back to find Pruitt in an argument with one of the delivery men. It was about a banjo or the condition of a banjo or its price, who knew? Pruitt held it in one hand; the neck was separating from the resonator and stuck out at an angle. Pruitt was swearing a long fizzling hot streak at the man.

"What the blue painted fuck is this?" he yelled. He shook the damaged banjo in the man's face.

He had a filthy mouth, he had shown up more than once with a torn collar, he drifted always toward the prostitutes who came to sit on the left side of the door in their dresses with dirty hems and spotted bodices, eating roasted peanuts.

Damon jumped between the two. The banjo was thrown to the

kitchen floor. The delivery man shook a fist at Pruitt and at the same time backed out the rear kitchen door, groping for the sill with his foot.

Damon said, "Pruitt, shut up."

Pruitt turned a long, slow calculating stare at both of them. "Trying to get a Goddamned banjo so I could play at this dance coming up." Then he spun around and snatched up a paring knife as he did so and stalked toward the delivery man. Damon stepped forward, Simon came behind him and laid hold of Pruitt's wrist while Damon twisted the knife from his hand. In the brief, sharp struggle the delivery man fled.

Pruitt shouted, "You son of a bitch . . ."

"One more time and you're gone," Simon said. "Do you hear me?"

Simon faced Pruitt down and stood until he turned away. Simon thought how he was wading through sludge to get to Doris, knee-deep in turmoil, insane people, one emotional cripple after another. Would it ever end, how would it end?

AT THE WEBB house, they found the dais where they were to play at the end of what was called the long room. The stand seemed fairly solid underfoot, covered with a flowery carpet. They came in when the ladies were still hurrying around laying out the refreshments on small tables against the walls, a cool evening outside. The whitewing doves fluttered down to the riverside with their heart-shaped cries and the bats of city hall began to stretch their wings and yawn. Simon's mouth went dry when he saw her come in the door of the salon. She was wearing a dark green dress with a low bodice. No hat; a white flower of some kind in her hair over one ear.

"Oh, how wonderful, here's our fiddler," Doris said in a low voice, a smile, a quick curtsey.

"Yes, here he is!" Mrs. Webb cast about herself distractedly.

"Put more of that there. Don't be so loud. You have a loud voice, Doris."

Simon bowed to the girl and looked into her eyes. "Good evening, Mrs. Webb, Miss Dillon."

He heard murmurs of the same from Damon and Pruitt.

"Yes," said the colonel's wife. She was inspecting all the silver sugar bowls. "More here, Doris." Then she raised her head to Simon, acknowledging him at last. "Oh," she said. A silence. "You're the fiddler that . . ." She seemed frozen with the silver in her hands and a napkin slid from her arm. "You . . . ," she started and then stopped. It was too late to get anybody else and even with conflict and misery staring her in the face she recovered. "You have the list?"

"Yes, ma'am," said Damon. He handed it to her and she bent over it.

"All very good. What is this 'Blarney Pilgrim'? This says 'jig.' I don't want any jigging to go on."

Simon turned to Damon and said, "Strike it." Damon opened his eyes very wide, reached for the list, then wet his thumb and smeared the ink and then wiped his thumb on his pants. He smiled wide-eyed at Miss Dillon and then winked in a great laborious contraction of one side of his face. A laugh burst out of her and then she put her hand over her mouth and looked down, still laughing. Mrs. Webb took the list again, stood beside Simon resolutely going over every song, and said, "Doris, stop that wretched giggling, would you please? Now, this fellow here, this fellow with the round drum, can he keep time?" She was flustered and asking stupid questions, angry, a little desperate. An angled and unstable kind of wrongness had come over her elaborate evening, this fiddler apparently the one accused of going about with Doris, too late, too late.

"Of *course,*" said Damon.

Pruitt turned his long, dull gaze to Mrs. Webb. "No," he said. "I just carry this drum around for looks."

"He can, yes," said Simon. He turned to Doris. "He will or I will strangle him." Doris put a finger to her lips in a shushing motion and tried not to laugh again, and then quickly picked up a tray of miniature butter cakes, paused, and, not knowing what to do with it, placed it pointlessly on another table.

"Oh!" Mrs. Webb tossed her head. "A sense of humor! We are all overcome with laughter!"

Colonel Webb came in with the cold air of the outdoors still about him and took off his hat. He poured himself a drink from the sideboard, tipped the glass up, emptied it, and set it down on the sideboard again. He stood in the middle of the room in order to be the cynosure of all eyes and gazed around himself with a slight smile. He saw Simon and his mouth dropped open. After a second's silence the colonel walked up to him.

"You're the fiddler from Los Palmitos," he said. His eyes widened a little. He was thinking, slowly but with great precision. "By God you are."

"Yes, sir."

"I forget who you were with."

Simon almost said, *I forget too,* but he didn't. "Thirty-fourth Indiana, band. I played G whistle on march."

"I'll be damned if you were. You were with Giddings. We never had any whistle players. You are an outright liar."

"Sir?" said Simon. Damon quietly stepped close to the two of them and pressed an elbow against Simon's side. "Sir, think of what you just said."

"I know what I just said. You came around begging for money after that dinner. You speak like a Southerner."

Damon gestured with his whistle. "Yes, Colonel, but people in southern Indiana speak like Kentuckians. Just across the river there."

"Who asked you?" Webb turned one way and then another as anger and suspicion grew in him. "My wife invited you to play here at this dance, but I swear there have been rumors of some irregularity involving a young person of my household and yourself going about to low whiskey houses. How did you get invited? She must have been out of her mind. Or misinformed. Or temporarily lunatic." His voice was rising.

"Colonel, Colonel." His wife floated up to him on the balloon of her hoop skirt. "The governor will be here before long. Watch your language please. The governor will be here. Please let us not have any ill manners and arguing, *please*."

Webb's eyes raked over his wife and past her and around the elegant decorations of the ballroom; he cleared his throat noisily, his face red. He glared at Simon, a look of both fury and indignation. Finally, with an effort, he turned away. "This is not worth my attention. Play your waltzes and stay onstage, fiddler." He strolled across the floor and began inspecting the tall windows. "There's specks on here. This glass is dirty. Why?"

Then he peered at the chairs against the wall and finally the silver tea sets, pretending indifference to the musicians, and came to stand beside Doris as she lifted one cube after another with silver tongs.

Simon rosined his bow slowly, watching. Webb stood too close to her. He wanted everybody to see him standing too close to her. He wanted Simon in particular to see him standing pressed up against the girl, bending over her. Carriages were pulling up outside with a *pocketa pocketa* sound of iron wheel rims on the gravel driveway, harnesses jangling. Doris moved away from the colonel and his hand shot out to take her elbow.

"You've tripped on your hem," he said.

"Indeed I have not." She flushed a bright pink and jerked her elbow away. Simon started to step down off the little stage, but Damon shot one arm out straight and thumped it backhanded across his stomach. Simon could almost hear his heart, it was almost a sound, a thickened bloody thudding. Mrs. Webb saw the colonel too, turned quickly with a stiff face, and said,

"Colonel, let go of the girl's arm, we must be in the hall to greet the guests." Then she hurried out ahead of him, pressing down her skirts at the sides as her hoops swung dangerously.

Soon the long room was filled with people circulating and greeting, swinging bells of hoops, military men in dress uniforms and businessmen in frock coats, one with the newest fashion in ties called a four-in-hand. Colonel Webb greeted Commissioner Davis, shaking his hand wildly, smiling. A man spoke urgently to Davis about being appointed county commissioner for San Antonio, another wanted a place as the postmaster, a thick man with a red face spoke of his gratitude for Davis's help in being named as sheriff, and the sheer volume of people talking rose to intolerable levels.

From the corner of his eye Simon saw the spare blond lieutenant who used to be a sergeant standing nearby, his hat in his hands. He had a vague expression, as if wondering where to put it. *Avoid that man,* Simon told himself, *if at all possible. He will remember you and the shirts and asking about Doris.* He turned away and they began the slow airs, one after another. After "Lonesome Boatman" Damon said in a low voice,

"'Blarney Pilgrim,' real, real *real* slow."

Simon laughed and said, "Do it"; and so they played it slow as a funeral march and could hardly keep straight faces as they did so.

The evening moved on; men went outside to confer with other men over bottles hidden in carriage footwells while Commissioner

Davis, who was bright and sparkling and seemed to be possessed of, or possessed by, an unending fountain of nerves and energy, talked without pause about Republican affairs and business affairs, great futures, shining horizons, the greatness awaiting Austin if only they could get the streets paved, about limitless opportunities, the Printing Bill, Negro schools, powerful committees, fearsome enemies lurking, Freedman's Bureau money, printing money, more cruel enemies lurking even more, days to come, pasts crushed under heels. Simon watched Doris when he could; she kept out of sight, shaking hands with guests and pouring tea. The lieutenant was bending to speak to her, smiling. In her dark green she seemed a lithe and velvety spirit balancing dire trouble in either hand. She nodded politely as he spoke, but her eyes flicked to the colonel.

A black man in a white coat began to move all the chairs against the wall and Simon knew it was time for the waltzes.

He lifted his bow and sailed into "Lucy's Waltz," slowly and carefully. To open the dance, Colonel Webb led Mrs. Webb to the emptied floor and they stepped out. The son of a bitch was a smooth dancer, Simon had to give him that. Commissioner Davis and his wife followed. Simon made his fiddle sing. No double-stopping. Clear notes of melody; *come and dance,* the melody said. *Glide and circle, take flight.* When the floor was full and crowded, when Davis and Webb and their wives had left the floor and half the men were half drunk he turned to Pruitt and held out his fiddle.

"See what you can do with 'Moonlight Waltz.'"

"Me?" Pruitt was alarmed.

"To whom am I speaking?" Simon gazed around the dais left and right.

"Just do it," Damon told Pruitt. "And shut up."

Simon stepped down from the dais and went straight to Doris Dillon. She stood demurely against the wall with her hands clasped in front of her. The white flower stood out against her black hair, the dark green dress showed off her white throat and arms. It was low in front. He put both hands behind his back and bowed and then held out his hand with the palm up as if he held there another waltz, and inside that another. It was hers to take, hers to brush away.

"Would you dance with me, Miss Dillon?"

"Yes!"

She gave the slightest indication of a curtsey, and then looked neither left nor right but lifted her hand to his shoulder. He placed his hand on her waist, and together they moved out onto the floor. That first step into the waltz with the left foot is like a boat into the rapids of the music, the first step into a long slide down a snowy glorious slope. A door opens into a palace made of lamplight, where all the men are just and courageous and all the women are beautiful and wise. They were in faultless motion together, his hand closed on her waist and all those emerald skirts flying out, her head on his shoulder. He lowered his head without touching her but still so close. He took in her scent of freshly washed hair, lemon and gardenia.

"Miss Dillon," he said. "Doris."

"We are in trouble," she said.

"I don't care, I don't care."

She gripped his hand tightly. She did not even see the other dancers. Moments like this in life are few. Very few. The music went on forever and ever and they moved from hesitation to sureness and then to a future between them, whatever that might be. All the tall windows were dark and swarming with the reflections of thirty dancers and floating skirts and the heartbeat pace of the waltz.

Simon put his mouth close to her ear and said, "Say when. No more delay, no more dithering. We will be married in the next town."

"Oh my God."

"Say when."

"In two nights. I will send a note by Mercedes."

"Yes," said Simon. "In two nights then."

"And you made a promise to me. You would not engage with Colonel Webb."

"In fisticuffs, no."

"Or shooting," she said.

"Or stabbing. Or drowning. I made a promise."

The colonel at last looked up from his inundation of words by Commissioner Davis and saw them; his face went blank with fury. The waltz cranked on, barely in the possession of Pruitt. It was getting away from him. Damon manfully fluted the harmonies and the timing in his ear.

At last it ended. Colonel Webb stared at them for a long time and then turned to talk to someone beside him.

Simon bowed; Doris curtsied. He returned to the dais, took back his instrument, and began to play "Death and the Sinner."

Now there would be trouble. He missed notes, played the A part three times. Damon picked up for him, playing amazing complications and arabesques on his C whistle. Colonel Webb remained in the room, talking, gesticulating, and always near Commissioner Davis. The dreadful Pruitt managed the rhythm well enough and at last the dancers fell to fanning themselves near the windows. It was eleven o'clock and so now it was time for the guests to go. Doris glanced at Simon once, smiled, and then took up her skirts and disappeared down the hall.

Webb came up to them as they were packing their instruments. Pruitt stood with the two pages of set lists in his hand. Simon blew the rosin from the bridge of his instrument, then looked up.

"Well," Webb said. "I am new to Texas. New to the South. I never heard of one of the musicians coming down from the stage in the middle of the performance to dance with one of the household maids." He nodded as if to himself. "No indeed. Never heard of it. Some strange new Southern custom."

Simon turned to him with both hands at his sides and looked him in the eye. He said, "Shocking, I know. I was overcome with admiration for your governess, Miss Dillon, and wished to dance a waltz with her."

Damon said in a low voice, "Simon."

Several other Union officers were nearby.

"I thought it was charming," one of them said.

"Why don't you shut up?" said Webb. The man flushed red and then turned on his heel and left. Two other officers quickly followed him. Mrs. Webb also sped out of the room, clearly from prior experience. Webb turned on Simon again. Damon stood stock-still, assessing the situation, and Pruitt gazed about with a wary look on his face.

Webb said, "It's very clear you are entertaining hopes of Miss Dillon. Aren't you? I am telling you, you are a common vagrant, and if you ever try to make contact with her I will have the sheriff take you up on charges. Any charge we can think of." He pulled at his coat front. "She is not for somebody like you, a tramp fiddler."

Simon turned pale but he kept his temper. He closed his fiddle case with a hard definitive snap like a gunshot. As far as Simon could tell Webb was not armed.

He said, "And so, who is she for then?"

"For someone certainly more refined, someone with a social position that doesn't involve common labor, and a tramp fiddler is common labor."

Simon closed his mouth tightly, thinking, *He said "common" about three times in a row.* Aloud he said, "And who are you to say who she can see and who she can't? I don't suppose you have consulted her in any way?"

Webb was silent for a moment and then he said, "Any more questions?"

Damon stepped up, whacking his whistle against his thigh in a nervous rhythm. "Yes. Where is our pay?" He was trying to change the conflict to one about money and not about Miss Dillon; money was safer, at this juncture, than love.

Colonel Webb glanced at Damon. "You don't deserve to be paid after that outrageous behavior." He stepped close to Simon and stabbed a finger into his lapel. "I did not pay you to come here and dance with the household help. She is not to flaunt herself about like a dance-hall girl. Not in my household."

Simon moved Webb's hand aside. "Don't do that," he said.

Damon was poised with the whistle in his hand and Pruitt stared, fascinated. "Simon, you made a promise," Damon said in a low voice.

Webb turned and shouted, "Thad!" A black man in a white coat came walking in at an extremely slow pace.

"Yes, sir?"

"Give me their money."

It was handed to him in a small, heavy cloth sack. Simon never took his eyes from Webb. Simon said, "And I want you to keep your hands off her."

"What did you say?" Webb gripped the sack. "An unbelievable lie! Your mind is in the gutter. The gutter. I'll be damned if I pay anybody to come here and say rubbish like this."

"It's not rubbish. You know it. And maybe your superior officers would want to hear about your accounts that don't add up."

Thad the doorman stood with his hands clasped in front of him and eyed Webb warily, with some fear, but he stayed where he was. He had clearly been through scenes like this before. Webb stared at Simon in a fixed way as if several conflicting thoughts were running through his mind.

"What the hell would you know about any accounts? You've been talking to her. She has lied to you. She's a pretty little liar. She's a little Irish demon." His hands moved restlessly as he shifted the money to his pocket and then out again. "Damn you, you can beg for your money like you did at Fort Brown, fiddler. And you're not going to get it."

Simon's eyes opened very wide. "And your wife knows it, Colonel. How you've laid hands on that girl. And your daughter knows it." He should not have said it and he knew it the second the words were out of his mouth.

The colonel took one quick step forward and hit Simon across the face with the cloth bag, heavy with coins. "Get out. Get out. All of you."

Damon kicked a chair between them but Simon didn't move except to blink. His face had gone pale and his lips were white.

Then Webb turned and stalked out of the empty ballroom; in one corner was a ribboned flower from somebody's hair, a forgotten handkerchief lay on a chair, a teacup had fallen and broken in a white scatter of porcelain. "Goddamn you," Webb shouted, and as he went he suddenly picked up one of the silver sugar bowls and threw it across the room and sugar cubes skittered all over the dance floor. The silver sugar bowl struck a windowpane and broke it. Then it rolled with a ringing sound to the wall.

CHAPTER TWENTY-FOUR

SIMON KNEW HE HAD to get her out of there as soon as possible. The mark of the blow stood out red on his cheek. He walked with wild thoughts streaming like a rapids through his mind on this night of broken teacups and shouting, this night of waltzes. When they were on the street he told Pruitt that he was no longer needed, to find employment where he could. Some hard words flew back and forth, but in the end Pruitt slouched away toward the little bridge over the San Antonio River, thumping the bodhran in one hand, and disappeared into the confusion of the Irish Flats behind the Alamo. After that, Simon was too angry to speak.

They went on toward the bridge on Fourth Street, toward Losoya. Damon walked beside Simon, running through melodies on his D whistle; waltzes. He poured them out into the dark city. He kept a prudent silence.

Beside a shoe repair shop on Commerce he said, "Simon, don't come back to the hotel. Find some other place to sleep. Stay out of sight until you two leave in . . ."

"Two nights."

"He's going to go for you one way or the other. I mean worse than beating on you with money. What you want to do is *abscond*."

Simon kept walking. "All right. I'll sleep in the buggy at Cassiano's. I owe about twenty-four dollars and fifty cents on the harness. I'll earn it in the next two nights at the Plaza House."

"No, *don't*."

"I have to. I have to pay what I owe. I will not run out of San Antonio owing money. And, of course, tonight we apparently worked for free."

Damon blew out a long breath. "Cheap son of a bitch. Very well, nothing is going to change your mind, I see."

They walked on in silence and finally they came into Main Plaza on the narrow little street called Dolorosa. The walls of the cathedral loomed on the other side. Damon said,

"And so, Simon, I will be on my way to Nacogdoches."

Simon's face changed. Sadness, maybe a kind of hurt at what was inevitable. They walked out of the narrow way toward the cathedral. The lights of the Plaza House shone out onto the wooden sidewalk and the dirt, the wheel tracks. Scattered bits of hay told of the hay market held there earlier in the afternoon, all gone now.

Simon stopped. "All right," he said. "Let's sit on the wall for a bit."

Around the cathedral there was a low wall enclosing the *camposanto* where San Antonio's proud old Spanish founders were buried: the Leales, the Bethancourts, Curbelos, Arochas. Their lacy cast-iron crosses surrounded the walk leading to the doors. Simon and Damon sat on the wall, both of them a little shaken by the near fight at the Webb house. Simon had come close to breaking his promise, breaking it into a thousand pieces. He laid his fiddle case on top of the wall beside him.

Simon said, "Well then." He stared at his boots while Damon rolled two cigarillos in newspaper and handed him one, lit both of them with a lucifer. They stared out at Main Plaza's dirt and litter, and low clouds raced over the campanile, the roofs of the town. Shouting and laughter from the saloons. Doors and windows here and there shone in squares of faint yellow candlelight.

"So tell me," said Simon.

"Yes," said Damon. "I have unfinished business there." He smoked. "I figured you were not going to wait it out for her contract to expire. I was thinking about it coming up on the freight wagons. And I thought, *Well, time to go back and straighten things out*. Back to the tall pine country." They watched a man stagger out of the Plaza front doors. He was silently drunken and deeply concentrated on putting one foot in front of the other. He managed to disappear up Soledad, past the Veramendi House and on into darkness in total silence. "I saw what Webb did. He was crowding her close, grabbing her arm. I saw she was afraid of him. I saw the old lady's face. Mrs. Colonel has been through this before. This ain't her first dog fight."

Simon flicked sparks and ashes onto a grave. After a moment he said, "Tell me about Nacogdoches."

"I need to go there and get my children back."

Simon lifted his eyebrows in surprise but remained silent, listening.

"I was a teacher there at that little university in Nacogdoches. I came down from Little Rock. Raised in Little Rock. Taught poetry, of course. Met a young widow—twenty years old with two children. Babies. Her husband was cutting down pine and had a tree kick back on him. He was a Hollis. That was their name, family name Hollis. Fairly well off people there in Nacogdoches. Got married. So then after two years she up and left me."

Damon sucked on the cigarillo and fought through his difficulty in speaking.

"Strange woman. Said she wanted to be a fortune teller. She

drank quite a lot. Laudanum too. Left with a group of people who wore various peculiar combinations of colors. Left me with the two small children. I loved them." At this his voice broke and he vigorously cleared his throat. "They were my own. Since babies." Once again he had to clear his throat. "Well. We made a little household, the three of us. Sammy and Rachel and me. Rachel was five and so serious about being the little mother of the house. I had a ring made for her keys and tied a ribbon to it and she went around locking and unlocking everything that had a lock on it. So proud. Played whistle for them evenings. Fireplace, sleepy children, 'The Lonesome Boatman.'" He paused. "Then they took the university building for a hospital. Confederate. I was out of work. Old man Hollis came and said he was taking the children. Said I was no relation and no job into the bargain. Said I was going to be conscripted anyway. That they were his blood kin, the grandparents. He had got a lawyer, had a ruling in their favor. We never did get along. He never did want her to remarry. The whole family was strange."

Simon waited and after a long silence he said, "And so he took them."

"Yes. A scene—crying, screaming, Rachel leaning out of the carriage calling to me, the sheriff riding alongside on a horse with four white legs." Damon looked up at the star-filled sky as if for some relief from the scene running through his head. "Bats," he said. "Belfries." They heard not only the whisper of bat wings but the long throaty groan of a nightjar. Damon said, "And so the next day I went to the sheriff's office. Tried to reason with him. He says, 'Hollis is my brother-in-law, he knows what's best for those children.' I said, 'I am legally their father.' Didn't matter, the judge had ruled in his favor. He says, 'You can go before the judge if you like and plead your case.' I said all right, by God, I will. He kicks back in his chair and hollers up the stairs, 'Verna! Bring me my robes!'"

Simon snorted out smoke, trying to contain his laughter. A bitter laughter. Then he took a deep breath through his nose and said, "So much for that."

"So much for that. At any rate, I went looking for money for a lawyer. Had some investments in New Orleans and there, amid the hustle and bustle of an occupying army, I got conscripted into the damnable Yankee ironclad navy. They needed hands. I was walking down the waterfront. '*Deep in the heart whose hope has died . . .*' Shoveling coal is in some way an antidote to hearts crushed by onrushing events. However. The captain was a lunatic, wanted speed, speed—he had us push that boiler to a hundred percent overload and then they hung a weight on the safety valve. Got away from them in Indianola—often referred to as desertion—jumped overboard—and then was snatched up by Colonel Rip Ford of the dauntless Confederate Army of the West, horsed and unhorsed. Shoved into the regimental band. Then you appeared with your fiddle in that stinking hot tent. And so. They are my children. Their names are Lessing, legally. Children need fathers. I am their father. I will go back and somehow get them back."

After a moment Simon said, "Well. Damon. I never knew."

"I never said anything."

"You don't have a discharge then, from either one."

"I do not. Probably on a list somewhere as a deserter. Yankees, I mean."

"Will you go back to teaching?"

"Not unless I can prove I was never with the Confederate Army, and in the course of attempting that, it's possible they could find out I deserted from the Yankees. Former Confederates are now not allowed to teach anyway. Or do much else, really."

"What about your investments?"

"Are you joking? They were in Confederate bonds."

Simon's chin drooped to his chest and he closed his eyes. He was for a moment discouraged with all of humanity's history of dismal marital confusions—the failures, the weirdnesses, and the tangled webs. He thought of stories in the Old Testament that recalled the hot jealousies and rages of men and women from ancient times when they used bows and arrows and swords, and no one had ever heard of a railroad or a telegraph and yet somehow the stories were just like modern times today in 1867.

But Damon was going to put it right for the boy and the girl, he was going to make it right somehow. Never underestimate the obstinacy and pure stubborn mulishness of an Irish tin whistler. What other kind of person would keep trying to wring melodies from those unresonant little instruments, would make up for their shallow tones with crans, cuts, rolls, and fills? He would not quit those children. Simon glanced over at the man with his beard-shadow and his Hardee hat tilted on his head, his white cravat and unbuttoned black coat with the C and D whistles sticking out of the pocket. Damon was staring at the dirt stretching away into Main Plaza.

He said, "Good luck, Simon."

"How soon are you going?"

"I'll stay until I see you're on your way. You are going to need a hand here and there. This is not going to be easy."

Simon stood down from the wall and took up his fiddle case and held out his hand to Damon. "Thank you," he said. They shook hands solemnly and then walked back to the Plaza House and into the kitchen for what they could find to eat while San Fernando rang out the hour of one in the morning.

DORIS UNHOOKED THE tapes and stepped out of her hoops. Mercedes sat before a vanity table with a long strand of her hair between her fingers, bent over a candle. "The animal!" she said.

She whisked the strand of hair through the flame. Little sparks and the smell of burning hair filled the room.

"Merci, what are you doing?" Doris calmed herself from the laughter and from thrumming nerves. She took in a long breath; her heart had been put crossways and it had not slowed down yet. She twisted the hoops into a figure eight, bent one loop into the other, and shoved them under the bed.

"This is a new thing, you burn off the split ends," said Mercedes. She blew away the tiny bits of ashes. "Now Dori, you know you can't stay here. We have to have a plan."

Doris realized she was gasping but in a slow contained way. She closed her eyes, opened them again, took the gardenia from her braids, and slowly began to undo the fifteen buttons down the front of her dark green dress.

"I know," Doris said. "I have told Simon I will be out of this house in two nights." She put her hands to her cheeks and smiled.

Mercedes laughed with conspiratorial delight as she brushed out her hair. Now all the split ends were gone and it was glossy as velvet. She looked around Doris's tidy small room. "*Dios te bendiga,* girl, at last we are going to be gone! Pack up," she said. "We will go out the window and over the roof. You are smart to say two nights. If you left now they would be waiting. Suspicious. Let two nights go, they are lulling, peaceful. Ha ha."

"It was Simon's idea. We were dancing and I said yes," Doris said. After a pause: "Simon has gone to the recorder there at city hall and has taken out our marriage license." She gave a small grateful laugh as Mercedes's eyes lit up. "He has a surrey and a pony." A small hesitation and then: "The pony's name is Tupelo."

"You see! From the first I told you! I love to be right. I am almost always right in these things." Mercedes got up and shook out her embroidered skirt, knocked more burnt split ends from her white blouse, and began to carefully and silently take all the clothes from Doris's trunk. "You must repack, here. Now your jewelry goes on the bottom."

"I don't have any but what I'm wearing."

"Never mind. All your music, then your underwear. You have too much underwear. Leave some with me, and I will give it a good home. Then soaps, then the white cloths."

Doris got up and then hesitated. "We can't get out with a trunk, Merci. I need a carpetbag."

"Yes." Mercedes put a forefinger to her lips. "You are right."

"I mean, if we went out over the roof it would be like dragging a dead body."

"Yes. And we would knock off the shingles. Shingles falling right in front of their windows, *fijate*. I will find one, my aunt has an old one. So let us now just lay it all out as to how it is to go in."

And so they practiced opening the window without noise, stepped out onto the slanting roof to judge the footing, whispering, trying not to fall into nervous laughter, crying *Shhh shhh!* to each other. And then two hours later, when Mercedes had gone to sleep, Doris sat at a slant on an armless chair with her legs out straight under the skirt, her dress unbuttoned and the front laces of her corset dangling. Her feet rested on the heels of her shoes. A grand feeling of freedom and exhilaration like a fast run on foot down an open meadow. She would soon be gone, gone.

The house sighed with luxurious silence now that the reception and the domestic collisions were dead for the night. She must find shoes with sturdy soles, not these Balmorals with their stacked heels. She would leave the hoops, she had two days to finish sewing a linen organizer with pockets, to knit the ribs on the last pair of stockings. Her sewing was in a cloth packet called a housewife, with razor, crochet hooks, sailor's palm, curved needles, straight needles, waxed thread, and silk embroidery thread. She remembered with a feeling of discouragement all the tools and utensils her mother had, for the fireplace and the butter and the cooking, the sewing frames. She and Simon did not even have dishes. *Mary, Mother of God, you will help us with all this, I know you will.*

It was going to be all right.

She would be gone into a land of roaming aboriginal creatures, with Simon, who was handsome and imperative in his desires and had the bearing of a working man, who knew music and could build a house. She wanted her life to be among working men. Her father was one and she had preferred his company above all others until she saw the fiddler standing alone in that landscape of spiny undergrowth, proud as Satan, pouring out a melody about death, about sinners. Better than the lieutenant and his account books in a stack, a good man but stuffed full of numbers like an arithmetical sausage and nary a note of music in his head. He wanted to go into law in the army, chasing down corruption by the numbers. Good. May he prosper. She would be gone at last from the Webbs and their crushed manners and the drink and their social terrors. God between herself and them. She felt as if she had shrugged off a heavy coat. In two days. Just two more days.

SIMON SLEPT IN the buggy with a blanket and left his rucksack at the Plaza House for Damon to care for; his few pesos and the revolver and the ring were in it. He awoke with confused thoughts or dreams of all the human and animal figures that stood in his way, figures of immeasurable antiquity that turned to face him with a stupid, powerful menace. He got a coffee and two crisp, fresh *orejas* at a stall, watching for the sheriff, a sheriff's man, Union soldiers. After tomorrow night they would go.

Up in the Plaza House's attic, as he was dashing hot water in his face, Damon stood at the door, observing him.

"Simon, let me give you a loan of the money."

"It's nearly a week's wages." Simon wiped shaving foam from his face. "I can't let you."

"Let me give it to you now," Damon persisted. He was dressed slim and black-coated and formal. "I'll collect from Pressley."

"Thank you, Damon, it will be all right."

That evening at the Plaza House Simon played with speed and verve, his hat pulled down over his face. There were great trials ahead. He must now become head of a family, responsible for his well-being and hers and the thought of it made him larger, as if he had gained several inches. He could make money anywhere with his fiddle and he intended to. He stood with his feet braced and the music sailed out of him and out of his fiddle. It ran in invisible currents through the cigar smoke; he and Damon bore down on "Mississippi Sawyer" as if to destroy it measure by measure and then lifted up "La Savane" as a peacemaker. Halfway through the night they saw Pruitt lurch through the front doors.

"Hey, hey!" He stared at Simon with a fixed grin. "I can come in here if I want."

Damon regarded him with a suspicious, alert expression but Simon was in the middle of "The Flowers of Edinburgh," and paid him no mind. Pruitt stumbled in to sit at a table near the front. Then at the door of the saloon Simon saw Doris; her slim figure and the heart-shaped bonnet.

She waved hesitantly at him. He paused with his bow lifted.

"Doris! What?"

Pruitt made a throwing motion at Simon and cried, "Play 'The Hog-Eye Man'! Let's hear it!"

An orange peel landed at Simon's feet. He did not even look down but called out, "Miss Dillon, don't come in here!" He held the bow and fiddle down at his side and called to a waiter. "Go down and escort her outside. Hurry."

But she walked in, into this abode of men and prostitutes, with her skirts in both hands and a desperate expression. Pruitt stood up, singing,

Sally's in the garden punching duff
The cheeks of her ass go chuff chuff chuff

Simon called out, "Shut up, Pruitt! Miss Dillon, I will meet you outside, what is it?"

She called out, "Simon, you must go, hurry! Colonel Webb has an arrest warrant . . . ," and at the same time Pruitt kept on singing about Sally and her duck and the line with the rhyming word and Simon's rage took hold of him as a fiend or a dark demon would possess a body. Pruitt turned and saw her and grabbed hold of her skirt in a thick wad in his fist and jerked hard enough to make her stagger. She struck at him with her bare hand. Then Pruitt cried out the last words of his life,

"Hey girl, let's hear that ass go chuff chuff chuff!"

Simon dropped his fiddle and jumped off the stage with his black coat flying open. With one powerful backhand swing he broke his fiddle bow across Pruitt's face. The broken half of the bow flew loose in a scarf of horsehair like a stream of smoke. Simon heard hoarse shouting. Pruitt's head flew back and came up again with blood springing red out of his face; a look of astonishment, then he rose from his chair. His hand went to his belt. He drew a knife, held it low, and with the other hand reached for Simon's coat. Damon had grabbed Doris and was hustling her outside. Clattering noise as Damon's D whistle rolled off the little stage. Pruitt's knife coming up underhand. Simon bowed his body back in an arc and the blade swept up his belly and parted his shirt in a line. A button of his vest went flying.

In his right hand was the other half of the broken bow, splintered sharp as a needle on one end. Simon shut his hand hard around the end remaining, stepped close when Pruitt's hand with the knife swept high in the air, and drove the sharp end straight into the place just below Pruitt's sternum. He drove it in with all his strength. Right through that loud striped shirt and into his heart. Blood shot out in a thin spray, fine as mist. A sudden pause. Everything stopped. Then the knife fell from Pruitt's hand and he bent low over the pulsing spray in his chest as if to contain it. He fell in segments, to his knees, his hands dropped, then he fell to one side.

Several men had hold of Simon's arms. Pruitt lay on the saloon floor with the fiddle bow sticking out of his chest and the horsehair in a white silky stream flowing over his shirt. His eyes were fixed, staring blindly toward the ceiling. There was blood everywhere. Simon half-turned to look for Doris, but then somebody had hold of his lapels. He called out for Doris, elbowed a man away, but then another pair of hands took him from behind, under his arms, twisted upward.

He was being hustled outside. He had no idea where Doris was or Damon either. He found himself in the hands of several large men, one of them wearing a star. Another one had his fiddle. He fought them all the way across Main Plaza and down the alleyway called Treviño between the cathedral and the Horde Hotel; from here and there in the shadowed city came lights and music. They were hustling him toward the jail behind the Bat Cave. They knocked him down and then hauled him to his feet again by one wrist and somebody behind him gripped him by the hair as if he would pull it out by the hank and shoved him forward.

By the time they got him into the jail and into a cell he felt several hot places on his face where they had struck him with fists or pistols. His shoulder joints hurt. He was bleeding from the wound on his belly. They wrote down his name in a book; other names were there and the preferred charges: epilepsy, pocket-picking, habitual drunkenness, evading service. *Simon, a fidler. Imployment musician. Charge homocide.* Misspelled. They slapped his pockets and then propelled him into a cell with a shove.

He went and lay down on a bunk for a moment to get his balance back. After a while he sat up. He kept one hand against his abdomen. His shirt was sticky with blood. He realized that a lot of it was Pruitt's blood. One man put an oil lamp on the floor in front of his cell and then left. The only man remaining was a thick fellow in a long dark frock coat, a short-brimmed hat, and a star. He turned the lock on Simon's cell door and put the ring of keys in his pocket. It was the man who had been thanking Davis for his help in getting the sheriff's position. At the dance. "The Moonlight Waltz."

The jail behind city hall was one long row of cells with a narrow corridor or hall in front of them. Down at the entrance a sort of ready room where they had written his name down. He had been taken to the end cell farthest away from the door. There was a window across from him in the thick wall, an unlit lamp on the dirty sill, straw on the corridor floor, and sacks of corn piled up along with a shovel and a box of old horseshoes, a boot, an auger.

"Well, then. I had a warrant for your arrest, fiddler, and I had some doubt about its legality but that is now a moot point. This is a hanging offense."

"Where is Miss Dillon?"

"I believe she's being escorted back to her place of residence. I am a friend of Colonel Webb's. Being fair here. Just so you know."

"All right." Simon stared down at the floor. "Is he dead?"

"As a doornail."

"Good."

The sheriff regarded Simon with an interested expression.

"I see you are unrepentant. It appears you were about to go tearing off somewhere with Miss Dillon. An *abduction*." The man's voice became high and tense and was heavy with stresses. "It seems you were planning on *abducting* her. *Seducing* her. A respectable girl. Not from this country. Unfamiliar with our ways. Looks like you talked her into coming into that saloon, a *notorious haunt* of prostitutes and drunks! Well. Fiddlers have their ways."

Simon sat on the cot with his hands dangling between his knees. *So that's how it is*. "Where's my fiddle?"

"Here." The sheriff lifted it from the windowsill. "You are a sort of predator. A desperado. Preying on young women."

"I want Damon Lessing to come and get my fiddle. In the meantime go to hell and stay there."

In the cell down at the other end of the long corridor a madman sang and spoke to the rank jail air in disconnected sentences. He sang snatches of Stephen Foster songs, spoke to an invisible man who was to write his name down in the Bible, they could see it there; he was Light-Horse Harry Lee, they could see it written down there. The one oil lamp threw long shadows down the corridor.

"Shut up," said the sheriff, and the madman shut up. The sheriff turned to Simon, leaned toward the bars. "You were not with any Indiana regiment, you were with Giddings. I checked. I asked around. You're from Paducah, you're a bastard, raised on the Ohio, a river that is just a running slum from Cincinnati to Cairo." He paused, waiting for Simon to ask him how he knew this. Simon was silent. "You want to know how we know this. Well. You're lately come and since you are not equipped with wings you had to have come up with the freights. So Colonel Webb asked around there and found a driver who knew you. Told him all he needed to know. Well. It appears that you were about to drag that young lady into a life of crime and drinking and who knows what else?"

"I won't have you or anybody speaking of her in that way," said Simon. "She can't be dragged. She is undraggable. Webb couldn't keep his damned hands off her. We were to be married."

"In your imagination. You are deluded. She is promised to Lieutenant Whittaker." The sheriff smiled. Struck a match to the lantern on the windowsill. The other one was going out. Shadows changed places on the walls.

"You made that up," said Simon. "You Goddamned liar."

"Say that again."

"You are a Goddamned liar." Simon lowered his head, raised it. "You kissed ass to get this sheriff job. You're not going to hang anybody."

"You're going to regret that. You watch your mouth." The man grew jerky with anger and the keys rattled.

Simon knew he should shut up, let it all calm down, but he had killed a man and his fury was still upon him and had taken hold of him, stopped here at this last minute when they were about to start for the Red River Valley, that beautiful valley, that treacherous river, and all this now standing in his way.

"Boy, they are going to execute you." The man's voice got louder, as if Simon were hard of hearing. "For murder!"

"Not without a trial."

"You're going to hang!"

"Bullshit."

"Is it? Is it?"

The sheriff was now red-faced and shouting. And then, at a loss for words, he picked up Simon's Markneukirche and lifted it over his head and slammed it against the wall. The upper and lower bouts sprang loose, the chin-piece landed on the far side of the corridor, and the strings dangled from the broken neck, still holding to the bridge.

Simon stood up in complete silence. He said nothing. The man seemed ashamed of what he had done and turned away with a thin, false laugh. He threw the neck with its dangling fiddle strings into the heap of grain sacks.

"You ain't going to be needing no fiddle where you're going."

Simon was still silent. He remained silent all that night and also the next morning. The blood dried on his belly. He opened his shirt and saw that the wound was not bad, it was only skin-deep. With an expressionless face he reached through the bars for a thick crockery cup of black coffee and flour biscuits wrapped in a newspaper.

"Visiting hours from eleven to two," said the deputy.

Simon sat down on the iron straps of the bunk with its thin cotton pad and ate and drank. The day passed in one impossible hour after another. It was cold. He turned up the collar of the black coat and shut it around himself. He heard Doris's voice; she was arguing with the sheriff. She was going to get a lawyer, she had a right to visit the prisoner, she was going to come back with a paper written by a lawyer, and he would be forced to allow her to visit Mr. Boudlin. He heard the sheriff say that San Antonio was under military law and she could go and ask the adjutant at the Vance House if she dared, give it a try, girl.

Simon sat in a daze, listening. The voices came from the front door of the ready room of the jail, and then he didn't hear her anymore. He sat back on the iron-strap cot. What could she know about American law, much less military law in an occupied state? Perhaps she even knew little about Irish law. Maybe the Irish had no laws, just whatever the English felt like doing at any given time. For her to come here meant that she was no longer in Colonel Webb's house. Where had she gone, where had she run to? And himself unable to help.

He squatted down to shove the tin cup back out of the bars, on the floor. The day passed; noises from the plaza outside. A bird darted to the window and flew down into the corridor to peck at biscuit crumbs. Perhaps it had escaped from the bird sellers.

CHAPTER TWENTY-FIVE

THAT NIGHT THEY BROUGHT in a big man who stank of alleyways and whiskey. They shoved him into the cell with Simon. The man stood there in the dark with his back against the bars, staring at Simon in the light of the one lamp that threw long shadows down the corridor. At the far end the madman called out for the fiddler to give us a tune. "He's the fiddle player," the madman said. "Sweet, sweet music. I loved his tunes at the Bull's Head. It is the Queen of Instruments."

The big man said not one word but advanced on Simon and with a swift punch struck him on the forehead. He would have landed the blow directly on Simon's nose except at the last second Simon saw it coming and ducked. He rolled off the cot and under it. The man got him by one leg, and dragged him out, and hit him again, in the ribs. Once, twice.

"Oh, he's killing the fiddler," said the madman in a small, feminine voice.

Simon got to one knee and rose up, close, inside the man's guard, with the heels of both hands together, and smashed up on the man's chin and at the same time took another terrible blow in his ribs. The man's fists were like stones. He heard a wet noise. The big man was bleeding badly from the mouth. Simon reeled back and got a knee in the hip. He had been aiming for Simon's testicles but missed, and Simon's hip bone took the most of it.

Simon realized the man meant to kill him.

That he was here because Colonel Webb had arranged for him to be arrested, brought in. Maybe paid him.

Simon was struck twice in the face in quick succession. He managed to keep his senses and his balance and his feet, got on top of the bunk and backed into the corner. He could feel blood running out of his nose and more trickling into his eye from a knuckle-cut on the forehead. He could feel the wound on his abdomen break open again and bleed down into his pants. When the big man closed in again Simon got in two hits with his fists, then took more blows to the face. The tiny cell was a cage for men to fight to the death with no place to run, nowhere to escape, and it smelled of the man's soiled clothes and hard whiskey breath, it smelled of the manure on his boots, while outside like a death knell the bells of San Fernando rang midnight.

The big man got hold of Simon's belt and flung him across the cell with such force that he ripped the belt clean out of its buckle and Simon struck the bars with a noise like a gong. Another punch; Simon dropped, the man struck his fist on the bars and grunted. Then he knocked Simon to the floor. He kicked at Simon's head but Simon managed, out of a sea of red sparks and swarming blotted blue figures, to turn to one side and took the blow on his ear. He doubled up his fists because he knew the man was going to stamp on his hands and he did, twice. Simon curled into a ball.

He lay still on the floor. Strange high harmonics sang in his head. The big man took a handful of Simon's black coat, now glossy with blood spots, but his attention was suddenly taken by some noise at the door of the jail. A boy's voice crying out, "Pa! Pa!"

The big man turned his head, quickly, then back again to Simon.

"Pa, what are you in for? Mama's coming!" A boy was jumping up and down at the window in the ready room. Bounding up and down outside, his face showing in the lantern light in repeated leaps.

"Shut up, Casey!" the big man yelled. "Go home!"

The man was printing blood on the back of his hand from his bleeding mouth like terrible sickening kisses. Simon lay watching the bars of the cell arrowing up into infinity over his head, disappearing into a bloody haze.

"Nah, she's coming! Went to yell at the sheriff! She'll get you out!"

"Go home, you little shit!"

"What'd you do?" the boy yelled.

There was more yelling. The deputy appeared; he came down the corridor and opened the cell, jerking the big man out. The deputy's boots were beside Simon's head. The man ignored him. They all went away.

Time passed. The bells rang one and then two. Simon managed to turn over, put his palms against the floor, and raise himself. His belt and buckle were dangling. Then he threw up, violently, all over the floor in a spasm that made his head feel like it was being crushed. He hung there a few moments, then finally got to his feet by going hand over hand up a cell bar. He knew he was damaged, but he couldn't tell how badly. He fell down onto the bunk. Felt the iron straps beneath the thin padding. He lay without moving.

Daylight. Noises from out in the plaza. Horses, wagons, shouts of vendors. It seemed to him that his parts were not all working. He tried to put one thought together with another in sequence. When they opened the cell door and gestured him out, he had to pause for a second when he sat up and wait until the cell stopped its strange circular perambulations. Then he stood and reached for the bars, held on to them despite the intense pain in his hands. Then he used those hands to carefully draw the broken end of his belt through the buckle. He wiped his mouth on his cuff. Then he stepped out. The sheriff clicked a set of handcuffs around his wrists. There she stood motionless down at the end of the hall, beside the desk. He was ashamed to look into her eyes with his face a mass of bloody red contusions, blood down the front of his pants, his lips swollen, and his wrists in manacles.

She stood resolutely, her face set in a kind of fierce, unmoving rage with her hands clasped in front of her. She wore the dark slate-gray jacket and skirt with a white collar and a little hat tipped like a garrison cap on her forehead. Then, her resolution gone, she suddenly put one hand over her eyes. Tears streaked down her face from under her hand.

"Oh, Simon," she said. "Oh, Simon."

Around her the strewn logbooks so carelessly dropped here and there, and on the wall a notice concerning rules of the jail. How prisoners were to conduct themselves. Beside Doris stood the blond spare man he had met so long ago at Fort Brown, at the surrender when he returned the white shirts. He had been a sergeant then.

"I *do* have precedence," the lieutenant said. He was talking to the sheriff. Simon tried to remember what his name was. Whittaker. Jacob Whittaker. Lieutenant Jacob Whittaker. He was in uniform, his shoulder boards with one bar on them, a gold stripe down his pants legs. "We are still under military rule. That will end shortly but it has not ended at the moment."

"Well Goddamn," said the sheriff.

"There's a lady here," said Lieutenant Jacob Whittaker.

The sheriff lifted his hat, murmured a few words about ladies not coming to jails. Simon remembered that the blond man had said *We hang them.* He, Simon, had killed a man. He felt that he was going to pass out. His head dropped forward and then he found he was able to lift it again. She managed a smile and pressed the backs of her hands against her cheeks.

"You must have water," said Doris. She stepped toward the water bucket, but the sheriff stood in her path. She said, "Get out of my way or I will have the eyes out of your head, do you hear me?" She stared him down and he started to object, to mutter, then he backed off. She brought the dipper to Simon.

Simon took it in both hands, turned it up, and drank all that was in it.

Whittaker said, "The tribunal will be at the Vance House and so I need a written confirmation from you that you are transferring the prisoner to my custody and authority."

Simon saw the sheriff writing and as he wrote he said, "Then where's the provost marshal? How come I'm sheriff then?"

"I have no idea why you're the sheriff." Whittaker reached out to take the paper. "Where are his possessions?"

"He didn't have nothing but a fiddle."

"Where is it?"

There was a long silence, shuffling boots. Then the sheriff said, "Well, there was a fight here and it got broke up." His voice had changed and now he sounded unsure. *Coward.* He turned and retrieved the remains of Simon's Markneukirche from a large basket that apparently served for trash. Somebody had thrown it all in there. Probably the deputy.

"Ah. I see," said Whittaker.

Doris didn't move for a moment and then she said, "Give it to me." She held out a hand. "You black villain. How *could* you?"

"No," said Whittaker. "Wait." From the floor beside him he picked up a large canvas bag marked U.S. MAIL. "Hand it over." The sheriff handed over piece after piece as if counting them.

"There was a fight here."

"You said that."

"I went home for the night, couldn't find a night watchman. They got into it."

"You'll testify about that later," said the lieutenant. "Under oath. That is a separate issue." He touched Simon's arm. "Let's go," he said.

"Where?" Simon didn't move.

"We have several places to go. It's going to be all right. Come, Simon."

Doris took up the front of her skirts in one hand and marched out the door to a light small surrey. It was their own, with little Tupelo brightly tossing his head and surveying with one eye his happy future. When they were seated, the lieutenant tossed the mail sack into the footwell, stepped aboard, and took up the reins. Before he urged the horse onward he said,

"Simon, now listen to me."

"Very well," said Simon. He closed his eyes, sat back with his wrists in irons and his slashed shirt, his vest missing buttons, his black coat littered with bits of hay and blood. He couldn't see out of one eye. His mouth was thick.

Doris pulled a handkerchief out of her sleeve and poured water from a canteen over it. He heard the rattle of the stopper chain, a familiar sound. She began the attempt to clean his face, one careful stroke after another. She made several choked noises.

"Don't cry," said Simon. "I'm all right."

Whittaker pressed back his eyeglasses and said, "We must appear before a tribunal today."

"All right."

"They are wanting to call Miss Dillon to testify and they will try to prove it was premeditated murder."

"No," said Simon. "She cannot. She's a girl from Ireland and doesn't know anything of this situation. No."

"Simon, be quiet and listen," Doris said. She wrung out the handkerchief, leaning over the side. The water she twisted out was bloody.

"Yes. Because she heard you say you would like to strangle Pruitt at the colonel's reception. They will question her about your relationship. Colonel Webb is pressing for this. He is not seated on the tribunal. The judge advocate, a Dutchman named Frelich, is a fair man. He is no friend of Webb's. No, be quiet, listen. So you will be married within the hour, as a wife cannot testify against her husband even under military rule."

Simon turned to the girl beside him to look at her carefully; her nervous brightness and her hair so untidy beneath the hat as if she had done it up in the dark. He needed some clue as to what was real and what might only appear real to somebody who had been hit in the head several times with great force. The activity of Military Plaza swirled about them, the bargaining and woodsmoke and rumbling of wheels.

She said, "Is that all right, Simon?"

Simon sat without speaking. He revolved the thoughts around in his head. He said, "Yes, darling. Yes." He paused. "I don't have the ring. It's in my stuff at the Plaza House."

"The ring, yes, all right." In this blinding sunlight of a February day she appeared anxious, confused, but then in the last two days everything had collapsed and fallen out of true; a hive overturned and events darting about like winter bees.

"Yes. Since Houston. It's in my ruck at the Plaza House." He moved slightly with the waves of pain in his shoulder, his ribs, his face. He leaned his bruised head against her forehead and then kissed her carefully on the lips. The lieutenant looked elsewhere. "Doris, I have long admired you from afar. Would you do me the honor of marrying me?"

"Since you ask," she said. And then, with a shaky smile, for she was looking into his battered face, "Yes."

"So is it settled, then?" The lieutenant shifted the reins and gazed, with iron resolve, across the plaza. He seemed to be studying the facade of the Horde Hotel with great interest.

"It is," said Simon and clasped her small hand in his two, despite the clanking manacles. "Doris, where are you staying?"

"With Mercedes. It is all right. I got out with a carpetbag, out a window, over the roof. Mercedes started laughing, it was a *scene*." She held his hand gently. It was swollen and several of his fingers were blue. "We are off on an adventure, are we not then?"

"Yes."

"To the Red River Valley."

"I hope. God, I hope so."

THE JUSTICE OF the Peace had a small office at the rear of the French building. He stood at his desk when he saw them come in and stared hard at Simon. He had a big nose and hollow cheeks and thick brown-and-gray hair. He leaned on his knuckles.

"Fiddler, I am sorry to see you like this."

"I clean up pretty good," said Simon. He made a vague, clanking gesture with his hand. "We want you to marry us."

"I saw you play at the Horde Hotel. 'The Highland Waltz.' Very moving, very polished."

"Thank you. Much appreciated. I was wondering if you could marry us. It seems kind of urgent."

"I know. The lieutenant has related to me the entire story. Very remarkable, very striking." The justice dredged up the thick marriage registry and placed it carefully on a high desk. He laid out steel pens and an ink bottle and pen wipers. "In this book are one thousand four hundred and seventy-one stories of human beings joining themselves in Holy Matrimony for better or for worse and done often in a heedless haste and others after years of senseless dithering. Often it does not work out and misery and parting are their lot; at other times mistakes are rectified and another attempt is made but human beings never stop trying their hand at matrimony, it seems to be a universal law. In this book you two are one thousand four hundred and seventy-two."

Doris and Simon stood before him like penitent schoolchildren, with Simon in his handcuffs and beat-up face having perhaps done something more felonious than was common.

"In here are Captain Jefferson Kidd and Maria Luisa Real, the oldest son of the Mavericks and his intended, the Huths of Castroville, Shanghai Pierce and Fanny Lacey."

Simon wondered if he said this to every couple that came to be married.

Lieutenant Whittaker listened carefully, his cap in his hand.

The judge nodded. "Yes," he said. "Only a small town on the edge of the world here in Texas, but still terrible things and wonderful stories happen, just like in the books. This is a book." He turned the pages, looking for the last entry. "This is a book," he repeated. "Great tragedies, gripping love stories, tales of uncommon heroism. Very profound, very thought-provoking. Enter your names here."

Simon wrote, dragging one hand behind the other because of the manacles. Doris stood on her toes to write her name, examined it, tipped her head back and forth, decided it was all right. The justice asked if there was a ring and the lieutenant said, in a rigidly controlled voice, "Here." He held out a thin band of silver, the kind you could buy at the Military Plaza market next to the bird sellers. The kind young girls saved for and wore on their forefingers to shine in the sun and glitter as they helped their mothers dish out tortillas and chilis, cheap and bright.

And then Doris said I will, and Simon said I will. He lifted his manacled hands over her head and laid his arms around her neck. He kissed her with great care because of his split lip and also so that he did not lose his balance. He felt her body pressed against him, ignoring the pain of the wound that ran from his navel to his sternum. He stood for what seemed to be a long time with his head bent and his face in her hair and nobody said anything. At last he lifted his handcuffed hands over her head again and stepped back. She looked up at him with wide eyes, and perhaps it was her vision, perhaps he had a glow around his head. He hoped so. He had little else. And so they were married. And then he went to his trial before the officers of the tribunal.

CHAPTER TWENTY-SIX

THE VANCE HOUSE WAS northeast of the plazas at Paseo and St. Mary's. It had been taken over by the Union Army, now simply the United States Army. In the main dining room was convened the last military tribunal of the Texas occupation under the auspices of the office of the judge advocate general this day of the twenty-fifth of February 1867 to consider the matter of a charge of homicide preferred against Simon Boudlin, age twenty-four, musician, resident of San Antonio.

Simon walked through the front doors with Lieutenant Jacob Whittaker at his elbow. Coming down the hall Whittaker took off his cap and said to him, "Listen, Simon, they wouldn't hang a fiddler. They'd hang a carpenter, a blacksmith, a gambler, or a horse thief but nobody would ever hang a fiddler."

Simon didn't laugh. What was in his mind was that they might not hang him but there was the possibility of several years behind bars in Huntsville.

"I am your counsel. Your defender." The lieutenant pressed back his glasses. He carried the mail sack in one hand and a sheaf of papers carefully annotated under his arm. This case would help him transfer into the judge advocate general's department. If he could win it. "None of us on the tribunal have to be lawyers, just chosen at random from various branches. The man prosecuting you is Captain Garth. It's his job, it would not be personal."

"Yes." Simon slowed. "Hold up a minute." He leaned against the wall, hoping the faintness would go away.

Whittaker waited patiently. "Take your time," he said.

Simon straightened at last. He said, "Lieutenant, I know you held Miss Dillon in great regard."

A long tense silence and then Whittaker said, "Love and war," in a stiff voice. "So it goes." The late sunlight glinted from his small round eyeglasses and the uniform itself seemed to hold him upright in a strict rectitude. "I wish the best for her. Selfless, very noble, I know. But she has made her decision and so deserves every good thing. That might or might not include you and by God it better." He held the mail sack in one hand, his sliding papers in the other. "I asked to be appointed your defense counsel. I will do whatever is in my power."

They walked on. The hall seemed endless. The wallpaper was a dizzying repetition of milkmaids with feet the size of pie wedges dancing in some kind of foliage. Two privates had been posted on either side of the double doors to the dining room. One opened the doors and then shut them as they passed through. Inside, Whittaker came to attention, tucked his cap under one arm, and saluted. The big man with the giant shoulder boards at the middle of the long table stood and returned it, sat down again. He was clearly Colonel Frelich. The other officers he didn't know. Had no way of knowing.

He stood before the board with his hands held low to hide the manacles. Doris had soaked her handkerchief and wiped his face, but there were still blood spots and stains on his shirt, his vest, his pants, rimming his nostrils. He saw that the butternut vest was not only missing buttons but it was cut through as was his shirt.

They began by reading aloud the military statutes that made the tribunal legal, then the state law against homicide in all its variations (willful, negligent, premeditated) and this went on until they finally came around to self-defense. Also charges of resisting an arresting officer and attacking another prisoner in the cells.

Simon was asked by Judge Advocate Frelich to describe what had happened.

He paused. Someone poured him a glass of water, but he didn't drink it because it would have been difficult with the manacles. It would have been humiliating.

Judge Advocate Frelich observed this and said, "You do not have to stand, you are injured. Sit down. Now, you had fired this Pruitt from off of your music band, did you not?" The man's stand collar bit into the flesh of his neck; the new spring sun shone on his balding head and the grain of the table, bounced off the opened law books, and reflected into men's faces.

Simon sat down in a chair pulled out for him. "Yes sir."

"So you differed. You had disagreements."

"No. There wasn't any disagreement. I told him we didn't want him."

An officer who was probably Captain Garth stood to speak. He said, "Someone has said that at Colonel Webb's dance they overheard you telling Miss Doris Dillon, the Webb family's governess, that you would strangle Pruitt."

"That's immaterial, it's unacceptable," said Lieutenant Whittaker. "Overhearing is not acceptable. Unless it was said directly to this someone, we could not consider it."

"Why not?" Judge Advocate Frelich looked around at the others.

Lieutenant Whittaker said, "Sir, the entire legality of military tribunals trying and sentencing civilians who are not in a state of rebellion is questionable. There are no precedents. We have to go with state law. That is the state law concerning hearsay."

Frelich shook his finger in the air. "Yes, there are precedents for trying civilians. Those who conspired to kill Lincoln all were hanged by a military tribunal."

"Correct. But they were in a state of rebellion and conspiring to incite more rebellion and an armed uprising. This is what you might call an ordinary homicide case, one civilian killing another civilian. Much better handled by state authorities, except there are very few local or state authorities at present."

Frelich regarded him in silence. Finally: "Are we proceeding with the prewar laws of the state of Texas, then, concerning homicide? Resisting arrest and so on?"

Captain Garth said, "We have to. We have no other."

"Very well. Again I ask you Mr. Boudlin, tell us what happened."

Simon said, "I sacked Pruitt and told him to leave the band. The next night he came into the Plaza House Hotel and sat at a table and started shouting for a certain song. I don't like to play it or sing it. It's uncommonly filthy. He was trying to embarrass me."

"What song?" Lieutenant Whittaker turned toward Simon, curious.

"'The Hog-Eye Man.'"

Several of the officers sitting around the table nodded in a knowing way. Garth made a wry face. Frelich gestured: *Go on.*

"Then Miss Dillon came to the door of the Plaza House and called in to me. She had something urgent to tell me. Pruitt kept on singing in a loud voice where she could hear the words, one of which begins with 'F'; I told him to shut up."

"Something urgent?" Frelich lifted his eyebrows.

"Yes, urgent," said Garth. "Colonel Webb had insisted that the sheriff put out a warrant for Mr. Boudlin's arrest. Miss Dillon had rushed out to warn him."

Frelich's foot tapped in a slow beat under the table. He said to Simon, "Then you are in a fistfight with this man."

"No, sir." Simon sat and tried to gather his words. "The fight with Pruitt was over in about thirty seconds."

"But you are beat up," said Frelich.

Lieutenant Whittaker spun an earpiece of his eyeglasses in one hand and then put them back on with slow care. "Mr. Boudlin was taken to jail, the cells behind city hall. Then apparently the sheriff put a man into his cell with him. Man called Tom Shettle, a notorious brawler. There are five cells back there, only two of them were occupied, and yet the sheriff put Shettle in with Mr. Boudlin, with the results that you see."

"The sheriff then is derelict in his public duty and liable for charges of battery."

"Yes, sir, but we will take that up presently. That is another matter."

Frelich settled in his chair in a certain indefinable way, with a slight narrowing of the eyes. The other officers had said very little. They were here for the fireworks and it appeared the fireworks were about to begin.

Frelich said, "Colonel Webb has no authority to order a sheriff to write out a warrant for anybody."

"Well, sir, we are not sure about military authority to enforce any laws whatsoever on civilians. We're under martial law and to tell you frankly, it leaves me confused."

"He has no authority," said Frelich in a stubborn voice, the voice of somebody who is not to be moved, not by arguments, gunfire, avalanches, or plague. "None. What was the warrant for?"

"Intention to abduct Miss Dillon."

Frelich laughed. "He invented that. It is no law. Not anywhere."

Simon listened to them wrangle with the law and thoughts about the law, what kind of law should be in force now that the war was over. What was military law as applied to civilians? Garth was eloquent, Whittaker came in repeatedly with allusions to ancient lawmakers, Frelich became bored.

"Be quiet," Frelich said. "All of you. Mr. Boudlin, continue. He was singing this song, this Hawk-Eye Man song. Miss Dillon comes in to warn you of something, this Pruitt keeps on singing. You tell him to shut up."

"Yes. Then she came in directly to the saloon, although I called out to her not to. It is not a place for a respectable woman. Then Pruitt grabbed her skirt and called out one of the lines of the song that was a terrible insult. He actually grabbed hold of her skirt and jerked at it as she came near him." Simon paused to regain his balance, his breath. "I hit him with my fiddle bow and broke it across his face. He came out with a knife and brought it up underhand. I had the sharp broken end of the bow in my hand and I stabbed him with it."

Silence fell. All talk of the law stopped. This is what the law came down to, this bar fight, this stream of blood spraying from a man's heart.

"And did he harm you?"

"Yes, sir. He got me in the belly."

"Let us see the wound."

They unlocked the manacles. Simon stood carefully and opened his vest, unbuttoned his bloodied shirt. The streak of the wound went from below his drooping belt to his sternum. A line of dried blood and swollen flesh cut straight up his abdominal muscles. Clearly a knife wound.

Frelich considered it a moment with an expert eye. He said, "This was meant to spill the guts. What is the word? I can't think of it."

"Eviscerate," said Whittaker.

"Yes, eviscerate." He gestured to Simon. "Enough."

Simon buttoned up and sat down again. A guard came forward with the manacles, but Frelich held up a hand and the guard went back to stand by the door.

Whittaker said, "So you see, he acted in self-defense."

Captain Garth said, "Perhaps. Perhaps. However, just the day before Mr. Boudlin stated that he intended to kill Mr. Pruitt at a public gathering and if you will not accept the words of the man who overheard him tell Miss Dillon that he intended to strangle Pruitt, then we will have to call Miss Dillon herself as a witness. I am sorry to have to do that. But this leads us to premeditation and I intend to pursue it."

"Pursue away," said Whittaker. "You cannot call her. A wife cannot testify against her husband, not by any law."

Silence.

"Eh?" Frelich leaned forward. "What?"

"They are married," said Whittaker.

"Since when?" Frelich leaned forward, attentive.

"Since this morning at eight o'clock by the San Fernando bells."

Simon, now that his hands were free, took up the glass of water and poured it all down his throat. His expression said, *Stuff that in your pipe and smoke it.* He set the glass down with a click.

"This is irregular," said Garth.

"In what way?" Whittaker regarded him with a blank face, innocent of all trickery or wrongdoing.

"Who married them?" Garth sounded a bit desperate. "Perhaps he does not have the authority. Was it a duly recognized Justice of the Peace?"

"Appointed by Governor Throckmorton. Or reappointed."

The officers sat back in their chairs. Whittaker noted arms crossed, shrugs.

"So." Whittaker pressed down his glasses again. "A wound clearly proving assault with intent on Pruitt's part and a great many witnesses to the same. All Simon had to fight back with was a broken fiddle bow. He defended Miss Dillon against assault and insult with nothing but a fiddle bow. There will be no testimony regarding prior threats, and I ask not only for acquittal of all charges but adequate compensation from Sheriff Patterson."

Again, a long, ticking silence. Frelich the judge advocate sat with the final word in his head, his right to pronounce guilt or innocence, his ability to override any vote by those officers inferior to him in rank.

"Compensation for what?" he said.

"His fiddle. The sheriff either broke it up himself or allowed a prisoner to do so." Whittaker bent down to the U.S. Mail sack and lifted it to the table. He stood, opened it, and lifted out every smashed, ruined piece of Simon's fiddle.

Frelich's mouth dropped open. "*Gott in Himmel!*" He bent forward and picked up the splintered neck with its delicate scroll. He turned it to see the maker's name on the inner top block. "This is a *Markneukirche*!"

Whittaker did not smile. He barely moved. He said, "Yes."

He knew he had won.

"This is a sin against God himself." Frelich turned a piece of the face in his hands; it had parted at the f hole. "Did the sheriff not have to write down the possessions the prisoner came in with?"

"He didn't even write down Simon's name properly," said Whittaker.

Frelich picked up one of the sprung bouts, moved his fingers across the rich, broken woods. He looked up at Simon.

"I don't want any compensation," said Simon. "It would take time."

Frelich carefully returned the pieces to the U.S. Mail sack. Watching him do it Simon realized that the Markneukirche had saved him one last time. One last time.

"Do you want this?" asked Frelich.

"I would like to keep the scroll."

Frelich drew the strings out of the hole in the inner rods, dropped them to the floor, and then expertly pushed the pegs in tight with the heel of his hand. He held out the scroll. Simon reached with his broken, discolored hand to take it. Frelich glanced down at his hand and then sat back. He gestured to the two privates to remove the accused. They stepped forward and Simon rose from the chair. They took him by the upper arms.

"Please wait outside," he said.

Simon sat on a bench out in the hall, leaning back against the wall with his eyes closed. He felt a tap at his shoulder and looked up to see one of the guards holding out a dipper of water. He said thank you and drank it down. It seemed his injured body could never get enough water. Then the guard lit and held out to him a cigarillo; Simon took it with a nod and smoked part of it, and then bent to toss it into a cuspidor. Fell back against the wall again.

SIMON WAS CLEARED of all charges. Verdict: self-defense. The bells of San Fernando rang out five o'clock. The bird sellers with their caged finches sat on the dirt of Military Plaza offering these captive wild creatures to any passerby. The fires of the evening were lit, the fallen leaves of the mesquites in the campo santo stirred among the graves like rattling minute petitions to the living, and the great shining paddles of Guenther's mill turned over the waters of the San Antonio River again and again as if searching for some running treasure that flows through our hands and is finally lost to the sea.

CHAPTER TWENTY-SEVEN

HE WASN'T SURE WHERE he was nor did he have much memory of getting here. He was looking up at the tiles of a roof overhead. No ceiling. Simon lay on a double bed with his eyes closed. What they called a *matrimonio*. Every hold-fast structure inside him seemed to have given way now that the tribunal was done with, now that evening had fallen. If he could lie very still the pain was held back, did not flood him. In this small room a calico curtain hung on a rope across the far corner, he supposed for clothes or privacy or both. A window with night behind it like the mouth of a deep well. A table beside the bed; on it were a basin of hot water, clean cloths, ointments, a candle. The smell of supper cooking came from the next room over. He opened his eyes when he felt his boots being unlaced and pulled off his feet, socks, then his belt unbuckled.

"Simon," Doris said. "I'm here."

"You are so pretty," he said, and his eyes drifted shut again.

"My dear."

"Is the door closed?" He spoke carefully, his voice was almost inaudible.

Doris said, "Yes."

He felt his trousers slipping off under the quilt, his drawers going with them. He lifted his hips and said, "Ow. Ow. God." She had dragged the belt over the terrible great purple bruise where the big man had kneed him, going for his testicles and hitting his hip instead. She kept the covers tucked around him.

"Oh, Simon, sorry." She gave that small quick lift of the head that showed how anxious she was and folded the pants over a chair. She sat down again beside him. "I never took off a man's pants before. You will be glad to know."

"I am leading you into a life of depravity."

He had trouble arranging his swollen mouth to make the *f* sound, trouble smiling.

"Shhh. No joking."

She kissed him several times on one unmarked place on his forehead. He tried to sit up, but she placed a hand on his chest carefully and pressed him back down. He felt the warmth of her hand through the fabric of his shirt, sank back.

He said, "Check the pockets."

He lay there and dissolved slowly into both pain and happiness, with his hands lying on either side like inoperable devices that had to be made to work again somehow, and watched as she dredged up a few coins, his small penknife, a tortoise-shell comb. One eye was black above and below and had almost gone shut; both cheekbones had contusions and torn skin. His entire upper lip was swollen and split. His ribs were splotches of blue where the jail maniac had kicked him.

"How did you speak to a tribunal like you are? The dogs, the black dogs. How could you argue before the law for yourself and you bloodied so?" She unbuttoned his vest and then the shirt. Bent to kiss him again, lightly.

"I had to."

"Now the shirt, please." Slowly she drew off the old vest and his arms from the shirtsleeves.

He said, "Where are we?"

"The house of Mercedes's family on Obraje Street, near Camaron."

"Good."

"Her husband is a carpenter. *Carpintero*. It is aye a sweet little house."

"Where's my hat?"

"Over here, on the floor."

He didn't say anything, thinking. Obraje, a block or two away from Flores. Flores Street was the wagon route out of San Antonio to the north. He tried to come up out of the fading feeling, to pull his thoughts together. They had to get their possessions retrieved and packed, they had to get out of San Antonio. Pruitt had friends. Webb had friends. Shettle the Unavoidable was probably lurching around the plazas seeking whom he may devour. He had to find a way to get money to Twohig's. He had to find another fiddle or he had no way to make money, not in the shape he was in and was going to be in for the next while. But he could play no matter what. *Maybe. I don't know how bad my hands are.* He would miss the feel of the fiddle neck in his left hand, against the heel of his thumb. The magic that was in it, that came to his touch and his call. Then he stopped thinking and simply lay there in the mellow lantern light to feel her hand and a hot cloth cleaning him up in one long stroke after the other and all the dried blood flaking away.

"Simon?"

She was holding a cup of hot broth in her hands, waiting. After a moment he reached for it and lifted it to his mouth. He saw her making little gestures unconsciously as if to help him but did not. He poured it down and felt, in a moment, the flush of nutrients flowing into his empty stomach, his bloodstream.

Voices in the next room and a tap at the door.

"Dorita!"

"What, then?"

"Give me his clothes." The door opened a crack and Mercedes's arm thrust through, she snapped her fingers. "I will take them to the washwoman."

She went away with the clothes. She had not asked to come in. There was a privacy between them now that none could enter without permission. It comforted Simon deeply, beyond words. Doris took the empty cup from him and then touched the hot cloth carefully to his mouth. Then he drifted away again but she called softly to him, "Simon, it's the doctor."

A man in a black frock coat with green edging had come to stand beside his bed. A military physician's markings. He saw Doris go to the door as if to leave but the doctor said,

"Are you his wife? You'll stay. I might need your help."

Simon thought, *He'll put me back together. Then we can go.*

The doctor flipped the sheet and coverlet back. Simon saw her look quickly away with a sudden flush of embarrassment on her cheeks and it made him smile, and then it was hard to keep himself from crying out at the doctor's probing. It was thorough and expert. The doctor first examined the long shallow cut down his middle. He pressed here and there to see if it was becoming infected. Then he ran his hand up Simon's skull, riffling the hair back, pressing carefully on his skull bones. Placed thumb and forefinger on either side of his nose, nodded. Then he bore down on his ribs and Simon made a low sound, shoved back against the dusty pillow.

"Fractures," the doctor said. "Right side. Other side's good."

Then he went over his neck, face, all the bones of his arms and legs, and then one hand after another. Simon felt himself sweating. His short-cut reddish hair was dark with it and stood up in cranky spikes. He saw Doris at the foot of the bed, looking everywhere but at him, and her cheeks were bright red.

When the man came to his left hand he tried to sit up again.

"That hand is not broken, is it?"

"Just lie still. No. Maybe a hairline fracture here on the first knuckle. I want you to keep it above your head and keep this splint on it for a week or so." The doctor flipped the covers back over him and then laid a piece of split cane alongside the forefinger of his left hand and with swift, expert movements bound it to his middle finger. "You may wonder why I know. There is fighting and brawling going on in this town such as I have rarely encountered. I have become the local expert on busted knuckles." He tucked in the end of the bandage and then took Simon's hand and placed it on top of his head. By this time Simon's white skin was glittering with damp. "So stop hitting people with your fists. Try an ax handle next time." He turned to Doris. "Mrs. Boudlin?"

"Yes?" She started up from the wooden stool where she had sat herself down with clasped, anxious hands.

"Bring that candle. Hold it in front of his eyes and move it back and forth. Simon, watch the candle and don't move your head. Just your eyes."

The doctor peered into his eyes and noted that they were tracking, that both irises were the same size. "Thank you. Set it back down."

He took a green jar from his bag and placed it on the little bedside table. Then he brought out a brown glass bottle and placed it there as well. "This first is for the cut. This other is laudanum. Thirty drops tonight and then thirty drops each day, morning and night." He turned to Doris. She was gazing at him as if he were some sort of divinity, the great healer, somebody who would save Simon's face and his hands. He said, "Don't use a spoon for the drops, use this." He handed her a glass rod with a tiny ball on one end and then turned to Simon and put a hand on his shoulder. "Nothing is broken. You will be tempted to do more than you should. But you have fractured ribs and severe contusions and I think the pain will put a stop to that."

"When can I use my left hand?"

"A week, nine days. You're left-handed?"

"No, sir, I play fiddle."

"Ah." The doctor stood back and thought for a moment, his hand on his mouth. "Yes. Lieutenant Whittaker didn't tell me that."

Doris said, "He asked you to come?"

"Yes." The doctor snapped his bag shut and turned to the door. "Now I have a delivery across town. Stay quiet, take your medicine, you'll be up and around in about six days."

He went out and shut the door behind himself.

She sat down beside him on the bed, took ointment from the green glass jar, and ran her fingertip down the long stripe of dried blood on his abdomen. The ointment sparkled. Her hair pinned high on her head was about to fall loose.

He said, "We don't have six days."

"I know."

"Between Webb and the sheriff."

"We are pursued by fiends," she said. "It's like a play."

"Yes. Darling." Words were failing him. "We have to find a freight convoy to join up. Going north. We have to get your baggage. Mine too."

"I can do all that." She smiled confidently. "I am the fiddler's wife and none dare cross me." She held up a fist. "I am dangerous." Simon laughed, then cried out at the pain in his ribs that it caused him. "So you must not laugh. I shall not be funny. And now, Damon came. He brought your rucksack from the Plaza House and left a note. He said he does not like to say goodbye."

"All right." He started to say "what is in the note" but to make a *w* sound he would have had to purse his lips and couldn't do it. His mouth seemed very fat. He said, "Read it to me."

She brought out a sheet of paper from her sleeve and unfolded it. Considered it. "It says 'Over the Mountains of the Moon, down the Valley of Shadow, ride, boldly ride.' I collected your money and paid for the harness. There is a man in Fredericksburg who has a Gaillard for sale. In good condition, name Koenig. God be with you both. Ever thine, Damon."

"Yes. Good. A Gaillard." He thought it to himself several times so he would not forget. Promise of a fiddle. Soon. In his hand. "Where is my rucksack?"

"On the floor by your hat."

"Look in it, sweetheart. See if there is a revolver in it."

She helped him sit up and then placed pillows and his rolled-up old Confederate-issue trousers behind him so that he was in a reclining position. She dropped to the floor in a welter of skirts and searched through the rucksack.

"There is indeed, Simon. But there seems to be two pieces of it."

"Hand it to me."

She brought over the frame and the cylinder, holding them clumsily. He dropped the rammer, pulled the pin, and put it on half-cock. He slipped the cylinder into place, secured it with the pin, and slowly lowered the hammer on the empty chamber. He reached down to lay the big revolver under the bed. This cost him some moments of lying perfectly still, waiting for the pain to subside again, especially in his left hand, where it radiated out of his first knuckle and crawled burning up his arm. She firmly placed his splinted hand on top of his head again. He watched as she dipped the glass rod into the bottle of laudanum and dripped thirty drops one after another into a glass of water. He drank it down.

"Darling, there is a ring in my fiddle case. Where's my fiddle case?"

"Here." She pulled it from under the bed. She opened it and saw the ring box, lifted the top to see the ring with its tiny peridot. "Simon, it is very beautiful!"

"Give me your hand."

He struggled to hold the ring and push it onto her finger. He got it on upside down but didn't seem to notice. She quickly turned it so that the stone was uppermost and leaned to kiss him again.

"There," he said. "Finally. Darling girl."

The night of the city fell in liquid sequential curtains, shadow after shadow, from the slow drowsy army horses in their paddocks on Government Hill who stood in silence under the alders there, and then over the ruins of the Alamo and then the river itself cast in deep shadow where a few canoas with a lamp at the prow made their way home. St. Mary's answered San Fernando as the old bells sang out over the plazas. A groaning noise as the millstones of the upper mill were disengaged for the night and the Guenther waterwheel lifted and poured, lifted and poured. Bats sailed out of the Bat Cave. Down Obraje Street a lone horse walked slowly. Laughter and clashing pans from the kitchen of this small house, the smell of woodsmoke.

He touched her face. He moved his hand like a block of wood. "You are brave," he said. "Brave and conniving. I love you. I love you so much."

She lay her head briefly on his chest and closed her eyes and said that she loved him as well and always would. They listened as the horse with its rider walked on by and the bells subsided. She took a long quavering breath. "By God it has been a hard day." Her eyes were shining with tears. He put his hand on her shoulder, beside her throat, and with his thumb he could feel the pulse of her heart.

"Darling, it's all right now. We're all right."

"Yes. In a moment I am going to undress and put on my nightgown." She cleared her throat and said this in a rather determined way, as if he might object. "And so, this is not to affright you with women's underthings." She sat up.

"I won't be affrighted," he said and smiled at her; that round small mouth, her candlelit skin. He thought of her light body beneath the severe dark jacket and its skirt, which drifted over his bedside in rumpled yards of material, and that she was his now and no one could ever take her away, not ever. The basin of hot water at her feet smoked in the cold.

"They are mysterious and complicated." She cleared her throat again.

"Sweetheart." He couldn't stop looking at her, her candlelit face. "Maybe I should tell you I have seen them before."

"No, don't tell me," she said. "Not now." She laid her hand on his arm and her hand had a slight tremor. She said, "Tell me about the alligator."

"Tomorrow. The alligator tomorrow."

She got up and stepped behind the calico curtain. He bent up one knee with a small involuntary noise and moved to relieve the pain in his hip. Thirty drops of laudanum and the pain was still there, but the secret of that drug was that he didn't care if it was. When she came out she was in a white nightgown that trailed on the floor; it had a high neck and long sleeves and an immense amount of lawn pouring out of a lacy yoke. She seemed lost inside it.

"Oh, Simon, I got the pattern size all wrong. It's a *tent*. It's a *circus* tent." She stood with her toes curled up against the cold floor and plucked at it, looked down at all the vast white yardage in dismay.

He laughed and then tried to stop himself. He bit his lips together and tipped his head back against the pillow and the roll of his old Confederate trousers. "Oh God, my ribs," he said.

"It's too big!"

"No," he said. "Could it be?"

"Well," she said. "I didn't get a chance to try it on, you see." She came to sit on the far side of the bed and laid her palm on his forehead to check for fever and trailed it down to rest on the bones of his shoulder, as if he were made of china, broken and only recently repaired.

"I see." His smile was slightly crooked. "This is not much of a wedding night, darling." She regarded her bare feet. Said nothing. When she raised her head again he saw a different expression on her face: unsure, apprehensive. "It's all right," he said. "I would like to throw myself upon your maiden body and ravish you, but the ravishing business will have to come later."

"Well, curses anyhow."

She gathered up a fistful of the white material and wiped at her eyes and her hands were shaking with nerves, with the events of this long and terrible day suddenly crashing down upon her dark head. He reached for her, ran his swollen, bruised hand up her arm. After a moment in which they could hear the singing whisper of the night wind at the window he said, "Let down your hair."

By this time the drug had left him vague and nearly wordless. She unpinned her hair and it came down in a beautiful tumble, thick and glossy. It was like rain. His eyes slid shut. At some time she fell asleep tucked in beside him. The lamp oil burned low. He awoke in the small hours before dawn and he lay awake and at first contented with the warmth of her body against him but then all the poetry of Edgar Allan Poe came back to him without any effort on his part, the dark-haired women who died or were spirited off or were themselves spirits. To make this go away he put his left hand on her head, felt the silky mass of hair beneath his splinted fingers. She slept and dreamed.

He saw all the hard road before them unrolling like a scroll and their names there, for better or for worse, written in the Book of Life.

ACKNOWLEDGMENTS

THANK YOU to my amazing editor, Jennifer Brehl, and equally amazing and tiptop agent, Liz Darhansoff, not only for years of seeing my writing into print, but also for walks, talks, levity, and friendship.

Much appreciation is due to my music group: Chuck (mandolin); Diane (dulcimer, piano, banjo); Kim, Kathy, and Mark (voice and guitar); and Tom, our fiddler. Thanks for putting up with me while I practiced the Irish tin whistle. I've learned so much over the years, and the fun and laughter were priceless. Here's to more years yet, with the blessing.

About the author

About the book

Read on

Insights,
Interviews
& More . . .

About the author

Meet Paulette Jiles

Jill Gann Photography

PAULETTE JILES is a novelist, poet, and memoirist. She is the author of *Cousins*, a memoir, and the novels *Enemy Women, Stormy Weather, The Color of Lightning, Lighthouse Island*, and *News of the World*, which was a finalist for the 2016 National Book Award. She lives on a ranch near San Antonio, Texas.

Behind the Book

About Simon

The character Simon first appeared in my previous novel, *News of the World*, as somewhat of a plot device: Captain Kidd needed somebody to stay with Johanna while he straightened his hat, brushed the dirt from his coat sleeves, and went off to give his reading. For some reason I liked the idea that the Captain and Simon knew each other the way traveling entertainers know each other, and I also enjoyed the idea of Simon sitting in a shop's bay window in Spanish Fort as the Captain passes by.

In *News of the World* Simon and Doris were used to act as temporary caretakers—babysitters, if you will—for Johanna. But after that scene was done and the Captain and Johanna moved on, somehow Simon and Doris—their story and personalities—stayed with me.

I play the Irish tin whistle in a band. (They are no longer made of tin; my whistles are made of carbon fiber.) Our band's fiddler, Tom, sort of morphed into—or informed the character of—Simon, not because their personalities are alike but because when Tom and I played together I could see how a fiddler performs and *thinks* music; so it was with our dulcimer player, Diane, and the two guitarists and singers, Mark and Kim. I found myself starting a new work with the triad of Simon and ▸

Behind the Book ***(continued)***

Doris and music taking precedence. After that, all the characters in *Simon the Fiddler* just came to me, and stories grew out of their struggle to survive and their struggle to entertain and make a living from their music.

Doris is a new immigrant from Ireland and has a long road ahead of her toward independence, for she has come over as an indentured servant, which was quite common in those days. In many ways, it is music that binds her and Simon together; she with her piano, he with his fiddle. And, of course, traditional Irish music is very close to what some people call "mountain music," which is in Simon's blood.

Developing a protagonist's personality is always absorbing work. Simon grew as the pages filled up, always in the context of what he *did,* his choice of actions, as much as written descriptions of his internal development or internal monologue. I genuinely like Simon; I admire his gumption and his perseverance and his integrity. As it is, I prefer to enjoy spending time with my characters and consequently those who are negative and unlikeable are dealt with briefly.

The other members of Simon's ragtag band are his Greek chorus, which as Wikipedia says often danced or sang: "In many of these plays, the chorus expressed to the audience what the main characters could not say, such as their hidden fears or secrets."

And, of course, those characters, too, have their hidden fears and secrets.

Excerpt from *News of the World*

Read on

ONE

Wichita Falls, Texas, Winter 1870

CAPTAIN KIDD LAID out the *Boston Morning Journal* on the lectern and began to read from the article on the Fifteenth Amendment. He had been born in 1798 and the third war of his lifetime had ended five years ago and he hoped never to see another but now the news of the world aged him more than time itself. Still he stayed his rounds, even during the cold spring rains. He had been at one time a printer but the war had taken his press and everything else, the economy of the Confederacy had fallen apart even before the surrender and so he now made his living in this drifting from one town to another in North Texas with his newspapers and journals in a waterproof portfolio and his coat collar turned up against the weather. He rode a very good horse and was concerned that someone might try to take the horse from him but so far so good. So he had arrived in Wichita Falls on February 26 and tacked up his posters and put on ▸

his reading clothes in the stable. There was a hard rain outside and it was noisy but he had a good strong voice.

He shook out the *Journal*'s pages.

The Fifteenth Amendment, he read, which has just been ratified on February 3, 1870, allows the vote to all men qualified to vote without regard to race or color or previous condition of servitude. He looked up from the text. His reading glasses caught the light. He bent slightly forward over the lectern. That means colored gentlemen, he said. Let us have no vaporings or girlish shrieks. He turned his head to search the crowd of faces turned up to him. I can hear you muttering, he said. Stop it. I hate muttering.

He glared at them and then said, Next. The Captain shook out another newspaper. The latest from the *New-York Tribune* states that the polar exploration ship *Hansa* is reported by a whaler as being crushed and sunk in the pack ice in its attempt to reach the North Pole; sunk at seventy degrees north latitude off Greenland. There is nothing in this article about survivors. He flipped the page impatiently.

The Captain had a clean-shaven face with runic angles, his hair was perfectly white, and he was still six feet tall. His hair shone in the single hot ray from the bull's-eye lantern. He carried a short-barreled Slocum revolver in his waistband at the back. It was a five-shot,

.32 caliber and he had never liked it all that much but then he had rarely used it.

Over all the bare heads he saw Britt Johnson and his men, Paint Crawford and Dennis Cureton, at the back wall. They were free black men. Britt was a freighter and the other two were his driving crew. They held their hats in their hands, each with one booted foot cocked up against the wall behind them. The hall was full. It was a broad open space used for wool storage and community meetings and for people like himself. The crowd was almost all men, almost all white. The lantern lights were harsh, the air was dark. Captain Kidd traveled from town to town in North Texas with his newspapers and read aloud the news of the day to assemblies like this in halls or churches for a dime a head. He traveled alone and had no one to collect the dimes for him but not many people cheated and if they did somebody caught them at it and grabbed them by the lapels and wrenched them up in a knot and said, *You really ought to pay your goddamn dime, you know, like everybody else.*

And then the coin would ring in the paint can.

He glanced up to see Britt Johnson lift a forefinger to him. Captain Kidd gave one brief nod, and completed his reading with an article from the *Philadelphia Inquirer* concerning the British physicist James Maxwell and his theories of ▸

electromagnetic disturbances in the ether whose wavelengths were longer than infrared radiation. This was to bore people and calm them down and put them into a state of impatience to leave—leave quietly. He had become impatient of trouble and other people's emotions. His life seemed to him thin and sour, a bit spoiled, and it was something that had only come upon him lately. A slow dullness had seeped into him like coal gas and he did not know what to do about it except seek out quiet and solitude. He was always impatient to get the readings over with now.

The Captain folded the papers, put them in his portfolio. He bent to his left and blew out the bull's-eye lantern. As he walked through the crowd people reached out to him and shook his hand. A pale-haired man sat watching him. With him were two Indians or half-Indians that the Captain knew for Caddos and not people of a commendable reputation. The man with the blond hair turned in his chair to stare at Britt. Then others came to thank the Captain for his readings, asked after his grown children. Kidd nodded, said, *Tolerable, tolerable,* and made his way back to Britt and his men to see what it was Britt wanted.

CAPTAIN KIDD THOUGHT it was going to be about the Fifteenth Amendment but it was not.

Yes sir, Captain Kidd, would you come with me? Britt straightened and lifted his hat to his head and so did Dennis and Paint. Britt said, I got a problem in my wagon.

She seemed to be about ten years old, dressed in the horse Indians' manner in a deerskin shift with four rows of elk teeth sewn across the front. A thick blanket was pulled over her shoulders. Her hair was the color of maple sugar and in it she wore two down puffs bound onto a lock of her hair by their minute spines and also bound with a thin thread was a wing-feather from a golden eagle slanting between them. She sat perfectly composed, wearing the feather and a necklace of glass beads as if they were costly adornments. Her eyes were blue and her skin that odd bright color that occurs when fair skin has been burned and weathered by the sun. She had no more expression than an egg.

I see, said Captain Kidd. I see.

He had his black coat collar turned up against the rain and the cold and a thick wool muffler around his neck. His breath moved out of his nose in clouds. He bit his lower lip on the left side and thought about what he was looking at in the light of the kerosene hurricane lantern Britt held up. In some strange way it made his skin crawl.

I am astonished, he said. The child seems artificial as well as malign.

Britt had backed one of his wagons under the roof of the fairway at the livery stable. It didn't fit all the way in. The front half of the wagon and the driver's seat was wild with the ▸

drumming noise of the rain and a bright lift of rain-spray surrounded it. The back end was under shelter and they all stood there and regarded the girl the way people do when they come upon something strange they have caught in a trap, something alien whose taxonomy is utterly unknown and probably dangerous. The girl sat on a bale of Army shirts. In the light of the lantern her eyes reflected a thin and glassy blue. She watched them, she watched every movement, every lift of a hand. Her eyes moved but her head was still.

Yes sir, said Britt. She's jumped out of the wagon twice between Fort Sill and here. As far as Agent Hammond can figure out she is Johanna Leonberger, captured at age six four years ago, from near Castroville. Down near San Antonio.

I know where it is, said Captain Kidd.

Yes sir. The Agent had all the particulars. If that's her, she's about ten.

Britt Johnson was a tall, strong man but he watched the girl with a dubious and mistrusting expression. He was cautious of her.

My name is Cicada. My father's name is Turning Water. My mother's name is Three Spotted. I want to go home.

But they could not hear her because she had not spoken aloud. The Kiowa words in all their tonal music lived in her head like bees.

Captain Kidd said, Do they know who her parents are?

Yes sir, they do. Or as much as he can figure out from the date she was taken. The Agent, here, I'm talking about. Her parents and her little sister were killed in the raid. He had a paper from her relatives, Wilhelm and Anna Leonberger, an aunt and uncle. And he gave me a fifty-dollar gold piece to deliver her back to Castroville. The family sent it up to him by a major from San Antonio, transferred north. He was to give it to somebody to transport her home. I said I would get her out of Indian Territory and across the Red. It wasn't easy. We like to drowned. That was yesterday.

The Captain said, It's come up two foot since yesterday.

I know it. Britt stood with one foot on the drawbar. The hurricane lantern burned with its irresolute light on the tailgate and shone into the interior of the freight wagon as if revealing some alien figure in a tomb.

Captain Kidd took off his hat and shook water from it. Britt Johnson had rescued at least four captives from the red men. From the Comanche, from the Kiowa, and once from the Cheyenne up north in Kansas. Britt's own wife and two children had been taken captive six years ago, in 1864, and he had gone out and got them back. Nobody knew quite how he had done it. He seemed to have some celestial protection about him when he rode out alone on the Red Rolling Plains, a place which seemed to invite both death and dangers. ▶

Excerpt from *News of the World* ***(continued)***

Britt had taken on the task of rescuing others, a dark man, cunning and strong and fast like a nightjar in the midnight air. But Britt was not going to return this girl to her parents, not even for fifty dollars in gold.

Why won't you go? said Captain Kidd. You have come this far already. Fifty dollars in gold is a considerable amount.

I figured I could find somebody to hand her off to here, Britt said. It's a three-week journey down there. Then three weeks back. I have no haulage to carry down there.

Behind him Paint and Dennis nodded. They crossed their arms in their heavy waxed-canvas slickers. Long bright crawls of water slid across the livery stable floor and took up the light of the lantern like a luminous stain and the roof shook with the percussion of drops as big as nickels.

Dennis Crawford, thin as a spider, said, We wouldn't make a dime the whole six weeks.

Unless we could get something to haul back up here, said Paint.

Shut up, Paint, said Dennis. You know people down there?

Well, all right, said Paint. I can hear you.

Britt said, There it is. I can't leave my freighting that long. I have orders to deliver. And the other thing is, if I'm caught carrying that girl it would be bad trouble. He looked the Captain straight in the eye and said, She's a white girl. You take her.

Captain Kidd felt in his breast pocket for his tobacco. He didn't find it. Britt rolled a cigarette and handed it to him and then snapped a match in his big hand. Captain Kidd had not lost any sons in the war and that was because he had all daughters. Two of them. He knew girls. He didn't know Indians but he knew girls, and what was on that girl's face was contempt.

He said, Find a family going that way, Britt. Somebody to drown her in sweetness and light and improving lectures on deportment.

Good idea, said Britt. I thought of it already.

And so? Captain Kidd blew out smoke. The girl's eyes did not follow it. Nothing could move her gaze from the men's faces, the men's hands. She had a drizzle of freckles across her cheekbones and her fingers were blunt as noses with short nails lined in black.

Can't locate any. Hard to find somebody to trust with this.

Captain Kidd nodded. But you've delivered girls before now, he said. The Blainey girl, you got her back.

Not that far a trip. Besides I don't know those people down there. You do.

Yes, I see.

Captain Kidd had spent years in San Antonio; he had married into an old San Antonio family and he knew the way, knew the people. In North and West Texas there were many free black men, they were freighters and scouts and now after the war, the Tenth U.S. ▸

Excerpt from *News of the World* ***(continued)***

Cavalry, all black. However, the general population had not settled the matter of free black people in their minds yet. All was in flux. Flux: a soldering aid that promotes the fusion of two surfaces, an unstable substance that catches fire.

The Captain said, You could ask the Army to deliver her. They take charge of captives.

Not anymore, said Britt.

What would you have done if you hadn't come across me?

I don't know.

I just got here from Bowie. I could have gone south to Jacksboro.

I saw your posters when we pulled in, Britt said. It was meant.

One last thing, said Captain Kidd. Maybe she should go back to the Indians. What tribe took her?

Kiowa.

Britt was smoking as well. His foot on the drawbar was jiggling. He snorted blue fumes from his nostrils and glanced at the girl. She stared back at him. They were like two mortal enemies who could not take their eyes from one another. The endless rain hissed in a ground spray out in the street and every roof in Wichita Falls was a haze of shattered water.

And so?

Britt said, The Kiowa don't want her. They finally woke up to the fact that having a white captive gets you run down by the cav. The Agent said to bring all the captives in or he was cutting off their rations and sending the Twelfth and the Ninth out after them. They brought her in and sold her for fifteen Hudson's Bay four-stripe blankets and a set of silver dinnerware. German coin silver. They'll beat it up into bracelets. It was Aperian Crow's band brought her in. Her mother cut her arms to pieces and you could hear her crying for a mile.

Her Indian mother.

Yes, said Britt.

Were you there?

Britt nodded.

I wonder if she remembers anything. From when she was six.

No, said Britt. Nothing.

The girl still did not move. It takes a lot of strength to sit that still for that long. She sat upright on the bale of Army shirts which were wrapped in burlap, marked in stencil for Fort Belknap. Around her were wooden boxes of enamel washbasins and nails and smoked deer tongues packed in fat, a sewing machine in a crate, fifty-pound sacks of sugar. Her round face was flat in the light of the lamp and without shadows, or softness. She seemed carved.

Doesn't speak any English?

Not a word, said Britt.

So how do you know she doesn't remember anything?

My boy speaks Kiowa. He was captive with them a year.

Yes, that's right. Captain Kidd shifted his shoulders under the heavy dreadnought overcoat. It was black, like his frock coat and vest and his trousers ▸

and his hat and his blunt boots. His shirt had last been boiled and bleached and ironed in Bowie; a fine white cotton with the figure of a lyre in white silk. It was holding out so far. It was one of the little things that had been depressing him. The way it frayed gently on every edge.

He said, Your boy spoke with her.

Yes, said Britt. For as much as she'd talk to him.

Is he with you?

Yes. Better on the road with me than at home. He's good on the road. They are different when they come back. My boy nearly didn't want to come back to me.

Is that so? The Captain was surprised.

Yes sir. He was on the way to becoming a warrior. Learned the language. It's a hard language.

He was with them how long?

Less than a year.

Britt! How can that be?

I don't know. Britt smoked and turned to lean on the wagon tailgate and looked back into the dark spaces of the stable with the noise of horses and mules eating, eating, their teeth like grindstones moving one on another and the occasional snort as hay dust got up their noses, the shifting of their great cannonball feet. The good smell of oiled leather harness and grain. Britt said, I just don't know. But he came back different.

In what way?

Roofs bother him. Inside places bother him. He can't settle down and learn his letters. He's afraid a lot and then he turns around arrogant. Britt threw down his smoke and stepped on it. So, gist of it is, the Kiowa won't take her back.

Captain Kidd knew, besides the other reasons, that Britt trusted him to return her to her people because he was an old man.

Well, he said.

I knew you would, said Britt.

Yes, said the Captain. So.

Britt's skin was saddle colored but now paler than it usually was because the rainy winter had kept the sun from his face for months. He reached into the pocket of his worn ducking coat and brought out the coin. It was a shining sulky color, a Spanish coin of eight escudos in twenty-two karat gold, and all the edge still milled, not shaved. A good deal of money; everyone in Texas was counting their nickels and dimes and glad to have them since the finances of the state had collapsed and both news and hard money were difficult to come by. Especially here in North Texas, near the banks of the Red River, on the edge of Indian Territory.

Britt said, That's what the family sent up to the Agent. Her parents' names were Jan and Greta. They were killed when the Kiowa captured her. Take it, he said. And be careful of her.

As they watched, the girl slid down between the freight boxes and bales as if fainting and pulled the thick blanket ▸

over her head. She was weary of being stared at.

Britt said, She'll stay there the night. She's got nowhere to go. She can't get hold of any weapons that I can think of. He took up the lamp and stepped back. Be really careful.